CONTAINMENT

B.A. HIPPSLEY

SEVERED PRESS
HOBART TASMANIA

CONTAINMENT

WWW.SEVEREDPRESS.COM

ISBN: 978-1-925711-90-5

CHAPTER – ONE

The day started weird and stayed that way. Sheriff Brad Eastman usually liked the TV on when he was getting ready for work, but this morning things were different. Cable TV was off. No signal. In fact there was no communication at all. He'd tried his cell phone and the landline. All radio stations were out, even the internet was down. Dressed in his County Police uniform, he glanced around his silent house, pulled his Stetson over his eyes and left for work.

Even at seven in the morning with the slight breeze, he could feel the heat on his bare arms, but he wouldn't have it any other way. He loved the country. He sucked the clear air in to his lungs and stood for a moment, taking in his ranch and skyline. Apart from vapour trails from two jets the sky was a beautiful cloudless blue. As he got into his white patrol car he flicked on the police radio.

"Station house calling Sheriff Eastman, do you read Brad?" It was Clara Benson, the station receptionist. She sounded edgy.

"Sheriff Eastman here. What's up Clara?"

"We got us a communications blackout here. The whole town's out."

"I thought it was just me. Okay, best call all the deputies in. We got to keep it calm, don't want to panic anybody. I'll be there in a while. Eastman out."

He started the car and drove towards town. It would take about fifteen minutes normally, but today he needed to put his foot on the gas. There could be a thousand and one reasons for this situation, but he didn't like to guess. He worked with facts. What he was sure of, was that he'd find a lot of worried people in Armstrong. He'd spent his entire life there. Built the ranch with his father and then married Helen. Now he lived alone and he'd grown used to it.

He saw his family and friends from time to time, but never by his own making. There'd been that first Christmas after Helen had gone. Uncle Joe had insisted he stay over; Uncle Joe and Aunt Em always had all the folks around. Hell, he spent most of his time there as a kid. But it had all been too much, everybody carrying on like before. It just seemed plain wrong enjoying himself, worse; it felt like betrayal. Since then, Eastman had made sure he'd worked all through the holidays. He was good at being *too* busy, besides there was always his duty. He'd thrown himself into the law and now he lived the law. There was no room for anything else in his life.

As Eastman drove into Armstrong, groups of townspeople were gathered in small clusters – worried townspeople. He slowed down as Jimmy Emmett walked towards him. Eastman wound down the window.

"Brad what in tarnation's going on? Nothing's working around here…"

"I'm as wise as you. Everybody, best go about your business as usual. I'll hold a meeting soon as I got something to say."

"Well, I got something to say; Armstrong's cut off from the outside world."

"Jimmy, I don't want any of that 'lights in the sky' bull. Not after last time. Do you hear me?"

Eastman wound the window up and parked in the station house lot. He looked around the high street. No kids. It was school time, but where were all the kids? In fact there was hardly anybody out. People were keeping their kids home. Then he looked over at Danny Hardman's hardware shop; it was full of people buying all sorts of things. Panic would bring trouble. Things could go south in the blink of an eye. He'd have to act fast.

****

Things were no better in the station house; people had filled the reception area, all demanding information. Eastman would first have to clear them out to get any work done. The reception area was spartan in the extreme. There were three plastic red chairs on one side of the room and a long low table with a small tropical fish tank on the other side. Clara Benson was sitting behind her desk at the top of the room next to the hall door. Clara had been 'Miss Armstrong 1998' and even now she had style, her curly blonde hair never out of place. Despite this, she was not the sort of woman you'd want to cross. Eastman walked to the desk, smiled at her, and then addressed the crowd.

"Listen up. I am none the wiser on this situation than you. But I can't sort this out with all this ruckus. So unless you got yourself a bona fide emergency, this facility is off limits to all civilians until further notice."

The throng begrudgingly began to disperse and gradually the station house returned to normality. Eastman began to make an assessment of the situation. The police computers were offline, not even the landlines were working. The only forms of communication were police radios and some old CBs although; neither could reach Burnsville, the nearest town, over ninety miles away. Jimmy Emmett was right; Armstrong was cut off from the outside world.

Eastman would have to send someone to Burnsville and let them know what was going on, but what if it was the same there? The same everywhere? Eastman forced such thoughts out of his mind. He had no time for speculation. Pollute the lake or poison the air – no problemo, but no Cable or cell phones and it's 'call out the Guard'!

A knock on the door disturbed him. Standing there with his practiced election smile, Mayor Tony Firth was the last person he wanted to see. Firth was desperate to be re-elected; and thanks to his particular brand of politics now that looked a certainty. The only other candidates were Olly Nixon and Veronica Redman. Firth had dirt on both. Olly liked to spend money; only thing was, it belonged to other people. Most folks thought that was the real reason he'd left the bank. Veronica, on the other hand, cared about the community, but she had a secret. A few years back, she'd had an affair with a married woman living in Burnsville. No big deal for city folk, but in Armstrong that sort of thing didn't go down well. Firth had used his 'connections' to highlight Veronica's past. Then the posters had started cropping up over town. Malicious personal digs at her, enough to start people thinking. It had the Firth clan all over it.

"Town wants action Brad! Hell, I want action!"

Firth made his way over to Eastman giving Clara an oily smile on his way. Firth always reminded Eastman of a second hand car salesman. He was the wrong side of fifty and looked it.

"Mayor, first of all we got to find out what's going on. We can't tell the town anything at the moment. And I'm not running about half cocked until I do know."

"I couldn't agree more there Brad. We need us a plan."

"I've pulled all my people in, cancelled leave. We need officers on the streets. This blackout is only affecting communications at the moment. The power seems all right for *now* but... our biggest problem is panic."

"Yeah, I passed Emmett on the way over here. He was standing on a box telling people to 'watch the skies'. People are banging on McReedy's Gun Shop to open up."

"If you call a town meeting for this afternoon, that should give me time to find out what's happening and come up with a plan."

"Not that it's a consideration, but it's the town elections in two weeks. Yours and mine. We both need to show we can lead."

"It's the safety of the people we need to think about, Mayor. I'm sending Deputy Koneg over to Burnsville. Then I'm going to see Chris Emery at the High School, see what he thinks."

"That sounds good. I've got an interview with the *Armstrong Bugle* in five minutes. I'll call a town meeting for midday. See you then."

Firth made his way towards the door, passing Clara on the way. "Clara, that offer's still open for my P.A. You'd make a hell of an addition to my team."

Clara fixed Firth with a cold stare, pinching her chin with her forefinger and thumb. "Tony, remember I got a job. *Here.*"

"Yeah, but I pay more than the county. Listen, take my card. Change your mind, then give me a call." Firth walked to the door and left the station house just as Eastman's deputies were walking in.

Clara watched Firth disappear through the door then threw the card in the waste bin. "Can't you arrest him for being a creep?"

Clara was right. Firth had probably overloaded the whole damn system trying to sell the town on eBay or clear his wife's credit card. The guy was a piece of work.

Eastman looked at his team: handpicked and every one as worried as the rest of the town.

"Okay, we need to sort this situation out before anything gets out of hand. I'm going to give you a quick briefing, but I want you all back on patrol in ten minutes. Everybody follow me through to the charge room."

"Sheriff, what about Gerard – should I call him?"

"Nope, he's suspended. I don't need him hanging about here."

"You're the boss."

"Clara, can you get hold of Vince Langley? I need to know why only the short wave radios work."

Vince Langley worked for the telephone company and knew every inch of the network. Clara nodded her head. Gerard 'T' Benteen was not in Eastman's good books. Eastman pulled the door shut and Clara was left alone in the room. She looked at the patrol map showing the position of all the police officers. Eddy Joe was the nearest; she'd send him to get hold of Vince. She reached forward and spoke into the police radio on her desk.

"Clara calling Deputy Eddy Joe. Do you read? Over."

****

Chris Emery had been just about everyone's teacher at the High School. He was the sort of man that people asked about getting married before they asked the minister. Eastman was sitting in the old school office and had just finished explaining the situation to his old mentor. Now he needed some answers.

"So there is no official line to all this then Brad?"

"I was hoping you'd come up with something, Sir."

Emery rubbed the palm of his hand across his grey bearded chin, deep in thought. This was beyond his understanding, but he wanted to help Eastman.

"It may well have something to do with 'Hurricane Molly'. Hurricanes can create all types of atmospheric anomalies. I suppose it's possible that such things could affect communication. Airwaves, satellites, the internet are all at the mercy of 'Old Mother Nature'. Though, I must confess, I have no positive evidence to support this theory."

"But that twister's nowhere near us, how…"

"Bradley, the Moon and the Sun can have enormous effects on Earth and they are much further away. Sorry I can't be of more help."

"Well at least I got something that makes sense. Firth will be more interested in the publicity this'll bring him."

"Tony Firth was a cheat in school. He's always been bad and his brother Peter is worse. The Firths are trouble. You watch them! How about the rest of the town?"

"Oh, I've heard everything from alien invasion, Al-Qaeda and the Chupacabra, not to mention the Men in Black theories."

"We've come so far and yet, we haven't really left the cave."

"I can't get used to this quiet. No classes then Sir?"

"I had to cancel them, nobody turned up today. Not my problem after next week, I'm calling it a day Brad. Doctor's orders."

"Sorry to hear that. People are sure going to miss you."

"Listen Brad, why don't you drop over sometime? Beth would be delighted to see you. She still makes the most exquisite pie in the county."

"Beth? Well thanks again, I'd better leave you to it. I'll see myself out."

As Eastman crunched across the gravel to his car, he felt a tinge of sadness; his old tutor looked tired and he'd certainly be missed. But there was also a deeper sadness. Mrs Beth Emery had died ten years back.

"Clara calling Brad, do you read? Over."

"Eastman here. What is it Clara?"

"Old Ben Burke reported something strange on his CB."

"CB? How'd he manage that?"

"Jim O'Brien and Vince Langley found that CBs work, so they set them up on the old Emergency Channel 9."

"Well that's something. What happened at Ben's?"

"His wife saw some vagrants over by the old Air Force base. They gave her a nasty scare. Can you call up?"

"Yeah, on my way. Eastman out."

****

It was some time later before Eastman arrived at the Burke farm. He was thankful for the extra police suspension as his car bounced about on the dusty farm road. Ben's farm had seen better days. Nearly all the fences needed replacing and the outbuildings looked fit for demolition. The snaking track finally brought Eastman to the Burke's run down house. The white walls had long since turned grey and the roof had started to sag. As he got out of the car, Ben came out to greet him. It was difficult to imagine that he was almost seventy-five years old; he still had a good head of hair.

"What's up Ben?"

"Some darn vagrants gave Erin a fright. She's shook up some."

Eastman and Ben walked into the sitting room. The room was badly in need of decoration and smelled of dog. Erin was sitting by the empty fireplace; Eastman could tell she'd been crying and was still clearly upset.

"You okay, Mrs Burke? I'm sorry, but I need to ask some questions. Can you tell me what happened?"

"I was walking over by the old base when I done seen them two."

"The vagrants?"

"Yeah, they looked real strange. I thought they'd been in an accident, so I went over to them. They was making real odd sounds too, like if they was hurt. I never heard folk make sounds like that."

"Mrs Burke, what kinda accident?"

"They was all messed up Sheriff, I mean them boys looked like they'd just walked out of an auto-wreck."

"Do you think they were on drugs?"

"Could be, but I tell you they looked mad as if they wanted to get me. So I ran away. But they kept on following me till I done lost them."

"Look Sheriff, nobody goes up there 'cept courting couples and folk that ain't up to no good. That place is less than three miles from us. It's kinda worrying. I reckon my Erin was lucky."

"I take the point Ben; I'll go up and have a nose about. If there's anybody that shouldn't be there, I'll move them off. That's all I can do. Oh, and Ben, I'd put that cannon away," said Eastman, pointing to Ben's pump action shotgun. "We don't want any accidents."

"You can't get the car up there Brad, since that tremor a while back. You gonna need a Jeep."

"I'll get the four-by-four and then have a look. I want you to lock up and stay safe. If you get any problems use the CB. Someone will come. I'd best get off. Morning Mrs Burke, Ben."

Eastman got back into the car and drove towards town. It was clear that Erin had been through an unpleasant experience and had been very lucky. Still, looking odd was hardly a felony, and in any case, that accounted for half the town. He'd need the four-by-four to meet up with Bill Merka, from the Parks Department. There'd been a lot of stolen cars dumped near the Lloyds' farm recently. Eastman suspected the Clayton brothers, but he had no proof. His list was getting longer.

****

Pulling up to the station house, Eastman could see Bill Merka standing by his Jeep. Eastman stopped alongside him, got out and walked over.

"You ready for some work then Bill?"

Dressed in his brown Parks uniform, Bill Merka was in his mid-forties. He'd spent nearly all his life working for the parks.

"What kept you Brad? I almost went without you."

"I've been up at the Burkes' place. Erin had a scare, some no-goods near the old airbase. I want to take a look around there later."

"Fine by me."

"Bill, I reckon we'll swing by the Lloyds' farm. A dollar to a dime says we gonna find something there. Then we'll head up to the Willis' farm. Maybe we'll run into George Lee."

"He's hunted those woods a long time, huh?"

"He was born in those woods – hell, he's part bloodhound."

Lee worked as a guide during the hunting season. Hardly an ecologist, he just didn't like folk 'messing up' his beloved woods.

"I spoke to Red Cloud yesterday, said he'd seen the Clayton boys up at the Lloyds' place. When they saw him, they just took off."

"Not much gets past that Indian. Hey by the way, when's that comet showing up?"

"Oh, don't you start. Mrs Peterson reckons it's gonna bring us all doom."

"Bill, you should be used to all that small town bull by now. You've lived here five years."

"Yeah, right. I asked Red Cloud to the tower for a look. You come too, if you want?"

"Appreciate that. May well do, if I can figure out all this crazy stuff," pondered Eastman.

"Okay, so what's the low down on this black-out thing Brad?"

"Bill, if I had me a dollar for every time I been asked that today, I could take the day off. Truth is, I don't know."

"Officially maybe, but you can tell me, come on."

"Saddle up." Eastman made time for Merka. That didn't happen with everyone, but he wasn't in the mood to discuss the situation further.

Both men got into their vehicles and drove off. The truth was that Eastman had no more idea than anybody else and that worried the hell out of him.

****

The men were driving towards the Willis' farm when they came across George Lee at Larson's Creek. Stepping forward he motioned them to stop. Pulling off the road both vehicles parked up on the grassy verge. The sound of the creek could be heard trickling by as Eastman cut his engine. George Lee stood with the peak of his Marine fatigue cap pulled tightly over his eyes. Eastman could still make out his drooping moustache and goatee beard. The bulky lumberjack shirt made him look a lot bigger than he was; in his arms he cradled his Remington hunting rifle. Eastman got out of his four-by-four and walked over to greet Lee.

"Heat starting up, George."

"Ain't so bad in the trees. I got some news for you."

"More cars? We just come by Lloyd's farm, found a stripped pick up over there."

"Nope. I heard some shots over at Dawson's Pool yesterday. I found some .38 calibre shell cases. Some sort of tent was set up, but they's all gone now."

"Any ideas where?"

"I done see some hikers this morning, boy and girl headed over to Highway 104. Could be the same folks?"

Eastman knew that Armstrong was a good ten miles from that point and he also knew the area was a maze. City folk were always getting lost there and with the heat set to soar, they could be in serious trouble.

"Obliged to you George, I'd best get over there and take a look."

Lee melted back into the woods and Eastman and Merka drove off.

Lee was a troubled man. It wasn't just the dumpsters spoiling the land, Eastman and Merka would put a stop to all that. This was way more serious. He hated Wal-Mart –'Yes Sir, no Sir, that's in aisle four Ma'am' – it wasn't right for him. It wasn't *man's* work. What the hell did any of them know about hunting and tracking? 'Jack' was the short answer to that one. No, the worst thing, the thing he hated the most was that he didn't have any options. When the hunting season finished so did the money. He shook his head in frustration. Then he saw tracks just in front of him. Heavy military boot prints, four, maybe even five guys had come this way in the last few days he reckoned. Whatever. He wasn't looking for dumb grunts; he was looking for game. His keen senses were alert for any sound or movement but... nothing. For the last few days it had been the same. Nothing. It was as if all the animals had left the woods. In his long experience, that only happened if something bad was going down.

7

CHAPTER - TWO

Brent Taylor scanned the sparse woodland in an arc left to right and back again; the less contact with people the better his chances of dodging the authorities. Relaxing from his crouching position behind a rocky outcrop, he spied no unwanted company and stood up. He was a sorry sight. His clothes were dirty and worn but on his back a large rucksack sat with surprising comfort; he'd been used to much heavier loads in Iraq. Longish, scruffy dark brown hair and a rough scraggly beard covered most of his rugged face. He needed a long, long time in a hot tub.

Soon, he'd need to emerge from the relative security and protection of the woodlands he'd been trekking through over the last few days. To get an accurate reading of his position, he reached into the side pocket of his pack and withdrew a grimy route map of the locality – stolen booty from a few days earlier. Taylor followed the hand-drawn line of his progress with his grimy forefinger and stopped at Highway 104. He let out a self-satisfied grunt, jabbing the point with his finger, as he recorded the miles he'd travelled. Not bad, almost twenty-five miles today. Looking at his desert boots he noticed that these were the cleanest part of his attire, well, apart from the spot of dried blood on the right boot. Pretty good for boots from a dead man, he mused.

How stupid he'd been to get involved, trying to help out. He'd first tried CPR on the man, but when it was obvious the guy was dead, Taylor had taken the boots. Then the damn cops turned up. Now the cops were looking for him.

As he reached the end of the tree line, Taylor's heart sank at the lack of cover in front of him. For as far as the eye could see it was just a long road, dissected by a featureless wilderness and nowhere to hide, *nowhere*. With no other option, he left the cover of the huge pine trees to continue his journey on the open road.

He'd gone about four, maybe five miles when he saw a dot in the distance behind him. The vehicle became larger and larger as it got closer to him. Taylor however, had ample time to take cover in the ditch and patiently wait for the Coca-Cola rig to thunder past. Boy, how he could do with some of that now!

Taylor realised just how thirsty he was and then how little water he had left. His throat was painfully dry and his mouth too parched to spit. He'd intended to fill his canteen at the small creek some miles back when he'd run into some hikers. One of them had shot at him with a damn pistol from the tent. Taylor had lost his canteen and had to run for it. He shut his eyes, rubbing his rough hand several times over his grimy forehead and cringed at how close that had been.

Taylor had to get more water; consulting the map he tried to locate the nearest water to him. A small river about three miles in the opposite direction should do it, he thought. It would drag him slightly off course and take him off the road, but the surrounding area was covered in trees. Besides, there was no other option; he had to have water. It would make a good pit stop and he could rest for a while. He wanted to be off the road before nightfall.

Nearing the river, Taylor could hear the soft babbling of the flowing water as it coursed over rocks and through the ravine. As he came into full view of the river it reminded him of that old movie *Planet of the Apes*, where Charlton Heston finds the waterfall. That's a damn good idea he thought; he was long overdue for a bath. After Taylor had selected his bathing area, he removed all his clothes and stepped into the sparkling water. The water was so cold it was almost painful, making his whole body judder. It reminded him of when he'd been a kid jumping into the reservoir.

Sometime later, he removed his clothes from the large rocks he'd used to dry them and got dressed. He'd never get served at a restaurant as he was, but at least he was a good deal cleaner. He hoped the lice had all died from the cold water. Taylor sat down to his makeshift banquet of shoplifted corned beef, cold beans and stale bread, washing them down with some water from his bottle. Raising his arms high above his head in a long, contented stretch, he lay back and contemplated his next course of action.

Looking at his map, Taylor checked the distance to his target. To his reckoning it was about ten miles or so north from a hick town called Armstrong. His target wasn't marked on the map – he hardly thought it'd have neon, Vegas style signs on it. More than likely, even the local rednecks hadn't a clue it was there. But he knew where it was all right. The man he'd killed for that information had also known. All he had to do was find it.

Taylor's mind started to drift back to those terrible events two months ago. His jaw clenched at the memory; but he did his best to block out the past. He knew he needed to be focused on the task ahead; he would not allow himself to become distracted now.

There'd be reference points; all he had to do was use these to work out where the place was. Taylor guessed the time by the position of the sun and its shadows and decided he would clear the road and then camp for the night. He'd gone only a short distance when the screaming started. He was able to detect a male and a female voice. Almost instantly the male voice changed from panic to pain. Taylor had covered only a few more paces when the male voice came to an abrupt stop. By contrast, the female voice rose to hysterical shrieks. Something dreadful was going down.

He tried his best to banish the screams to that dark area of his mind; the place he kept all the other screams. Determined, he marched on with the harrowing wails ringing in his ears. Instead of the female's screams getting further away, the awful din was getting closer. He was now aware she was behind him some way back. Taylor turned and saw a young, dark haired female in her mid-twenties with blood on her legs and hands. Her eyes were like huge white flashlights, staring right through him.

"Stay there, you're safe now," he called in his most reassuring tones. "What the hell's happened here, what's your name?" The girl just looked blankly at him and pointed to the small ravine from which she'd just come. He knew he'd have to follow her, so he took her hand and she pulled him down the path.

"Work with me here, where's your cell phone? You gotta call 911…"

"They, they attacked… started biting Paul and…" She stopped, unable to continue.

"What, animals? What?" Taylor demanded.

"Not animals, I think they were *people*."

Taylor felt a cold sweat start to develop, that cold type of feeling you get in the gut with bad news.

"Did you say people?" he said in a slow, low voice.

"There."

Taylor slowly turned from the girl to follow the direction of her quivering, bloodstained finger. He already knew what he'd find because he'd seen it before, but it still filled him with utter revulsion and horror. On the ground, two crouching figures were bent over the torn and mangled body of a man. They were holding large chunks of the man's flesh and were feeding on it, totally oblivious to Taylor or the girl.

"Move back, they're not interested in us," he said in a soft, low voice, taking her arm to lead her away.

Seeing one of the ghouls holding the man's severed hand with his ring still attached, was too much for the girl and she started to scream. Taylor reacted instantly and grabbed her around the shoulders.

"*Shut up!* You gotta shut up," he hissed at her.

Her voice rose in both pitch and volume, screaming uncontrollably. His warning however, came too late as one of the attackers turned slowly to look at them. Its colourless opaque eyes seemed to stare straight through Taylor. Then it drew its grey lips back to reveal broken and jagged teeth coloured red by its victim's blood. To Taylor's horror it started to get up with a jerky stiff motion and shamble towards them making a rasping noise as it moved ever closer.

These were as mean looking as the ones he'd first come across two months ago, and they had the same bad table manners. Pushing the screaming girl to one side, Taylor aimed a well-directed kick at the thing's left knee with brutal force. The limb broke easily, the white of the bone protruding out of the trouser leg. The thing fell to one side; unperturbed, it started to crawl towards them.

****

They'd travelled less than five miles when Merka sounded his horn and pointed to a broken gate. It was Parks Department procedure to maintain all its fences. Eastman and Merka stopped their vehicles and walked over to the gate. The land had hardly changed from before the time of the first settlers. Here they could follow the path leading up river from Hinckle Point to Highway 104. Then they heard the screams, anguished screams of terror coming from the direction of Hinckle Point. Both men ran down the narrow lane to the sound of the screams.

As they rounded the bend, Eastman took in the picture: a roughly dressed man just like a hobo, standing by a female hiker. The girl was hysterical. His first reaction was that the hobo had attacked her, but although she was covered in blood, the man didn't have a speck on him. Both were standing with their backs to Eastman and Merka – they were staring at something else.

As Eastman got to where the pair were standing, he saw a second guy covered in blood crawling toward the girl and the hobo. Eastman presumed he was on PCP or the latest happy drug. Matted hair stuck to his head and grey skin clung to his bones. But it was the eyes that struck Eastman. The colourless blobs were dead man's eyes. He wore some sort of tattered coveralls that looked as if they'd come from a dumpster. Directly behind him was another man, bent over what was left of a dead male.

To Eastman's horror, this second man was eating from the body. This was no 'shoot out' or bad wreck where Eastman got to scrape the bits up. He'd heard of cannibal murders, insane people that took a perverse pleasure in eating human flesh. This was different. These two were *ravenous*; tearing at the body like a Coyote with a road kill. It was now obvious that the hobo *was* protecting her from them and he'd placed himself between the men and the girl. The first man stumbled towards the young woman and the hobo, emitting growls and snarls, his outstretched fingers reduced to bare bones.

"Stop where you are and stand still!" Eastman shouted, holding one hand in the air, the other on his holster.

The man took no notice and continued his lumbering advance. These were no ordinary 'crack heads'. They were sick with something, and it was the type of 'sick' you didn't want to get. Eastman called his instructions several times, but they went unheeded. The man was starting to get too close for comfort. Suddenly, the hobo sprang forward and took the Colt 357 Magnum from Eastman's open holster and stepped back calling to Merka as he did so.

"Put the pistol on the ground and step away. Now!"

Merka looked at Eastman, but he'd no choice other than to do as he was told. The hobo had the drop on him. Both he and Eastman were now at this wild man's mercy. The hobo looked directly at Eastman and spoke in very deliberate, icy tones.

"You want to arrest *that*? You can't arrest that, dumb ass!"

In one smooth fluid movement he turned, aimed and fired, hitting the man's chest, dashing him to the ground. The heavy 357 Magnum round punched a dime-sized hole in the front and then smashed out the back, striking the second man in the arm, breaking his elbow. He hardly seemed to notice as he continued to gnaw on the dead hiker.

Eastman had been the county police marksman instructor for a long time; he knew the shot had gone through the heart. He watched in disbelief as the first man started to get up. The hobo fired a second shot, hitting the man in the stomach. Eastman saw the bullet go clean through, cutting his spinal cord and embedding itself in a tree. The man bent in two like a plastic drinking straw. Either one of these hits was enough to kill someone. As impossible as it was, Eastman saw the man start to crawl towards them.

The hobo turned and looked right at Eastman and he knew by this man's eyes, this guy was used to killing people.

"This is the only way to deal with these things."

The man turned from Eastman and in the same casual way you'd swat a fly, shot the first man through the left eye, stopping him dead. Then with the same detachment, he shot the other man through the back of his head and the dead hiker through the left temple. All were perfect head shots. Eastman knew there was only one round left in the chamber. As he watched the killer walk towards him, all he could think was that he hoped Bill could get the guy before he reloaded.

The hobo stopped a few feet away from him, then miraculously gave the pistol back to Eastman with the last round unfired. Merka covered him while Eastman cuffed and booked the hobo. He stood and looked at the carnage he'd just caused with a detached manner that unnerved Eastman. This boy was bad news. Eastman was thinking fast, how to move the hobo to the patrol car, when Frank Jorgan and his two boys Larry and Kurt arrived. The Jorgans were local farmers; they lived on one of the many farms outside the town. All three were armed and fired up as they started towards the hobo.

"You the dirt bag that attacked my wife?" Frank Jorgan growled at the hobo, levelling his shotgun at him.

"Simmer down Frank, he's in my custody."

"Don't care, I'm gonna blow his damn head off."

Frank Jorgan aimed his Remington shotgun directly at the hobo, but Eastman stood in the line of fire. He'd never been one for rough justice.

"Okay, Frank, ease off, there's been enough killing done. Put the weapon down before somebody else dies."

Jorgan could see that Eastman was in no mood to argue and lowered his shotgun. As if for the first time Jorgan took in the full extent of the gruesome scene. Eastman could see Jorgan and his boys were riled up. They were a tough bunch but not trouble makers.

"What you say about Nancy, Frank?"

"Some creep was on my farm and grabbed Nancy, roughed her up some, but she locked herself in the house, then he left."

"She alright?"

"Yeah,'cept for some scratches."

"Did she get a description or something?"

"Said he was weird looking, kinda poorly. She got spooked real bad."

The hobo edged his way forward. "Listen pal, I never attacked your wife. I been here all the time. Was she bitten?"

"What's that to do with you?"

"Look Sheriff, you've seen some bizarre things here," the hobo continued, "those bodies are contaminated; you need to be careful. Ask yourself, they look *normal* to you?"

Eastman could tell the hobo was uptight, maybe even scared. This was not the same man who minutes earlier had executed three men. He was sure this guy was a loon yet, with his own eyes he'd seen someone moving about after they should've died. What if these bodies did have something wrong with them? Some sort of disease. This notion worried him, but for now there was police business to deal with.

"Okay, Bill, Frank go get the vehicles, bring them back here. Then I'll call in for backup. Larry and Kurt can stay with me."

Eastman passed his keys to Jorgan and watched as the two men headed back down the track. He didn't want to risk this hobo on the narrow track; there was no telling what he'd try. Eastman wanted him in plain view at all times. The girl was shaking but a lot calmer now. The boys were talking to her and had moved her away from the scene. They were about the same age which seemed to help he thought. Eastman viewed his captive with suspicion and curiosity.

"You! Over by that tree!" Eastman shouted at the hobo, "and don't even think about giving me any God damn problems."

The hobo called over to the brothers, "Did your Ma get bitten? It's important. If she did then you need to watch her."

"Don't speak to him boys! And you! Just shut up!"

"Why for Mister?" asked Kurt.

"If she was, then she's gonna be crunching on your bones very soon."

"I'm gonna bust your filthy mouth!" screamed Kurt running towards the hobo but Eastman quickly stepped in front of him.

"Easy up there Kurt, he's just sassing you! He's not worth it."

After a moment or so Kurt calmed down, then Eastman rounded on the hobo.

"Shut the hell up or next time I'm gonna let them have you."

Eastman had the feeling this was going to be a long day. One thing was certain; this man with no name had more questions than answers.

CHAPTER – THREE

Sheriff Eastman's office was a somewhat drab but serviceable room. On one side stood several grey filing cabinets topped with a number of box files. The walls were adorned with various achievement certificates, largely relating to law enforcement. On a metal wall shelf, sat a multitude of shooting awards and trophies. A large window overlooked the majestic mountain range that dominated the town, the tinted glass keeping the glare of the sun at bay. Even at this time of day it was hot. A large mahogany desk occupied the rest of the room. Positioned amongst the functionality of the desk accoutrements, was a small photo of an attractive blonde woman.

Eastman finished the entry in his private diary and closed the book. He was still unable to fully understand what had happened earlier. What bothered him the most was trying to understand the motives of the hobo. What kind of a guy shoots three people after disarming a lawman and then gives the weapon back?

Deputy Mitch Chattman had processed the suspect's paperwork as soon as they'd returned. However, the hobo still hadn't said a thing about the shootings. The female hiker, Rose Gane, had been sent with Deputy Jedrey Bodien to the health center for Anne Lenski to check over. Eastman wouldn't have been surprised if she needed further sedation after Hinckle Point. Hell, even he felt like something a little stronger than the black coffee he was drinking. The intercom on Eastman's desk suddenly burst into life.

"Yeah Sheriff, it's Mitch here. Can you come to the charge room now please?"

"I'm busy right now Mitch."

"No, I mean *now*. There's something you gotta to see."

There was something in Mitch's voice that told him this was important.

"Okay, I'm on my way."

Running his fingers through his black hair and sighing deeply, he began slotting his gun belt back through the belt loops as he walked out of the office. He had a gut feeling this was going to be another weird thing to add to the list.

****

Walking the short distance to the charge room along the corridor, he passed the hulking figure of Deputy Gerard 'T' Benteen coming out of the rest room.

"Hey Brad, where you off in such a hurry there, boy?"

Eastman was still 'smoothing over' Benteen's most recent indiscretion.

"I thought you were suspended. What you after… getting in my good books?"

Moving his head in a low arc to avoid Eastman's gaze, Benteen said "Okay, okay, so I was a little out of order that's all, said I was sorry."

Eastman looked his old High School buddy up and down, enjoying his awkwardness. It did Benteen good every so often to know who was boss. Eastman regarded Gerard as a good lawman, but he sure could fly off the handle.

"You're lucky that guy dropped the charges, don't get smart with me."

Benteen nodded his head. Lesson learned. Eastman decided that since Gerard was about he could do some work. He'd known Benteen all his life and the guy had always been headstrong. Benteen was a powerfully built man; he was over six foot, full of muscle and mean. During their High School days it was only because of his place on the football team that Benteen hadn't been thrown out of school. Eastman had spent many hours working with him on his academic studies and trying to keep him out of trouble. Even now as a peace officer, Eastman knew too well that Benteen was still a handful. There were always allegations against him. Benteen loved to fight. The complaints were never upheld; no one wanted to have '*Mr Kick Ass*' on their case. This was his official nickname, however, nobody was ever dumb enough to say this to his face. Despite the trouble he caused, there was never any malice in his actions. He'd batter some guy for a misdemeanour one day and pull his truck out of a ditch the next. Benteen sure was a complicated kind of guy.

"Gerard! Since you're here you can do some work, come with me."

"Sure thing, Brad. You okay after this morning? Jedrey told me what happened. It sounded real rough up there."

"He took my firearm and killed three people, what do you think?"

****

The charge room was small and practical with no windows. Two small holding cells occupied almost one half of the room, while the charge desk and processing station covered the rest, consisting of a photo booth and a desk with printing equipment. The strong odour of printing ink filled the air. Mitch Chattman stood with a worried look on his face. The same look a kid gets when he's done something wrong.

"Okay Mitch, what you broke?"

"Sheriff how many bookings have I made?"

"Mitch, if you got me down here for God damn twenty questions, you *will* be handing out parking tickets before this day ends. I promise you."

"He means it too, college boy," said Benteen, drawing immense enjoyment from Chattman's predicament.

This outburst served only to increase Chattman's already heightened nervous state. A small bead of sweat rolled down the side of his face and he shifted his stance awkwardly.

"Well, what I mean is, I've made loads, so I reckon I know what I'm doing that's all."

"Mitch is there a point to this? Because I'd like to know before I die of old age."

"Yeah, for a trainee Fed you ain't exactly making much sense there, *boy,*" Benteen goaded, savouring Chattman's discomfort even more.

Not wishing to incur the further wrath of his boss or lose face in front of Benteen, Chattman managed to spit out a reply in his defence.

"I processed that guy you brought in. I done everything that I normally do, but when I got to taking his prints... *he had no prints.*"

"Exactly what do you mean he had no prints?" questioned Eastman.

"What I mean is; there are no prints. His fingertips are smooth as a saddle blanket."

Eastman took a long hard look at his deputy; Mitch had worked there for over a year, he was a college boy, a smart kid and a good cop. His application for the FBI had been approved and he was in the process of leaving town to start his selection. So what the hell was he talking about?

"Look" said Chattman, showing Eastman a set of prints and a close up of the suspect's fingertips.

The boy was right; the prints were totally smooth as were the shots of the fingertips. Without looking up from the prints Eastman said in a low voice, "I knew that creep was odd. None of this is good. Mitch, we still out of touch with everybody?"

"Yeah Sheriff, I tried all ways to contact HQ and the FBI, no good."

Even with the fingerprints, without the FBI central database, they still wouldn't be able to get a fix on this guy.

"I reckon it's about time we had a good old-fashioned word with this crazy S.O.B. don't you Brad?"

Looking at Benteen, Eastman nodded. They'd have to use a tougher approach with this guy.

****

The jail held four standard cells, each constructed with reinforced eight-inch thick steel bars and a heavy-duty door. The jail's windowless walls were cinder blocks, over-painted blue. Two large strip lights provided the only source of light. A simple table and chairs were the only furniture.

Eastman walked to the table area, picked up one of the chairs, turned it back to front and sat with his arms resting on the back of the chair. The suspect was the jail's only resident and he lay on his bed with his eyes closed. Eastman looked directly at the hobo – he knew he wasn't asleep. He'd killed three men in cold blood and yet he seemed completely at ease. He was a cool character. He was about six foot and though not overly muscular, he was fit and able, despite obviously having lived off the land for some time. His clothes were exactly the type Eastman had seen on countless vagrants, dirty and ragged. Except the boots – they looked almost brand new. He had a rough beard and unkempt fair hair, but he still looked in better shape than any hobo Eastman had seen. This was no ordinary vagrant. He was mean and dangerous, but now he was contained, like a venomous snake.

With a sudden explosion of noise that jolted Eastman from his chair, Benteen hit the cell bars with a baseball bat. The hobo seemed completely oblivious to the incident and remained motionless.

"Reckon he's dead, Sheriff?" Benteen mocked.

"I hope not, we want a little talk with him. I don't have to tell you how serious this trouble is, do I?"

Eastman looked for any response from his prisoner. There was absolutely none.

Catching Benteen's gaze, he raised his eyes. Benteen flew at the cell like a raging bull.

"You better talk to me you *freak* or I'll break your God damn face off!"

The force of the bat hitting the metal reverberated around the room with such impact, even Eastman winced.

"Now cool the hell down there, Benteen, it's no good if you break his jaw. I'm sick of telling you that!" Eastman quite enjoyed the play-acting.

"You ain't going nowhere, boy! 'Cept to your grave. We got the death penalty here," roared Benteen.

"I said that's enough, now sit the hell down!"

Landing a hefty kick on the other chair, Benteen sent it flying into the wall with a crash, before leaning against the wall.

"You're going nowhere, so you may as well talk to me. I saw you kill those two guys with *my* gun so you can't deny that. Now just talk."

The hobo moved his hands away from his eyes and swinging his powerful legs over the edge of the bed, looked directly at Eastman.

"What'd you do with the bodies? Where are they?"

Now the guy had spoken, Eastman pressed his advantage.

"Why are you so interested in them, I mean they're dead, right?"

"You just don't get it do you? *They're still dangerous even after they're dead*!"

Eastman noted a rise in the other man's voice that sounded close to panic. He was on to something here.

"Yeah, what you get out of it boy? You still a murderer."

Benteen was back in play.

"You dumb ass country boy, you can't murder them, *they're already dead!*"

Raising his eyebrows, Benteen widened his eyes and looked at Eastman, whistling through his teeth. Eastman might have agreed this guy was crazy, had he not been there.

"Mind telling me your name and *exactly* why you don't have fingerprints mister?"

During his long experience in law enforcement, removing someone's fingerprints was never done for a good reason. It generally meant they were trying to hide something or from someone. Eastman's gut reaction was that this creep was on the run. From the ease with which he'd handled the pistol, Eastman would lay odds that he was a professional killer. The hobo looked at his hands, then looked back at Eastman but he said nothing. Eastman fixed him with a long hard stare.

"You got some kind of connection with those 'people,' that much I do know."

The hobo returned Eastman's stare and rubbed his chin between his grimy forefinger and thumb.

"Those things are contaminated, you understand that, right?" he said, in slow deliberate tones.

As if to signal the end of the interrogation, he swung his legs back onto the bed and shut his eyes. As Benteen strode toward the cell, Eastman motioned him to stop. It was clear that this bozo wouldn't volunteer any more information. They'd need to employ another tactic.

"Let me tell you mister, prints or no prints, name or no name, we *will* find out who you are." Eastman decided to conclude the interview and both men started to leave the room.

"Sheriff, you need to cremate those bodies and you need to do it right now."

Eastman looked at the prisoner. What the hell was with this guy? Eastman and Benteen left the room and headed for Eastman's office.

****

Eastman sat behind his desk and spread his fingers, then joining them like a ribcage at the tips, looked at Benteen through the gaps.

"Well that went really well. He's playing his own ball game with his own rules. I'm going to nail this bum, Gerard."

Eastman realised that Benteen was unusually quiet and this worried him a lot.

"Okay, what's eating you?"

"Nothing…we... look Brad, we got work to do that's all."

"Yeah I know. I'm going over the med centre to talk with Anne."

"I ain't talking about those bodies; I'm talking about the blackout. We got to get us a plan to deal with that."

"Gerard, we got a meeting with Mayor Firth this afternoon, we'll do it then. First we've got multiple homicides to deal with, remember?"

"Brad, the way I see it, is we got ourselves a situation here that we gotta deal with pronto. You need to get your head squared and sort this out."

"What do you mean get my head squared?"

There was a tone in Benteen's voice that Eastman didn't care for. And he wanted to get to the bottom of it.

"Brad, I know what you went through at Hinkle Point; I… no, no I don't know, I wasn't there. It must have been tough; a guy takes a lawman's gun and then murders three people in front of him. That's just a crock. I know you want this guy bad, but there's other things need doing. Psycho guy is in jail and murdered guys are in the morgue, none of them are going anyplace soon. We got us a town full of spooked citizens who can't even call 911. When it gets dark, some people are gonna see this as a free for all garage sale."

Holding up his hand, Eastman looked at Benteen and shook his head. They were some way to calling out the National Guard and somebody had already suggested that.

"Now wait there, before we all go declaring a full blown state of emergency here, Firth will cover it this afternoon."

"Aw, crap! Brad, Firth's a fat clown. He's gonna turn up with election posters; he ain't interested in no damn emergency plan. It's you the town look to; they want you to run things."

"Tony Firth is the legally elected Mayor – not me. It all has to come from him, Gerard."

Replacing Firth would be like a kind of martial law. Even if Benteen was half right, that's not how he worked.

"You been out there and seen what's going on recently?"

"Yes of course I have," began Eastman but Benteen interrupted him.

"When I found out what was going on I came into town, even though you done suspended me and all, to see if I could help. McReedy's gun shop had idiots lining up in the middle of the road, I near run Bill Gardener down. I shut McReedy's and sent those bozos home. It ain't good out there buddy and it's gonna get worse. At night people are gonna start popping rounds off all over the place. They'll panic and we gonna get casualties. You need to take your head outta your ass and take over, damn it!"

Eastman rubbed his eyes. Benteen was right. The hobo was going nowhere fast and neither were the bodies. The current emergency had to take priority over this freaky case. Maybe Benteen was right, maybe he had taken it all too personal; after all it was his gun the guy had used.

"Okay Gerard, we're going to call a meeting here with just our people and we need to deputise more townsfolk. I want a list of all the military guys and we need to organise citizen patrols for the duration."

Eastman reached into the top drawer of his desk and pulled out a silver deputy badge. Tossing the badge up and down in his hand like a dime, he eventually threw it to Benteen.

"You'll need that and I need you. Consider yourself un-suspended Deputy Benteen."

Benteen gave Eastman a wry smile and nodded. "You know it, boss."

"Gerard you get your butt out there and get all our people together and tell Clara to make those lists. I'm gonna see how Anne's doing; I'll be back for the meeting here at one."

CHAPTER - FOUR

Armstrong dated back to the Old West but hadn't really prospered until the 1960's when the US Air Force had constructed a listening post there. Most of the town's two thousand inhabitants were the descendants of the original military personnel. There'd been a thriving sawmill and logging plant, but those were the boom days. The break-up of the Soviet Union rendered such military establishments obsolete, shutting the base. The decline in timber sales had closed the logging plant and last year the sawmill had moved to another county.

To any tourists who ventured there, Armstrong seemed to meet their perception of the typical mid western town. They viewed through romantic eyes, a quaint old town that had stood still since the 1960's. For the people who lived there, the reality was somewhat different.

Sitting in her car, with the air conditioning blasting out cool air, Doctor Lenski pushed her sunglasses onto her long dark hair and took in the sights of the town. Among the faded stars and stripes of the flags that draped along the avenue, yet another For Sale sign had appeared. The shop beneath it sat empty, it's once clean and bright windows now dirty and smeared with window polish. Five years ago, there'd been all sorts of shops and diners on Main Street. Now they'd all but gone, replaced by an ever-growing number of empty shops, each one as faded as the hopes and dreams on which they'd been built at one time built on someone's aspirations.

Anne had noticed the increase in small groups of men, standing about, idly talking. Two years ago these men would have all been employed, but now there was hardly any work. The closure of the sawmill had hit the town hard, badly affecting the economy and promoting a mini exodus. Whole families had moved to find work. She remembered how painful it had been for everyone.

Although unemployment was high, the people got by, working in whatever capacity they could. A lot of the guys made a living as guides for the tourists. This was only seasonal; the rest of the year they had to rely on welfare.

Shambling down the sidewalk was the unkempt form of Robert Pool. His New York baseball cap pulled down over his eyes, his hands thrust firmly into his beer stained vest, he was drunk again. He was always drunk. After his son was killed in the war, he'd hit the bottle and lost his shop. Anne treated more people for alcohol abuse and depression than any other single ailment. Times were bad.

What struck Anne the most was the way in which the picket fences and lawns were well kept, while the window and doorframes were often rotten. It reminded her of the stories her Grandmother had told her about Krakow during the war. The way, in which people swept the doorsteps, even though the street had been half destroyed by German dive bombers. She said it was an attempt to retain normality and retain some small dignity.

The blaring sound of Peter Firth's horn shook her from her contemplations. The lights had changed to green and he was in a hurry to get to Barney's Bar on Second Street. Firth had a number of business interests in the town that made him a regular income, all far from legal. As he recognised her, he slowly drove past in his brand new Cherokee four-by-four Jeep. Anne caught sight of his lecherous gaze and it sickened her. In her late thirties, she was an attractive woman and she knew it. Although Firth was handsome in a rugged type of way, he thought far too much of himself. His wife, Mary, had recently given birth to their second child. She was already walking about with a black eye and cut lip. Last year he'd beaten her so badly she'd been admitted to hospital and he'd been arrested. Sheriff Eastman had been forced to drop the charges at Mary's insistence. The man was a pig.

Averting her eyes, Anne turned left off Main Street and headed towards the health center. Anne liked 'her town' and enjoyed the work she did there. She also liked the way in which the town had welcomed her when she'd moved there. After her husband had died it had made her feel good to be valued and needed again. Driving past Brockman's TV and computer shop, a small group of people caught her attention. They were all staring worriedly at the blank rows of TV screens.

****

As Anne drove through the gates into the health center grounds, she checked her cell phone. Still no signal. The whole town was in a communications blackout and people were starting to worry. Leaving the car, she walked across the parking lot towards the health center, eager for the cool air conditioning. Even the shade from the roadside trees in the town gave little protection from the hot Montana sun. The air was so still and hot it generated a shimmering, hazy effect in the middle distance.

The health center was new; the newest building in the whole town, built when the town still had money. Although minute compared to the city hospital she'd worked at, it suited her well. Next to the Wal-Mart store and the High School it was the town's biggest employer.

As she entered through the metal and glass automatic doors, she stepped into the cool foyer of the health center. A long high wooden desk dominated the reception area. The walls were a clean bright cream and the smell of antiseptic filled the air. Coming out to greet her was the familiar form of Nurse Elle-May Wellman.

"Morning Doctor Lenski, what ya make of this blackout thing?"

"Are we still offline here?" Anne deliberately ignored Elle-May's question.

"Yeah, even the phones are still off."

"What about emergency calls, how are we dealing with them?"

"Well Deputy Bodiene dropped some CB radios off for us to use and the EMT crews can still use their radios in the ambulances, so that's okay there, but nobody's going to be able to call us without a CB."

Anne tried her cell phone one more time but was not surprised to find that it was still dead. She turned to Elle-May.

"Can this day get any freakier, do you think?"

****

21

Sitting in her surgery, Anne checked over her patient list; not one soul had turned up. She guessed that in situations like this people discovered they didn't need the doctor after all. A loud rapid knocking on her door disrupted her musings.

"Yes come in."

It was Elle-May and she was in a hurry.

"Doctor, we got a situation. Eddy Joe called in and said there's been a multiple shooting up at Hinckle Point. Jedree said Brad Eastman and Bill Merka are up there."

Anne felt a slight flush of panic that briefly knotted her stomach, but she shrugged it off – this was an emergency.

"Elle-May, get the crash team ready. Looks like we need to earn our pay after all."

****

Looking out of the main doors, Anne was the first to see the ambulance followed by Jedree Bodiene's squad car. There were no wailing sirens or any sense of urgency. Eddy Joe had already radioed ahead and told them that the three shooting victims had been pronounced dead at the crime scene. However, a sole female had needed sedation. Eddy Joe hadn't identified the victims. Anne's immediate priority was the female but she desperately wanted to know about Brad.

"Elle-May, take this woman to the treatment room, I won't be long."

As Anne went to open the first of the dark green plastic body bags, Bodiene stepped sharply up and stopped her.

"Sorry Doc, contents non-viewable. Sheriff Eastman's orders."

That answered her unspoken question and a sense of relief flowed over her.

"Uh-uh, me doctor, him cop, remember?"

"Whoa there Doc! The Boss said don't touch until he speaks to you himself."

Anne could tell that Bodiene was serious and she decided to let it go.

"Who are they Jed?"

"Don't know Doc, most likely to be drugged out vagrants I expect, not sure. Be glad it ain't Brad or Bill though."

Sam Cortez, the morgue attendant, opened the steel morgue shutters for the EMT crew and silently wheeled the three bodies in.

****

Anne had just completed her examination. Rose Gane sat on the edge of her bed in the treatment room, rocking herself gently back and forth. Although she'd replaced her bloodstained clothes with a hospital gown, her short dark hair was still matted with dried blood. The girl was in a deep state of shock but other than that, she hadn't suffered any injuries except minor scratches to her legs. Bodiene looked over at Anne. "Doc, you think she's gonna be able to talk to us?"

Anne shook her head; the truth was she had no idea. People in this state of shock could be silent for days, sometimes even weeks. Anne was aware that her patient had already been sedated at the scene; this would soon start to wear off. There was a knock at the door and Nurse Garcia popped her head around the door.

"Elle-May said I should come sit with her a while, Doctor Lenski."

"Okay, Maria I've finished for the time being. I think Elle-May must be telepathic or something, thank you. Keep an eye on her and any change just page me; I'm only in my room. Jedree, you want to come with me a minute?"

"Reckon I best stay here Doc, just in case she speaks, I don't want to miss nothing."

"We'll only be outside; I don't want to talk in front of the patient, that's all."

"Umm, yeah okay then but I don't want to stray too far from the door."

Anne and Bodiene stood in the cool shaded corridor, just out of earshot of the treatment room.

"Jedree, what's with the body bag thing? It sounds weird!"

"Eh, what you say there Doc?"

She shook her head; she'd need a more direct line.

"Why can't I touch the bodies? It's *my* health center!"

"Cause the Sheriff says they're dangerous."

"Why are they dangerous? They're dead."

"He reckons they all got some kind of contamination thing going on there."

Contamination? What were they dealing with? Jedree wasn't the smartest, but he'd been a peace officer a long time and clearly this had unsettled him. She needed to talk to Brad if she wanted to proceed with this.

"What happened Jedree; do you know who shot whom?"

"This guy, maybe a crack head, just shot them three and then Brad arrested him. He's down town right now in fact… that's all I know Doc."

Elle-May cut their conversation short.

"Hello Jedree. Sorry to interrupt here, but Sheriff Eastman's on the radio for you."

Elle-May smiled at Bodiene and then walked off with Anne to the main reception, where the radio was kept. It had been some time since Anne had used a two-way radio set but she quickly remembered her military training. She'd been in the US Army reserve during *Operation Restoration*. It was strange how something like a radio brought back the memories of her late husband, Paul. They'd served together as army doctors. Soon after, they'd returned to their civilian jobs and married. She felt a strange feeling of reassurance at hearing Brad's voice over the radio.

"Hello Anne, its Brad here, is everything alright with you over there?"

"Yes, what happened up there this morning, you okay?"

"I'll tell you when I come over later, but the important thing is I don't want those bodies touched."

She detected a level of concern in his voice but she wanted to know more about the new arrivals at the morgue. If there was any risk of contamination, as the town's doctor, she would demand that he tell her.

"Listen Brad, why are the bodies dangerous, what's wrong with them?"

"Anne I can't say on an open channel, but *don't* have any contact with them. Wait till I get there."

"I *have* to examine them, it will make no difference if you're here or not, I need to know what we've got here. Now I'm going to do it with or without your say so."

"Listen Anne, my suspect said they were contaminated and dangerous. I've seen them in action and I think he's right. If need be, I'll get Jed to arrest you. I *mean* that Anne."

If they were that dangerous, then she needed to carry out tests to see what was wrong with them. He had to realise that it was just as dangerous to keep this in the dark.

"Brad if this is some kind of communicable disease and I'm not saying that it is, we need to know what we're dealing with here. The longer we delay, the greater the risk to us all. I know you're worried but you *got* to let me find out what's wrong with them."

Eastman's reply seemed to take forever but eventually he said. "Okay…you win but under one big condition: if you're gonna do it, you dress like a God damn condom, I mean full protection."

"I *will* be careful. When can you come over?"

"Later, I got to interview this creep first. You just take care with those things. See you later. Out."

'*Things*' what an odd term he'd used.

"I want to look at the bodies. Elle-May can you man the fort for a while?"

"Yeah, the place is like a morgue in any case, off you go and have some fun, honey."

****

Anne stood in the morgue, covered head to foot in protective clothing. She had no idea of what to expect. A defective strip light flickered over the three examination tables, casting shadows of the dead around the room. She decided it was best to use the portable theatre lights. The three bodies were still covered in the green plastic body bags they'd arrived in.

Under normal circumstances the attendant would have already removed the bags. However, because of Brad's instructions they'd been left bagged. Only one had been identified. This was Mark Lebel, a tourist from Houston and definitely not a local, Bodiene had said. The other two were completely unknown, with no I.D. She decided to examine Lebel first. It always felt somehow better to work on someone who had a name. It seemed to allow her to empathise with the dead. Anne began to open the bag and realised just how nervous she was, although it was probably all the hype created by the talk of a mysterious contamination. She'd spent hours in this room examining the dead, but though she could not identify why, she now felt very uneasy. It reminded her of the type of feeling experienced in her Gran's old cellar.

Opening the bag, she cursed her clumsiness in tearing her latex glove on the bag zipper. Pulling the zip down slowly, she glimpsed the extent of the injuries. It took her a few moments to completely remove the bag and the clothing from the body. Surveying the wounds, it looked as though a large animal had attacked the man, possibly a mountain lion or similar. There were large cavities torn out of the abdomen and his right hand had been severed, leaving a nasty jagged wound.

The next most obvious wound was a bullet hole through the right eye. She judged by the wound, particularly the exit wound, that it had been from a large calibre weapon. More than likely a Magnum, with almost certainly a heavy loaded round to cause this damage. This was evident by almost twice the damage to the back of the head that she'd have expected. Anne found this particularly interesting; Jedree had said that the 'crack head', as he'd called him, had shot all three with, she assumed, the same weapon. Brad used a heavy load in his pistol, which was also a magnum. Had Jedree got it wrong? Had Brad shot this man? What were the odds of two similar weapons using the same type of ammunition being involved in the same incident? If this guy had been dead at the time the animals had attacked him, why had he been shot in the head?

On closer inspection, it was clear that the other wounds had been inflicted not by a large animal but several smaller ones. Lebel's limbs also bore a number of small bite marks. The bite radiuses of these injuries were certainly not consistent with a large animal. Anne noticed a white object in one of the leg wounds and as she removed it, she discovered that it was a tooth. To her surprise it was a human crown. Could this have come from the man himself? She carefully checked his teeth – all were intact. The awful discovery hit her like a sledgehammer. The bite wounds were not animal but human. The creature that had caused the damage was undoubtedly *human*. Her mind reeled under the implications of the gruesome find. The stories of crazy backwoods people murdering strangers were all made up, weren't they?

Uncovered, the male bodies gave off such a strong odour that it was almost overpowering. Apart from the gunshot wounds, neither body had any visible damage. However, it was almost impossible for Anne to tell because of the high level of decay. The first of the bodies had been shot through the chest; there was a second gunshot to the left eye, which had exited through the back of the head. The second body had been shot through the back of the head and the left arm, almost severing the elbow. It was obvious to her that the same Magnum type bullets had also caused these wounds.

Both bodies displayed a puzzling level of decomposition. They seemed to be in an advanced stage of decay and yet they were still full of fluid, with no evidence of rigor mortis. As she made her first incision, the smell of putrifying flesh filled her nostrils and made her gasp for air. She backed away, holding the back of her hand to her mouth, the foul odour stinging her nostrils. She'd never experienced such an incredible deathly stench in all her professional career. After several minutes of work and with the ribcage now broken, she had a clear view of the exposed internal organs, or rather what was left of them. Each of the organs resembled a shrivelled piece of rotting fruit. What struck Anne the most was the state of internal decay; even the bone structure had advanced to an abnormal level. It was obvious that something was very wrong with these bodies.

****

Anne sat drinking a cup of black coffee in her office. She put the cup down and massaged her throbbing temples. After the examination she'd taken blood and tissue samples and sent them to Conrad Brown in the lab. She hadn't the faintest idea what was wrong with the bodies. This was the sort of situation that required expert advice. However, with communications still out that was impossible. She was completely on her own and she felt vulnerable. The findings had raised more questions than they'd answered.

The discovery of cannibalism was bad enough, but the other two bodies just didn't add up. It looked to her as if both males had been alive when they'd been shot, but that was impossible given the condition of the bodies. She'd have to wait for the toxicology report from Conrad before her next move. To her surprise the telephone on her desk started to ring. Could be that the blackout had come to an end. She hoped so.

"Hello."

It was Elle-May.

"Brad Eastman just called; he's coming over now."

"Oh thanks, send him up when he gets here will you? Are the phones working now?"

"No, not the outside lines. Vince Langley from the Telephone Company connected them in here, like a kinda intercom. We can use them here, but we can't ring out."

Anne could hardly wait to see Brad Eastman's friendly face. It surprised her how a simple thing like being able to use the phone again lifted the mood and made her feel less isolated.

****

Sheriff Eastman made his way to Anne Lenski's office through the near deserted health center. The lack of patients in the building created a very strange if not unnerving feeling. He wanted to see if the Gane girl could be questioned, but first he needed to check on Anne. He realised that maybe he'd sounded harsh earlier. He wondered what reaction he'd get as he tapped on her office door.

"Come in!"

"Hello, do I need a white flag?"

Dr Lenski shook her head and got up from her seat to greet him. "No but only if you remember that I call the shots with the medical matters, Sheriff Eastman."

'*Sheriff Eastman*' that wasn't exactly what he'd expected. He detected a tone in her voice that reminded him of his old High School teacher or even worse, his mother. With a wave of her hand she motioned him to a chair and eventually smiled at him.

"Did you do the tests on the bodies yet?"

"Brad, what happened up there this morning?"

Although he knew that this question was coming, he still felt unable to talk about the troubling events, even to her. Shifting awkwardly in his seat and tapping his chin with his fore finger he began.

"It looks as if the two hikers were attacked by some vagrants or something … then … this guy shot them."

"The same guy you've got in jail? Brad what happened to those vagrants?"

"You got 'em here Anne, remember?"

"No, I mean the two that attacked the hikers, where are their bodies?"

The look of bemusement on Anne's face surprised Eastman, why had she asked such a dumb thing; he'd already said those two had been shot, where did she think they were?

"You got em right here; *you've been looking at them all morning.*"

"Brad, what I have here are two dead bodies. *Dead bodies* that have been shot. I'm talking about the two attackers."

"*They are* the two attackers Anne."

"Don't tell me those two attacked anybody, they've been dead about a month or more."

She must have got it wrong; they were ill maybe even dying, but they were definitely not dead.

"Anne when the suspect shot these two they were still very much alive and moving about."

"Brad that's not possible, it's just not. I'm telling you, the degree of decay on the two bodies means that neither of them would be able to function enough to *move about*, let alone attack anyone."

Eastman knew what he'd seen, but he also knew that the state of them was the same kinda mess he'd seen on bodies fished out of the creek after a month or more. "I ain't gonna argue with you, I know what I saw and when they got shot they was still moving and …"

Just as he was about to explain further he was cut short by the ringing of Anne's telephone.

"Yes...oh Conrad...have you got the results? Right, well what have you got? Look, either you know what you have or you don't. There's no 'not sure'."

Eastman could see by the reaction on Anne's face that something was not as it should be. She wore a deep frown and was uneasily rubbing the top of her pen against her cheek.

"I'll come right away. Conrad, don't show anyone else."

As she replaced the receiver her eyes darted from the telephone to Eastman's and his instincts told him all was not right.

"What's up Anne, bad news?"

"Conrad found something with the toxicology on those bodies. He wants to see me."

"Yeah, well let's go take a look at what he's found then."

Both left for the health center lab without saying a word. Eastman hoped that they'd found something to shed a bit more light on this mystery, but he'd a feeling that things were going to get a whole lot more complicated.

****

The lab was a small well-lit box of a room. The strong smell of disinfectant permeated throughout. A set of large windows overlooked the car lot, bouncing sunshine off the medical equipment onto the far wall. As Eastman and Dr Lenski entered, Conrad Brown was drawing the blinds to cut out the hot sun.

"Conrad where are the slides?" asked Dr Lenski.

It was obvious that she did not want to waste any time. Brown looked over at her and pointed a long finger at the worktop area, nodding a brief acknowledgement to Eastman at the same time. The worktop was littered with various types of medical equipment and near a powerful electron microscope was a set of blood slides.

"Doctor, the slides are from each of the three bodies you examined earlier and they're from *exactly* the 'bloods' that you gave me. I just want you to know, there are *no* mistakes."

"Why would there be?"

"You best check for yourself, that's all I'm saying."

Brown rubbed the sweat from his forehead. Although Eastman had no idea what either was talking about, it was part of his job to judge people and situations. This guy Brown was like a cat on a hot tin roof. Was he trying to hide something or was he scared at what he'd found? Whatever, it was plain to see that he was a worried man.

Dr Lenski placed the first slide under the powerful lenses and adjusted the magnification back and forth. After a few seconds examination, she replaced the slide with the other two samples. Moments later she shook her head, looking directly at Brown.

"What are these? Where's the slide from the bodies gone, Conrad? These aren't even proper blood samples. I don't know what these are!"

Her tone was sharp and irritable. "Doctor, I've checked and re-checked and *these are* the 'bloods' you gave me."

Brown's reply seemed almost desperate as he tried to convince Dr Lenski he'd done his job.

"Look, here are the phials you gave me, they've still got the samples in them and this is your writing. I know what you're thinking because I thought it too. But as crazy as it looks, the samples are right."

Dr Lenski looked long and hard at Brown. Then she took the samples from him and placed them under the microscope. After further examination she puffed out a long breath.

"*This is incredible*…you're right Conrad…I…I have to agree. I've never seen anything like this before! I'll need to run further checks but…"

Eastman looked at Anne. She'd discovered something but he couldn't fathom any of it and he needed a straight explanation from her.

"Mind letting me in on this big discovery?"

Turning to face him on her swivel chair she eased herself off the seat and went to a bookcase, selected a book and gestured him to join her. She placed the heavy textbook on the nearby worktop and leafed through the pages. Looking at Eastman she pointed to a photo.

"Brad, do you know what that is?"

He looked at the image; it was a photo of something that had been magnified many, many times but he had no idea what it was.

"Nope, but I'm sure you're gonna tell me."

"It's a healthy human cell. No matter who you take a cell from, if it's healthy it will look like this. Even diseased cells will appear similar."

Lenski took Eastman back to the microscope and placed one of the blood samples for him to examine.

"Now you look, tell me what you think that is Brad?"

Eastman adjusted the eyepiece to enlarge the image clearly enough to identify. The object looked nothing like the picture in the book. It was a dark, bruised colour, not so defined as the cell in the picture and with faint wispy tendrils. It looked plain ugly.

"Is it a cell or something? It doesn't look like the picture … I don't know…"

"Ten out of ten Brad, it is a cell but that cell stopped being human some time ago."

Eastman was now confused. She'd said even diseased cells still looked human and yet she'd just said these cells were not human. What the hell was she going on about?

"Anne take it slow, it's been a long day."

"Brad, whatever source contaminated these bodies it has mutated, or taken over if you like, the very cells that makes up our bodies. *Whatever they are, these bodies are no longer human!*"

CHAPTER – FIVE

Taylor was sitting on his bed staring at the bars of the cell. He was in a world of hurt. Worst of all he knew it was his fault. Not because of the shootings, that needed doing. No, it was because he'd been dumb enough to help that damn fool girl. He should've just kept on walking but no, he'd had to get involved, again.

That was his problem. Like the man at the road accident or the girl being mugged some months before. In the war, he'd hated the casual indifference to killing from both sides. He'd been forced to detach himself from the situations he'd encountered in order to survive. Killing was not an easy thing to do but being killed would be far worse in his book. By and large this strategy worked. But for now, he was locked up in Jerksville USA.

These rednecks had no idea what was hanging over their heads. He'd been dumbstruck when the cop had tried to arrest the creature. He smiled as the image of the thing in a court room on trial flashed into his head. Had his reactions been that different when he'd first come across these things? The bottom line was, from the cops' point of view, he'd simply murdered two people in cold-blood and done it with a cop's gun.

It worried him that some small town quack would likely blunder about with the bodies and infect half the town. Well, he'd more pressing matters to contend with. When these clowns managed to reconnect to the world they'd get to know all about him. It wouldn't be long after that, that ZerTon would come for him. The thought filled him with utter dread. He needed to escape; there was no way he was going through all that again.

"Hey Benteen. What gives with this crummy dump? You hillbillies forget to pay the telephone bill?"

There was no response; he'd have to raise his game plan a notch. He needed to provoke this ape and fast.

"Is that the official line or don't you understand the question? I mean they don't keep you around for your deductive skills. You're just a heavy in a uniform."

To Taylor's dismay, Benteen just sat looking through a pile of reports, completely ignoring the attempts to provoke him.

"What's wrong, Eastman keep you on a chain too long? He hasn't let you beat on anyone today? Would you like to beat me?"

"Close your hole, hobo. All I can hear is blah-blah from you."

"Aw, I get it. You used to get beat on. Your redneck Pappy done break your GI Joe? Or maybe it was *Barbie*?"

Benteen slammed his hand down on the desk, the noise echoing like a pistol shot in the concrete room. Then he spun himself around on his swivel chair and glowered at Taylor.

"You got one hell of a lot to squawk about, considering you're behind *my* bars. Ya low-life bum!"

"You da BIG man. Or is it just your fat mouth that's big? Come on, no one to stop you now is there?"

With a low rumble, Benteen rose up from his chair and drew himself to his massive height. He fixed Taylor with a wild stare and advanced towards the cell, fists clenched and arms rigid at his side. This was it, thought Taylor.

"I'm gonna tear you a new ass, you God damn freak!"

"Hold up there Deputy," called Eastman from the doorway.

He was walking into the room with Dr Lenski. Benteen shrugged his huge shoulders, grunted and moved away from the cell. "Sorry Brad, but that boy's got some mouth on him."

"Well, that's good, 'cause he's going to need it. Can you get someone over to Mike Goodman's place? They've reported trespassers."

"Sure Brad. See you later, Doc."

As Benteen left, Eastman shot him a reproachful glance. Gerard was not the best person to baby-sit this guy. He looked at the hobo; this drifter was a dangerous unknown. It was obvious that he'd just tried to play Benteen. Anyone crazy enough to want to pick a fight with him was *very* dangerous.

"Okay drifter. Dr Lenski here wants to ask you some questions. You'd do best to cooperate."

Dr Lenski looked him up and down. "I'd like to know more about these bodies we have. They've got some peculiarities about them. I don't understand."

Taylor shifted his position and stretched out on his bed with his hands behind his head. Then he turned his head to look at Dr Lenski, giving her a long stare before he answered.

"They're not safe, even dead. Even then, they can still get you. Sort of complicated, Doctor."

"You said that they were contaminated, *contaminated* with what?"

"You wouldn't believe me if I told you. Don't poke about with things you don't understand."

"Why not let me be the judge of that?"

"I'll tell you this. Don't think you've seen the last of these things. Take my advice. Burn those damn bodies. Now if you don't mind, it's kinda noisy in here and I need some shut-eye."

"Wait, I need more if I'm going to..."

"Don't waste your time; he's not gonna say any more."

Both Eastman and Lenski walked out of the room and into the hallway. Eastman knew it was pointless to continue to question the guy. Besides, there was work to be done.

"Anne, I'm going to talk to Rose Gane, see what I can come up with. Then I'd better start sorting out the volunteers."

"I can't believe that guy not wanting to help us. Yet he warned us about the contamination. What do you think he meant about not seeing the last of these things?"

"Hate to think, but he knows a lot more than he's letting on."

Despite the heat, she shuddered as a sudden chill swept over her.

****

Eastman was sitting in his office with Benteen when Dr Lenski walked in.

"Is it true what Clara just told me about that girl Brad, has she left?"

"I went to the hotel and Mrs Jackson said the girl left a few hours back. Took all her gear and slipped out. I've sent some of my people out, but she could've gone anywhere."

"We have to find her. She's going to be confused with all that's happened."

"Look Doc, there's miles and miles of nothing out there, if we knew where she was at then we'd go get her," Benteen said.

"Gerard's right, she could be walking, she could've hitched a ride and I don't have the manpower or the resources to mount a search. I'm sorry."

"So what, you're just going to let her go?"

"Anne, don't forget this girl is a material witness to three murders, if I could find her I would. If everything were normal then I'd put an APB out, hell I could even call for the county chopper. State Troopers would set up roadblocks. But we're on our own. I got to think about the people here."

Dr Lenski nodded and lowered her gaze. She knew Eastman was perfectly right but hated the idea of this vulnerable girl alone in the wilderness.

"Okay it's time for the meeting. Gerard, you've got the store until I get back. Anything up, you know where I'm at. You gonna come, Anne?"

"Yes, but I'll sit in the audience if you don't mind. There's nothing I can contribute at the moment."

****

The town hall was the heart of Armstrong. It had been one of the first buildings constructed and had grown over the years. In its day it had been a grand building but it had seen better days. The midday sunlight flooded into the hall through the high-set sash windows, illuminating the countless dust motes lazily drifting in the air and gleaming off the polished wooden floor.

Eastman and Firth sat on the stage facing the assembled townspeople. The old hall had never been built to hold this volume of people. Eastman noted that many people were standing with still more outside. This situation was the biggest thing to hit the town since the Cuban missile crisis. Judge Carmille called order and handed the floor to Firth, who stood up and launched into his speech.

"We woke this morning and found us in a communications blackout, that's what this meeting was supposed to be about. Now we got us another situation. Three people died up at Hinckle Point this morning. That's plain awful, but as mayor of this town I gotta look after our interests first. That's just the way it is. The Sheriff here's got the low-down on all that. Then we'll get back onto this blackout thing. Sheriff over to you."

Eastman got up from his chair and looked out at the anxious faces peering back at him. Not only were these people worried about this bizarre situation they now had three murders right in their front yard. However odd the murders were, he would use plain and simple police procedure to deal with them, it was the other situation that could bring trouble.

His glance fell on Lenny Kovak, the editor of the *Armstrong Bugle*. Problem was that nobody had told him that, as he sure as hell thought he was on the *New York Times*. Eastman knew full well this guy could be a real pain in the ass. He'd have to watch him.

"At about 9:30 this morning Bill Merka and myself came across a dead body. During the course of this discovery the suspect shot and killed two men. This suspect is now in custody. There was also a female who was being treated for shock at the medical centre. She has since absconded. I got people looking for her but in the current situation; I'm limited to what I can do. Now, this is an ongoing investigation so I don't have a lot to go on. But none of these individuals are local folks. I know this is big…"

Kovak sat up and called out, "Sheriff, when you say absconded, had she been arrested? Is she a danger? Do you have any motives at this time? I mean any connections to the bank job in Burnsville last month?"

"Lenny, you're gonna give yourself a heart attack. Simmer down a while. This girl was a victim and poses no danger; I already said this is *ongoing*. Like I was about to say, I know this is big news but it's under control. Right now we got us another situation we need to deal with. That's this blackout and that concerns all of us. The Mayor will say a few words about that."

Firth stood up and began his address.

"At the moment we got us a situation we don't fully understand. We got no communication with the outside world. But that don't matter none, we come through floods, snow and a hell of a lot more than no Cable. I'm going to lead you through this. We all gotta stick together as a town. I got my people chasing the cause of this down and as soon as I got some progress I'm gonna let you know. We still got our power and we can use the old CB radios so we ain't all done in and…"

Kovak interrupted him. "Mayor, is it true that Deputy Koneg said that the town is cut off in both directions?"

"Mr Kovak, saying things like that's gonna get people spooked. We don't want to cause a scare."

"I'm not looking to scare anyone; I just want the truth. Mayor, are we totally cut off? The people have the right to know."

Eastman could see there was a danger of the meeting degenerating into panic as people started to call out in concern. They wanted to know what had happened. Eastman rose and with a loud voice announced, "Max Koneg drove towards Burnsville but just outside our town limits is a huge crater blocking the highway. He tried going north toward O'Brien's Ridge but most of O'Brien's Ridge is now on the Highway. Both Highway 104 routes are blocked."

Eastman used the stunned silence to continue, "This doesn't mean we're trapped. There are tracks running through the countryside to Burnsville. But they're only for those who know how to use them."

"That's just great but what about the rest of us?" called out Oscar Majors.

Eastman knew Majors from High School but he'd left town years back and gone to the city. He'd recently come back and taken over the General Store, after Mr Miller had died.Eastman could see that Sarge was getting agitated. Sarge was dressed in his combat fatigues and cut an imposing figure as he stood up and called out.

"Why the sudden need for everybody to run screaming to the hills? One side of Highway 104 is darn near 90 clicks of desert to Burnsville. You get a blow-out there and the sun will get you. The other side of the highway is the mountains, you get trouble up there and the grizzlies will get you. We just need to sit tight and let this blow over."

"Sarge is right. Anyone thinking about private expeditions can forget it. If the time comes, then we'll send an organised convoy for help. But that's not going to happen," said Eastman.

"I gotta agree with the boys there," said Firth. "We got no need to run from the town. What we gotta do is work together on this. Anyone who's worried by this can talk to me and, of course, Preacher Goodman. Sheriff Eastman has a few words to say then we'll wrap it up."

"Thank you Mayor. We can't use 911, so I want volunteers to help out. I need about twenty people. They're gonna patrol the town and any folks needing help can let them know. The teams will have CB's or police radios. I asked Dan Brockman for as many sets as he can get. "Mayor, you can authorise that from the town fund. Next thing I need is any military reservists and people on leave; turn up at the station house in *uniforms* with everybody else at seven this evening. Right now, we need to be good neighbours to keep the town safe, just check on each other. Well that's about it for now."

"One last question, Sheriff is there any connection with the blackout and these murders?"

"I'll take that Lenny," Firth said. "There is absolutely no connection and these are separate issues. You can trust me on that."

****

Marv Glitzman was a geek and he'd be the first to admit it. He collected Smurf toys and wrote poems. But it was his body that caused the problems. He was too skinny and too tall. Mr Donovan, his Phys Ed teacher, called him 'fragile'. He hated sticking out from the other kids. There was one other thing: he was the new kid. The new kid that just couldn't do any right. He'd moved from the city about a year ago, but his dad reckoned that in a place like Armstrong, outsiders were always outsiders. He was desperate to fit in. This was why he'd agreed to come on this stupid trip.

Conrad Firth was a boy that no one liked; in fact most kids avoided him. He was the Mayor's son with cash to burn, but he was trouble. They'd starting hanging out together as something to do in school. Some other like-minded kids had joined them and now Conrad thought he was the leader of a 'bad ass' gang. He got into trouble in town but his family would see that it never amounted to anything.

He'd planned this trip for weeks; the gang would take some gear and camp out by the old airbase, but with all this excitement today they'd nearly called it off. Conrad had persuaded them to carry on. However, it wasn't through loyalty to Firth that Marv had agreed to continue. It was Britney Patrick. She was a vision of beauty with long blonde hair and eyes as blue as…

"Hey keep up Marv, you're slowing us down," called Conrad, completely ruining the moment.

Conrad was well in front of the rest except for Britney who was just in front of him. She was wearing 'those' pants that Marv liked. How long he'd waited for this trip, now all he had to do was pick his moment with her. His father had wanted to call the whole thing off, but Conrad had lied about where the gang was going to camp.

The old base had a serious 'spook' factor about it. Everyone in town had been too busy and with Eastman gathering his posse, they'd just slipped out. Tony Arcado had brought some of his old man's Bourbon. That left Jenha Galway and Ruby Carson. They were invited along because they were the only ones with tents.

"Hey, how long till we're there?" Jenha asked.

She was tired of lugging her tent up the incline and now it was getting dark. She hadn't wanted to leave town with all the commotion going on, but she couldn't let the others down. Even so, she wished that someone else would carry the tent.

"I'll have a look up ahead," Conrad called back.

As Conrad sped up and disappeared over the crest of the hill, Marv quickened his pace, drawing level with Britney. With Conrad out of the way he could see his chance of being with her. But what would he say? Making small talk with girls was not his thing.

"Hi. A bit cooler now," he ventured, looking over at her.

She shot him a sideways glance but said nothing. Britney Patrick was from the other side of town. Her parents owned several properties and regarded themselves as 'people of substance' but she'd never been good at making friends. She found most people in the town plain dumb and did her best to stay clear of them. Conrad was different, he was like her, he didn't care what people thought of him and he was exciting. She looked at Marv. He was a geek but he was good at schoolwork. She knew that if she got him to help her, then her grades would improve and she could move out of Armstrong.

"So, Marv, what do you make of all this today?"

"I...well better than watching the grass grow," was the best he could manage.

Both of them laughed. Suddenly, a figure erupted from the foliage on the trackside, brandishing a large knife. It was dressed in a black robe and under the hood was a disfigured skull. Shrieking insanely, the figure rushed at the terrified group. Marv barely had time to react; he shot a kick at the figure's hand and sent the knife soaring into the air. The other kids were riveted to the spot screaming, too shocked to move. Then the hooded figure started yelling back.

"Ow, you God damn fool; you could've broken my wrist!"

Everyone stopped screaming and looked at the figure in bewilderment. Marv reached out and pulled the rubber mask off, revealing the assailant. The kids erupted into angry outbursts.

"Real clever there Firth. I done just about messed my shorts!" Tony Arcado shouted.

"That was a dumb thing to do up here, you creep," called Britney.

"Aw, come on guys! Can't you take a joke? Nobody got hurt - except for *me*, that is. Who the hell do you think you are Marv? Chuck freaking Norris?" said Conrad defending himself.

Jenha was comforting Ruby who was close to tears.

"Yeah, well good for Marv. He should've kicked your stupid head off!" she yelled at him.

"That was cool. Where the hell did to learn to do that dude?" asked Tony.

Suddenly Marv was the unexpected centre of attention; his face felt like it was on fire as he turned bright red. His eyes darted about, as he frantically struggled to think of a reply.

"My Grandpa fought in 'Nam and he taught me a few tricks, that's all."

Marv watched as Conrad went around each of the gang almost pleading with them to carry on. He'd been brought crashing down and Marv was surprised at just how good that felt. He wasn't the only one; Britney was enjoying it also. Then she looked directly at him. It was a strange look with a faint smile. It was the type of look that made him glad he was wearing loose pants. Eventually Conrad successfully persuaded the gang to continue and they moved off. Marv began to think this expedition might not be so bad after all.

****

Taylor lay on his bed keeping a watchful eye on his captor. This new guy had replaced the gorilla. His gold nameplate read 'Deputy Bodien' and man, was he a real hillbilly. He'd spent the last half hour or so drooling over a copy of *Guns and Ammo.* Taylor had managed to piece together that Eastman had organised extra patrols to cover the night hours. Taylor had taken more information from them than they'd got from him. Eastman was not from the same breed as the other cops, that much was clear. He was no ordinary flatfoot, he was smart and that made him a threat.

"Hey, hillbilly boy. When's chow time?"

"Call me that again and you don't get no chow, *boy*."

"What's going on out there in any case?"

"Ain't no concern of yours. Hush up now, I'm reading."

"If you're not feeding me, then how about one of them lights off?"

"Clara's gonna bring some food at eight – it ain't half seven yet. I don't want no wise cracks outta you when she turns up, either. You hear me?"

Bodien switched the strip light off in the nearest cell, affording some shade.

Taylor lay back on his bed, placed his hands behind his head and linked his fingers, sighing heavily. How the hell had he got mixed up in all this crap in the first place?

CHAPTER - SIX

Jimmy Red Cloud looked up at the full moon, thankful of its guiding light. Although nothing but a rough mountain track, he treated it like most folk would treat the sidewalk. He'd walked the five miles from his home and almost reached the Parks Department observation tower, a trek he'd made many times before. Tonight though, something wasn't quite right.

There was a certain something in the air. Everything was still and silent and it shouldn't be. Where were the nocturnal animals, the hunters and the prey? There was something else too; he couldn't shake the feeling that he was being watched. He looked about the heavily-wooded area, the tall pine trees reaching into the clear night sky, his keen senses alert, but all he could smell was that same stench of death. First he'd thought it was coming from a large animal, but the odour had followed him for miles and then vanished. Now it was back and worse than before.

Covering the ground the way he had, he figured it would be another hour before he'd reach the tower. He was meeting with Bill Merka. For a white man, Merka had a real feel for the land and Red Cloud liked him. They'd started working together some two years ago and Red Cloud had volunteered as often as he could. Tonight Merka had invited him to help record a meteorite shower. It was due in over the highest peak and he'd have the best view in the county on top of the tower.

Red Cloud had tried to call Merka on his cell phone and landline but both were out. The kids he'd seen a while back seemed to have been using their cell phones, so perhaps it was just Bill's? They'd been heading up towards the old Air Force base with camping gear. He'd kept out of sight. He knew that some whites got freaked when they came across Indians and things were odd enough as it was.

He'd spent countless hours hunting these hills though he'd never felt like this before. Animals could sense things that people couldn't. Maybe it was the comet that had spooked them. He tried to rein his imagination in; he was sounding like one of the old men. Spooks and spirits, all that bull was long gone.

The only spirits he'd seen on the reservation came courtesy of Mr Jack Daniels or worse, Moonshine that could turn a man blind or mad. Too many on the reservation drank and drank too damn much. He never touched the stuff and he wanted no part in that old hokum either. That was for tourists, like the couple he'd seen in the SUV some days ago. He'd stopped by to warn them of the park's fire regulations. They'd seemed okay but it was obvious that the nearest either had been to a real Red Indian was a re-run of *The High Chaparral* on TV. Most whites were shocked to find that Indians didn't use 'um' every other word and that annoyed him.

Red Cloud stepped up onto a small rocky outcrop and in the distance he could clearly see the lights of the tower. He tried his phone again, still nothing. Stepping back onto the track he was suddenly seized by a sense of overwhelming anxiety. There was that stench again. Sickly, sweet – a rancid stink. He was sure he was being watched. He could feel the eyes on him. It was such a strong feeling that he spun around, his eyes darting all about him. There was nothing. He still couldn't explain it. Now the hairs on his neck were standing up. He was desperately fighting the urge to run, but he still didn't know from what?

****

Marv couldn't stop thinking about the look Britney had given him a while ago. It was the look that girls gave boys when they're hot. That's what Mike Travis had said and he knew about such things. Damn, was she hot! Which was more than he could say about the chill night air; he guessed it made up for the day's heat. He glanced around at the others. Jenha and Ruby were sticking like glue to Tony, who was just behind him, while Britney walked ahead. Conrad had been way out in front but now he'd dropped back, walking along with them. Marv was surprised at how bright the moon was. He could easily make out the tree line and even the track wasn't that difficult to see. There was a steep rocky drop either side of the narrow track.

"Hey Conrad, where's this place at?" Tony called.

He was about done with all this walking and he wanted to show the rest he could drink strong Bourbon, none of that watered down crap. He'd been sipping it neat since second grade although if his Pa ever caught him, he'd be for it. This walk just seemed to take forever.

"Yeah, do you even, like, know where this place is?" Britney was mocking him.

She thought it good to keep people in their place. Conrad had had about enough of the lot of them. He'd gone to the trouble of organising this whole trip and now they were crapping on about whatever. Worst of all, his wrist hurt. Marv had been oh-so-lucky back then. All that kung fu bull didn't worry him none, he could've done that if he'd really wanted to. Damn. He knew this place was up here somewhere, he just couldn't recollect exactly where.

Conrad looked back at the others, their faces lit up from their cell phones. Who the hell did they think they were gonna call he thought? A sudden movement from the trees made the group stop. Everyone looked towards the place the sound had come from. Conrad shone his torch, but its dim beam barely reached the trees. Then they heard it again; somebody or something was crashing about in the undergrowth.

"What was that?" Ruby murmured nervously.

"Oh, that's just the maniac airman," Conrad joked, mimicking a spooky voice.

"Yeah, then who's that?" Britney pointed up the track.

Marv looked up ahead. There was a figure moving toward them, but it was too far away and dark to get a fix on. He knew if this was another trick, then Conrad was likely to get thrown over the side, rocks or no rocks.

"If this is another one of your lame jokes, I'm sure not laughing," accused Britney.

"It ain't none of my doing. Maybe it *is* the maniac airman?"

Conrad was enjoying every second of it. The figure kept on walking towards them. As it drew closer, it made directly for them and Conrad started to back away. The guy sure looked loaded, the way he was lurching about. Things were starting to get heavy. Although Marv was still unable to see the guy, the odour from him was sickening, like something rotting. He heard Conrad call out to the guy but all he heard back was a strange growling sound. The figure let out a fearful screech and then without warning, lunged at Conrad, grabbing and clawing at him. It knocked the torch from Conrad's hand as he desperately tried to push him away. Conrad lost his footing and fell backwards, the assailant clawing at his face. Jenha ran to help and started to pull at the attacker, who then turned on her. Conrad pushed the hapless girl directly at the attacker. She screamed as the creep took a large bite out of her arm and then greedily began chewing on the flesh.

As the others went forward to help, three other figures emerged from the darkness with hideous shrieks. One pulled Ruby's head back and bit into her neck, sending an arterial spurt into the night air, falling as crimson rain on the others. She rasped for air and clutched at the assailant as he continued to gnaw at her throat. Ruby lost her footing and together with her attacker, fell down the embankment, crashing through the foliage onto the rocks below. It was too much for Conrad who broke away from the first attacker and ran, terrified into the woods.

Britney grabbed Jenha and called to the others. "Come on, let's get out of here!"

"Wait, what about Ruby? We gotta get Ruby!" wailed Tony.

"She's had it dude!" Marv screamed, pulling at him.

"What if she's just out cold? What...?" Tony pleaded, pushing Marv's arms away.

"There's too many, they're gonna get us too, if we don't go now!" yelled Britney.

The situation was helpless; there were just too many to fight. They had to run. Fortunately the attackers were slow and the kids managed to out-distance them easily. As they ran away into the night, they couldn't help but think of Ruby's fate.

****

Benteen was sitting in his squad car. He glanced at his watch; it was after one AM. He'd never seen Armstrong so quiet. *So far so good,* he thought to himself, though it was more than a bit odd to see the streets completely deserted. Brad had done a good job. He'd split up the volunteers into small groups, each with a police squawk-box and given them areas of town to patrol. The service people had turned up in uniform like they'd been told, which as Brad said 'put more uniforms in view.'

Sarge, of course, was in his element. He loved it, barking out orders here and there, but so far it seemed as if he was doing a good job. Benteen just hoped Sarge wasn't going to get all crazy or pull some dumb ass crap. Benteen agreed it had been a good idea for the volunteers to be unarmed, not good to have too many nervous guns about. It wouldn't take much for lead to start flying.

Benteen had driven right around the town and despite Brad not having ordered a curfew; nobody was out, apart from the patrols. Folks had just decided to lock the doors and batten down the hatches. All the bars had shut, except Barney's Bar, but then they already knew that was going to happen. However, without customers, Peter Firth had to shut anyway.

On the whole, the town looked as if it was pulling together, which was just as well. Benteen had lived through some tough times in the town, but generally speaking, people just got on with it. This, however, was the strangest thing he'd ever seen.

There had to be some real good explanation for all this crap and, hopefully, this situation would sort itself out soon. Then they could nail that creep in the cell. Benteen really wanted to get even with that bum. He knew Brad always did everything 'by the book' although, every now and then, you had to skip a page or two. He'd get all they wanted from this guy, given the chance.

Why always let the Feds get the credit? He shook his head in frustration, reached forward and started the car, then drove off. It was the end of his shift; he needed to get some rest before the morning. He was going to slowly drive around the town for one last check before handing over to Jedree. Everything was as it should be, with the good folk of Armstrong all safely tucked up in bed.

****

The kids were hopelessly lost. They'd left the track and had run blindly into the woods putting as much distance between themselves and their attackers. They'd been on the move for hours, every noise or movement in the woods spurring them on further and further into the unknown. They'd no idea who the people were but they knew that not even crazy people acted like those things.

Now the gang found themselves at the bottom of a steep ravine. Dense trees blocked out the moonlight, reducing their vision still further. Marv looked at the others. Over the last few hours, by some kind of unwelcome twist they'd come to regard him as the leader. It was a case of the blind leading the blind; he'd no more idea than them.

He wished he'd listened to his Grandpa more about tales from 'Nam but, back then, they'd just sounded too way out. Like some kind of war comic. He remembered it hadn't been until the funeral and seeing that general with Grandpa's Silver Star, that Marv had realised that the stories had been true. If only he was with him right now.

He still couldn't get Ruby out of his mind, her screams and the blood. If he'd been faster or there hadn't been so many of those things...The fact was, she'd been killed; there was no way she could've survived that fall. Then he flushed with anger at the thought of that punk, Firth, bugging out.

He was brought out of his thoughts as Jenha let out a pitiful gasp. She was getting worse. He could see by the light of Britney's cell phone that the bite area was an ugly dark colour. She also had a high fever. God knows what had been wrong with those things; maybe they had rabies or something.

"Okay Marv," said Tony, "what do we do now? I mean you know, right?"

"Marv, we got to get her to hospital," pleaded Britney.

"Look, I...Well..." Marv was lost for words and at a loss as to what to do.

"Conrad did this to me," sobbed Jenha, "it's his fault."

"Aw, it's the fever," said Tony. "She's talking bull."

"No, no she's not, he pushed her," said Britney. "I seen him."

"That ain't so; he wouldn't do that, not Conrad."

"Yeah he did. He pushed her at that thing, just so as he could save his rotten skin and then he took off!" Marv concluded.

It was all too much for Tony who burst into floods of tears. Marv watched as the other two sat and shivered. He had to come up with something or they'd end up the same as Ruby.

"Look, it'll be light in a few hours then we can see where the hell we're at. We don't have any choice; we gotta go back the way we just come. We gotta find that track."

****

Stallone was barking again. Al Paxmore cursed the dog, flicked on the bedroom light and got out of bed. His wife Jill looked on as he tried to find his slippers in the small bedroom. She watched, trying not to laugh as her husband struggled, cursing, to find them. It was unlike Stallone to create such a ruckus, she thought.

"Al, didn't you say that a dog always got a reason for barking?"

"This is the third time tonight, damn mutt. We gotta get up in four hours!" he yelled. He was far from happy.

"Well, just get him in, no need to fuss so," reprimanded Jill.

Al walked the short distance down the hall to the solid wooden front door. She watched as he unlocked the door, lifted the heavy latch and called the dog. The chill night air made her draw the duvet to her chin. Stallone came bounding in, ears flat against his head, eyes wide like dinner plates and tail tucked between his legs. The dog hid behind Al, shaking with fear. Something was wrong, very wrong.

"What's up with him, Al? He's all weirded out," called Jill from the hall doorway.

"Aw, it's just some old coyote," said Al, closing and bolting the door.

"Well ain't you gonna look?"

"Nope, the only place I'm going is back to bed."

Al walked past her and headed for the bedroom and climbed back into bed, pulling the duvet over his head. As she got into bed next to him, she thought he should really take a look. But they did have an early start, so perhaps it was best to leave it. She reached over and switched the light off. Jill lay back and listened to Al fidgeting about but he'd soon be asleep. She shut her eyes knowing it would take her ages to drift off.

They both worked in the town; she was a nurse at the health center and Al worked in the grocery store. She'd always wanted to be a nurse; even as a little girl she'd liked to help people. After college, she'd taken her nursing exams and landed the job at Sunnyvale Rest Home. But then, about four years back, the health center had opened and she'd worked there ever since. She and Al had been married ten years next week. They'd had more good times than bad, but the bad times had been pretty bad.

Like a whole lot of others, Al had lost his job when the sawmill shut. It had devastated him. He'd started drinking, then shortly after, he'd become suicidal. It had been tough to keep it together. Al was better now since he'd taken the job at the store. It had given him a new lease of life. Although Armstrong was hardly a Metropolis, it was way too busy for them. That's when they decided to buy the Reynold's although, strictly speaking, it wasn't really a farm; they had open space and lots of land.

They'd made some money on their town house, but even though Al had done most of the work himself, putting the place right had left them with hardly anything. Four miles outside town, they had to commute to work every day but it was worth it. They both enjoyed the peace of the country; it was the perfect retreat. Jill liked to paint and Al was at his best woodworking – who needed TV?

The blackout had really worried a lot of people but up here on the farm, they'd hardly noticed. Elle-May had asked all the staff to be ready for any situations and Gerard Benteen had made sure that all her girls got a CB radio. Jill's PA had used one years back, in fact, most folk had used them in the days before cell phones came along. She and Al had brought the CB home but they'd soon had enough of hearing all the other people jabbering on. Now it was silent in the other room. Jill turned onto her side, yawned, and wondered what the next day would bring.

Stallone was still agitated and now she could hear him whimpering; there was something bothering him. Suddenly, he started to howl. What was it Al had said about dogs always having a reason for barking? As far as she could recall when a dog howled like that, it meant death.

CHAPTER - SEVEN

For a change, Eastman was glad to hear his alarm sounding its wake up call. He sat up in bed and swung his legs onto the wooden floor. He massaged the side of his head with his fingertips and sighed. He'd spent one of the worst nights he could recall, tossing and turning. But it was the nightmare that had affected him the most. It seemed to go on and on, all damn night. It was the kind he got after Helen's funeral, only worse.

Night-time terrors were supposed to vanish with the light – that was the rule his mom used to tell him. He could still see the confused images in his head: Armstrong, blood on the streets and people screaming. The town full of vague, shadowy figures, just out of focus. There seemed to be a battle going on, he just couldn't make out with whom. He told himself it was just his mind dealing with the stress of the past day, but in all honesty, it had disturbed the hell out of him.

He stood up, stretched wearily and walked out of the bedroom towards the living room, the early light revealing the remains of last night's supper. Pouring himself a large glass of chilled water, Eastman looked at the telephone on the unit in front of him, almost willing it to ring. His one consolation was that the situation in the town couldn't have got any worse; otherwise Clara would've called him. He reached over and picked up the landline. Dead. The TV and his cell phone too. Whatever was happening, things weren't finished yet.

****

It had been light for several hours and though the sun was still low in the sky, the kids knew it would start to heat up very soon. In the grey light of dawn, they'd managed to find a path leading up from the woods. They were sitting now on a rough vehicle track, a vast landscape spread out before them. Recent tyre prints told them the track was in use; at least there was a chance that somebody would find them. Britney suddenly stood up and pointed down the track.

"Guys, it's a car. Look!"

A large black four-by-four stopped a short distance from them, its engine still running. It was impossible to make out who was in the vehicle through the tinted glass.

"Oh, guys we're safe!" shouted Tony, standing and shaking Marv's arm.

Marv grinned in relief at his friends, then approached the vehicle. "Hey, can you help us please? We've been attacked!"

As he got closer, the vehicle revved its engine and then, without any warning, drove straight at him. Marv narrowly escaped being hit as the Jeep raced past, throwing up stones and dust as it sped by. The kids hurled abuse at the jeep as it disappeared into the distance.

"Where's he going?" Tony shouted in disbelief.

Marv looked at Jenha, she was no better. Beads of sweat ran down her pale drawn out face. He was powerless to help her, or was he? There was something Grandpa had said about getting lost in the hills. If he could just remember what it was…?

"I know where we are," announced Marv. "That, over there," he pointed to a small creek, "is the start of Dawson's Pool. That's gonna take me right back to town."

"Oh yeah, and how do you know that?" Tony said.

"Something Grandpa used to say. If you ever get lost in the mountains you gotta find a stream and follow it down, sooner or later you gonna get to a town. That's the way people build towns, because the water runs down to them."

"What you mean, *you're* gonna follow the creek?" Britney inquired a hint of concern in her tone.

"I said I knew where we were. We're not far from O'Brien's Ridge. Now, there's a whole mess of farm tracks around here. Somebody's gotta come along here on the way to Armstrong. They just gotta."

"Like hello! What you mean, you're gonna follow the creek?"

"Look Britney, Jenha's never going to make the journey. You two stay with her and get a lift. I'm gonna try for the town. It's the only way."

None of them liked the idea but they all agreed it was the only option left. With a backward wave Marv set off. It would work out just as long as he didn't run into any more of those things.

****

Eastman was sitting in his office leafing through the day's orders. The blackout, much to his dismay, was still ongoing. On the plus side however, the town had spent the most peaceful night he could recall. So far this morning people were getting on with everyday life. Then his intercom crackled into life. It was Clara.

"Sheriff, I just got a call from Ben Burke. Erin's been attacked by some vagrant. And Brad, Ben's shot him."

"Shot him?"

"He killed him, Brad."

This was all he needed first thing in the morning, another death. But right now he was just concerned for the old couple's safety. "Clara, they all right?"

"Ben said the creep bit her on the hand, otherwise she's alright, I guess."

"Tell Ben I'll be right there. Clara, get hold of Gerard and let him know what's about."

"Sure thing Brad."

Whatever happened, he needed to get to the Burke place. As he picked his hat off the table and made toward the door, he wondered if this biting attack was connected to the events at Hinckle Point.

****

Bill Merka was worried. It was very unusual for Jimmy to miss a chance for stargazing. When Merka had asked him a few days ago, Jimmy had been thrilled at the opportunity of watching the meteorites from the tower. It would have taken a lot for him to miss that. Though with all that was going down, anything could have happened. Jimmy lived on his own, so even if the phones had been okay, they'd still have had to wait until he turned up; there was no one to give him the message.

Merka was standing outside the observation room, using his powerful binoculars to scan the region. The one hundred foot high circular tower afforded full visibility in every direction. The concrete and steel structure stuck out like a sore thumb in the idyllic setting. Even on such a warm day as this, the wind caused him to shut his eyes.

He loved the outdoor life but there was other work to get done. He shook his head, opened the door and went back inside. The observation room was surrounded by glass panels where people could sit and view the vast expanse. Jimmy called it 'the fishbowl' and Merka thought that a fair description. He sat back in his swivel chair and slowly spun himself round until something caught his eye.

High up, on a ridge overlooking one of the small lakes, were the Clayton brothers. Their unmistakable orange truck had stopped at the summit. After a short time they drove away out of sight. He'd have liked to have known what they were up to but whatever it was, he was sure it was no good. Merka thoughtfully drummed his fingertips on his chin and went back to his logbook.

****

Eastman stood looking at the body on the floor by Ben Burke's chicken shack. The shotgun blast had obliterated the head, leaving only the lower part of the jaw and neck intact. The condition of the hands, and the general stink, told him immediately this body was the same as the ones at Hinckle Point. This one was wearing some type of tattered lab-coat and lanyard. Despite being covered in Lord-knows-what, he could just make out the word 'Medi-Tek' printed on it.

There were also two bullet holes in the chest, which he was positive Ben hadn't put there because these were 9mm pistol rounds and they'd been there for some time. Ben only used a shotgun. Eastman scratched the tip of his nose, breathed a deep sigh and went back into the house.

Both Erin and Ben were shaken, that was plain to see. Ben had bandaged the injury to his wife's left hand. On the mantelpiece just behind her, Eastman spotted an old wedding photo; they'd been married a long time. This was no social call. The old folks explained what had happened and it sounded like a clear-cut case of self-defence. Ben was no murderer, but Eastman had to follow the law – Ben had shot and killed somebody.

"Ben, the ambulance is coming for Mrs Burke. She's gonna need that hand checked and I have to take you down town."

"Now wait one darn minute there Bradley Eastman, you're not taking my Ben no place, y'hear me?"

"Now Ma," began Ben, "It's only right…"

"Ben done shot that varmint, 'cause he just kept a coming! He wouldn't hear no sense! What's a man to do, 'cept protect his kin? Shame on you Bradley Eastman!"

"I know it was self-defence Mrs Burke, believe me I know. But Ben killed a man. I gotta take him in."

"Don't go on so woman, I ain't no killer, Sheriff ain't saying that. It got to be done legal. Ain't that so Sheriff?"

"I'm not charging him with anything but I gotta arrest him, that's the law."

Eastman did not like the situation one bit but that was how it was. He walked to the front door as he heard vehicles on the track. Looking out from the door, he could see two squad cars and an ambulance heading towards the house, kicking up clouds of dust and he walked onto the porch to greet them.

****

Robert Pool clutched the bunch of fresh flowers to his chest as he made his way down Corman Street. Today was his son's birthday and he was headed for the cemetery. He'd had to get the flowers from Wal-Mart. After that last time, Mrs Kronberg had banned him from her shop. Still, at least he'd used her vase, not the floor. Getting cut short was a hell of a bad thing. Wal-Mart was about the only place he could still get served, but even they had standards.

When he visited the grave, he always made a special effort to clean up and stay off the booze. Sobriety was not a condition he liked. His normal world was safe and fuzzy and viewed through the bottom of a shot glass. He was used to being ignored, folks crossing to the other side of the road, averting their gaze or just blanking him. All that came with being 'the town drunk', but things were different today. People were oblivious to each other, let alone him. It had been the same in Wal-Mart; everybody had been dashing about, frantically clearing the shelves.

He couldn't remember when this blackout thing had started and to be honest he wasn't interested. However, he was now aware of a new feel to the town. Panic! Not the type where people were running about screaming – this went deeper. This was the type of fear where neighbour killed neighbour, just for gas.

On the sidewalk just in front of him, was the burly figure of Sarge in combat fatigues. He was between two guys, reading them the riot act. Whatever their beef with each other had been, it wasn't worth riling up Sarge. He was one of Eastman's posse of helpers and he looked like he was having a ball. Sarge had left the army but the army hadn't left Sarge. When Pool looked at him, it was a painful reminder of his son.

Robert Pool Junior had been killed just two days after his twenty-second birthday, in the last stages of the war. When they brought him home, Pool had wanted to see his boy right away. The Sergeant at the base said the body had been classified as 'non-viewable'. It took a week before they released the body and then the casket had been closed. Around then, reality had taken a back seat and the bottle took over. It was the only way he'd got through the last two years. The bottle was his best and only friend. It never judged him and was always there when he needed it.

As he crossed the corner of Reno and Norton, he noticed that some of the buildings now had shutters up and cinder-block walls had replaced some of the picket fences. This was siege mentality and it reminded him of the race riots some years back in the big cities. Even Joe Lester had put a metal fence on his lawn.

Pool had heard some guys talking about a bunch of stuff that had happened over the last few days. Shootings, murders and other things – none of it sounded good.

He couldn't tell what reality was anymore. Take the guys he'd seen in the woods the other night, the ones in yellow suits and gasmasks. They'd been carting off dead bodies. He was pretty sure of that and he knew he ought to tell somebody. The problem was, that he just couldn't recall if it had been before or after he'd seen the giant yellow ducks at Dawson's Pool. If he told Eastman, he'd be in a rubber room for sure. Eastman had already taken his hunting rifle and truck keys. The only one to have really helped him was his old High School buddy, Tony Firth.

All this thinking had given him an almighty headache and his shaking hand fumbled in his pocket for the cure, but he'd left the hip flask on the table. Damn! He tightly shut his eyes and blew out a long deep breath. He needed to hold it together. He was only a few blocks away from the cemetery; surely he could just make that? Turning the corner, his gaze fell on Barney's Bar.

Like a beacon in the wilderness he could almost smell the comforting nectar beckoning him. The cemetery was so close... was one drink too much to ask? What if it wasn't open yet? Bull! Barney's was always open. One drink wasn't gonna do any harm, besides it was on his way. Pool drew the back of his hand across his dry lips, tucked his shirt in and crossed the deserted street towards the bar.

****

Elle-May sat on her chair at the nurses station watching Norris Zillman manoeuvre Mrs Bakeman's wheelchair through the narrow doorway. The whole matter was complicated by Mrs Bakeman's weight problem and the fact that poor Norris weighed no more than a wet dollar. As the commotion got worse, Elle-May began to wonder what would give out first, him or the chair.

Mrs Bakeman was a woman of colourful language but Norris kept his cool, much to Elle-May's admiration. What a lousy first day for the guy. The thought had crossed her mind that as the senior nurse, maybe she should intervene but she'd had enough. Any second now that woman would be out of her hair. With one last push, Mrs Bakeman was out of the building and in the charge of her poor husband. Norris swept his thinning hair back onto his head and lent against the hospital doorway, beads of sweat running down his thin, angular face.

"You done well there Norris," called out Elle-May.

"She was a powerful woman. I never heard cussing like that afore."

"Don't mind her none, you're gonna hear that again. You got her Thursday as well. Now best make yourself useful and make up Bed four."

As Norris left the room, her face broke into a broad smile. He was going to have to shape up fast if he wanted to work here. She shifted her gaze out of the window and watched poor, worn-out Mr Bakeman struggling to get his wife into the SUV. She was a total contrast to Erin Burke. It was still hard to take in that Old Ben had killed somebody. By all accounts, he blew the creep's head off. He had it coming though, attacking an old woman like that. Elle-May hadn't seen the body but the ambulance boys said it was just like the others – rotten. Brad

Eastman had given them all strict orders not to go anywhere near the bodies. She wasn't going to argue. Some things were best left well alone.

City folk always went on about how dull small towns were. Right now she'd be happy with dull. All this was starting to get too much. These murders and other stuff, it was like one of those trashy novels her sister read. Looking on the bright side though, she got to see a lot more of Deputy Jedree Bodien. It was true he was no oil painting and maybe not the sharpest knife in the drawer, but he was a good honest man and he looked cute in his uniform. She was woken from her thoughts by the loud voice of Nurse Brown.

"Hey, where is everyone? This place is like a graveyard!"

"Hush up there girl, that ain't even funny. Jill's on her way in and Anne's over at Mary Firth's place."

"She had another 'accident'?"

"Yeah, kinda looks that way. I'd love to give that bum a baseball bat in the kisser."

"Peter Firth is gonna get it someday. Can't something be done about him?"

"They can't pin anything on him if she won't press charges."

"There's gotta be other ways to skin a rabbit."

"Forget it." Elle-May screwed her face up and clenched her fists. "Benteen already tried that, Brad put his ass on ice. So you see it's sort of difficult."

"See what ya mean. So we got another murder in the..."

"Careful how you go there Zoë, Ben did that in self-defence. The creep bit Erin."

"I didn't mean...is she okay?"

"She got shook up some but nothing that a band aid can't fix. I sent her home with some antibiotics. She'll be fine. It's just a bite."

****

It had been several hours since Marv had left them on the track. Britney and Tony had moved Jenha under the shade of a large tree. She was now unconscious. A lone buzzard circled slowly overhead as the fierce sun climbed ever higher; soon the shade would surrender to the ever-increasing temperature. Britney and Tony were out of water; they'd given the last to their friend. All Tony had was his bottle of Bourbon but now all he wanted was some plain water. Both of them were sat next to Jenha, ever watchful for the traffic Marv had said would be using the track. There was also the possibility the mysterious four-by-four would return, which was not such an attractive notion.

"Britney, what if them things got Marv? I mean what if nobody's coming to git us?"

That unpleasant thought had crossed her mind but somehow she doubted it. Marv was a tough kid and for a geek, he was all right. If anybody would get back, then it would be him.

"If he runs into any of those freaks, I put my money on Marv."

Just then she caught sight of an old white pickup heading towards them. Both Britney and Tony stood up and began waving frantically to attract attention.

Jill and Al Paxmore were still tired from the previous night. Al had got up early to check for any evidence of unwanted visitors but had found nothing. Stallone was in deep disgrace. None of those dog treats that he adored and loved hiding under the old chair for a month. Now they were heading for town. It was a journey they made almost every day. Today Al was driving; he thought Jill went too fast.

Jill flicked through the radio channels but only the sound of static filled the cab. Suddenly, she called out, pointing at some people in the middle distance. The morning rays had turned the whole desert pink and Al had to squint into the early sunlight, but could just manage to see two figures waving at them.

"I reckon they got themselves some trouble," remarked Al.

As they pulled up alongside, Jill recognised them as being Britney and Tony. Then as she got out of the truck she could see Jenha, under the tree, lying pale and still.

"Okay," called Al, "what's going on here?"

It was obvious by the sorry state they were in that something bad had happened.

Both kids were now in floods of tears as they poured out the events. How could people do such things? While Al was doing his best to calm them and retrieve as much information as he could, Jill went to Jenha. It was clear she was in a desperate way. However, it was the bite that intrigued Jill the most.

Britney had just said the wound had been made only a few hours ago. She must have been mistaken; this wound was at least a week old, thought Jill. It looked bad and smelled worse. She could even feel the heat from the wound. Jill stood up and looked at the two kids; she needed to handle this with delicacy.

"She's in a real bad way here. We've gotta get her to town quick."

Al could hear the urgency in his wife's voice and ushered them into the vehicle. "Everybody in the truck, we gotta go now."

They loaded the kids into the back seats of the truck. Britney and Tony sat either side of the unconscious Jenha. Jill took a bandage from the first aid box and attended to Jenha's wound, then got into the driver's seat. It was Al's turn as the passenger now. Jill knew it was a matter of life or death for the girl. She put her foot down hard and the truck shot forward, leaving a cloud of dust.

CHAPTER - EIGHT

Tony Firth pulled into the long driveway of his mansion, the gravel crunching under the chunky tyres of his BMW. La Fontaine House was the sort of place that most people could only dream of owning. His solid stone, six-bedroom house was set in two acres of pure peace and quiet right on the edge of Armstrong, but it hadn't always been this way. His great grandpa, Austin Firth, had acquired the land (then a fur trader's post) from a French trapper, way back.

Over the years the various Firth generations had extended the house and land until it had reached the present size. When Tony Firth's parents had died he'd inherited the property and bought his brother, Peter's share. He wanted the family home, the place where he'd grown up more than anything else and nothing would stop him.

Walking up to the oak door he could see his wife Bridget in the front room, in her favourite spot on the leather sofa. She'd been something in her day but now her looks were maintained by cosmetic surgery – the price of the good life. Her family had been a big name in the town, owning both sawmill and lumberyard in the town's hay day. But with the recession taking hold, profits had gone down; that's when her father had decided to sell the shares. He died shortly after, leaving her the estate but there'd been that thing with the IRS.

Even Firth had been surprised at how fast she'd gone through the remaining money and now she was broke. Oh yes, she had expensive tastes. Bridget was high maintenance and she liked to spend. He used to joke that all his pay went on Bridget's shopping trips; truth was that in those days it did. He pushed the door open and went inside.

The interior of the house was as lavish as the exterior. Firth had used as much wood as he could. This was the best American wood that money could buy. Wooden panels encased the living room with ornate stone block columns holding up the ceiling. Above the huge stone fireplace, pride of place was a painting of the current generation of Firths. His eyes fell on Conrad's face and he wondered where the boy was.

"Well, you got any news, what did Eastman say?"

He looked at Bridget's plump face with its rose red lips and peroxide blonde hair and pondered what to tell her.

"He wasn't there. I got to speak to that ape, Benteen. He said we got to wait till Eastman gets back."

"That ain't no use to us. We got to get out and look for our boy. Tony, it ain't safe out there. Eastman should be here, where the hell is he anyhow?"

"Benteen told me he was up at the Burkes' farm, some kinda trouble there."

"What kinda trouble?"

He wasn't in the mood for tact. "Ross Murphy said he saw an ambulance and squad car heading toward there earlier."

"Tony Firth, you need to get out there and find that boy."

"Ain't so easy, when the boy lied where he was going. I went to see the other parents and they got no clue where their kids are at either."

"I don't care about the other kids, our boy's missing…"

"Benteen said they aint regarded 'missing' until they've been gone for twenty-four hours. That's the law."

"To hell with that crap! What you the mayor for, if you can't look after your own folk? Now git back out there and start mayoring. Damn it!"

The trouble was, she was right and he knew it. All these years of greasing palms and doing favours, half the town owed him some. However, he'd no intention of provoking any conflict with the law. During this situation, that sort of thing could easily be taken as causing trouble for the town and that turn could cost him votes.

Sure he wanted to get out after Conrad but it would have to be done with Eastman, above board and legal. Bridget wouldn't understand his motives, so he knew he'd have to use some double talk. His whole political career had revolved around saying one thing and doing something totally different. If it was good enough for the suits in Washington, then it was good enough for him.

"Hell, you're right. I'm going back up there to demand they set up a search team. Yes sir."

Politics was nothing if not an act, he thought as he walked out the door. But where was that damn kid?

****

As Firth drove down Leonard's Boulevard toward Main Street he was surprised at just how many people were about. They were queuing outside shops, standing in neat lines from the doors to the sidewalk. Kirk's Bakery had shut and people were banging on the closed door. People in a panic, just because of a blackout – how dumb was that?

He didn't miss that darn QVC channel that was for sure; gold jewellery, workout gear, saucepan sets - Bridget lived for all that crap. Bleeding his bankbook dry.

Driving past the shops and townsfolk, he began to think how best he could use the current situation to his advantage. If he could somehow appear as the town's saviour, it'd guarantee his re-election.

Just then, he caught sight of his brother outside Crowns' fruit shop. Firth didn't really want to see him but it was too late to turn off, his brother had already seen him. It wouldn't do for him to been seen with Peter at the moment because of the mess he was in with Mary. The whole town knew that Peter was a wife beater. But even that wasn't the real problem. The problem was that his dumb brother made no secret about it and as mayor, Firth found the whole situation embarrassing. Worse still, Peter had taken up with good old Slippery Sally, some tramp who'd seen more action than the US Marines.

None of this helped Firth's public image. Peter ambled up to Firth's car and playfully tapped the roof. Firth wound his window down and looked at his brother. He had that look of self-assurance that irritated Firth so much.

"Well howdy big brother, how's it hanging?"

"Stow it, I ain't in the mood. Conrad's missing."

"Missing? I only spoke to the little shi…I only saw the kid yesterday."

"Did he say where he was going? I mean, any kinda clue could help here."

"I know there was a girl involved 'cause I sold him some insurance. But I don't know where they were headed."

"Insurance? What's my boy want with insurance?"

"Now come on, when a boy goes off with a girl it's good to have some insurance against any, let's just say, *accidents*."

"Rubbers? They're just kids, for God's sake!"

Fortunately for his brother there was now a crowd of people in earshot. It wouldn't do to make a scene.

"Oh, come on. I did you a favour. I reckon you don't want any extra additions to the family."

Peter walked over to the passenger side of the car and got in.

"In case you ain't noticed I'm in kind of a hurry, so don't make yourself too comfortable, will you?"

"Look at them, just look at them," Peter said, pointing to the people in the streets. "Running about buying up everything in sight. The hardware store's sold out of kerosene and Joe's put a limit on the batteries folks can buy. What happens when all the stuff's gone? Who they gonna run to? I'll tell you. Me, that's who."

"Yeah and what makes you think that, Mister?"

"I got me a warehouse full of stuff. Food, gas, tools – you name it, I bought it. I did a deal with Benny Arnold and he gave me a discount too. When the town runs dry, I'm gonna open up shop. 'Course the price is going up."

"Sounds good, but what if everything's back to normal this afternoon? You gonna lose out. You got dead stock then."

"Like I said, I got a good discount. I'll make back, even if it takes a while. I thought maybe you'd like a piece of the action…"

"Hold on there, I got an election in two months. I can't get mixed up in any shady dealings."

"There's nothing shady about this. I got receipts for the lot, its legal. All fair and square."

"Yeah true, but folks are gonna see it as…well, unethical."

"Hey Tony, remind me will ya, when did ethics ever bother you?"

Firth studied his brother; there was no doubt about it the boy had an eye for a hot deal. Maybe there was a way he could get a share and still keep his nose clean.

"Okay, I suppose I could act as a silent partner but I ain't bank rolling this and my name stays out of it, you hear me?"

"Oh man, you won't regret this…"

"Well I'd better not! Look, I gotta get going, we can talk turkey later. Just don't forget, I'm the *silent* partner."

Firth reached over, opened the passenger door and waved his brother out onto the sidewalk. He knew Peter hadn't offered him a cut through brotherly love alone; he'd needed some financial muscle to broker the deal. If Firth was going to part with cash, then he was going to make sure it paid off. Nothing was for nothing in his book. He looked at his watch; time to give Eastman a call. He started the engine and headed to the station house.

****

Eastman was studying a map of the surrounding countryside. How Firth disliked Eastman. Even as kids they'd never got along. He'd poke his nose in and speak his mind and stand up for folk, even when he'd nothing to gain from it. He was the sort of guy that Firth just couldn't reach; to Eastman money was just that, money. Even now, sitting opposite him in the sheriff's office, Firth didn't get him.

"The thing is," began Eastman, looking up from the map, "for someone to be reported missing they gotta be missing for twenty four hours. Strictly speaking, these kids got a few hours to go yet."

Was he just gonna sit spouting the law? His boy was missing – what the hell were a few hours?

"My boy and four other kids are *missing* right now, why ain't you looking for them?"

"Hold on there Tony, I said 'strictly speaking.' With all this craziness going down and all that up at the Burkes' this morning, I was gonna say we need to find them and fast. Okay, Conrad told you they were going to the Galway's place to camp, only that was just a lie."

Firth had already told Benteen all this. They were just wasting time. Time that they did not have.

"I called over there and Bob Galway said the kids hadn't been there, so I met the other parents. They said that they'd been told the kids were at my place."

"I gotta try to figure where we can start to search, I don't want us going off half cocked. Is there anything that could give you a clue, no matter how small?"

Firth had thought over and over again about this and the only thing that came into his mind was the Pandy Woods.

"It's probably nothing, but a few days back Conrad said how much he'd enjoyed camping out up the Pandy Woods with me last year. I recall him saying he'd love to go back, that's all."

Eastman looked at Firth.

"The Pandy Woods are real close to Bill Merka's tower; I'll call and ask if he's seen anything. Meanwhile, can you get some good people for a search party?"

This was more like it. Now at least they were talking about search parties. "Sheriff, what happened at Ben's place?"

"Erin got attacked and Ben shot the punk."

Firth could hardly believe his ears; Ben Burke had shot somebody?

"I hope he peppered his raggedy ass."

"Ben blew his God damn head off. I had to bring him in for questioning."

"You got Ben Burke in a cell?"

Firth was shocked; Ben was a feisty old bird but harmless. The thought of him in a jail cell was hard to take, even for Firth.

"Hell no, he's helping Benteen put ration packs together for the search party. It was one of those 'things' he shot. Believe me; he wouldn't have had a choice. He's free to go after the Judge sets his bail this afternoon. We want Ben out ASAP."

Firth and Eastman rose to get out of their chairs when Eastman's phone rang. "Clara...funny, I was about to contact Bill just now...somebody else missing...no, just the kids...tell him I'll get back to him soon...yeah, we'll be out right now."

He replaced the phone.

"Clara said that Bill Merka told her Jimmy Red Cloud's gone missing. He was supposed to meet Bill last night but he didn't show."

Firth was worried. As Indians went, Jimmy was pretty reliable. When he said he'd be some place, he'd be there.

"What you gonna do, Sheriff?"

"The Pandy Woods are a fair stretch; we gonna need lots of manpower. I want you to start getting people together. You know the type of guys we need – good trackers. Benteen will lead. I've got some loose ends to tie up and then I'll come and join you."

Eastman got up and showed Firth to the door.

****

As Firth walked across the street to a large congregation of townspeople, he could feel the heat on his bald head. A lot had gone on in the last few days and you'd have to be some kinda sap not to think it was all connected. If Conrad had gone to sow his wild oats then that was the last thing the boy would want his folks to know. Damn brat! Suddenly, Marv Glitz's father cut in front, stopping Firth in mid stride.

"Tony, what's happening about the search?"

Firth looked at the man and fixed him with his best look of concern. Sam Glitz and his boy had moved from the city about a year ago. He ran the print shop on Main Street and Firth had put a lot of business his way recently. With practiced sincerity, perfected over the years, Firth took Glitz by the shoulders and spoke softly to him.

"Sam, me and the Sheriff have decided to launch a search party but no need to worry. The kids are gonna show up. I'm going to get some men together."

A large crowd had gathered near the Post Office; it was time for Firth to play to his audience. This was vote-gathering time.

"Some of you will know by now that five of our kids are missing. One of them is my boy, Conrad. Also missing, is Sam's boy, Marv, Jehna Galway, Tony Arcado, Britney Patrick and Ruby Carson. They went out camping last night and they ain't come back yet. Now, most likely they gonna come in like lost sheep, but with all this commotion going down, me and Brad Eastman have decided we gonna go find these kids."

He looked at the faces gathered around him; he had them in his palm now.

"Now our search area's gonna be the Pandy Woods. It's a big old space, so I want some good volunteers, people who know the area and can track. Anybody who wants to help out be back here in forty minutes and ready to roll. We're gonna need enough people for at least five groups, maybe five a group."

"I'd like to take a group," called out Sarge. "I got me more than enough experience."

Firth looked at the crowd's reaction. It wasn't good, judging by the head shaking and muttering going on. Although he knew Sarge had the experience, he was also a fruit loop and not to be trusted. But with Sarge came the vets' vote and after all...

"Appreciate that Sarge, but I think you're gonna be more use in town. We need some people left in charge..."

"Yeah, no offence there Sarge," cut in Billy Yardman, "but people wouldn't trust you to fetch them back safe."

Firth had to agree with Yardman. In fact half the town agreed, though few would admit to it. Sarge was able to help with the patrols in the town and he was good at that, but leading a group in the woods, well that was another thing.

"What makes you all so sure those kids are up there in the first place?"

"Because Sarge, that's where folk go with their families when they go camping."

"*Families* maybe, but the kids all go to Hinckle Point or the old Air Force base and..."

"I've told Conrad if I catch him up that air base, I'll leather his hide. Look Sarge, you got a hell of a lot of experience in military matters but these are kids we're looking for. And I know that base is the *last place* to look."

"Mayor, I'm gonna ask one last time. You go to the woods but let me have some guys and I'll search the old base. Now that's fair."

"Sarge, I don't have the manpower to waste, besides, no one will go with you. Sorry, but that's how it is."

"Did all of you always listen to your folks? I know where I'm headed and I aim to fetch them kids back here."

Firth watched in silence with the rest of the crowd as Sarge strode off down the street. Turning to Sam Glitz, Firth patted the man's arm.

"Sam, since we've got some time spare, I wanted to talk to you about that second poster of me."

Firth led Glitz to the print shop; well, business was business after all and he only had two months before the election.

CHAPTER - NINE

Al Paxmore gripped the edge of his seat as Jill threw the truck around yet another sharp bend. The journey had turned into a white-knuckle ride, but it was the kind of ride you only did the once. It was times like this he wished he'd never taught her to drive. Admittedly, it was vital Jenha get to town; he knew that all too well. There just didn't seem too much of a point if they all got wiped out on the bends.

"Jill, maybe you could leave some of the damn wheels on the ground next time?" Al griped as he held the sides of his seat.

Before she could reply, a loud commotion erupted from the rear of the truck. Jenha was convulsing violently. Tony reached forward to help her and recoiled in shock as trickles of blood ran from the corners of her eyes.

"Mrs Paxmore you'd better, I mean...!"

Jill shot a glance at the interior mirror; at this speed it was too dangerous to risk anything else. The girl was crying blood!

"Okay, kids," she called, "don't panic, I can see the town."

They were about ten minutes away, but she doubted if the girl would make the journey. Suddenly, Jenha started vomiting. Thick, dark, foul smelling liquid exploded from her tortured face, splashing about the rear of the vehicle. Britney tried to hold the girl's flailing arms while Tony held her head, just as Jenha vomited directly into his face. Tony drew back and wretched as he wiped his face.

"Jill, you'd better stop, that kid's in a bad way," Al cried out.

"Can't. She'll never make town if I do," came the frantic reply.

Al knew that was the truth. They just had to keep going.

"You kids hold on," he called as Jill threw the truck around another bend.

He turned around in his seat for a better view of the scene behind. Jenha had stopped convulsing but her body was still shaking. It kinda reminded him of the way you get with the flu, all shaky, but there the resemblance stopped. This was like no flu he'd ever seen. The boy was covered in gunk, his hair, eyes and even his mouth. It made Al want to throw up just looking at him. He'd always thought Britney a snob but looking at her now, she seemed a different kid. She was covered in Lord knows what, but she'd stuck with the others.

The stink in the car reminded him of diapers and rotten meat and he quickly cranked down the window. The rush of air did nothing to take the stench away. Everything seemed a whole lot calmer now; the girl had stopped moving about. It was a hell of a way to start the day.

"Mrs Paxmore," Britney called softly, "I think Jenha's stopped breathing..."

"Britney, I want you to check for a pulse. Can you do that for me honey?"

Jill shot a sideways glance at Al then back at the girl. She could try CPR but it was not something she'd relish. Just then, Tony cried out.

"No, she's all right. Look, she's moving her hand. It's okay."

Britney desperately felt for a pulse – any pulse. "Yeah, yeah I got it!"

She looked at her friend, draped on the seat just like a ragdoll, head slumped on her chest. She wished that above all else she'd made more time for the girl. The truth was she'd hardly even noticed her before this. Jenha didn't have any money; she was a nothing and nobody. When they'd set off yesterday, she'd just been the one with the tent.

Jenha Galway made a sudden rasping noise in the back of her throat and lifted her eyelids revealing a set of colourless orbs. Shakily she moved her head around to look at Tony, and then peeled her lips back over her teeth in a cruel snarl. Like a creature possessed, she began to claw at his face.

It was the noise coming from the girl that affected Al the most. Her voice didn't seem right any more. Hell, it didn't even sound human any more. The snarling shriek chilled him to the bone.

"Pull over, we gotta calm her down!"

As Jill was about to stop the truck she felt her head jerk backwards as Jenha caught hold of her long auburn hair. Al and Jill fought to break the demented girl's grip but it was too late; Jill lost control of the truck and ploughed into a roadside fence, sending clouds of dust into the air and bringing the truck to an abrupt halt.

****

Ethan Mason watched with interest as the situation developed outside the Town Hall. Eastman and Benteen had been arguing with Tony Firth, but they'd been too far away for him to hear. Was it only him who could see the disdain those two had for each other? There was trouble heading their way. Big trouble.

It looked as if half the town had turned up to see the search party off. Some were genuine well-wishers, others were there because they didn't have any place else to be. He looked around the group; pretty much all white folk. But Armstrong was like that. He'd spent his whole life here but Monica, his wife, was from Houston and she'd always been uneasy about there being so few black people. She'd moved back with the girls some months ago because the Armstrong branch of the bank had shut and she'd had to transfer. At least that had been what they'd told people. They'd found it difficult to sell the house and so he'd decided to stick with the General Store for the time being. He'd tried Wal-Mart for a while but George Lee gave him the creeps. He was one of those survivalist nuts and he carried a hunting knife with him, everywhere. Even as a kid he'd been odd. Mason liked it where he was and he had a good friend in Al Paxmore who also worked there at the store.

The group of roughly twenty-five or so volunteers had gathered around a collection of four-by-fours as they waited for Benteen to fetch some extra CB sets. Mason squinted up at the midday sun perched above the Town Hall. This was going to be hot work and all because of that little runt, Conrad Firth. He'd led the others on a merry ride, lied to his folks and then got lost. What a bum.

Mason recalled the time Conrad Firth had stolen from the General Store. Oscar had wanted to tell the cops but Firth's old man had done some kinda deal and Oscar got the planning permission for his lock-up. That was how Tony Firth did a lot of his business. He watched as Firth worked the crowd, shaking hands, smiling and joking. What a sleaze. No wonder Eastman had left Benteen to deal with him. The two cops were like a double act, but they kept the town safe. Benteen and Firth moved to the front of the group just as Mason began to think he'd melt.

"Okay folks, can I have your attention? First of all we appreciate so many of you coming forward today. Now we all know why we're here and we know what it is we gotta do, so I'm gonna let Gerard here say some words."

"Thank you Mayor. Okay, just so as no one forgets what we said. There are four groups: the Mayor, Deputy Chattman, Kate Black and me. Each group got one police radio and a few CB sets. Now listen up, real careful. You gotta keep a watch on the range of these things. If you go too far you gonna be out of range, then you gonna need to use the flares. Just remember to fire them things towards the town. We ain't fixing to have no forest fires out there. It's hot and dry. Each of us got our own areas to cover, just use the maps. Ain't no need for anybody to get themselves lost out there."

Well at least with Benteen running the show things would get done properly, thought Mason. He looked at Mitch Chattman and Kate Black. Two college kids but they were smart and Kate used to run his kids' swimming lessons. He liked her. He'd seen Sarge all done up in his army gear earlier and Mason was glad he'd gone off on his own. That kinda guy could be bad news, real quick. Suddenly, to his left he could see Frank Jorgan and his boys making their way through the crowd to Benteen's group.

"Sorry we're late Gerard... uh Mr Mayor, only my Nancy done taken sick."

"No bother. Frank I'm gonna ask you and the boys to leave the guns in the truck. We don't need any guns; we're looking for kids, not bears. Right, anyone got themselves anything to say?"

Mason looked around him but no one had anything to say except Firth.

"Lenny's here to take a couple of shots for the paper, can we get around the Jeeps?"

Mason couldn't believe it; the man was turning the whole thing into a PR stunt. He really was priceless. Mason looked on in disbelief as the search team crowded into the photo shoot. Then after several minutes he heard Benteen calling them to order.

"Okay, if we all quite done now? It's a quarter after twelve. I want us up at the start position in under half an hour. We gonna work on till six and finish up at position four..."

"Tarnation boy, say where?"

Mason looked around to see who had just spoken, it was Henry York. Henry was a regular at the store and had to be at least eighty plus. Mason glanced over at Benteen to see what he would say.

"Position four is Aldridge farm gates. You sure you up to this, Henry?"

"Yep. You just gotta speak up a bit. Can't stand all this darn mumbling."

Mason shrugged his shoulders and blew out hard. He was beginning to wish he'd stayed home.

****

Jill Paxmore opened her eyes as she felt someone tug at her arm. Everything was hazy and the sound around her was just a din. Gradually her hearing returned and she heard Al calling her name.

"Jill! Jill you all right?"

Jill rubbed her painful neck. She knew she'd been out cold. The inside of the car was a mass of swirling dust. Slowly taking the picture in, she could see Al had gashed his arm.

"Al your arm. What...?"

Then with a rush of fear, she remembered what had happened. Her neck hurt too badly for her to look into the rear of the vehicle. She had to release her seatbelt to do so. Tony was curled into a tight ball in the far left of the truck and Britney was holding a rucksack up against Jenha, who was still raging. She was hurt bad. She'd impaled herself on the fence post Al had taken with them. This was the type of injury that should've killed her. The shock, let alone the internal injures ought to have been enough.

"Mrs Paxmore, she's just like those things that killed Ruby!" Britney yelled.

"Are you and Tony injured, darling?"

Jill's main concern was for the other two kids. Jenha was way beyond the help Jill could offer up here.

"I think so, but Tony's all zoned out. I don't want to look at her anymore."

It was the eyes that freaked her the most. Dead eyes. All those horrid noises and now this damn wood thing stuck right through her was all too much. Why the hell couldn't she just pass out or die?

Al looked at the situation; the whole thing was surreal. Pal Yantos' 2 x 4 fence post was sticking out of this kid's gut. If that wasn't enough, the thick brown gunge pooled on the floor was like no blood he'd seen before. What was more, she was still trying to get at the other two kids, moving from one to the other. She reminded him of an eel with its head cut off. Dead, but not knowing its dead. But this was no darn eel.

"Kids, I want you to get out of the truck and come to us. Can you do that for me?"

Britney waited until Jenha's attention had transferred to Tony, then dropped the bag, un-did her belt and leapt out of the truck. Safely on the road she began attracting Jenha's attention. To her dismay, Tony just lay on the seat.

"Tony! Tony, get out now! Come on, move your lazy ass!"

Al walked around to the rear door and pulled on the handle only to find it locked from the *inside*. The only way to get at the boy would be through the truck. He cursed the panic stricken boy under his breath. Al rubbed his hands through his hair and kicked at the ground sending a mini dust cloud into the air. Then he had an idea.

There was some old sacking in the trunk, if they could get that over the girl, stop her biting and clawing, then they could tie her up. That way they need not worry about getting the boy out. Al went to the rear and fished out a large grubby hessian sack and rope then walked up to Jill.

"What you got that for?"

"I'm gonna put this over her and then we gonna tie her up. It ain't right, cause she's hurt and all but there ain't any other way for it."

Jill eased herself out of the door and lent up against the truck. She knew she'd got whiplash and it hurt like hell. Looking at the thin bedraggled Britney and Al's arm, she'd just have to get on with it. Al squeezed her hand firmly, gave her that special smile and they both walked up to Britney.

Britney looked at the sack and rope in Al's hand.

"You gonna put her in a sack?"

"We gotta restrain her. I'm gonna put it over her head then we gotta tie her arms. It's the safest thing for us all."

"Why is she like this? I mean, she should be dead or something! I don't know…"

"Easy now. She could've gone into some sort of shock. The body's got some strange ways to deal with stuff."

Jill patted her arm.

"Let's get this done."

"I don't think its shock. She's got some kinda disease."

"Okay, I'm gonna put the sack over her head and Britney, you slip this noose around her arms. All you gotta do is pull it tight – I'll do the rest. Jill, you bang the hell out of the window. Everybody set?"

They all moved to their positions. Jill started to bang the glass on the side of the truck, drawing Jenha's attention away from the door. The girl's efforts were feeble compared to earlier as she half-heartedly swiped at the window. Seeing his chance, Al quickly opened the door and slid across the seat towards the girl. He could clearly see that the fence post had skewered her to the rear seat. He dashed over and pulled the sack over her, securing it tightly over her head and shoulders. Jenha reacted violently but couldn't get free.

"Kid, get her arms," yelled Al, as Britney brushed past him and slid the rope over Jenha's wrists.

Jenha moved her head from side to side but as Al adjusted the sack and rope, she struggled less and less. Al was able to reach the door handle near Tony and open the door. Then both he and Britney got out of the truck. Jill fully opened the door and caught Tony by his arms. He was completely still and his eyes shut. He looked awful. Jill gently shook him and called his name. Slowly Tony opened his eyelids and looked at her through bloodshot eyes.

"I don't feel too good." His voice was rough and laboured. The boy was in a hell of a state though she couldn't see any obvious injury to him. She sat him up in the car and took his pulse. It was racing.

"Al, she all secured up?"

"Yep, we best get ourselves going. Sorry kids you gonna have to sit in the rear, but we'll be back in town real soon. Best if you don't make any noise though."

Reluctantly, Jill buckled Tony into his seat and closed the door. She looked over as Britney closed the door and fastened her seat belt. Jill walked to the front passenger seat and motioned Al to the driver's side.

"You gonna have to drive, I can't move my head."

Both Al and Jill climbed into the truck, shut the doors and drove off. Al looked up. In the distance, a military helicopter buzzed over the treetops.

****

"I can't believe you sent Erin home before I could run tests!"

Anne Lenski was furious. Of all the stupid things her senior nurse could have done, this took the can. What if the person who'd bitten Erin had the same infection as those at Hinckle Point? What if Erin was now infected? What if...? There were far too many 'what ifs.' Only Brad, Conrad Brown, and she knew anything about the so-called 'contamination' and of course the guy in the cells.

None of her medical team had any real idea of the potential danger. So was it fair to unload on Elle-May in this way? Anne was aware of her face being flushed and the fact that she'd been on at Elle-May for some time. Her anger quickly subsided and was replaced by embarrassment as she calmed down.

Elle-May found it difficult to look at Anne pacing around the office. Boy was she mad. Generally pretty much all of them had a good working relationship and everyone got on. So after she'd told Anne about Erin Burke and how'd she'd sent her home, she was surprised when Anne had bustled her into the office. She'd been standing there for the last few minutes but even after explaining what had happened, Anne had still gone on and on. It felt kinda like High School when you'd done something wrong. Why the commotion? Sure, she'd sent Erin home without Anne looking her over, but since when did the doctor need to check on a few old stitches? At least now it seemed as though Anne had settled down a bit.

"Elle-May, I owe you an apology. I had no right to go on so."

Anne reached forward and placed her hand on Elle-May's arm.

She recalled the long, lonely winter nights when she'd first moved to Armstrong. She hadn't known anyone; she'd just filled her weeks with toil. Then, one night after work, Elle-May had brought in homemade blueberry pie and some wine. The pie was to die for and though the wine had tasted like vinegar, Anne appreciated the sentiment. With Elle-May what you saw was what you got. She was loud and vivacious but one of the best nurses Anne had ever worked with, and she deserved to know what was happening... but not just yet.

"From now on, every bite, every scratch, in fact all injuries need to be fully tested."

"Tested for what? What we looking for Anne?"

"Any kind of abnormalities, anything that looks wrong, that shouldn't be there."

"Anne I know you can't tell us what's up here, but how serious is all this?"

"I just don't know Elle-May. I just don't know. But we're on our own until we get outside help."

It angered Anne to be so much in the dark. All she had to work on was the crazy test results that made no logical sense and the ravings of a killer. If this was some sort of contagious disease then she was obligated to warn her staff and the town. However, without firm medical evidence, in the current situation that would lead to panic. Brad would not thank her for that. Still, there needed to be some sort of official statement.

"Look Anne, it was just a small bite. I would never have let Ben take Erin home if I thought something was wrong. I'm real sorry. I reckoned after all they'd been through that was the best way."

"And you were right. Let's forget it. Wait a second; I thought Ben was in the station house?"

"Yeah well, it was the darndest thing. Tony Firth posted his bail and they let him go."

"Tony Firth?"

"Cross my heart."

"I'll call up at the farm and bring Erin back for some tests. I've got to know if she's clear or not."

With that, Anne left the office, leaving Elle-May to ponder on the morning's events.

****

Ben Burke looked across the fancy white linen table top at Erin Burke. She looked so fragile sitting there with sunken eyes and a bandaged hand. They were waiting for Bill Gardener to collect them and take them home. Ben cast his eyes around the small room. Neither of them had ever been in Aunty Betty's before. Ben had always regarded the cafe as being 'too grand' for him. But here they were amongst all the fine china and Sunday best stuff. The tea-room was full of folks sitting at little round tables. He knew every one of them and he and Erin were as good as any of them.

"What you thinking old man?"

"The first time I clapped eyes on you was just across the sidewalk there."

He pointed out of the window to the now vacant dressmaker's shop.

"Cept then it was the blacksmiths. You recall my Pa was fixing your Ma's old Ford? I just couldn't keep my eyes off you."

"Oh, hush up, you old fool – that was near fifty years or more."

"You hush, I'm a thinking here, woman. Always with the last word. Tarnation! I done forgot what I was about."

"That don't matter none, how'd you get out of jail so darn fast? You broke out or something?"

"Nope. The Judge set my bail and told me I had to stay in town."

"Well that ain't no difficulty. Nobody's leaving anytime soon. Who posted your bail? How'd you get out?"

"Tony Firth," said Ben, peering into his teacup.

"Looks like he done paid his Pa's dues then."

"That was a long time back."

Erin reached across the table and held Ben's hand.

"Pay no mind to it. What's done is done, that's the way things are."

Ben looked up at his wife; she was the wisest woman he ever did come across. It was high time he got her home and safe.

"Erin, I been thinking about that man I killed."

"He done give you no choice. You had to do what you did..."

"No, *no*! When I saw him on our land and you hurt, I just wanted to kill him."

"Now looky here, Ben, you did what you had to do, what any man would have done. Otherwise I reckon we'd both be dead right now."

She was right and he knew it. After he'd gotten back with Hound Dog, the dog had started snarling at the back door. When he opened the door, the first thing he'd seen was Erin with her hand all bloodied and that man grabbing at her. He felt a powerful rage well up in him; he had to protect Erin. As he pumped the shell into the breach, he wanted to kill the guy but as he eased off the safety catch and started to squeeze the trigger, he just couldn't do it. Not in cold blood.

He called for the man to back away and when the guy turned to look at Ben, it was like looking at some sort of a 'thing.' It wasn't just the rotting face or even the eyes. He could tell the thing was evil; the face was full of hate. It was like it had *no soul*. That was when he knew he had to kill it.

"Ben, I...I..."

Erin reached out to him before slumping onto the table, sending the cup and cake crashing to the floor. As her head rested on the tablecloth, he noticed blood trickling from the corner of her left eye.

CHAPTER -TEN

Eastman slowly sipped at his coffee, looking around the people gathered in his office. Clara sat opposite him taking notes with her pad. Vince Langley sat next to her with a nervous look on his face. Pat O'Brian was still standing in the centre of the office. It was clear O'Brian knew his stuff on radio communication, but he'd lost Eastman on this theory of his. He was just going to have to run through it again.

"Okay, Pat you kinda lost me there a while back. Now in plain language, that even I can understand, why do you think this is all manmade?"

"Right, let's just forget frequency modulation and wave lengths. I been around radios longer than I care to mention. I spent twenty years in the Navy in the wireless room. *I know radios.* This is all to do with the god damn weather. Any kind of weather anomalies, sunspots or whatever is damn well gonna affect everything. No cell phones, no landlines, no TV, no radio, not even emergency bands. *Nothing!"*

Eastman reached across his desk and turned up the volume on the police radio.

"Yeah, but the police radios *do work.*"

O'Brian moved to the radio and turned the volume to zero.

"That's my point. *They shouldn't do."*

Clara had sat through the meeting listening to Pat's argument for the last ten minutes. So what if she didn't get all that techno mumbling, his other stuff made sense. Only last week, she'd had the feeling there'd been somebody on the line. True, nobody had spoken but every time she'd picked up the office phone there'd been that strange echo. Not for long, maybe a second or so but long enough.

She'd told Brad but he'd been busy with that bank heist in Burnsville. When she'd told Vince Langley, he'd agreed with her. Then before they got around to telling Brad, all this other stuff had started.

"Brad, that kinda fits in with what I told you about the phones last week, just before the blackout. Maybe they are connected."

"Oh, for heaven's sake Clara, not you as well! What's it with you two? Are you gonna join Jimmy Emmett? Because you're sure not on this planet."

"Sheriff, on a good day with my old CB I can hear people from Burnsville atop of Bilton's Peak and my home base can reach Europe. Why now are we down to less than ten miles and why only short range sets?"

Eastman wasn't buying this 'manmade' crap. Why would anybody want to cut off a town and who'd have the ability to do so? It just didn't add up. There just wasn't enough to go on; he needed more facts.

"Vince, you got anything sensible to add here?"

Langley was a man of few words. He did his work and that was that. The only reason he'd turned up was because Eastman had asked.

"All kinda folks rang the depot last week complaining about interference on the line. Almost all thought that someone was listening in. I think it's deliberate."

"If you're looking at some kinda conspiracy theory here people, then you forgot one thing. Not only can we not get out, but the outside world can't get in. Now somebody's going to work that out soon. You can't just isolate a whole town."

O'Brian leaned forward and gently tapped his chin.

"Maybe a big town or city, but not way out here. How many damn people you suppose gonna want to contact Armstrong at the same time? We're on our own."

"All right, so just suppose this is deliberate. How'd they manage to blank a whole town?"

"That's the easy part. All they gotta do is broadcast a blanket frequency that covers all other damn frequencies in the target area. That'll block the signals. When I was on the *Barack Obama* we used radio jammers to block the Syrian gunboats. We just shut their whole comms systems down, left them dead in the water. If you got the savvy you can even isolate different bands and control the range, that kinda thing."

"Yeah sure, but you're talking the US Navy there and..."

Max Koneg knocked on the door and thrust his head around. His face was both agitated and excited at the same time.

"Sorry to bother you Brad but it's important."

Eastman gestured him into the room and waited for the news. It was obvious that something big had happened; Max wasn't given to this type of behaviour.

"Jill and Al Paxmore just brought some of them kids back. But they're all in a hell of a mess."

"Sorry guys but we gonna have to leave things for now."

Eastman got up and left the office with the others following behind.

****

Tony Firth dabbed at his bald head with the already sodden handkerchief. He'd forgotten just how hot it could get in the hills and even in the trees this was hot. He just didn't have the frame to trek about up here anymore. Boy, was that brat gonna get it when he showed up. He'd gone too far this time, hauling half the town out on a day like this. It was bad enough with all this other crap going down but hell, this was prime election week. That damn boy was gonna get grounded till he was fifty. Conrad had it far too easy and Bridget darn near ruined the boy. She just didn't know when or even how to say *no*. Firth's father had never been one to spare a whopping, in fact he'd handed them out like cotton candy at the county fair.

He looked around at the tired and hot faces of his motley crew and shrugged. Glyn McDowall, Miguel Bonzzoni, Billy Boy, Ross Murphy and Danny Hardman. They all owed him some form of assured loyalty and that was the only reason they had come along. Still, he needed them.

"Hey Tony, where we at now?" Danny Hardman called out.

He was tired and more than a little mad at Firth. They wasted a whole lot of time on the meadow because Firth had assured them the kids would be there. That had been a bunch of crap; now he was convinced they were lost. Firth had given

Ross Murphy the task of scout because of his so-called tracking abilities. The fact was that Murphy couldn't find his butt with both hands. Hardman was fast losing patience with the whole thing. There had to be an easier way to pay all that money off than this. He kicked his expensive hiking boot at the loose earth.

"Look, I'm sure that Dobson's Barn is just over that ridge and past those trees."

"Ain't that what you said last time Tony?" Glyn McDowall said. He was a powerful man used to hard work but this was crazy. The heat was just too much for a trail like this. He stopped and adjusted the straps of his day pack then took a long swig from his canteen. The small frame of Miguel Bonzzoni caught his eye.

"Hey Miguel, you run up there and tell us where we all at, boy."

Miguel Bonzzoni looked at McDowall standing there, giving orders. He was the kind of man you kept away from especially if you weren't white. Miguel knew he'd have to be careful how he responded, but he didn't want to lose face in front of the others.

"If I run up there you had better be ready to carry me home. Too hot, I think."

McDowall shot him a long stare and let out a humourless laugh.

"I sure never realised that you people felt the heat. Well, I'll be."

Billy Boy sniggered quietly at the exchange; his weaselly face formed an uneasy smile. It wasn't that he liked McDowall or even that he disliked the Mexican, he was simply relieved that he wasn't in the firing line. He moved his weedy frame forward.

"Hey, guys what's that up ahead?" said Hardman, pointing to a large white metal object partly obscured by large trees.

Firth led the others toward the object and as they drew closer they discovered that it was a camper van. If the owners were about then maybe they'd seen the kids. Approaching from the rear the thought briefly crossed his mind that it was possible Zack and Luke Clayton had dumped it. Then he saw the guide ropes were attached so unless they'd taken up camping it was unlikely to have been them.

"Hello there, anybody about? We're looking..."

Firth stopped dead as he rounded the front of the camper van. From the driver's door to the mid section was a mass of bloody handprints. A set of plastic garden furniture was strewn across the floor along with food and plastic plates. The remnants of a once colourful awning hung off the partially demolished aluminium tent frame. Blood covered the whole area. As they began to file in behind Firth, the others took in the full extent of the ghastly scene.

"What in hell's gone on here?" Hardman whispered.

Firth looked about the area. There'd been a hell of a fight, the awning had been torn apart and everything thrown about. A Grizzly could do all this and more. Looking at the handprints on the white camper, this looked as if it was people, and more than one. The thing that puzzled him the most was where were the owners? The table had been set for two and there were only two chairs. Then he looked at the van.

"We gonna have to check the van, guys."

"What in hell for?" Murphy spluttered, still in shock.

"Do you see anybody about here? Maybe they're in the van…"

"Yeah, what if they are hurt or something?"

"You volunteering, boy?" McDowall mocked Miguel, gesturing toward the camper.

"No, no I'm not a fighter, I…"

"Why don't you go Glyn? You're always telling us how tough you are?"

"Screw that Tony! Hardman's closer than me."

Hardman moved back from the side door as if he'd been scalded, shaking his head.

Firth's gaze fell on Billy Boy then Murphy. Billy Boy would be lucky even to get the darn door open, so that left Murphy. Then he had an idea of how to use the situation to gain support. The worst thing he was likely to come across would be the dead campers. Unless it was the nut that'd killed them, of course.

"Okay, I'll go in but you *warriors* be ready for anything. You got that? See if you can make out anything inside the van. I don't want anybody creeping up on me."

The men peered through the windows of the camper, but all the curtains had been drawn. The brown cloth made an excellent and irritating barrier. Apprehensively, Firth approached the side door and slowly pulled the handle down. The bloodstained door creaked open. Firth cursed the fact that no one had bothered to bring a flashlight and slowly stepped inside. As he entered the campervan, adrenaline surged through his body, he felt for a light switch near the door but found nothing.

He tried to open the curtains but they were secured by some type of cord; he desperately fumbled to open them in the pitch black. His mouth dry, he could feel his heart pound and he fought the urge to run. After what seemed an eternity he managed to open a blind, flooding the interior with light. As his eyes adjusted to the brightness he scanned the van and within minutes he'd searched the whole vehicle. There was nothing.

"He's been in there a long time fellas," remarked Billy Boy, moving nearer the door. He hoped nothing had happened though he was sure happy it wasn't him in the van. Then Firth emerged from the doorway.

"Nothing. It's empty."

Firth stepped down from the van and leant up against the side, massaging his temples.

"Nothing," echoed Miguel.

"Everything is neat and tidy, beds all made up. No blood and *no bodies*. Whatever happened it happened fast."

"You'd better call this in Tony."

Hardman glanced over at the others.

"Now wait up there guys. If I do that, then Benteen's gonna turn this whole damn area into a crime scene and no one's gonna keep searching. We never gonna find them kids."

"Tony, we got Lord knows what going down here. We gotta report this," demanded McDowall.

"If it was your boy, would you be so quick to give up, Glyn?"

McDowall lowered his gaze, deep in thought as he looked away.

"Yeah but Tony..."

"Leave it Ross! We gonna follow Tony on this."

McDowall moved to join Firth. Without a sound, George Lee appeared from behind the camper's front and stood looking at the carnage.

"Jeez, George, you scared the crap outta me," said Firth, stumbling backwards.

"What you doing up here?"

"I was fixing to help out with the search. I done saw you and reckoned I'd tag on."

"Think this was bears, George?" asked Billy Boy, nervously wrapping his arms around his chest.

George Lee squatted down near the remains of the bloodied torn awning, brushing his fingers over the ground, staring intently at the area. After a few moments he shot up like a coiled spring and silently walked to the front of the vehicle, gesturing to the upturned table and chairs.

"Ain't no bears."

Hardman rubbed at his eyelids, shaking his head. He'd never got used to all this 'mystic man of the woods' bull, but he remembered how Lee had found those climbers back last summer, when everybody else had given up. Even the hounds hadn't been able to find them.

"Then what?"

"There's a mess of all kinda footprints leading to the chairs. All the blood is up here," he said, pointing to the front of the vehicle. Then he walked a few feet towards the rear of the camper.

"Then you got these big old army boots coming right in behind the first set."

Cradling his rifle in his left he jabbed out his other arm and pointed to a tree in a direct line past the plastic furniture.

"See them holes? They's bullet holes. *This ain't no bears.*"

Miguel stepped anxiously forward.

"What you say George, these people been shot?"

This was all getting too much for Miguel, here he was up the mountain searching for some lost kids and now there was a gun nut on the loose. And the only one with a gun anywhere near was standing right in front of him.

"Ain't up to me to say. I ain't the law. But it don't take darn near ten people to shoot two folks sitting in chairs. You'd better call this in, Mr Mayor."

"We already been through all that. I want to find them kids now. I don't want to waste time waiting for Benteen to show up. We gonna call it in later. Will you track for us George?"

Lee looked at the others and it was some time before he answered.

"Yep, reckon so. Where you all headed?"

"Good man. I was sure that Conrad would've taken them to The Meadow but I was wrong. So now we gonna follow the search grid and head for Dobson's barn and..."

"Dobson's barn? You done gone round in a circle, that's in the other direction."

Firth rounded on Ross Murphy.

"I thought you knew where the hell we were going! Eagle Scout you told us? *Eagle Scout my ass.* How far we out, George?"

"Bout three miles, if you're lucky."

"Can you get us to the barn?"

"Yep. We gotta go join the old airbase track then a ways up; we go back into them woods and the barn's right there."

Firth was relieved that Lee was with them on this; at least they could get on with the search. If they *had* got lost then Benteen would be furious. If he found out that they'd deliberately ignored the search plan that was something best not thought about. He walked forward to Murphy, stared at him until the man looked down at his feet, then snatched the survey map from the rucksack pocket and handed it to Lee.

Lee shook his head and held up his hand. "Got no use for one of them. They's made by city folk."

Then he strode off with the others following close behind.

****

Elle-May placed her rubber gloves into the contamination bin and looked intently at Zoë Watson. Both were in shock. Al and Jill Paxmore had brought Tony Arcado, Britney Patrick and Jehna Galway in about ten minutes ago. Tony and Britney had checked out just fine but Jehna Galway by all the odds should be dead.

"Elle-May what in hell's wrong with that girl? We ought not to have tied her up like that."

Even with her spine cut clean through, she'd gone crazy and tried to bite them. Norris Zillman had brought some restraints and they'd bound her to the bed. In all her years of nursing, Zoë had never seen anything like it. A fence post had impaled the girl and cut through her backbone. Even with pain-killers that should have knocked out a horse, the girl was still awake. They'd tried to plug the wound as best they could but the stuff coming out of it sure wasn't any kinda blood she'd ever seen. The whole thing was way too freaky.

"Zoë, we had to restrain her, there's nothing else we could do. I don't know what's up with her, it's sure beyond us. Look, make real certain you don't get none of that stuff on you. I gotta talk to Brad Eastman."

Zoë washed her hands and watched Elle-May leave the room. Alone in the treatment room, she could still hear that girl's awful wails. She shut her eyes tightly and concentrated on last week's ballgame results. The rough paper towel scraped her sore hands; she smoothed moisturiser on them and made a mental note to ask Lenski for more prescription cream.

Eventually, all she could hear was the rhythmic tick-tock from the wall clock. She looked up at its large round face – was that the time? She should have gone home half an hour ago; she just knew Elle-May would need her to stay. Damn! It was times like this she wished she'd never quit smoking.

****

Eastman was sitting in the nurse's rest room listening to Elle-May as she explained about the test results she'd taken. It was obvious this virus or disease or whatever the hell it was, was infectious. The drifter had been right all the time but he still wasn't to be trusted.

Jehna Galway's folks wanted to see their little girl and though they had every right, he couldn't allow them, not when she looked like *that*.

"Elle-May, has anyone else got this bug?"

"Nope. Tony Arcado, Britney Patrick, Jill and Al all checked out clear. I'm keeping Tony and Jill for observation. Tony's real shook up and Jill got some whiplash but nothing to do with the bug."

"What about Britney Patrick and Al?"

"I've sent for her folks, she's fine and Al's gone with Jill's brother, he's gonna hang around for Jill."

Eastman had already interviewed everyone from the group; there seemed little point in keeping people in hospital with nothing wrong with them. Jill's brother lived in town so it would be easy to get hold of Al if need be.

"I still can't believe what happened to poor Ruby. How are her parents?"

"I just came from there, Father O'Donnell's with them now. I sent Jedrey and Eddy Joe with the coroner to bring the body back. I just called in to ask you something before I meet up with them. Bob and Jane Galway want to see Jehna, is that gonna be possible?"

"No. I wouldn't advise that. Not like she is. Before we got to work on her you could see light through the hole in that poor kid's gut. I sure don't know what's keeping her alive; I swear it ain't natural."

"Maybe, but how can I stop them seeing their own kid?"

"I've tried knocking her out but it just doesn't work. We got her under restraints with tape on her mouth. It's like...well...it's like she's *possessed* or something. You gotta stop them from seeing her."

"How? How am I gonna do that?"

"Maybe you could tell them she's been isolated for medical reasons. There's all kinda protocols for that sort of thing. Anne would know best."

That sounded as if it could work. They could see her through a window and that would calm them a while. Seeing her all wild would not serve any kinda purpose. Sometimes things were best left unseen.

He fought for control as his last images of Helen on the roadside flooded into his head. Her crushed and broken body, still smiling at him through the shattered windshield. Putting on a brave face just for him. Unable to help, he'd watched her die in front of him. Painfully, he dug his short fingernails into the palms of his hand, hoping Elle-May had not noticed.

"Anne? Yeah, where is she?"

"Oh, she went up the Burke's place to check on Erin a while back."

"That's funny because Erin's been taken ill in town. She's on her way here right now. Anne wasn't there and her car's not in the lot."

"Maybe she's on her way back?"

There was a knock on the door and Elle-May got up to answer it. Max Koneg entered the room and walked up to Eastman. He had that look on his face; the one that always meant trouble.

"Brad, sorry to bother you. I just come up with Ben Burke."

Eastman shifted forward in his chair, looked at the man and nodded his head.

"Yeah."

"Well it's probably nothing but we got to talking and he said that there was two of them fellas up at his farm *not one*. Just thought you should know."

Eastman shot a worried glace at Elle-May and got up from his seat.

"Reckon I'd best look for Anne. Max, you stay in town. Son, you're the only lawman I got."

Eastman nodded his head and left the room.

****

The group had been walking for hours over the increasingly rough ground and the going was getting worse. As the incline gradually transformed to a near vertical rock face, George Lee indicated the point where they'd need to turn off to join the air base track. Murphy watched Lee clamber up the steep embankment towards the track. As Lee reached the hill he looked over his shoulder beckoning the others to follow, then disappeared from view.

Ross Murphy trudged along behind the others with his hands thrust deep in his pants pockets, like a scolded child, every once in a while muttering and cursing to himself. It didn't bother him none that Tony had given Lee the navigator's role; it was less for him to do. Anyways, all this damn walking was getting too much like hard work. It was no good everyone blaming him for getting them lost, when it was Tony that'd changed the route. He took quick stock of the others. Lee had been striding ahead over the rough, rocky path like a goat, but then nothing ever seemed to faze the guy. A way behind him was Tony Firth, still trying to be the leader, but now he was dragging his tired butt along.

McDowall was finding the going tough but Murphy knew that the 'big man' couldn't lose face in front of the others – especially Miguel. Miguel had been lucky to steer clear of McDowall on this expedition so far, which was just as well. The little Mexican was smart, maybe smarter than they gave him credit for, but not smart enough to avoid being mixed up with Firth.

Billy Boy was just the gofer, plain and simple. He did anything Firth told him to do. But Hardman, now he was something else, he was a real odd fish. Talk was that good old Tony had some serious dirt on him. That was Tony all over, that's how he bought loyalty.

As they began their steep ascent, Lee suddenly appeared and called down to them.

"Mr Mayor, you'd best take a look at this."

One by one, the group clambered up the incline and stepped onto the summit. The tree-covered wilderness stretched out in all directions as far as the eye could see. The road was a patchwork of broken tarmac; it was hard to remember that this had once been one of the town's main roads.

Lee was crouching looking hard at the road. Firth and the others walked over and looked down at the same area. Lee was pointing to a reddish section of the surface. However, it was the blood-stained pink sweater that caught their attention.

"That there Mr Mayor," said Lee pointing at the shaded ground "is blood. This here area's covered in it."

Irregular patterns of congealed blood dotted the area as if somebody had splashed red paint all over it. It was obvious there'd been a violent struggle fought here; its aftermath spread the whole width of the road.

Firth reached down to take the sweater.

"Who's...?"

"I know who that belongs to; she was in my store buying tent pegs a few days back. Jehna Galway," said Danny Hardman, dipping his head sadly.

Firth dropped the garment like a hot coke and began to shout. "Conrad! Conrad!"

Lee sprang up and stood directly in front of Firth. "Hush up there, Mr Mayor."

The blood rushed to Firth's head and he felt sick to his stomach. This was unlike anything he'd experienced before. When his old man died, Firth had gone through the motions of the grief-stricken son; done what was expected of him. The truth was, he'd waited a long time for the moment when he, Tony Firth, was the head of the family. He didn't want to lose Conrad. He had to find him.

"George, Conrad's out there someplace. I gotta find him. Do you understand?"

"Reckon so. Whoever done this likely done the camper. I reckon they're sure to be about."

"We gotta call this in," said McDowall, striding up to Firth. "This whole damn thing's gone too far."

"Guys!"

Billy Boy's whiney voice scratched through the air from the opposite side of the road. The others looked over at him standing near the edge of the road, a few yards away. He was looking down at something over the edge. Lee walked briskly over with the others following at his heels. As they reached Billy Boy, Miguel Bonzzoni was the first to speak.

"Sweet Mother of God!"

Miguel struggled to take the gruesome picture in. Far below lay the body of a man, dashed on the jagged rocks. Nearby, were the dismembered remains of at least one other body, but it was difficult to tell. Miguel could make out a leg and what was possibly a chunk of torso and maybe a head. He'd never expected to see this kind of thing here, not in Montana.

As a kid he'd managed to avoid the gangs and cartels back in Mexico. A lot of his friends had not been so lucky, but his father had been a carpenter, a good honest trade. Miguel worked with him and there'd been no time for all that. One day they'd stumbled across an execution site, the childhood memories of mutilated bodies once again filled his head.

His parents had moved to Armstrong to get away from such things. His sense of horror was soon replaced by fear and desperation. Could Lee be right? Was the person who'd committed these acts still around? For all the talk from the 'big men' they were defenceless and alone.

Firth placed the back of his hand across his mouth and drew in a sharp breath. Then without taking his eyes from the scene, he said to the others: "Somebody's gonna have to get down there and take a look. Any volunteers?"

"It ain't going to be me," barked Murphy, moving swiftly away from the edge, vigorously shaking his head.

Firth looked around at the others. There were no takers; his gaze fell on Lee.

"George you up to that?"

"Yep."

Billy Boy watched as Lee made his way down the dangerous slope. He guessed most folks would have needed a rope but not Lee. He held his rifle in one hand while using the other to balance. With his back-pack slung over his shoulders he may as well have been walking on the road. Billy Boy admired Lee and considered him almost kin; in many ways they were. He knew the others measured them as white trash. Billy Boy lived in the tiny trailer park outside town and Lee lived in his mountain shack some place in the hills. However, that's where the resemblance stopped.

These guys were following Lee about like lost kids. This was Lee's environment and they needed him to survive. Even Firth had done as he'd been told and shut up. How Billy Boy wished he was like Lee.

It seemed to the others that Lee had taken an eternity, but now he was making his way back up to them. Stepping onto the road, Lee stood in front of Firth, raised the peak of his US Marine cap a few notches and fixed Firth with a grim stare.

"What you find George?"

"The guy's been dead for days. There's just one body and that's a girl. Don't know where the rest of her is but I found this." Lee held up a small yellow knapsack with a teddy bear motif printed on it and handed it to Firth.

"What's this George?"

"I reckon Mayor you the only one here with the authority to open this." He pushed the blood-spattered bag at Firth and stepped back a few feet.

Gingerly, Firth took the tattered bag from him. Then he turned the yellow bag around in his hands and slowly opened it. The tag inside read Ruby Carson. He looked at the others.

"Ruby Carson. It's Ruby Carson's."

Firth dropped the bag to the ground. Out of the five kids that were missing it looked as if at least two had met with a grisly end. Firth thought of the twisted remains on the rocks and the likelihood that the other body was Ruby Carson. His gut churned as the notion struck him that Conrad could have met the same fate. He had to find him; the others would have to help.

"Okay, there's still some daylight hours left, let's get going."

Firth marched up the road with no real clue of where he wanted to go, but he had to do something. Then he stopped abruptly as he realised no one had followed him. He turned to face the group and stared at them, waiting for someone to speak first.

"Tony, enough already! We're all going back. It's gone beyond looking for some missing kids. There's some damn nut up here killing people. We need the law for this."

"McDowall's right," Hardman agreed. "In case you haven't noticed, George is the only one packing artillery here. This is way too dangerous. We need our guns."

"Yeah, screw that. I ain't going no further," said Murphy, moving towards Hardman and McDowall.

"Whatever! Fine. I don't need none of you anyhow."

Firth threw his arms up in disgust and walked up to Lee.

"George, I gotta ask..."

Lee held up his hand and shook his head. Sure, he felt sorry for the Mayor but McDowall was right, things had changed. This was no place for town folks. The others were all done in. They had no water and no clue.

Yeah, he could carry on, maybe even find the boy or this creep, but it was the law's job not his. They had the tin stars, not him. Whoever had done this was one nasty SOB. He'd killed at least three people and Lord knows what had happened to the other kids. It was just as well not to think about that for now. But there was a whole bunch of stuff that just made no sense.

Why were the soldier boys at the camper and what about the guy on the rocks? He looked like he'd been dead a while, then why hadn't any critters had a go at him? He decided that he'd have to get this bunch home and then he'd come back with the law.

"Sorry Mayor, you and the boys here ain't up to it."

"Tony, we want to find them kids just like you but we can't stay no longer. We ain't leaving you up here neither."

McDowall walked up to Firth. "You're coming with us even if I gotta drag your sorry ass back."

"No need of that," said Lee, pointing behind them. "We got us some company."

The group turned to look in the direction of the old track leading to town. A small convoy of two squad cars and an ambulance was winding toward them. It looked as though they'd all be spared a long hot walk after all.

****

Anne Lenski walked up the drive towards the Burke house, her feet crunching over the rough ground as she went. House calls over the past few years had persuaded her of the use of practical footwear. This was the first time she'd visited the house and although she knew them well, both Erin and Ben were relative strangers to the health center.

She passed Ben's battered old blue pickup as she climbed the steps to the weather-beaten porch. Two old and worn wooden rocking chairs sat facing towards the mountainside. She imagined them sitting there watching the sunset go down beyond the mountain. Standing in the porch, Anne knocked on the shabby door and waited. When no reply came, she called out and tried the door, only to discover it was locked. She called again, and then decided to try around the back. A small narrow wooden path led off to the left of the house and after a short time she came across a stone-walled back garden.

Anne pushed the much repaired wooden gate open and stepped into the enclosure. The garden was full of shrubs and potted plants and an ancient looking glasshouse was filled to the brim with delicious looking vegetables. Vivid red tomato plants and the strong aroma of fresh mint wafted through the air.

However, the stark reality remained that this was a crime scene. Remnants of yellow and black plastic police tape hung lifeless in the breeze lazy afternoon. A tin of bright green paint lay on its side, the spilled contents solidifying in the hot sun, testament to a task never completed. Directly in front of the glass out-house was the white outline of a figure, the intruder that Ben had killed. Jack Larson, the coroner, had attended the scene. Anne had been at Mary Firth's house and missed the call.

Over the last few days there'd been too many violent deaths and she'd found herself dwelling on her time as an army doctor in Iraq. There, violent deaths had been a daily occurrence. Looking at the white figure outline, her thoughts drifted to Paul.

What had gone through his mind when the Jihadists had dragged him from the aid tent? What had been his last thoughts on that day in Syria? What would her last thoughts have been? He'd been in the wrong place at the wrong time and he'd died just because he'd been an American, as simple as that. Nothing profound; just a victim of racial and religious hatred.

She tried the door and lifted the catch but as she was about to enter the dilapidated structure, she saw reflected in the glass window a figure through the open gate. She turned around and walked back down the path towards the gate. If it was Ben or Erin then she didn't want to startle them, so she called out to let them know she was there. As she left the enclosure she caught a fleeting glimpse of the figure disappearing around the corner of the house.

"Ben, its Dr Lenski. I just need to talk to you. Ben?"

She turned right and followed the pine end of the house until she came to a small extension. She called out once more and as she rounded the corner she came face to face with the figure. It was neither Ben nor Erin. Its lipless face was etched into a grotesque sort of smile and as it opened its mouth it let out a raspy shriek. The lifeless transparent eyes stared right through her. Terrified, she stumbled backwards as the creature lurched at her, its hands reaching out like claws.

CHAPTER - ELEVEN

Ben Burke was scared. Not like the time he'd flipped the car; this was a different scared. He sat in the tiny treatment room, holding his wife's fragile hand. Rows of beeping machines with little flashing lights surrounded them, and the brilliant white walls hurt his eyes. He knew that all these contraptions were keeping Erin alive and he was thankful, but he just wanted her home. When he'd thought of death, he'd always imagined that it would come to them in their own home, in their own bed, on their terms.

Ben looked at Erin, her features barely recognisable through the plastic face-mask; just a frail old lady, but back then when he'd first met her that had been different. She and her cousin had been standing by the open door on the hot summer night. Hank had asked the cousin for a dance and Ben had been left with Erin and that had been the start of it. Some weeks later he'd asked her Pa if he could walk her out.

Old man Harris had been a stern faced old coot and he'd taken an instant dislike to Ben. But Ben was persistent and eventually he got his way. The two never got on, so when the old coot suddenly dropped dead, it was no great loss. The following year, Ben and Erin married and she moved into the Burke farmhouse. It had been a long time since they'd had a woman about the place to fuss over them. Ben's mother died when he was a child and his father had thrown himself into the farm but farming was also Ben's life. However, the same could not be said for Hank. He'd never liked the lifestyle and had always waited for the chance to quit. As soon as he was old enough, he joined the army.

Although the farmstead was modest, it was still large enough for them to loan areas of land to people. Tony Firth's father had farmed one such plot for years but that arrangement had cost them dearly. With Hank leaving, the workload had increased for everyone and Erin had also needed to pitch in with manual work. They were hard times but also among some of the best. Then the Union Pacific telegram had arrived, changing things forever.

He remembered how his father had wept in the barn that day. Ben had never seen him like that, even when Ma died. Hank had been one of the last Americans to die in the Korean War. A week later, Pa died. The death certificate said 'heart attack' but Ben knew it was a broken heart. He and Erin had suddenly become people with property. It had taken him years to get used to the idea. They didn't have much, but what they had was all theirs. Yet it wasn't worth a thing without Erin. He looked down at her and a tear slid down his wrinkled old cheek. She was all he had left. If only she'd wake up.

"Ben. Ben!"

He looked at his wife but the sound was coming from the doorway. Elle-May was standing in the room, clutching a notepad, beaming back at him.

"Sorry Ben, I figured I'd fix up some food for you. Just wanted to know what you wanted?"

Food was the last thing on his mind; still it was good of her to ask. He slowly shook his head and raised his weary hand.

"Obliged to you but I ain't rightly hungry now."

"Maybe so, but if you don't eat something soon, you'll be in the next bed."

He shut his tired eyes for a few moments. The day had taken its toll on him; he was so worn-out. It made no sense to make himself ill. What use would he be then? Perhaps she was right. He looked over at Elle-May, smiled and nodded his head.

"Two runny eggs and a plate of beans will do me just fine, if you've a mind to?"

"Sure thing. We aim to please."

"Just asking, when's the doc gonna see Erin?"

"She went up to your place 'cause she thought you were back home. She's gonna be back real soon. Don't worry; I'll go fix the eggs."

With that she gave a little wave and walked off down the corridor. It wasn't that he didn't appreciate all they were doing; he just couldn't stand all the fuss. The sooner the doc got there, the sooner they could get home, the happier he'd be. As Ben squeezed Erin's hand he couldn't help but think: what was keeping Dr Lenski?

****

Eastman's rugged boots crunched heavily on the gravel as he passed Anne Lenski's car. The barn was the only place left to look. Where the hell was she? As he cut through Erin's withered flowerbeds he became aware of a faint pounding coming from the direction of the barn. As Eastman drew level to the small wall at the side of the house, his eyes darted about. Across the yellow expanse of Ben's top field, Eastman could make out two of the creatures beating on the barn door and wailing loudly.

Ducking behind the wall he slowed his breathing and cautiously stuck out his head for a better look. Above the door about twenty feet up, was the hayloft and through its opening he saw Anne Lenski. Eastman drew his pistol and stalked closer, trying not to alert the creatures. His jaw dropped when suddenly, Anne started calling out to him.

"Brad, just listen don't talk. I'm okay. They're not interested in you; they hunt by sight and sound. As long as they can't see or hear you, you're invisible."

The things that were trying to break down the door were certainly oblivious to him – maybe she was right. As he moved closer, his mind frantically tried to come up with a course of action. The thought of trying to subdue these things was out of the question. That left him with the second option. He disliked the notion of just killing them out of hand. However, after Hinckle Point he was not prepared to take any risks. As much as he hated the prospect, there was no other way; he levelled his pistol at the back of the nearest creature's head.

"Don't shoot them. We can't just kill them, there has to be another way… Brad, please?"

Eastman looked up at her in disbelief. Had she lost the damn plot? He widened his eyes and shook his head. Loony as a coot. Yet, *maybe* there was some other way. Neither of them was in any immediate danger; Anne was safely behind a solid wooden door and after all, he was armed. These things were never going to win any races. Taking several steps backwards, he knew he'd not have much time as soon as he started to talk. He'd have to be direct and precise. He called out in a hushed voice over the creature's mournful wails.

"I'm going to distract them from the barn. When they follow, you get the hell out."

His luck was in; the creatures took absolutely no notice and continued to pound the door. He decided he would carry on until they noticed him.

"Is there any way into that barn other than this door?"

The nod of her head prompted him to continue.

"Great, when they start to follow me, get out and hide just there, out of sight," he said, pointing just left of the outside barn wall.

Then just like the last dime on a payphone, his time ran out. The larger of the two creatures stopped the infernal pounding and slowly turned its head to look over its right shoulder, looking for the next target. Brownish drool trickled out between the broken teeth and dripped down its ragged bearded chin. Then the creature let out a chilling screech as it lurched towards him. Eastman drew back; this did not rank as one of his best ideas.

The first time he'd seen one of them up close he'd felt a whole range of emotions; fear, revulsion and horror, but there'd been something else. At the time he just hadn't been able to figure it out; now watching this thing stalking him, the answer hit him like a right cross. *Anger*. The type of anger that's difficult to separate from hate. This puke ugly critter saw him as part of the food chain. Just another lump of meat. Eastman's eyes narrowed to pin points and he felt the pressure build in his trigger finger. He hadn't felt like that since he'd caught the drunk who'd killed Helen. Then he remembered he was a lawman.

Eastman holstered his Magnum and looked at the second creature, still bashing the door. The plan needed both of them to follow him. He stepped back a few feet, picked up a medium sized rock and scored a direct hit on the second creature's head. Letting out a loud grunt, the thing stopped and turned to look around. Eastman brought his hands together like thunderclaps, yelling at the top of his voice. The excited creatures lost interest in the barn door and slowly started to follow Eastman onto the field.

"Anne, I'm gonna lead these dead heads away from the barn, up to the top and then I'm coming back. I'll holler when it's clear for you to come out. Anne, don't take any chances."

"Be careful."

Eastman led the two creatures in a ghoulish 'follow the leader' away from the barn, calling to Anne to leave as he went. The creatures moved no faster than a slow walk and like Anne had said, they seemed unaware of anything other than their intended prey. They also seemed incapable of coherent speech and just let out a constant groan. He doubted if there was anything anybody could do for these poor souls.

Eastman kept an even pace far enough to be out of reach, but not so far that they lost interest. When he reached the battered fence at the top of the field, he turned and touched the brim of his Stetson, bid the creatures farewell then ran towards the barn. Soon he was standing next to Anne and he placed a reassuring hand on her shoulder.

"Listen there's not much time, I'm gonna lead those two into the far end of the barn. Then I'm gonna high tail it back out. You gotta be ready to bar that door soon as I'm clear."

"Now hold on there. You're going in there with those two? That's not such a good..."

"Anne, either we trap them in there or I'm gonna have to shoot them. I can't risk them roaming around. Now, you with me on this or not?"

"I don't like this one bit. Just be careful."

Eastman nodded his head and handed her the wooden bar for the door. It was a solid piece of timber and he reckoned strong enough to hold them. He ushered Anne behind the barn side and swung the single door wide open. This further obscured Anne. He wanted the dead heads to see him only.

"Anne stay out of sight until I get them in the barn, but be ready when I come a-running. I need to know, do you think there's a cure for these things?"

"Well I..."

"I'm risking my life here."

"I don't know. I really don't know. But I'm sure going to try."

Eastman put his finger to his lips and nodded his head towards the right hand corner
of the barn. Both creatures now only feet away, Eastman peered into the unlit barn. The interior was large enough for about two pickups; enough room for him to manoeuvre around the things. He just hoped the barn was empty. He stepped forward and cautiously entered unknown territory.

His eyes quickly adapted to the gloom and he could make out Ben's tractor and beyond that was the hayloft entrance. There appeared to be no obvious second exits. Stacked right at the back of the barn was a small wall of hay bales. For his plan to work they'd have to get uncomfortably close to him. Too far and they'd grab him, too close and they'd definitely get him. The timing had to be perfect; there'd be no time for any mistakes.

Allowing them to get in close, Eastman jumped onto the bales and in the same movement, jumped back onto the floor. The distraction complete, he dodged past the outstretched grasping hands. In a move that would've made his old football coach happy, Eastman sprinted toward the daylight. Suddenly his foot connected with something buried under the straw covered floor. In horror, Eastman saw the barn floor rushing up to meet him.

With an impact that knocked the breath out of him, Eastman lay face down on the hard ground, stunned. After what seemed an eternity, he felt hands clawing at his boots and grasping at the legs of his pants.

Rolling onto his back, Eastman kicked out with his right leg, catching the creature in the face. It flew backwards under the savage impact and when it sat up Eastman could see its jaw hanging down at one side. Just in time, Eastman saw the second creature about to fall onto him. Eastman brought his left leg to his chest and kicked out like a piston as the creature fell forward. He felt a sickening crunching feeling as the dead head's rib cage crumpled. Leaping to his feet, Eastman bolted for the open door, stopping just long enough to retrieve his hat.

"Anne, here I come!"

As he exploded out of the gloom, Anne started to push the wooden door shut. He grasped the door and slammed it closed, while she slotted the bar into the heavy duty metal latch with a resounding crash. Anne grabbed his shoulders and pressed him close.

"What took you so long?"

Eastman raised his eyebrows and blew out a long sigh, holding up both hands in a mock surrender, then whipped his head around as the creatures began to pound on the door.

"Is that going to hold them?"

"That's good timber. It'd take a truck to bust that open. C'mon let's get back to town."

"Brad, where are Erin and Ben? I tried to get into the house but one of those guys attacked me and I ran for the barn."

"*Guys*? I don't know what the hell those things are but they ain't guys."

"I don't know either, but until we know otherwise, they're just sick."

Eastman took a long look at her. How could she think these were still people? Still, he must be as dumb as her since he'd gone along with it all. But that was just like Anne Lenski, always fixing to cure things. He shrugged his broad shoulders and gave a weary nod.

"Ben and Erin are both safe at the hospital. Erin got bitten and so did Jehna Galway."

"And the others?"

"I'll tell you in the car."

"Brad, I want to know right now, what about the others?"

"Yeah, okay. Ruby's dead and Conrad's missing. But the others are fine. Jill and Al got busted up a bit too, but I think they're okay."

Eastman watched as her gaze shifted from him, into the distance. Her face turned to a puzzled expression as she pointed to something on the horizon. He also turned to follow her stare.

"Is that...is that a...?"

"Helicopter. Yep sure is."

In the clear blue sky a small dark helicopter was hovering just above the tree line in the distance, facing directly towards them. Although Eastman was no helicopter expert, he recognised the aircraft as the type State Troopers used for search and rescue operations. Underneath the nose he could clearly make out the orb that housed the thermal image camera. He wasn't sure of the function of the other bumps and balls but sure as hell, this was no Sunday picnic chopper.

"Can he see us from over there?"

"He's looking right at us. He can't fail to from that distance."

Anne started to jump up and down waving her arms above her head. Eastman joined in by waving his hat. Maybe it wouldn't do any harm to highlight their position. To his astonishment, the helicopter suddenly shot vertically into the air and disappeared over the horizon leaving the sky clear except for a flock of startled birds.

"Brad, what the hell was that all about?"

Eastman looked at her and shook his head. He'd stake his hat on the fact the chopper had seen them. It just had to have. If it was some kind of rescue team then he was sure they'd have orders to make contact. It gave him that feeling he always got in the gut when he just knew something was not right. There was a lot of odd stuff going down and he needed to get to the bottom of it. No matter that he was a cop; he hated mysteries.

"Anne, I think it's time we left."

****

Perched on a large rocky outcrop, Sarge scanned the area in front of him with his binoculars. Pine trees, boulders and lots of rough ground. But no kids, only the river as it coursed by. He'd trekked this region since his boyhood and there was always something to catch the eye, but not today. As he clambered down he adjusted his back-pack, then briskly walked off. Wasn't it just typical of half-assed civilians to get it all wrong? The search grids that Benteen had drawn up were far too large, you could march a whole darn battalion between them. Where was Eastman when you needed him? He ought to have been leading the search or at least coordinating it but no, he'd gone off someplace. That left Firth as the C/O and what a clown he was. He'd probably already got himself lost or eaten by bears before he'd even found the kids.

What was it with that guy? Why the Sam hell didn't he guess where the kids would be? Since the flyboys had pulled out of Armstrong, the old listening post had been a magnet for kids; they got up to all sorts of antics. Kids did things and went places to get away from their parents.

As he walked into the woods, Yardman's wise crack still stung like a hornet. Yardman was the sort of guy that had done nothing and been nowhere but the honest truth was that half the lamebrains in town agreed with the bum. Of course none had the nuts to tell him face to face, but he'd heard the jibes: 'here comes GI Joe' or 'it's Soldier Boy' and a hell of a lot worse.

He shook his head; they just didn't get it, none of them. Even now he was dressed in full combat order because it was appropriate for the job. He wore it everywhere, no additions or embellishments, just the dress code and what he was entitled to wear. He never tried to pass himself off as a 'serving' soldier and if anyone ever asked, he told them he was 'US Army *retired*.'

The uniform gave him a much needed purpose and a link to the military. He was never going to be a civilian. No sir! He needed to remind the town he still 'had it' and maybe that's what he needed too? He wore the uniform because he was proud of his country and proud of the US Army. That was something those 'numb nuts could never understand.

They thought he had a bruised brain; that he'd been thrown out on a Section 8. Sure, after the war, he'd had problems – everybody does, but he'd worked with the shrinks, popped all those damn pink pills and listened to endless mumbo jumbo. Eventually, he'd been passed fit for duty, but combat was a thing of the past. Game over.

Sarge stopped and took a drink from his canteen; he took the opportunity to quickly scan the immediate horizon. Damn kids! Of all the times to go AWOL they had to go and pick one of the hottest days this year. And it figured that brat Conrad just had to be involved -just like his Pa, a no good trouble-maker. Still, he was here to rescue, not to judge and the other kids seemed okay. Not that he was an expert on the matter; he'd never found the time for kids. Yeah, he'd been married but he'd always been away on deployment some place or other. She'd run off with the cable guy. TV wasn't the only thing that slime ball had plugged.

So no kids, no wife and no job and here he was looking for a bunch of dumb kids. But at least he figured his motives were genuine, unlike others. It was election time and Firth wanted votes and this was one hell of a sure way to get them. Sarge wasn't interested in getting credit for finding the kids; he just wanted to find them, and before Firth.

A set of footprints suddenly caught his interest a few feet ahead in the soft ground near the river. He looked at the prints then crouched down for a closer inspection. There were a set of recent sneaker tracks but the most interesting of all were the bare footed prints. Who the hell would not wear footwear over this ground?

The prints led alongside the river and into the undergrowth. As he followed the direction with his eyes he heard an unexpected noise to his front. The undergrowth exploded as a wide-eyed figure lurched at him, bloodied hands clutching at the air.

****

Benteen was sitting at Eastman's desk, his big arms folded on his equally powerful chest. He was studying the search grids on the map. It was a huge area to cover, difficult enough in normal times, when you had the manpower and air cover: they had nothing except good intentions. Mostly, everyone had been late at the checkpoints; they just hadn't been able to cover the grids in the agreed times. What he didn't want was for people to get lost and add to the situation. He needed to get out into the action, but with Brad away he was the only one left to run the show. Sitting this side of the big desk for a change gave him insight into how frustrated Brad must feel. There was a lot to be said for just following orders.

He'd been out earlier and the streets were buzzing about with people. Folks had also gathered outside the town hall and the station house. Luckily the mood was calm, almost as if they were waiting for some kind of parade to roll on through. Benteen was still mad at Yardman for getting Sarge all fired up earlier; now he'd gone off on his own just to prove a point.

Sarge would have been more use in town but on the other hand, at least he was out of Benteen's hair for a while. There was too much going on for a place like Armstrong. With that Galway kid all messed up in the hospital and the possibility of Ruby Carson dead, it looked as if things couldn't get any worse. Then there was a knock on the door; seconds later Clara walked in holding her pad. Her face was full of concern as she spoke.

"Gerard, I got us a shopping list. I just had Jedrey and Eddy Joe on the radio; they're with Mayor Firth and his party. They got a body but they can't say if it's the Carson girl. It's in bits."

"Poor kid."

"That ain't all. They found a camper van a couple of miles from where they are now, no bodies, but plenty of blood."

"Tell them boys I'm coming up. I don't want them going off half-cocked and walking into anything. What else you got on that list?"

"Jimmy Emmett reported seeing a helicopter near the Burke farm a while back and..."

"Yeah sure, don't tell me, ET was flying it."

"No, but Brad and Anne Lenski are up there remember? And Bill Merka reported some type of drone near the tower."

Things were getting stranger by the minute and he was stuck behind a desk. Then again, perhaps at last the outside had come to take a look at what was happening?

"Clara, I gotta call the search off. There's too darn much going on here. We need them folks back. Get the teams on the radio and tell 'em to head back, pronto."

With the likelihood of more deaths at the camper, he wanted to get everyone back to town safely. If there was some kind of killer on the loose, town was the safest place.

****

Sarge looked across at the wide-eyed figure sitting against the rock. Its eyes were fixed on something in the middle distance; Sarge had seen that look so many times before on people in combat, it was known as 'the thousand yard stare.' This boy was on the point of both nervous and physical exhaustion. It was clear he'd been to hell and back. However, what worried him the most was the blood encrusted rock the boy clutched in his right hand.

Sarge recognised him as being the printer's son, some kind of Jewish sounding name like, Goldberg or something. So he knew he'd found one of the missing kids. Problem was, where were the others? He looked at the blood-stained rock and started getting an uneasy feeling.

"Hey son, I'm here to help you. I need to get us back to Armstrong for the medics to check you over. Can you understand me?"

Since the kid's dramatic appearance, Sarge had calmed him down and for the last ten minutes, he'd just sat there and said not one darn word. Something so traumatic had happened that the boy had all but shut down. Sarge was painfully aware of how that worked. He'd blanked the events in Syria immediately after his Hummer got hit. Sometimes the mind blocked things as protection. But they couldn't hang around all day; he wanted to get them home.

"Look boy, we gotta get moving. I don't want to sit on my ass all day and you need checking over. But first I need you to drop that hunk of rock."

Sarge saw the boy's eyes flicker as he let the rock slip from his bloody hand. Still watching the boy for any reaction, Sarge reached into his pocket for an empty chip packet, and carefully placed the rock in the bag. If the boy had done anything, Sarge wanted the rock for the cops to look at, besides he didn't want any incidents on the way back.

"Silver Star?"

"Affirmative. That's right boy."

Sarge pointed to the medal on his ribbon band.

"Gramps won his in Vietnam."

"I got mine in Syria, along with a mess of other metal. I could've done without the last lot."

As the boy started to rise to his feet Sarge heard a commotion to his left, followed by a strange growling noise. The boy drew back, his face a mask of terror. Sarge didn't know what was behind him but he knew it wasn't going to be good. He spun around to confront whatever was there. He narrowed his eyes and his mouth opened slightly. He'd seen hundreds of guys looking like this one; the only difference was that they'd been in body bags.

The guy's lips had rotted away, leaving two rows of jagged, decayed teeth and fluid dribbled from the mouth as he moved towards them. Sarge noted that he was wearing some kind of hospital gown and the bare feet were worn to the bone. How the hell could somebody get to look that bad and not be in a box? As the apparition moved ever closer to Sarge, he heard the boy shout out.

"Don't let him touch you mister, they're poisoned!"

They? Sarge looked from the boy to the guy, then like a light switch he got it. This kid had come across whatever this guy was before. The dark thoughts Sarge had about what had happened to the other kids were unfounded. It was one of these guys the kid had whacked, not the other kids.

"Hey kid, what's with this punk?"

"They killed Ruby!"

For all he knew, this guy could have some kind of rabies but one thing was certain, Sarge wasn't about to let this mush face get any closer. He only ever gave the one warning; Sarge deemed that more than enough.

"Halt! Don't come any closer."

Sarge was not remotely surprised when the nightmare just kept coming. He allowed a few steps, and then landed a hefty kick to the guy's stomach, bowling him into a tree. Satisfied that the danger had been removed, Sarge dusted his gloved hands together and turned to face the boy.

As he started to speak, he felt skeletal fingers grasp his right shoulder, then the boy screamed out a warning. Sarge broke free of the grip and brought his elbow crashing into the attacker's chest. Wheeling around he saw the decomposing features of another one, inches away from him. Sarge connected a powerful upper-cut to his opponent's jaw and his foe staggered back, showering broken teeth and part of his tongue into the air, before crashing to the rocky ground.

Out of the corner of his eye, Sarge detected movement to his left. The first of his attackers was now moving forward. The thing that struck Sarge the most was the injury to the chest; several ribs were poking out of the filthy gown. It was obvious the chest had caved in and yet he was still standing.

Sarge grabbed the boy's arm and pulled him away. Sarge and the boy would have to break away and fast. However much he disliked the notion of leaving these things roaming free, if they remained then he would be forced to kill them out of self-defence. Since he'd no idea what was wrong with them, he had no intention of being saddled with murder.

"Come on son, time we left this party."

"Marv. My name's Marv Glitzman mister."

"Well okay then. *Marv Glitzman*, time we left this party."

Sarge looked at Marv and gave him a dry smile. This kid had guts and he was happy to have him on his squad. Whatever was wrong with those two creeps, it was pretty bad, but they damaged easy and moved real slow. Still, with a few miles left to town, this was by no means over.

CHAPTER – TWELVE

Jimmy Emmett walked down Harris Street, watching the stunned faces of the passers by as he went. The news about Ruby Carson had hit the town hard. Although the search teams had returned not more than a quarter hour back, the news had gone through the town like wildfire. He'd overheard Billy Boy talking with some others about the RV and the Carson girl. Although he couldn't recall where, or even who'd said it, he was pretty sure the girl had been cut up with a chainsaw.

The other big news was that Sarge had brought back Marv Glitzman. Although Jimmy wasn't a big fan of Sarge, the guy had done well. So with all this, Jimmy had already worked out the cause a while back. It was his considered opinion backed up with years of experience with conspiracy theories, the only people with the power and ability to shut down a whole town had to be Uncle Sam. He even knew where the air force base was located.

Some weeks back, in the dead of night, he'd seen lights at the base and some kind of construction work going on. It was common knowledge that these old bases went down miles below the surface; the perfect place for their operation. Hidden away from everybody, they were conducting some sort of experiment on the town.

He was pretty sure the attacks were also connected to the blackout. They could have brought the infected people to study. What would happen if they were used as some kind of weapon? His mind was on fire with conspiracy theories. This was big, the biggest thing he'd ever discovered. But the trouble with this place was that no one would ever listen.

He walked slowly up and down Harris Street, his mind reeling under the implications of this revelation. Outside the flower shop, he saw just the type of guy who would listen. Emmett walked up to Chris Emery. Now here was a man who knew about everything.

"Hi Mr Emery, what you make of all this? I got me a theory that…"

"Hank Emmett has a theory, now this, I must hear."

"Its Jimmy, Hank's my Pa."

Something was wrong here. Emmett looked at Emery; he was a mess. His grey hair was standing up on one side of his head, as if he'd just got up and he had a few days' worth of stubble on his face. But the strangest thing of all was that he was still wearing his pajama top. However, none of that was Emmett's problem, he was on a mission and fit to burst.

"I think that the blackout and the attacks are linked …"

"Absolutely dreadful about Ruby. She is…or rather was, one of my students. Who could have done such a horrible thing?"

"Well that's what I'm trying to…"

"A lot of people about Hank, is there a game?"

"Game? No, they're headed to the town hall or the police station – waiting for official word, I suppose."

"Official word? No, you'll find they're protesting the war. Outrageous! Should never have got involved."

"Syria? But we pulled outta there last year."

"Syria? What's Syria got to do with anything? I'm talking about the Vietnam War. You'd know that if you paid attention in class, Hank Emmett. Now I'll see you Monday, have a good weekend."

Emmett tugged at his ear lobe and rolled his eyes as he watched Emery walk away down the street with his blue and white pajama top sticking out of his pants. That was the thing with this town - nobody ever listened to Emmett. Take last week, for instance. He'd met Sarge in Wal-Mart and was busy explaining some of his pet theories on JFK's assassination. He'd just started to explain away the second shooter theory and how Oswald had used a teleport, when suddenly Sarge had gone crazy, chasing him from the store with a rolled up fishing magazine.

The only reason he'd stopped was because Benny Arnold, the manager, had chased after Sarge because he hadn't paid for the magazine. When Emmett looked back, Sarge, Benny Arnold and the guard were laughing at his expense. Well they'd be sorry when the

G men got them. Of course, he could always tell the cops but even they weren't interested.

Yesterday he'd been advising a bunch of people about leaving the town as one of the safest options, when Gerard Benteen came raging up like a bull, purple-faced and cussing. Benteen had threatened to charge him with 'subversion and incitement to cause panic' and a whole lot of other stuff he'd never heard of. What a disgraceful way for a lawman to behave. Emmett wanted to report it to Eastman but he'd disappeared as well.

Emmett neared the station house and was surprised at the large crowd of people gathered there, with the same worried faces. They wanted answers. They needed answers. Bernie's Burger Bar and Spinelly's Kool Ices had set up in the street. God bless America and free enterprise. He'd give Kool Ices a try later, but the burgers were best left alone, he'd heard stories about where Bernie got his meat. From the other side of the street he could see Firth and Benteen standing on the steps of the jailhouse. Were they going to say something? he wondered. Then they disappeared inside. Yeah, that was the thing with Armstrong, no darn communication.

****

Benteen and Firth were standing in Eastman's office, Benteen behind the desk and Firth in a state of agitation. The tension in the room was thick enough to cut with a table knife.

"Look Gerard, I know things are rough at the moment and it's all on you, but you gotta get people back up there. My boy's still missing."

"Preciate that Mayor. Under the circumstances it ain't safe for anyone going up there."

"Yeah, that includes my boy, damn it. Gerard I want boots on the ground up there right now!"

"We got us a maniac up there attacking people. He's already killed one of our kids. I'm sure as hell not risking any more of our folk, until we get us a new plan. Now I'm sorry but that's the way it's gotta be."

Benteen was trying to hold his temper; it was a downhill battle. He'd just about had enough of this fat, bald, pain in the ass. For two pins, he'd throw him in the slammer, Mayor or not. However, as the senior, in fact the only peace officer in town, he had to respect the man's status.

"I know Brad's not here to tell you what to do, but for this one time maybe you could manage a thought all by yourself and damn well get up there and look for Conrad!"

Benteen glowered back at Firth – this was typical. He was used to getting what he wanted. Even allowing for the fact his son was missing, it was clear that Firth had put others in harm's way for his own ends. Benteen had a responsibility to uphold the law and keep the people safe. He was not about to send anyone into the mountains without a revised plan. If there was some nut out there then he'd need armed rescue teams and folks who knew how to use firearms - not just gun owners, who brought them out every other Sunday, but folks who could look after themselves. George Lee had shown him some 9 mm slugs he'd got from the RV site; it was unlikely the things Eastman or Ben had seen could use guns. That meant somebody else could be on the loose.

"Look, you may not respect me but you sure as hell are gonna respect this uniform. *Now, no one's gonna go up that God damn mountain till I get me a plan!"*

"Now, see here you..."

"Anybody got a beef with one of my officers best come see me first, Tony."

Both antagonists whirled round to see Eastman standing in the open doorway with Anne Lenski just behind him. They were hot and tired and Eastman was in no mood to mess about. He walked across the room to stand alongside Benteen.

"I'll let you boys talk," said Anne as she hurriedly left the room.

"Okay, I've told the people outside, we gonna have a meeting in about twenty-five minutes in the Town Hall. Gerard, what's happening here?"

"Well Brad, we got us all kinds of situations. I called the teams back 'cause as well as those freaks, I got reason to think there's someone armed up there. I can't put other folk at risk but..."

"Whatever," said Firth, "but you ain't worried about Conrad. He's still up there on his own and you two are sitting doing nothing!"

"Faced with a whole bunch of unknowns, Gerard's right. *Nobody's going up there*. Do you want our people coming back in body bags? Tony, I don't like the idea of one of our kids up there with all this going on, but we gotta have a plan."

"Then just let me and some guys go up there. Damn it, I gotta do something!"

"I can't do that and you know it. We only got a few hours of good light left. By the time we get organised and up there, that light is gonna fade. That means we'll be searching in darkness. We'll go at first light, organised and with a plan."

The logic finally sunk in and Firth slumped into a chair holding his head in his hands. They were right; by the time they got up there they would have lost the light.

"Brad what you want me to do?"

"Just go home; you look done in. Try and get back for the meeting but nobody's gonna blame you if you can't. Tony, if Bridget wants a scalp, tell her come get mine. You done all you could up there."

Eastman watched as Firth nodded his head, dragged himself from the chair and trudged out of the office. Closing the door, Eastman looked at Gerard. There was a lot to go through and hardly any time to do it.

"What we got?"

"We brought Ruby back, all the bits we could find. We got some other developments too. Firth found an RV – looks like some violence went down. George Lee dug up some 9 mm casings at the scene; it looks as if they were machine guns. No bodies, just blood. Then Sarge and Marv Glitzman ran into two of them things you met with."

"How's the boy? I mean where'd he been all this time?"

"After the attack up on the road, when Ruby got killed, he led the other kids to safety and then went for help. He followed the river to town, killed one of them things and came across Sarge. A regular hero."

"Marv Glitzman did all that? Where'd he think Conrad went?"

"Ah, well that's it you see. Conrad cut out after Ruby died and ran into the woods, arms in the air, screaming like a blind faggot at a weenie roast. But there's something else we got to look at."

Benteen rubbed his jaw awkwardly before continuing. "Marv and Britney Patrick swear Conrad pushed Jenha Galway at one of them creatures."

"*And?*"

"So after it took a chunk outta her, he left the others on their own."

"Does Firth know about this?"

"Just you, me and the kids."

Eastman sat back in his chair, deep in thought. That girl was in a bad way; the thought someone would have deliberately caused her suffering annoyed the hell outta him. If this was the case then Conrad would be in serious trouble, just the same as if he'd thrown her to a mountain lion. This put a whole different slant to the picture, yet they still had to bring him back. It would be best if they kept this to themselves a while, at least until they'd more evidence. He looked over at Benteen and gave a friendly nod.

"So, do you really think we got us a maniac up there?"

"Could be, but I thought that folks would take to the maniac notion rather than the zombies. Where the hell are these things coming from anyways?"

"Don't know buddy, but I captured two up at Ben's farm. We gotta bring them back..."

"Hold up there, what you done Brad, arrested them?"

"Anne thinks there's a possibility of a cure. So we need them alive."

"What about you? You think she can set things right?"

"Don't know, but the thing is, she thinks so. If she's right, then every one of them we kill is murder. There's gotta be a better way. I want you to get a team together and fetch those two back here. But be careful."

Benteen sucked in deep and shook his head.

"How in hell you suppose I'm gonna do that? These damn things are killers!"

"We can use that gear we catch dogs with; you know the poles with the hoops on. Twist it around the neck and use the pole to control them. You gonna need to cover up and use heavy duty gloves. It's not gonna be easy but it's not impossible. One other thing, don't take chances; if you gotta kill them, aim for the head."

"There've been reports of a helicopter thereabouts."

"Yeah, we saw it up at the farm. It looked like one of them search types, you know, like the ones we use."

"Reckon it saw you?"

"It was a way from us but yeah, it couldn't have missed. Listen I'm gonna get ready for the meeting. Anne's agreed to cover the medical stuff; I'll go fetch her in a bit."

"You want me to tag along Boss?"

"Nope. You watch the store and organise some guys to round those things up."

Benteen nodded his head and watched Eastman leave the office. The thought of trying to round up two of those things worried him. He had no issues with doing it himself; he'd just grab the dumb freaks and throw them in a horsebox. What worried him was that he'd need to get others to do the job while he sat on his butt. Kicking his boots off, he shut his eyes and sighed deeply. Man, he could do with a beer right now.

****

Ethan Mason had the misfortune of bumping into Will Yardman on the way to the town meeting. Will Yardman was a redneck troublemaker. He never had a good word to say about anyone. Ethan knew Yardman from school and never liked him. For the past ten minutes or so, Yardman had talked at him about his restricted views of the day's search. Mason had lost count of the times Yardman had said 'I would have done it this way or that way.'

In reality the man did nothing; he was on welfare and lived in the house his parents had left him. Periodically, Mason nodded his head or shrugged his shoulders, feigning interest; it was best not to aggravate the guy. Ray Johnson had also been drawn into the one-sided conversation but he stood to one side. Every so often, Mason looked at him and raised an eyebrow or rolled his eyes.

"And look at that Sarge, now everyone thinks he's a freaking hero. What the hell for I gotta ask you?"

"Well Will, he did bring that boy home and..."

"Ray, you dumb blob. That kid was only up the damn road, he'd have soon come back without that ape. Hey no offence there, Mason. He sure ain't no hero."

"Well, they gave him the Silver Star."

90

Mason looked at Yardman. "That gotta count for something."

"You boys forget he let four of his guys burn to death in that bushwhack?"

"Hold up, Sarge was exonerated of all charges."

"I don't know what zonorated means. But I know a no good coward when I see one, sure enough."

"That's not what I read," Mason countered heatedly. "Sarge rescued his team despite being shot up and he couldn't get at the others because of the crossfire. Now that's a fact."

"Says who, boy?"

"*Says me!*"

Sarge grabbed Yardman around the throat in a vice like grip.

"For the record, Willy boy, I lost two of my team trying to get them guys' outta that wreck. I wasn't about to lose any more. I knew they was still alive 'cause I heard them screaming; I still can. I'm gonna take that to the grave. That's my punishment. You ever bad mouth me again; I'll tear your rotten heart out!"

Sarge released him, gave him a cold stare then calmly walked away. Yardman fell back against the wall, gasping for air. Mason looked at Yardman's ashen face then noticed a damp patch spreading from his crotch. You didn't mess with people like Sarge. Both Mason and Johnson walked away and headed for the Town Hall.

****

"So, you're telling us that there are more of them things running about," Tom Price called out from his seat. "Well just how many?"

Eastman and Anne Lenski were sitting on the stage. Eastman looked out at the densely packed hall. He was feeling the heat, but it must have been near unbearable amongst the throng of people.

"Tom, like I already said, the attacks support there being a number of these people out there. But if you're looking for a number… I can't tell. We gotta have more evidence."

Bob Galway stood up. "How many more people must die before you get that evidence? My child is in the hospital. How many more are gonna end up there? What are you doing to sort this out?"

"Bob, I know you're upset, but I'm doing the best I can with the resources I have. I'm gonna need to bring in some extra measures. From today onwards, I'm introducing a dusk to dawn curfew. The only people on the street will be those with legitimate business. And the patrols will now be armed."

"Sheriff Eastman, since Mayor Firth is not here, I have to ask you as a town councillor, have you discussed these 'extra measures' with him?"

"Miss Redman, I know this sounds kinda heavy but we need to be ready for anything. At the moment we've been lucky, these people – or creatures – have only attacked outside the city limits. Now I want us ready if that changes. But no, I haven't asked Tony as yet."

"Well my farms outside the city limits Brad, and Alice and the kids are a mite worried about all this," shouted Buck Willis.

Eastman looked over at Buck and Alice sitting with the two kids, Julie and Ron. There could be a problem with the outlaying homesteads. In fact, it'd been some time since he'd seen Mike and Susan Goodman. He shot a quick glance at Anne, this was more difficult than he'd imagined. He could've done with Firth or even Benteen. The buzz of the gathering had risen in the last few minutes, sounding more and more like a swarm of angry hornets. He watched as Lenny Kovak pushed his glasses on his head and rose from his front row seat. Now here was trouble.

"Sheriff, for the last ten minutes or so, we've sat here and listened to you, but there's a lot you're not saying. Benteen told us he thought there was a maniac on the loose. So is there some nut as well as these things to contend with? And have you established a connection with the blackout yet?"

"I can't comment on that first question and as for the second part, we have no direct evidence to support that notion."

"What about the helicopter and drones that've been reported, any comments there?"

"Dr Lenski and I both saw a helicopter up at Ben's farm, but as yet we've had no contact from the outside."

"Where are these things coming from? What are they?"

Eastman looked over at Rudy Goldsmith.

"All the bodies we've recovered are people from outside of town. So whoever they are they're from away. Why the hell they've pitched up here I don't know. As for what they are, I'm gonna hand you over to Dr Lenski."

"Hello. Now I've heard a lot about Ebola and even rabies over the last few days. Since the Ebola catastrophe some years back, strict medical checks are in place that identify all traces of Ebola. No one wants a repeat performance of all that. So I'm happy to tell you, it's neither. Nor is it airborne like the common cold. All my evidence so far tells me this virus has to be ingested into the bloodstream from direct contact with body fluids and blood. But other than that, this is a completely unknown class of disease. It is however, highly contagious and deadly."

"So how's it work?"

Kovak patted his notebook with his pen. "I mean what exactly happens?"

"You have to understand that to date I've only had dead people to examine, so I don't know the full course of the disease. However, once infected, the virus starts to mutate the victim's cells and causes the internal organs to break down. The whole body starts to rapidly decompose and..."

Rudy Goldsmith stood up.

"Sorry Bob, I know your kid's...well, bitten, but doctor, is there a cure for this thing?"

"There may be a cure for this thing, I just don't know yet. The people who are infected are still *people* until I find otherwise. I would point out that all those in the later stages of this infection have been violent and dangerous. They should not be approached at any time."

"Yeah, I'd just like to add something to that Anne," interrupted Eastman, getting to his feet. "Now as Dr Lenski said, at the moment we need to treat these people as sick. But they will do their best to tear a chunk outta you."

The burly figure of fire Chief Ron Virdon called out from his seat.

"What's the best way to handle them Brad?"

"They don't listen to any kind of reason; if you get yourself into a situation with one of them, high tail it. If you have to defend yourself, strike at the head."

Veronica Redman waved her arm in the air for attention.

"Dr Lenski, how can we tell if someone's infected, I mean what should we be looking for? Are there symptoms?"

"Bear in mind, the only cases I've come across so far, have what I'm calling, *Stage Two* or deceased. So I can't comment on Stage One, or newly infected. Stage Two are very easy to spot; they show signs of advanced decomposition. They seem unable to communicate but fortunately have greatly reduced mobility. I also think there's some degree of brain damage."

"Sarge said they got dead man's eyes," said Kovak, with a nervous laugh. "So doctor are these dead people?"

A hushed silence fell over the room. Sitting next to Ethan Mason, Ray Johnson clearly heard him utter the word *Jumbie* under his breath. Then as Eastman concluded the meeting, Johnson lent over to Mason.

"What you say?"

"My family was brought here from the Caribbean. My Gran used to scare us with stories from the old land, about the Jumbies."

"What the hell's a Jumbie?"

Mason looked at Johnson and spoke in a low voice, "The spirit of the dead."

****

Tony Firth poured himself a generous Brandy and fell back into his favourite brown leather armchair. He swished the dark liquid around in the large glass then swallowed, savouring the moment. He let the effects of the drink wash over him as he tried to make sense of the day's events.

He'd imagined Bridget ranting at him for being unable to find the boy, but she was nowhere to be seen, which was just as well because he wasn't in the mood to deal with her yacking. Even now, he just could not get the image of that little pink bag from his mind. The thought of what had happened to the poor girl and how she must have felt, made him shut his eyes tightly. No family should have to go through that.

Then there'd been the RV. He'd never experienced that kind of fear before; his heart began to race at the memory. He knew he needed to get a grip. Then of course there was Conrad. The boy was still missing and despite his best efforts, Firth couldn't get rid of the feeling of guilt at letting the boy down. He'd always set his political ambitions before the boy and he'd lost count of the birthdays and other times he'd missed because of business matters.

Firth took another gulp of his drink; the notion of electioneering was a million miles away. Was it the effects of the brandy, he wondered, or was it something else? If this was some sort of wake up call, he hoped it hadn't come too late.

He moved over to pour another glass and thought about Eastman's meeting. He was in no shape to attend and he wasn't even sure he wanted to. Eastman and

Lenski would have to manage without him. That Redman woman would be there too, no doubt milking his absence for all it was worth. But who the hell cared?

His thoughts were broken by a sudden crash from upstairs. He called out but there was no answer. He eased himself off the chair and headed for the staircase and called out again. And still the stony sound of silence. Firth started to climb the elegant wooden stairs, his mind reeling.

If Bridget had fallen asleep then she'd surely have heard him and answered by now. Then he spotted a set of muddy footprints heading to Conrad's room. Bare feet! His heart began to pound and he felt sweat run down his face as he turned the doorknob to the bedroom. Firth flung the door open and saw his son standing in front of him, bloodstained and covered in muck, holding his arms out to his father.

"Conrad!"

CHAPTER – THIRTEEN

Frank Jorgan put the letter in his pocket; no matter how many times he'd read it, it still wasn't going to change a thing. In fourteen days time Mr Bishop would foreclose the mortgage. The farm, the home where they'd lived for the past forty years, would be taken off them. He looked around the small kitchen, watching as Larry put away the last of the crockery. That was Nancy's chore but she'd taken to bed, sick. He'd kept the letter from her. In fairness to Bishop, he'd done his best to slow things down, but with no more money he'd no other option than to take their home. Jorgan turned to see Kurt bring the untouched supper tray back into the kitchen.

"She left it then son?"

"Yep Pa, said she'd try some time later."

He placed the tray back on the kitchen table and went to help his brother. It worried Jorgan that his wife had taken sick. It wasn't her way, but the worry from the farm and that crazy man had taken its toll on her. He looked at the boys and it saddened him to think that in a few days' time they could all be homeless. If only that darn idiot Seavers hadn't cancelled his order with them, they'd have enough to get by.

"I'm gonna see Ma for a while, get your work clothes on before I come out. We got us plenty of work to do before dark."

He left the room and walked the short distance to the master bedroom, then gently pushed the door open. The small room was just light enough to make out Nancy, even with the top window ajar he could still detect that odour. He called out softly to her and moved to the bed. She sat up and raised her hand to him. She looked dreadful; her matted hair had stuck to her head and she was running a high temperature. He sat beside her and took her hand. The faint scratches of a few days ago had now become three ugly brown furrows, oozing pus.

"You don't look none too good Nancy, how's that hand?"

"True to say I've been better, but don't fret on. I just wish that boy had clipped his nails some. I hope you ain't wrecked my kitchen between you all?"

"Nope, but I..."

"I can always tell when you're worried. It's the bank, what they say?"

What was it with women; did they all have second sight?

"I had a letter off Bishop; he's trying to stall for more time, no need for you to worry. I got me a few irons in the fire yet."

Lying didn't come easy to a man like Frank Jorgan, but he saw no sense in adding to her woe. They'd lost near a whole day's work with the search, but it had been the right thing to do. The Lord had said 'love thy neighbour.' Folks was in trouble, folks needed help. They still had a few hours' light to load the trailer and get the produce over to David and Betty Lloyd's farm. Then of course there was Tony Firth's offer but that was a last resort. It had to be, with a man like him.

"What you got planned then Mr Jorgan?"

"The Lloyds have given a fair deal for some of our stock, if I can get it to them by tonight, they'll pay out right away. Now we got us some daylight hours left and if we work through the night..."

"Just hang on there, you been out with them boys all day and in case you forgot, you gonna help search tomorrow as well. Now how you gonna manage that, Superman?"

"All we gotta do is load up. We can be at the Lloyds' and back here afore daybreak. I'm telling Brad Eastman I got too much on. Anyways, who gonna look after you?"

"Now wait just one minute there, you given your word to help out and..."

"Be sensible woman, you're not well. They gonna have to manage without us. We got work to be done."

"No husband of mine is gonna break his word on account of me. You can fetch my sister up here and she can look after me. But you're going on that search."

Why in tarnation was the confounded woman so obstinate? It wasn't that he didn't want to help, but he had responsibilities to his family. If they got back in time they could grab a few hours before they had to meet. He could drop the boys in town and go fetch Iris and then meet up with the search teams later. It would be tight, but it was the only way.

"Nancy Jorgan, you're a hard woman to please. I guess you've gone and won again."

"Well ain't that what you married me for, to get my own way? How the boys? How they holding out?"

"They done real good out there today, outpaced anybody else. They done us proud, I let Kurt say Grace this supper."

"What about those jobs, did you have a word, like you said?"

"I spoke to Benny Arnold; he said there'd be work for them by the end of the week. I mean they still gotta go through the interviews and such, they never gonna work the tills, but they're good workers."

"That's good news. Now, I'm gonna rest a while then I'll set that kitchen to rights."

"No need you obstinate critter, we done it all. You ain't gonna like it, but I'm looking to get Doc Lenski up here first thing."

"I don't have time for no medical people poking about with me. Those two bears in there," – she jabbed a finger towards the kitchen – "I birthed right here in this house, in this bed, just you and me. No need of medical people in this house. You hear?"

"I ain't listening to you. For once you'll do as I say. Now I got some work to get on with."

He leant forward and tenderly kissed her forehead. He was bringing that woman back here no matter what Nancy said. He closed the door and wiped the back of his hand across his mouth. The next two weeks were going to be hard but with a woman like that behind him, he could just about do anything.

****

"I tell you, it's just cuts and bruises, the boy's fine and he point blank refuses to go to hospital."

Tony Firth was in the sitting room explaining to Bridget what had happened.

"He didn't say a word up there."

Bridget blew on her rose red nails. "Well, where the hell's he been till now?"

"After those things killed Ruby they all got separated, I guess he wandered about all that time and then made his way back home?"

The real reason of course, was that those kids had run scared and left Conrad to it, all alone. That Glitzman fink taking all the credit: 'hero,' what a crock! The time wasn't right for that now, but he'd get it all sorted later, show them his boy was the real deal.

"Whatever, but Tony, you gotta take him for a check up, he looks awful."

"He's just whacked. It's gonna stress him even more if they start prodding him about. Don't forget, Eastman's gonna want to know all sorts. Let him chill, play on the computer a while, we'll take him in the morning."

"Okay, but I ain't happy. You'd better tell Eastman he's home safe though. He can call off the search in time."

Eastman was about the last one he wanted to tell; he'd be over in no time with his little notebook for a statement. Firth wanted the time to get the boy's story right before it went official. He wanted to know everything that had gone on up there. Once things had been said, it'd be too late to get a retraction. Conrad looked rough; he'd been through a lot.

"Look Bridget, I don't want Eastman over here snooping and asking darn fool questions, until we talk to Conrad ourselves."

"Don't be so damn stupid! You gotta tell him Conrad's back. Half the town's gonna be looking for him tomorrow."

"All I'm saying is that we should wait, that's all."

"And all I'm saying is, you get your ass over to the station house right now! I'm gonna fix him something to eat. What you still doing here?"

Firth marched towards the front door, picking up his car keys from the brass door hook as he went. Dumb woman! She had no idea how something like this could go wrong. It would be he and Conrad who'd carry the can, not her. Of course, he believed the boy's story, what he didn't want was for that tin star to get it all wrong and start taking things outta context. But damn it, she did have a point; he didn't want a mess of egg on his face when the search teams turned up. He pushed the front door open and walked out to his car. Dumb woman!

****

Benteen was dead on his feet; they'd been at these maps for hours. He looked over at Brad rubbing his eyes; if Brad had to keep going then so did he. It reminded him of High School, just like the times he and Eastman had stayed up cramming the night before a test. Well, more like Eastman doing Benteen's work, with him looking on.

"Gerard, I think we've about covered the search grids. If we keep a narrow pattern and then widen as we go, I reckon by the time we reach the top we'd have about covered the whole damn range."

Brad had drawn up a much tighter grid and the checkpoints weren't as far apart, giving the teams more time to report. It'd been good to run the store for a while, but it was good to have Brad behind the 'big' desk.

"Sure thing boss. I've got a list of all the guys best suited for tomorrow; only thing is we still don't have enough with experience and good gun sense. I don't like the idea of some Sunday shooter popping rounds off up there. Maybe we can mix some of them guys in with the four-by-four boys?"

"Yeah, that works for me; it'll restrict their use of the guns if they're in vehicles. Is Sarge still up for his one man mission?"

"It would be one hell of a job to stop him. Yep."

"It's just before ten now, we'll send the night patrols out and then bring down the curfew."

"Brad, I just got to thinking about the homesteads, are we going to bring them in at some time?"

"I don't think it's time to circle the wagons just yet, but those folks are on a branch out there. We can start sending the patrols out there tomorrow."

Benteen nodded in agreement and both men turned towards the door at the unexpected knocking. Eastman walked to the door and was surprised to see Anne Lenski with an armful of fast food. He smiled at her as he called her into the office.

"Well, I never realised you'd taken to delivering this stuff," joked Eastman as he took the food from her.

"Careful or you'll have to tip me. I just thought you two wouldn't have had anything to eat and being 'men' you'd both think you could manage without."

Benteen reached over and took a food bag and a plastic coffee cup.

"Even if *he* forgot his manners, I sure appreciate it Doc."

"It's a pleasure Gerard, at least there's one gentleman in the room," she said with a touch of devilment in her voice.

"Oh, don't you go siding with him; he's only just worked out how to use the hand driers."

Eastman made space on his desk and the three sat down and began to tuck in to their overdue supper. Eastman gave his seat to Anne and he sat on the edge of the desk. It had been a long and tiresome day and a little downtime went a long way. Anne sipped at her drink as she glanced at the diagrams on Eastman's whiteboard.

"It all looks very impressive. Have you about finished with the grand plan for tomorrow?"

"All done, Captain Lenski."

"I was a Doctor, Brad, not a strategist. Did you bring back the two in the barn yet?"

Eastman nervously looked at Benteen, then looked at Anne.

"They weren't there when he went back for them."

"What? There must have been another exit. Damn!"

"No, not exactly. Gerard, you got the ball."

"Someone let them out. The bar was off the door and there were heavy truck prints there abouts. The kind the military use."

"The military? How'd you know that?"

"Some time back I used to drive for the Guard up at Burnsville. The military use a special tyre. I'd know them treads anyplace."

"Brad, what's going on here? I mean first that helicopter and now an army truck?"

"It looks as though someone didn't want us to get our hands on those two."

Suddenly, Eastman's radio set burst into life, it was Clara's voice.

"Brad you got yourself a visitor. It's the Mayor, shall I send him through?"

"Yeah, send him right up."

Benteen moved to hide the treasure. "He ain't getting his paws on the fries."

Eastman didn't really want to see Firth right now; however, the guy did have a vested interest in the following day's proceedings. And now they had a working plan to show him. It would also be difficult not to involve him in the search. There was a light tapping on the door and Eastman called Firth in.

"How you feeling Tony?" Eastman got up to greet Firth as he entered the office.

"Sorry about the meeting but I was done in." He nodded to Anne and Benteen before his eyes settled on the fast food feast.

"Hey, this all looks nice and tasty, guys."

Benteen scowled as he leaned forward to grab the bag of extra fries, clutching them to his chest as he sat back down. In his view, the bum had no right to get involved with police business. He hadn't been there to support Eastman and Lenski with the meeting, and it seemed typical of him to turn up when something was going on. God damn slob!

"I reckon I owe you an apology for this afternoon Gerard. I was tired and upset. I'm real sorry."

Eastman shot his deputy a sideways glance, rolling his eyes as he did so, and Benteen reached forward and shook Firth's hand.

"Yeah well, that's big of you Tony."

With the pleasantries over, Eastman decided to take the opportunity to grasp the bull by the horns.

"There's a couple of things I need to run by you, admittedly a bit late but still. I've imposed a night time curfew, starting at ten tonight."

"A curfew? Brad, that kinda thing gotta be discussed and approved before a ruling like that gets passed. The police can't just go introducing a curfew."

"I know, but since neither you, nor Judge Carmille was present at the meeting, I did what was needed."

"Yeah, but Brad..."

"Tony, we've been lucky so far, these creatures have only attacked outside the town. Imagine what could happen if they got into the town? There are a lot of scared people out there; it wouldn't take long for an accident to happen."

"Sheriff's right there Tony," Benteen pitched in. "We got a lot of nervous guns out there just itching to shoot something. Curfew's about the best thing."

"I...well, in that case...yeah, you did the right thing. It's a good positive action and it's covered by the constitutional right to bear arms under times of threat. You get any objections to it, Brad?"

"Veronica Redman said it was a 'gross infringement of civil rights' and un-American. Some people agreed."

"I might have known. Well, it's not. Best take no heed of her; just slip her a copy of

'Swimsuit weekly' or whatever the hell her kind reads and let me sort it out."

"So I've got your backing on that?"

"Darn right. Brad, what this town needs is a strong lead and that's what I'm...we gonna give them."

"That's a weight off my shoulders, thank you. I'd like to show you the search plans for tomorrow." Eastman started to gather the maps and paperwork.

"Um... I'd like to say something about..."

Just then Clara's voice cut through the room like a razor.

"Brad, they got themselves an emergency at the hospital. It's one of those things!"

Eastman flicked over the talk button and called into the machine,

"Call in all available units. I'm on my way. Anne I reckon you should stay..."

"Forget it! That's *my staff and my health center.*"

Eastman knew there was no point arguing and he didn't have the time. He led the others from the office, heading for the health center.

****

As Eastman ran the short distance from the deserted reception area to the treatment section of the health center, he met up with Joe Lester. He was standing in his dressing gown, still attached to his IV drip.

"In there, in there I tell you..."

Joe pointed to the next bend in the corridor and Eastman and Benteen, guns drawn, sped around the corner. The treatment section was a series of individual rooms. Directly in front of Eastman was Norris Zillman, eyes wide with terror, his uniform dotted with bloody hand-prints as he held the door to the treatment room shut.

"I got it trapped in here."

His voice had a manic tone as he vigorously gestured with his head towards Treatment Room 1.

Eastman noted the blood trail leading to the body of Nurse Zoë Watson, slumped against the wall to his right. Her throat had been ripped open like a wet grocery bag, exposing the inside of her neck. Anne Lenski rushed to tend the woman but sadly shook her head. Eastman moved to the treatment room and gently prised Zillman's hand from the door, motioning him towards Lenski. Eastman placed the left side of his body against the door and held it shut. Then, holding his revolver in his right hand, he beckoned to Benteen.

"We go on three. One. Two. THREE!"

Eastman shouldered the door as Benteen forced it from its frame. The small room was covered in blood. On the blood-drenched bed he could see Ben Burke lying with a creature feeding noisily from his near decapitated body. With a sudden rush of horror, Eastman realised who it was.

"Erin!"

The thing stopped and, still crouched over its feed, turned slowly to look at the two standing in the room, throwing back its head and letting out a hideous wail. Then it started a sluggish but deliberate walk in their direction. All vestiges of Erin Burke gone, Eastman drew back the hammer on his pistol and sent a heavy grain 357 Magnum bullet smashing through her brain. His gun arm fell like a lead weight; he shut his eyes and muttered a faint prayer. Mitch Chattman's voice erupted from the corridor.

Firth was backed up against the drinks machine with a snarling Zoë Watson, less than two feet away from him. Mitch Chattman and Eddy Joe were standing some feet away, weapons aimed. Chattman called out another warning, then with no option left, fired three 9mm shots into her upper body.

The impact from the rounds knocked her sideways but she continued her advance. Firth tried in vain to fend her off, but her grasping hands caught his sleeve and she dragged his hand towards her gnashing mouth.

For the second time that day Eastman had no choice but to fire. The single round ploughed through Zoë Watson's head and thudded into the concrete pillar just behind her. Benteen looked back at Eastman, gently nodding his support.

"The head, you gotta get the head."

Coming towards the group was Sam Cortez, holing a fire axe in his hands.

"Jeez, you took your time."

"Sam, where is everybody?"

Anne Lenski was concerned. "After Erin killed Zoë, Elle-May barricaded everyone in the day room. We figured with the shots, you guys must have turned up."

Eastman walked over to Anne and took her arm. "You alright Anne?"

She tugged away and gave him a venomous stare. "You killed Zoë Watson right in front of me. What the hell happened to taking them alive?"

"Another few inches and you'd have your stage zero patient, starting with Firth."

Lenski wrapped her arms around her body and stared at the bloody handprints on the wall.

"This whole damn place is contaminated! We've got to keep people away until it's cleaned and..."

"How'd Zoë do that? How'd she get up like that? She was dead. *I seen her dead.*"

Anne Lenski looked over at Norris; he was sitting on the floor and shaking like a leaf. He was perfectly right but she had no idea how to answer him.

Eastman called his officers to him. "Okay fellas, I know it's a mess here, but we gotta keep people away from the bodies and blood. Get your latex on and don't touch anything."

Firth caught hold of Eastman and warmly shook his hand. "I owe you big time buddy. She almost got me back there."

"That's why we need a curfew and armed patrols."

"You're damn right. No problem there."

"Tony, we gonna need a statement on all this come tomorrow morning. Can you make a start on it for me?"

Firth nodded in agreement and walked off towards Anne Lenski. Benteen had organised a containment area around the contaminated sections. The last thing they wanted was further infections. Joe Lester was sitting, watching all the bustle with a casual air, tutting away to himself every now and then, as if to some hidden agenda. Eastman called Benteen over to his side. There was a lot to get on with.

"Gerard, pretty soon we gonna have half the town at those doors, curfew or no curfew. But nobody's getting in here until its safe. Now you're in charge. I got something to do."

"I'll call in some of the guys. Where you going, Brad?"

"To do something I should have done a long way back."

Firth watched as Eastman left the corridor. Where'd he think he was going at a time like this? No matter, it suited Firth to have him out of the picture awhile; he had questions for Lenski. He moved alongside her and took his chance.

"Anne, I'm so sorry about Zoë, she was a wonderful person. I feel kinda responsible for what happened."

"Tony, that wasn't Zoë anymore. You can't blame yourself for that."

"Snapping at me like that, I thought I'd had it. Is that what happens when you get bitten?"

"No, not if I can find a way to stop it."

"But it's gotta be a bite right, I mean that's how it starts?"

"It can come from the smallest scratch. Anything that causes contaminated fluid or blood to get into your bloodstream can cause infection. What I really need is someone in the early stages. If you're worried I can test you right now?"

"No! No, no need she never got that close."

He withdrew, putting his hands up. "It's been a long day Anne. I'm headed for home. Guess I'll see you in the morning?"

Firth waved his farewell and started for the exit. No one noticed him leave. There was no way he was handing Conrad over for tests for her to experiment on. He was safer at home.

****

Taylor's eyes were adjusting to the dark, he'd worked out that lights out was anywhere between 21:30 to 22:00. The hillbilly pie he'd eaten sat like a rock in his gut. They'd had a busy day judging by what he'd gathered. It was surprising what Intel could be obtained by just pretending to be asleep. At least one of the missing kids had been killed while another was still lost. But as far as he could tell the other kids had been brought back. Some guy called 'Sarge' had brought one kid back on his own but there was something about a run in with two, possibly three of the creatures. This was bad news; it showed an increase in the threat level. This could lead to some type of intervention force being involved; if it wasn't already there.

The most interesting part of info however, had come about half an hour ago. One of the redneck's radios had blurted out there'd been some kind of incident at the hospital. The old guy, who'd been in jail for killing one of the things a day back, had mentioned his wife had been bitten and was in the hospital. There'd also been an infected kid there too. Now if these bozos hadn't been careful then either of these two could have attacked someone.

Suddenly, brightness from the strip lights flooded through his eyelids. Eastman was striding into the room towards his cell, but this was a different looking Eastman than he'd seen previously. He unholstered his revolver and pointed it directly at Taylor, drawing the hammer back, with a loud metallic click.

"There are people dying in my town, good people and I've just had to kill two of them myself. Now, tell me what I want to know, you lousy son of a bitch! *Or I'll blow your God damn head off!"*

Yeah, Eastman had a very different look and Taylor had seen it on so many guys in combat. It was that look that meant someone was going to die. He knew this was a turning point, something had happened to tip this guy over the edge. Taylor would need to be very careful if he wanted to come out of this in one piece.

"You need to think very carefully about what you say in the next few minutes." Eastman eased the safety catch off the weapon, "I want to know what these things are, what you got to do with them and who the hell are you anyway?"

"They're the result of a failed medical test."

He stopped to gauge the other man's response. He was still alive, that was always a good result.

"Keep talking."

"ZerTon was a pharmaceutical research company conducting tests, experiments into cures for this and that. This one went wrong, creating the things you've seen."

Taylor had developed a heightened sense in reading people. Facial expressions, body language, even a shift in stance. The blood had returned to Eastman's whitened fingers, as he relaxed his grip. However, the pistol still remained trained on Taylor.

"And you, what's your connection with all this?"

"Mind telling me what you're doing there, Boss?"

To his surprise, Taylor had failed to notice the arrival of Benteen in the cell-block. Benteen slowly walked into the room and stood at an angle to Eastman. Worryingly, Taylor noticed Eastman gave a flash of anger, once again tightening his grip on the pistol butt.

"I gave you instructions, now leave me the hell alone and get them done!"

"No can do Brad. What you doing, target practice? You know the rules about weapons in the detention area."

"Gerard, will you just get the hell outta here!"

"You running a private neck tie party here boss? 'Cause it sure looks that way."

Was this some kind of 'good cop bad cop' routine? Taylor doubted Benteen's ability or indeed, intelligence, to carry out such a ruse.

Eastman shot Benteen a sideways glance. "Gerard, you stay outta this, you hear me?"

Taylor watched as the big man lowered his eyes and moved back from Eastman. Just how far was this cop going to take this?

"I was a PI."

Taylor focused on Eastman and continued.

"The people I worked for were hired by a rival Pharmaceutical outfit to spy on ZerTon. I discovered their secret and then they discovered me."

"Now, don't tell me... and then you escaped?"

Eastman narrowed his eyes and glared at Taylor. "You gonna have to do better than that."

"Somebody shut them down but not before they shut us down, permanently. They took our office out and murdered my boss, fitted me up and I went on the run."

"The thing is you see, you and those things pitched up here at exactly the same time. Now it seems to me, if you're trying to get away from them, wouldn't you be running the other way? That kinda rains on your parade."

"I got a death bed confession off a guy who said that ZerTon had transferred operations to this area. I wanted to shut them down."

"Aw, Brad. How much of this horse crap you gonna fall for? This guy's full of it!"

"Listen Eastman, that baboon over there is too dumb to even understand what I'm saying here. But you, you've seen things these last few days that have taken you to the *Twilight Zone*. You gotta wake up and smell the coffee, before it's too late."

Slowly Eastman lowered his pistol, clicked the safety catch on, and eased the hammer forward, holstering the weapon.

"Okay, you made a good case, but I'm sure as hell you've got a lot more in that head of yours. For now at least we've made a start. Now, how about a name for you, Mr...?"

"Taylor. My name's Brent Taylor."

CHAPTER -FOURTEEN

Bridget Firth sat in her most comfortable chair picking the remnants of roast chicken from her flawless teeth; implants, the result of too much candy as a child. She kicked her pink fluffy slippers off her feet and drew her tanned legs up under her. The Roman numerals on the wall clock confused her but Tony said it showed class. She checked the time on the TV remote, it was almost midnight. If he wasn't back soon, she was going to bed. He'd probably stopped off to see that no-good brother of his.

There was something going on with them. She'd never liked Peter and it wasn't all to do with him beating Mary – she didn't like her either – the guy was just a creep. Even after all this time, it still infuriated her when she thought about her wedding reception. She put up with him for Tony's sake, but she hated him anywhere near Conrad.

At least Conrad was looking better after his bath; she'd dressed his wounds and made him freshen up. Although he'd refused anything to eat, he'd told her about his ordeal. It annoyed her to think of the way the other kids had left him to save their hides. He'd desperately tried to save that poor girl and the others had used it as an opportunity to run away. But at least he was safe now.

She'd even given Conrad the candy bar that she'd been hiding from Tony. He was always going on at her about that lousy diet; she'd had more than enough of it. He wasn't exactly an oil painting himself. It always made her laugh when he put sun-screen on his bald head. She looked up at the clock; just after midnight. Then she heard the key turn in the front door.

She switched on the ornate glass chandelier, fully illuminating the room and watched as Tony trudged toward her. He looked terrible. His face was pale and drawn and his eyes were red and puffy. If she didn't know better, she'd have sworn he'd been crying.

"Jeez, Tony you alright?"

"I watched people die tonight."

She listened in stunned silence as her husband related the events at the health center, barely able to grasp that Erin, Ben and Zoë had all died. Zoë was in her keep-fit class for God's sake.

"That's why we gotta keep him here...Bridget. Bridget! Are you even listening?"

"Yeah, yeah. But if he's sick we gotta take that boy to the doctor."

Firth brought his clenched fists to his face and roared loudly, "Damn it woman! That's the last place we want to take him!"

"And what you got figured, Mr Mayor?"

"What if they already knew about this thing? I mean, what if that's why we're cut off up here?"

Bridget didn't like where this was going. She remembered the stories about Ebola; the authorities had done some pretty scary things and it wasn't that long ago.

"So what you getting at?"

"They'd have to stop it from spreading, right? Even if that meant killing people?"

"Who the hell is 'they'?"

"A few days back, Robert Pool came to me half outta his skull..."

"That ain't nothing new."

"He told me about how he'd been walking home one night, then he'd seen a bunch of guys in yellow suits herd some people into a gully and shot them dead."

That really was the limit. Pool was an idiot; he'd tell you he'd been playing cards with the Easter Bunny if you'd listen. She knew that Tony and he were old high school pals but this was just plain dumb. Tony looked as if he'd been through the mill, but he was just talking crap now. She got up from her seat and marched over to him and stared right into his face.

"Tony, you expect me to trust anything that guy spouts?"

"He picked up a couple of M16 shell cases and gave them to me. I didn't believe him either, until he took me to the spot. The area had been cleared and a bunch of trees were cut down in a semi circle. But just outta the area, I found a tree with some M16 bullets in it."

She pressed her fingers to her temples and shut her eyes.

"What you trying to say? I don't get it!"

"That amount of firepower, you gonna get bullets all over the place. They cut the trees down and cleared the ground to hide the evidence."

"Tony, will you listen to yourself?"

He continued, "But they missed one tree."

"And that proves what?"

"That there were people up there shooting, which means there's at least some truth in what Rob said."

"Then why didn't he go to the law?"

"He was too scared."

"In fact why don't *you* tell Eastman?"

"Eastman! Eastman gunned down Zoë in front of me right after he killed Erin Burke."

"Not more than ten minutes ago, you said Eastman saved your life."

"He and the others could have captured those people but they just killed them. What if Eastman and the others hand the infected people over to the guys in the woods? They're in on this. Don't you see?"

Now he sounded like that fool Jimmy Emmett. Then Bridget began to think about the danger to Conrad. Tony had said you only needed a scratch to become infected. Conrad had lots of bruises and he also had cuts and scratches. She couldn't be sure if her husband thought Conrad was infected or not? If he was ill then the hospital had to be the best place for him. What if Tony was right?

"If you're one hundred percent, and I mean one hundred percent sure that I'm talking bull, take these and you drive him to the health center, right now."

Firth took his keys and tossed them at her.

She caught the keys then turned them over in her hand, then she looked at Firth. "Okay, what are we gonna do Tony?"

****

Eastman surveyed the search teams on the sidewalk in front of him and the people who'd come to see them off. He'd spent the last half hour or so going over the routes and checkpoints and what was needed of them. The search teams were divided into three mobile patrols of three four-by-fours, and three five-man foot patrols, with a rapid action Jeep to act as a run about.

The thing that troubled Eastman the most was the level of weapons. They were armed with everything from handguns to military assault rifles and even a few crossbows were being toted. This was a rescue mission, not an invasion. He looked over at Benteen and the Judge: there was still no sign of Firth. With or without him they'd need to make a start soon.

"Judge, I think we're going to have to get underway," cautioned Eastman, looking at his watch.

"I agree Brad. We can't wait all day for him. I'll leave the taking to you."

Carmille turned to face the crowd. "I'd just like your attention for a few seconds."

He clapped his hands above his head.

"Before we get on with the search, Sheriff Eastman has a brief statement about last night."

The crowd fell silent and all eyes fixed on Eastman as he took centre stage.

"At a quarter after ten last night, there was serious incident at the health center. This incident resulted in the death of Zoë Watson and both Ben and Erin Burke. The situation was brought under control by the Sheriff's Department and there is no danger to the public. The health center has been closed as a temporary measure and should re-open later today. I'll answer briefly any questions but remember this is an ongoing investigation."

The citizens exploded into a frenzied buzz of excited racket. Not surprisingly the first to fire questions was Lenny Kovak.

"Sherriff, have you got the person who did this?"

"There were no suspects involved."

"So who killed them?"

"No comment at this time."

"So does that mean they attacked themselves or...wait? *Did the police kill them?*"

"No comment at this time."

"Sherriff, did the police kill those people?"

"Lenny, that's enough for now," interrupted Carmille. "We're making another statement later today. Now we've got lots to do, so no more questions."

Eastman nodded and began his address. "First off, I want to thank you all for turning up here today and for showing your support."

He moved next to Benteen.

"Let's remember what we're doing here today. We got a child lost in the hills; he could be hurt or trapped, but we gotta fetch him back. Doctor Lenski and Fire Chief Virdon have put together emergency packs for all the teams."

He held up a backpack with a rolled silver blanket attached.

"A big thank you to them!"

"Now I can see a lot of shooting irons out there. This is a rescue mission. I don't plan on invading the next county. These guns are for protection only. I don't want anyone out there causing problems. One last point, Jimmy Red Cloud has been listed as missing, so be on the lookout for him too. You'll be working close to the tower and Bill Merka here,"– Merka raised his arm in acknowledgement – "is going to help coordinate. Now anyone got any questions?"

"Yeah, I got me a question."

Glyn McDowall stood dressed more for war than a rescue.

"What happens if we come up against this maniac?"

"Call in for help and keep an eye on him. No need for a gun battle. Is that clear to everyone?"

The last thing Eastman wanted was someone like McDowall taking the law into his own hands; that was a darn sure way for people to get hurt, or worse. He looked around for any other contributions and then caught sight of Ramon Tuco, hand raised. Eastman didn't know a lot about him, other than he'd moved to Armstrong recently with his wife and two kids. He was a small man, but with a frame that was suited to outside labour. He was dressed in rough old denim pants and jacket, with a pair of rugged boots on his feet. Tuco had a backpack but was unarmed. Eastman signalled to him to speak.

"What about these creatures Sheriff, what we do if we meet them?"

"Just observe and call in. Under no circumstances do you let them touch you. That's real important. Let's move on out."

"Well done there Brad."

The Judge looked at his golden wrist watch.

"Where in Tarnation is that Firth?"

"Yep, you'd have thought he'd been here, on account it's his kid we're looking for."

Eastman nodded to Benteen in agreement. They could wait no longer, the search teams had to make full use of the light. Frank Jorgan and his boys had also failed to show up which was odd. Frank was like a reliable watch, always on time. He turned to Benteen.

"Gerard, where's Frank Jorgan? I'd have bet my last dollar he'd have been here."

"Well Brad, it ain't exactly common knowledge," he continued in a low voice, "but Frank and his people have hit hard times."

"Hard times how, d'you reckon?"

"I was up at their place a day or so back and they had them a barn sale, I mean they was selling everything, pots and pans even that ancient *John Deere* tractor. I got to talking with Frank, he told me they'd run out of money."

"Jeez."

Carmille drew their attention to Tony Firth making his way towards them, the sun reflecting off his sunglasses. Eastman couldn't make his mind up whether he was late or just making a grand entrance.

"Sorry, guys I reckon yesterday all but done me in. Brad, I got the statement you wanted ..."

"Brad's already made a statement."

Carmille was in no mood for Firth. "As the Mayor you need to be setting an example here, not making excuses. Now maybe we can get this started?"

It was not wise to get on Judge Camille's wrong side and Firth let the remarks go. Carmille owned a lot of the town and had a great deal of influence. He'd also been responsible for cleaning up the town with Sheriff Buck Mitchell around the time the Firth clan had all but escaped being run out themselves.

When the teams were at last ready to depart, Eastman gave the signal to move out.

"Tony, I want you to take one of the mobile patrols. I got your instructions here." He handed over a plastic map case to Firth.

"Sweep up past Ben's farm, then branch out."

Eastman noted the odd look that Firth gave him and watched as he got into his vehicle and drove off. Eastman looked on as the last of the teams meandered out of town, then he headed back to his car.

****

Britney and Marv walked down the path from Tony Arcado's house and headed into town. They were both troubled by their friend. They'd all experienced bad dreams after their ordeal but Tony's were way out. He'd dreamt he was a butterfly that ate all the other butterflies. They'd told him that it meant nothing, but it had spooked them. People had been talking about the 'the great rescue operation' having left. But neither of them could find in themselves any interest in finding Conrad.

"Do you think they're gonna find him, I mean alive?"

"Don't be so lame," chided Britney. "I hope one of those things got him."

"How can you say that?"

"Marv, I don't know what I mean. These last few days have been the worst of my life!"

"Yeah, me too, but we're gonna hold it together, we owe it to the others."

When they'd heard about the dreadful events at the hospital, they'd both come to the conclusion it had been Jenha who'd killed the people. Try as they might, they were unable to convince each other differently; the memory of the events in the Paxmores' truck was impossible to forget.

They sat on the bench overlooking Abe McReedy's Gun shop; it seemed to have a constant stream of people. People were going into the shop empty handed but leaving with bags of stuff.

"Looks like everyone's getting ready for a war. I bet McReedy's shelves are bare."

"Is that what you think is going to happen Marv, a war?"

"That guy Sarge said if any of those things get into the town all kinds of stuff could go on. We gotta be ready, that's all."

"That's too freaky, it gives me the creeps."

What they needed was some fun. As if on cue, Britney punched his arm and gave an excited shout. "Come on, let's get some candy."

She sprang up and produced her purse. "I'll pay."

He scratched his head and got up. "Well in that case, lead on."

****

The sound of their footsteps echoed on the wooden floor of JM's convenience store as they headed for the candy aisle. Marv noted that the usually well-stocked shelves were run down: in some areas completely stripped. Britney tugged at his arm as she pointed to Bob and Mandy Galway shopping in the other aisle. She started to move towards them; Marv caught her arm and shook his head. The time was not yet right.

They completed their selection and went to the long glass counter to pay. Britney smiled at Mr Martinez as she handed him the money. Javier Martinez was a jolly round little man with a large drooping moustache hanging under his hooked nose. His pot-belly stuck out over his pants. He'd run the store for as long as anyone could remember and despite the arrival of Wal-Mart, JM's was as popular now as it had always been.

"Britney and Marv, I'm sorry your money is no good today," Martinez said pushing her hand away.

With her eyes and mouth wide, Britney was dumbfounded. She turned to Marv only to see him with a similar reaction. What had they done to deserve this? They could feel the eyes of the other shoppers burning into their backs. Her whole head flushed as she stared at Martinez.

"Your money is no good today, because you are my two little heroes," Martinez beamed with delight as he clasped her hand. "You brung those kids down on your own. That was amazing. No charge for the candy and I give you soda pop and chips free, too."

The two kids had no idea of what to say as the jolly man handed them the items. Marv turned bright red as he saw the faces smiling at them. He was not accustomed to being treated in this way; the limelight was something new to him. He smiled back awkwardly, there was a time when he'd have just run away, but those days had gone for good.

Mandy Galway's sister slammed her shopping basket down on the wooden floor and marched angrily up to the pair, stopping inches away from them. Her tearful eyes burrowed right into Marv and her whole face contorted as she spat her words at him.

"You two 'little heroes' have done real nice out of this, but what about my girl, what about her?"

"Mrs Galway I'm so sorry..."

"You're so smug, Britney Patrick, with your big house and money. You never even showed for her birthday. What do you care?"

Britney watched; her body trembling and tears running down her face, as the Galways headed for the door.

"It should be you lying in that hospital!" Mandy's sister yelled and with those words ringing in the air, she was gone.

****

Eastman was talking to Clara at the station house reception area. He told her that it was vital they kept track of the search groups. Each party had one radio set including the police sets being used by Benteen, Koneg and Eddy Joe. This was adequate to provide the teams with reasonable communication. Pat O'Brien had managed to set up a booster receiver for Merka and although it only had limited range, Merka could relay communication from the CB teams. It was enough to reach the station house – but only just.

"Clara, I reckon that's about it for now. Keep your ears open for anything from them." He handed her the route clipboard.

"I'm gonna find Anne but I'll be back soon."

Clara would have to watch the store for a while. He didn't think there'd be any news; they'd only been gone half an hour. He wanted to talk to Taylor, but he knew that Anne would want to ask him a cart-load of questions too. The last time, Taylor had produced as many questions as he did answers. Without the police database Eastman couldn't even tell if Taylor was this guy's real name.

There was some stuff that made sense and there was no denying the creatures were real enough. But all that stuff about being an undercover PI and the mad, bad drugs company was difficult to swallow. There was no place in this area where you could set up a secret base. Still, he wasn't going to get anything done here, he had to find Anne. As he turned to leave, Frank Jorgan's deep voice cut across the room.

"Sorry I'm late Sheriff but Nancy's gone missing."

Jorgan strode across to stand in front of the desk. He looked uptight.

"What you mean, missing?"

"The back door was wide open and the kitchen was upside down and there was some blood on her pillow."

"Okay, now Frank let's slow down here and start at the beginning."

"I got back from the Lloyds' place with Iris, to look after Nancy but when we got back to the farm, she'd gone. We started looking for her, but then I thought I'd better get some help."

"Have you got any reason to think somebody else was involved? Any tracks?"

"Nope, the only tracks were hers."

"A dumb question, but how'd you know they were hers?"

"They was bare footprints. When she was a girl she lost a toe on her right foot. These was her prints all right. We followed them to the rocks, then we lost them in the stream."

"I know it's easy for me to say but try not to worry. I'll send some of my people up with you and the boys."

"Appreciate that Brad, but my boys are still up there looking for their Ma. I reckon that hand of hers drove her crazy."

Her hand! Of course. How could he have been so stupid? There was every likelihood that she'd transformed. Why else would someone head barefoot over rocks and into the wilderness? Frank's boys were in more danger than either of them could imagine.

"I'm gonna send you back with one of my officers and some other guys. I'm sorry but I gotta stay here. I got people all over the mountainside."

"Yeah, sure thing Brad, I understand."

"Frank, if Nancy's not well I need you all to be careful with her. She may not be herself."

"What you saying there Brad?" He fixed Eastman with a cold stare.

"I'm just saying she could be confused and..."

"I know what you're saying. You think 'cause she got herself injured, she gonna be like one of them things. Like last night. But you're way wrong, she's just ill, not a monster!"

The sad thing was there was nothing Eastman could say that would make Frank see otherwise. As Jorgan left the building, Eastman looked glumly at Clara.

"Clara, can you get hold of Mitch and Jedrey? Ask them to bring some other guys too. Frank's gonna need some help."

****

Zach Clayton was a rough kid from the wrong end of town. But here he was, sitting in 'The Beast' reading one of Luke's comic books. It had been Luke who'd given the bright orange Chevy four-by-four its name; they'd built it up over the years, some legal parts, others not so legal, but now it was their pride and joy. It was also one hell of a chick magnet and the other guys hated him for it. If anyone asked what they did for a living, Zach would tell them 'auto traders'. He'd spent his childhood learning from his Pa about taking cars apart in the chop shop. There was a darn sight more dollars to be earned doing that than working in some store in town.

Zach tossed the comic into the rear of the truck and looked out at the surrounding woodland. The bright sunshine bounced off the tinted glass, betraying the encroaching heat of the day. He lazily flicked through the CD tracks and wondered where the hell Luke had gotten to? His curly brown hair jutted out from his baseball cap as he surveyed the track. Then, just in the distance, he saw his brother running towards him. Within seconds Luke was clambering into the truck.

"We gotta move. Half the town's on us. Let's go man!"

Zach looked at his brother, his thin frame shaking with exertion and beads of sweat running down his bright red face. He was sure the boy was about to have a heart attack. Luke really was not the sharpest of tools. But, with a gearbox and a full set of alloy wheels under a tarpaulin in the back and no bill of sale, maybe it was time to haul ass. Zach hit the gas and shot off. The Beast slunk into the woods like a great orange metal tiger.

"Look man, we gotta cool it. With all that's going down, it's too risky."

"Ever thought of the upside Lukey boy?"

"Huh?"

"With all this ruckus going on, everybody's taking on like a bunch of turkeys at Thanksgiving. I heard me that Eastman's called a curfew in town. Know what that means?"

The boy's blank stare made it obvious that he did not. Zach continued, "It means we can do what the hell we like without any meddling from the law."

"Yeah, well what about that helicopter darn near buzzing us off the road. The cops are on to us, I tell you."

"You ever see a police helicopter all blacked out like that? That weren't no cops."

"You reckon it's something to do with all that crap in town?"

"Maybe?"

"Well we got to tell someone. Ain't we?"

Zach stopped the truck and looked at Luke.

"The wind only gotta change and we get the blame. It's about time we got something for nothing. Right now, nobody gives a damn about us. We start blabbing and we got us half the town up here."

Zach didn't want to spend the coming winter up in the mountains. With just a couple more deals they'd have enough cash to get away for a few weeks, even months. But first they had to deliver the merchandise.

"A couple more jobs then we made enough to take a vacation somewhere warm. You'd like that, little brother."

"What we gotta do?"

"A day back I swung past the Woodridges' place. Mike Woodridge got himself a new Dodge parked up. I didn't see nobody about no lights no nothing. I reckon they gone someplace else."

"So why'd they leave the truck there?"

"Who knows? I reckon we slip by there tonight and have a darn good look. We can have that truck re-sprayed with new plates by tomorrow."

"A vacation? You really mean that? Anywhere we like… then how about Disney?"

Zach looked over at his brother and smiled. He could think of other places than Disney, but what the hell; at least Orlando had nice weather.

****

Taylor sat on the edge of his bed, looking at Eastman and Dr Lenski who in turn sat looking at him, like a Mexican standoff from one of his favourite movies. They were just behind the red safety line, the area deemed safely out of reach from those in the cells. At least with the good doctor in tow, Eastman would have to behave himself, no more Magnums. However, if he wanted to get out, Taylor would still have to win this man over. After an awkward interval, Eastman spoke first.

"Okay Mr – Taylor, we're gonna ask you some questions. Dr Lenski wants to ask about a whole bunch of medical stuff. You *will* cooperate. Are we clear on that?"

"Mr Taylor, you told the Sheriff that the condition of these people was the result of some 'failed' cure; a cure for what?"

Taylor slapped the palm of his hand against his forehead with a resounding whack.

"Do you still think these *things* are people? Worse, you think you can cure them – is that it? There is no cure! Lady, you can forget AIDS, Ebola damn it, even cancer. When you get this thing, it gets you – The End!"

"How do you know, are you a doctor?"

"If the people who invented this crap couldn't find a cure how the hell are you?"

"What is this disease? I mean do you know how it works?"

"I've already told you how it works."

"Yes, I know about how people become infected, but how can I treat it?"

She needed to know about the symptoms, how the infection worked, how long before the infection took hold and many other questions. If she was to stand any chance in fighting this appalling thing, she needed to know what it was.

"I'm no doctor; I can only tell you so much. Once they're infected, they get flu-like symptoms, then this fever sets in, like no other you've seen. They just burn up in front of you. Some dip into a coma and by the time they wake it's too late."

"I seen somebody get infected and almost instantly, they got up and went for someone. Now there was no darn coma there, mister!"

"Depending on the severity of the wound they can transform within minutes but it's never longer than three days. The closer the injury to the brain, the quicker they change."

"Why the brain?"

"The doctors said the virus makes its way to the brain. In military terms, take the command centre out and you win the battle."

"Did ZerTon try to find a cure for this?"

"Sure Doc, but there wasn't one. As soon as you get infected, the virus attacks the organs, and by the time you turn, your insides are just a bag of mush."

Anne Lenski sat forward pinching the bridge of her nose and sighing deeply. The stark reality hit her. Brad and the others had been right the whole time; these things were no longer people. How could she have been so dim for such a long time? It was obvious that such tissue damage had to be terminal; she'd thought it was just the dead ones she'd examined, but all the infected were like it?

"How are they able to keep moving in such a state?"

"They take a lot of structural damage; you can pump holes in them or blow bits off, but you take out the brain and that's it, game over. Like I said Doc, 'command centre'."

Since the first time Eastman had met Taylor, he'd watched his reactions all through the question sessions; this man had hardly given away a thing. Although Taylor was very good, every now and again he'd let his guard down. Eastman had seen a chink in his armour. He didn't buy this guff about Taylor and the creatures turning up at the same time as a coincidence. Eastman needed more information on the man himself, what made him tick, where he came from and what he really wanted in Armstrong.

"Okay, you said you were a PI on a mission. Start convincing me that's all true."

Taylor held his head in his hands, shut his eyes and allowed himself to drift back to the point when it had all begun.

There was no way in hell this cop could ever understand...

****

Taylor entered the large, brightly decorated room. It looked more like the office of a law firm than a private investigator. His feet sank into the plush blue carpet as he walked across to the desk. Gary Richmond was sitting behind his green leather-bound desk. His expensive Italian suit served as a stark reminder to Taylor that now Richmond was the boss. Just behind Richmond, there hung a large, wooden-framed photo of their old unit.

Richmond had been in his unit for some time before leaving to set up an investigation service. He was now well connected and established. In the beginning it had just been good fun. Taylor had offered his military skills in surveillance and observation to whomever of Richmond's clients wanted them. As the clients got bigger, so did the money, but it was never really about the money with him, it was the excitement he thrived on. He loved it.

"Sit your bones down Brent," said Richmond, ushering him to a seat.

Taylor sunk into the chair and let its extravagance swallow him up. This was the sort of chair you could sleep in. He studied Richmond's face. His dyed blonde hair made a sharp contrast to his deep tan and since their last meeting; Taylor noted that he'd had his teeth whitened.

"We got us a mission. A real mission. Interested, Captain?"

It had been a long time since someone had called him that. He nodded his head. Richmond continued.

"This isn't cheating wives or husbands, this is serious Intel gathering. We've a new client. A big pharmaceutical outfit wants the low down on a competitor. Industrial espionage. I've hit the big time, buddy. These guys are loaded."

Taylor could almost see the dollar bills in Richmond's eyes. He knew pharmaceuticals were big business, but it was the thrill of a real covert operation that interested him the most. He sat further back in his seat and placed his arms on the arm rests.

"Okay. What do they want?"

Richmond opened a suitcase and handed him a thin red plastic file.

"This is ZerTon. These guys are so sharp they've got all the big boys worried. You get inside; grab as much info as you can then bring it back here."

"How do I get in and how'd I know what to look for?"

"We've got a guy on the inside; you meet up with him and he'll tell you what you're after. There are plans and blueprints of the whole place in this file. You just got to find where to get in."

"What's it about? I mean do we know?"

"It's a need to know operation Brent, but I can say that ZerTon are on the brink of a big cure. It'll be like the old days, you'll see. But I tell you, this thing is global and we got us a piece of the action. It's a walk in the park."

****

Clara's voice cut through on Eastman's radio set, "Brad, do you read. Over?"

"Yes, go ahead. Over."

"I had a call from Wal-Mart; they got themselves some kind of incident. Over."

Eastman looked uneasily at Anne. "What kinda incident. Over?"

"I don't know. They lost contact before they could tell. Over."

"Okay, send the nearest unit. Over."

"Sorry Brad," her tone sounded anxious as she continued, "Jedrey left with Frank, Kate is at a traffic accident and Mitch is the other end of town. You're the nearest. Over."

"Yeah, copy that. I'm on my way but Clara, dispatch those other units, I may need back up. Out."

"Brad, why don't you wait for the others? I mean it would be safer if there's trouble."

She was right of course, but he couldn't risk anyone's safety. If it was real trouble, he needed to get there fast. He couldn't hang around for the others; they'd have to join him.

"Anne, we're done for now. I don't want you here with him on your own. Best leave and I'll catch you later."

Anne collected her notes as she left with Eastman. Taylor pondered whether he'd ever see either of them again.

CHAPTER - FIFTEEN

Benny Arnold's office was perched on the third floor of the Wal-Mart store, overlooking the town of Armstrong. The office was a small rectangle with white painted walls and a green carpet – utterly functional. Benny Arnold normally regarded this as his boardroom, his seat of power, but not today. The imposing form of Sheriff Eastman strode into the room, talking on his radio.

Benny Arnold was a tall, thin man. His pasty complexion and greying hair made him look much older than he was. He'd started on the bottom rung of the ladder but had always been in the right place at the right time, and over the years had progressed to assistant manager. When the previous manager Alan Barns, was re-located to another store, Arnold had been appointed temporary manager. Shortly after, his position had been made permanent, a fact which somehow he'd never quite taken in. However, being in charge often brought unexpected responsibilities.

The trouble had started just after the store opened this morning. There'd been a large crowd outside since first light, waiting for the doors to open. Benny watched on the CCTV as people raced about the half empty aisles, anxiously searching the bare shelves. Jane Pready, the floor supervisor had tried to calm the situation but then Paul Washington became abusive. Arnold and his security man, Joe Levine had arrived and called for the police.

"No Clara, it's under control here," said Sheriff Eastman "Some folk got a bit hot headed, that's all. Kate's out front with the volunteers. Over."

"Do you want any more back up? Over?"

"Negative. No sense in any more guns down here. Out."

Eastman advanced on Arnold and leant on his desk, glowering at him. Arnold found it impossible to hold the other man's glare; he averted his eyes. He felt threatened and uncomfortable, feelings that he was unused to having in his insular domain, atop the world.

"Benny, what in hell were you thinking?"

"Now take it easy Brad," Arnold tried to assert himself, "this is all legal, no law's been broken here."

"Let's just leave the law to me shall we? You and I got family and friends out there who can't get the things they need. Why? Because you sold it all to Peter damn Firth..." Eastman slammed his hat onto the desk.

"...and you wonder why you had a riot here?"

"It was a legal transaction, it isn't my prob –"

"It sure as hell is your problem. The next time you got a shop full of Paul Washingtons wanting stuff you don't have, you tell them it was a 'legal transaction.'"

"I just never thought of it like that."

"Benny, you're not talking some cotton candy here. If it hits the fan, and I reckon it will, then people will want all kinds of supplies, supplies which Firth will charge the earth for."

Arnold put his hand to his head and slumped back in his chair. Firth had turned up with five grand in cash and bought everything from duct tape to cordless screwdrivers and then some. It had been obvious that Firth was intending to make money but Arnold hadn't made the connection. It wasn't as if he could order up replacement fresh stock. It had gone and there was nothing he could do about it.

"If I could get it all back," he said, shrugging despondently, "but I can't."

Eastman rubbed his fingertips over his chin in a circular motion. "Perhaps you can't but I sure as hell can. Where'd he take that stuff?"

"I got no idea."

"Who'd he have with him, did you see anyone?"

"He was on his own. Is it important?"

"Nope, I'll just have to make a house call that's all."

"Brad, what should I do with the rest of the stock we got left?"

"We gonna have to talk about emergency rations. Start getting all the shop owners together to see what we can do."

He watched as Eastman left the room. If the guy was going to pay Firth a house call, then Firth best be elsewhere.

****

As Benteen and Eddy Joe drove the department's four-by-four past Ben's house, Benteen shook his head in disbelief. It was still hard to think of Ben and Erin dead, especially the way they'd died. He wondered what would happen to their farm. As far as he knew, the pair had no living relatives in the area. Something like this was bound to make a man question his own mortality. Benteen had no folks left, at least none that he knew of. What would happen to him, when he was gone; would anyone even care?

Eddy Joe nodded at the farm.

"It's hard to take in what happened to Erin and Ben. I mean, the way she turned on him like that."

"That wasn't Erin or Zoë last night. They were God damn monsters."

It was clear to Benteen that the real cause of all this bedlam was that bum in the cells. All this had started with his arrival. Even if Brad had been taken in, Benteen didn't believe a word of it. If he was ever alone with that nut, then he'd make him pay. Clenching hard on the wheel, he turned left and led his small two-vehicle convoy past the barn. Just ahead, he could see Firth's motley crew parked up; everybody was out and looking towards the tree line.

Benteen stopped his four-by-four and looked at Eddy Joe. "Grab your M16 and get the guys out."

"Gerard, do you reckon they got one of them things?"

"I don't know. Let's go see."

The whole area was tranquil, soft rolling green pasture led down to the shallow river. The only discernable sound was the hum of men's voices. Eddy Joe gathered the group to him and Benteen cast his eye over his posse: Austen Colt, Ray Johnson, Ramon Tuco, Ethan Mason, Boulle and even Preacher Goodman. So at least they had God on their side. Satisfied that everyone was present,

Benteen beckoned with his hand for them to follow, covering the ground in great strides towards the other group.

Boulle caught Benteen's attention; he was a rough kind of guy, powerfully built, in his late thirties with short black hair. He was one of those guys Benteen just did not get. The man was a no seeker; he was the last person Benteen would've imagined to be in something like this. Some years back, Boulle had thrown his lot in with Peter Firth, but they'd had a falling out and now they hated each other. Boulle had no real interest in the community and yet here he was, a volunteer, looking for Peter Firth's nephew.

Preacher Goodman was an altogether different character. He was well known and much liked in the community. A young man with a wise head on his shoulders; he'd come from Houston, some years back and taken over from Preacher Hall. He'd thrown himself into his work and although he was from the 'God squad,' even Benteen got on with him.

"Well Mayor, where's this guy?"

Firth pointed to an area just beyond the tree line.

"Jim-boy saw one of those things just over there."

"Well I thought I did," interrupted Jim-boy uncertainly.

Firth continued, "Some of the guys wanted to take a look. I said we'd best call you."

"Sure done the right thing. Me and Eddy Joe will take it from here. You guys can carry on with the search."

Benteen started forward with the other deputy then Firth suddenly caught his arm. "Look, far be it for me to interfere, but I reckon that's kinda dangerous?"

"How so?"

"It don't make any sense you two risking your lives when you got all of us as back up."

"Yeah, I mean what if there's more than one?"

Benteen looked at Roody Goldsmith, his thin frame poorly suited to such an exercise. He was more at home in the town hall than hunting. Sure, he was sporting a powerful hunting rifle with a scope that cost more than a week's wages, but the guy was a Sunday shooter. There was certain logic to what Goldsmith said, but out of all the men there were only a few he'd trust not to shoot each other.

"Okay, we'll search in an extended skirmish line, no more than four feet between each man. I don't want no safety catches off, or weapons cocked, or your butts will feel my boots."

"How you want us to do this, guns in the front and unarmed guys at the rear?"

Austen Colt had a good point. He was an experienced man who knew how to use his AK47. He was wearing a Russian ammunition vest full of magazines for his AK. It amused Benteen to take the rise outta him for having a name like Colt but always using Russian stuff. But he was one of the few men Benteen trusted around firearms. The rest had chrome plated pimp guns.

"What you brought that Commie piece of crap with you for, Austin?"

"This baby can outshoot, outrange and outdo that M16 of yours any damn day of the week 'T' and you know it."

Benteen looked at Colt and suppressed a smile. There were very few people who could get away with using his middle name and less who knew what the 'T' stood for. As Eddy Joe formed the group into the skirmish line, Benteen gave them the last instructions.

"Listen up. We gonna hold this formation the whole time. Nobody shoots nothing, 'less I tell 'em first. We looking for tracks, any tracks, so keep your eyes open."

Holding up his hand, Benteen ordered the group forward into the dusty heat of the midday sun.

****

Ramon Tuco took a long drink from his water bottle. He was hot and tired. They'd spent almost two hours searching for this Firth's guy. He was thankful for wearing his old boots and not the new pair his wife had bought him for his birthday. Firth had insisted they search for this phantom but now everybody had had enough. Benteen had finally called a halt and now his troops were back at the starting point, much the worse for wear. Benteen and Eddy Joe were a few feet away from Ramon but he could clearly hear that neither man was happy about the diversion.

"What a total waste of God damn time." Benteen thrust his canteen back into his back pack. "A God damn goose chase!"

"Reckon I agree with ya. I walked my feet off, but I never seen nothing up there."

Most of Benteen's search team were clustered around the two deputies. Ramon agreed that it had been a needless waste of time and effort, but only Benteen and Eddy Joe were prepared to say so. A few feet away, he could see Firth and Murray Scott talking; Firth stopped and looked over at Benteen.

"Maybe there weren't no tracks 'cause there weren't anything to leave 'em in the first place."

"You got a problem there Gerard?"

Benteen turned to square up to Firth, who was now standing a few feet away, flanked by Scott and McDowall. The hum of conversation ceased immediately, everybody awaiting Benteen's response.

"Nope, but maybe Jim-boy made a mistake – happens all the time."

"I saw him too."

"Yeah well, then maybe you made a mistake too." It was not in Benteen's nature to back down.

Scott tilted his head to one side, shifting his body as he did so. "Sounds like you're calling the Mayor a liar there, deputy?"

Ramon Tuco's eyes darted from one man to the next as the mood changed from tense to volatile. It was well known that Scott was one of Peter Firth's strong arms. Tuco had seen him beat up a guy once outside Barany's Bar; he was the kinda person who got off on that thing, and he was built for it. A shock of cropped white hair crowned his boxer-like features and a broken nose completed his harsh appearance. Standing in his tan body warmer with his heavily tattooed arms folded across his chest, he looked every bit as mean as Benteen.

Benteen walked right up to Firth. "I ain't calling *no one a liar*. The word I used was *mistake*." He turned to Scott. "Look it up, if you can read…"

Colt stepped up to Benteen. "Gerard's right, stress can make folks see all sorts of things, things that ain't always there."

"Gee, that's just swell. Not only do you think I made the whole damn thing up, you think I'm crazy as well!"

"That ain't what I'm saying here. We spent all that time tramping about and we never saw no evidence. Not one scrap."

"Well, maybe you're just not as good a tracker as you think you are."

Ramon winced; he was sure that if looks could kill then Firth would be in a pine box. Benteen took two steps forward and stopped directly in front of Firth. Just like a crap game, everyone was waiting to see how this would play out. To the left of Benteen, Ramon could see Boulle inching his way forward. He was looking intently at Scott; it was the kind of look that went right through a man. There was unstated business between these two.

"If there'd been anything to find I'd have found it. And we wouldn't have wasted all that time, like a bunch of idiots."

"Think I don't want to look for my boy or something?"

"Guys, guys, let's simmer down a notch here shall we?"

Preacher Goodman moved briskly in between the two, placing his hands on each man's arms. He smiled broadly, then turned to Benteen.

"Gerard, now wouldn't you agree that if whatever or whoever we've been looking for went into the stream, then we'd have no tracks, right?"

"Sure, but I didn't see no prints to begin with."

"Fair enough, but with a bunch of guys stomping about down there, is it possible that any tracks could have been destroyed?"

"Well…I guess…"

"Tony, since tracks could have been destroyed, then it may have been impossible for Gerard to find any, agree?"

Firth rubbed his fingers over his mouth and shot a sideways glance at McDowall before nodding to Benteen.

"Yeah, yeah that's possible."

A buzz of chatter erupted around the small group as people nodded in agreement. McDowall placed his hand on Firth's shoulder and gave a cheerful grin and Scott took a few steps back. When Ramon looked to see where Boulle had gone, he'd already melted back into the throng. However, Goodman had not yet finished and called out in a loud voice.

"Gerard, we don't want to forget what we're all doing up here and Tony best remember that Gerard's up here looking for your boy."

Benteen and Firth acknowledged each other and the respective groups made their way back to the vehicles. Ramon walked alongside the two lawmen; he'd a feeling that things were far from resolved, then he heard Eddy Joe voice his opinion.

"Well that sure cleared up that, I'd say?"

"That what you think?"

Benteen stopped dead and slowly turned to look at the other lawman.

"I smell a rat, a two legged bald rat. That fink is up to something, I just don't know what."

"Aw, come on man, Preacher's already said about the tracks and..."

Benteen gave him a scornful retort.

"Your Momma drop you on your head or something? Nuts to the tracks! I'm talking about that fool goose chase he lead us on."

"I don't get you."

"Firth didn't want us back on that search. Each time I said about getting back on the case, he come up with reason after reason not to. He was all about finding that thing. Don't you see?"

"No, I don't see." Colt sent Benteen a bewildered look. "I don't get the connection here. If there was a guy up there and he just wandered off, that doesn't mean he wasn't there ever. What if we just couldn't find him?"

"Bull! Brad said those things hunt on sight or sound. They ain't the fastest of critters, so it can't have got far. Now, all us crashing around is sure gonna bring some attention."

"What you saying there, he was more interested in that guy than his son?"

Benteen jabbed his finger at Eddy Joe. "Like I said, something's not right here."

To Ramon nothing would have been more important than finding your own flesh and blood.

"If it was my boy up here, I would not waste my time on a crazy guy, I tell you this."

Benteen looked at Colt and Eddy Joe then touched the brim of his hat and winked at Ramon.

"Now there's a man who knows the real deal when he sees it."

Ramon Tuco clambered aboard the Jeep with Preacher Goodman. Maybe those devils and the blackout were not the only things to worry about.

****

Eastman walked up the steps to the solid wooden door and rang Peter Firth's doorbell. As he waited for the answer he looked about: just an ordinary detached town house. A dilapidated cinder block wall enclosed the overgrown lawn and a small stone path led to the double garage. An ordinary house, like any other, but bought from the dirtiest money you could imagine.

Eastman caught sight of Mrs Grison's twitching curtains; he smiled and tried the door again. He heard the latch scrape back as the door opened a fraction. He recognised the figure of Mary Firth standing just inside the gloomy hallway.

"Mary, can I talk to Peter?"

"He's not here."

"Can I come in? I need to know where he's at, please."

The door opened just wide enough for Eastman to pass. Mary stood aside, shutting the door behind her. Her thin frame was topped by long straggly auburn hair that looked as if it needed a good brush. The light blue dress she was wearing had seen much better days, like its owner.

"I said, he's not here and I don't know where he is."

As she stepped into the light he caught sight of her swollen lip; it infuriated him but he was here on other business. They moved into the sparsely furnished living area. Two brown leather chairs occupied one side of the small room, a damaged wall cupboard on the other side. The tiny portable TV seemed out of place on the huge glass fronted, wooden cabinet. Eastman noted the fist marks in the inner door and the broken photo frame in the next room.

"You know Mary; you really ought to have those stairs or that cupboard door fixed. You know the one that keeps on whacking you? I'm darn good at DIY, perhaps I can fix it?"

"What's he done this time?"

"He cleaned out Wal-Mart and darn well near caused a riot."

Eastman set down his hat on the TV.

"I need to find him."

"What's that to do with me?"

"Mary, if things turn bad here, then people won't get the stuff they need, 'cause Peter's bought it all up. Folk are gonna be forced to buy it from him. What if they don't have the money?"

"He's out till all hours with that whore."

She walked to the window and gazed out.

"I don't know where he is anymore."

He caught a glimpse of the marks on her wrist. He'd known Mary since college and it pained him to see her like this. But they'd been down this same road before; she had to be the one to act.

"If you know where he is, tell me. With all that stuff, he's gonna hold the town to ransom. Things are gonna get out of hand. People are gonna suffer. Do you want that?"

"Why don't you try his girlfriend's house? I'm sure they're real snug. Now please leave."

She opened the living room door and gestured him to leave. Eastman nodded his head, collected his hat and moved towards the hallway. He'd have to find Firth on his own.

"Brad, wait! He's gone to that lock up Barney uses; he went there with a truck, just now. Don't let on, or he'll kill me!"

Eastman turned around and reached out, taking Mary's sunglasses off. Her tearful, blackened eyes looked sadly back at him. He held her hand and she let out a painful yelp. Eastman clenched his fists and cursed under his breath.

"Why the hell do you put up with all this crap? Just say the word and he's gone. He's gonna hurt you real bad one day."

She lowered her eyes and for the second time, Eastman headed for the front door, his heart leaden with sadness.

"He's my husband."

Eastman shut his eyes and sighed deeply as he opened the door and stepped out into the bright sunshine.

****

Leona Arcado neatly folded the hand towels and placed them on top of the wicker basket outside the bathroom. She was in her thirties and a slim, attractive woman. She normally wore her dark brown hair up but today she'd allowed it to flow over her shoulders.

She looked across at Tony's closed bedroom door; it was best to leave him rest, Vinnie had said. It was all right for her to miss a shift, but for him to miss one was a sin, or so he'd made out. After all that had happened at the health center, home was the best place for Tony.

All this talk of infection had done a good job of scaring people half to death. So she'd rung Molly at the Post Office and told her she'd not be coming to work that day. She looked at her watch; it was time for something to eat. Leona walked into the kitchen to make her son a bite to eat.

She liked the idea of the bungalow being all on the same level. Although small, Vinnie preferred the term 'compact.' The wood finished kitchen was as perfect as you'd expect from a husband who was a carpenter and a good one at that. She opened up the fridge and selected one of Tony's favourite pizzas, Hawaiian, with a thick base. She picked off the mushrooms; Tony hated them. He said it made the food taste 'funny' and for years he'd believed his pizza came devoid of mushrooms. She tossed the offending vegetables in the trash and slid the pizza into the oven, selecting the right temperature before sitting down to wait for it to cook. She looked out of the window across the street and watched as Marko Vega picked up his upturned trash-can, his trash strewn across the sidewalk. He'd just retired after years in the bank and had too much time on his hands. He blamed cats. He always blamed cats but this had been Robert Pool, out of his skull last night. Perhaps she should have told Vega but she liked Robert and he could do without the hassle.

Leona looked away from the show; she had other things on her mind. She was worried about the effect things were having on Tony. He'd become withdrawn and for the last few days he'd just holed up in his room. Then there'd been those freaky dreams he'd told them about; Vinnie had played them down but she could see they had gotten to the boy.

When Britney and Marv had come to call, he'd perked up a lot and it had been good to hear them laughing. It was disgraceful the way Mandy Galway had treated the kids in JM's, sure the woman was overwrought, but she'd no cause to behave like that.

The aroma of freshly cooked pizza signalled that everything was ready. She took the piping hot pizza from the oven and placed it on a tray, with a glass of cola and some cutlery and set off for the bedroom.

She called out to her son and then placed the tray on the floor in front of his door, before swinging the door open. She entered with the food tray and called out again. Tony lay on his side, facing the still drawn curtains. As she placed the tray on the bedside table, she was tempted to leave him sleep but he needed to eat, even if she had to feed him herself. She reached out and gently shook his arm, then once more with added effort. His head lolled back towards her and she screamed at the pools of blood gathered in the corners of his eyes.

****

Eastman sat in his patrol car watching out from the side lane leading from Wilmot Road. The locality was a nest of lock-ups and garages, even at this time of day hardly anybody was about. The area had once been a hub of activity, with trees and the smell of freshly cut grass: that had all long since disappeared. Now the grass was overgrown and many of the lots were vacant. Most of the people he remembered as a kid had died, whilst a lot of other people had moved to look for work. With the street lamps out, the place was a virtual no-go zone after dark.

Wilmot Road lay directly in front of him and just beyond that was lot thirty-four. This belonged to Barney Branigan. It had originally been just a small compound with a garage, but at some time or other, Branigan had acquired Matt Henson's lock-up also. The whole area was now enclosed by a high wall, leading on to the sidewalk. Just above the wall, Eastman could clearly see the white roof of a large delivery van. As he watched, the van periodically bobbed up and down, an indication that the vehicle was being unloaded or even loaded up.

Aldo Kolp came into view, carrying a six pack of beer. Kolp was one of Peter Firth's heavies; he was the kind of guy that looked suspicious even going into his *own* house. He was oblivious of Eastman and entered the compound via a large, brown, wooden door. Eastman reached down between his seat and the car door and picked up his nightstick. It was a piece of kit he seldom carried, let alone used, but it was a useful midway point between bare knuckles and a bullet.

As he made his way across the street, Eastman kept one beady eye on the compound; the last thing he wanted was for someone to spot him now. He stopped by the brown door and listened to the subdued voices inside. He could hear two voices; Kolp had to be one, he couldn't make out the other. Eastman gently pushed the unlocked door open and went inside.

Just to the left of the door stood Kolp and another member of team Firth – Don Breck. Breck always reminded Eastman of a large Forrest Gump but he had no notable track record and was largely regarded as the outfit's driver. Both men had their backs to him as they drank their beer. The whole lock-up was piled high with Wal-Mart products – everything from band-aids to power tools.

"You boys got yourselves one hell of a stock-take going on here."

Eastman gave a wry smile as the two goons spun around in total surprise.

He walked further into the compound, locking his thumbs behind his large silver belt buckle as he did so. Barney Branigan's large brutish frame stepped out from behind the truck.

Although way past his prime, he was still someone to watch out for. His hard green eyes fixed on Eastman.

"We got a bill of sales for this whole pile…" He walked up to the others.

"…and this is private property, Sheriff."

"That an invite for me to come back with a search warrant there Barney? 'Cause if it is, then this is gonna be the start of one bad day for you."

"Ain't nothing wrong here."

"Glad to hear it."

Eastman made his way to the blockhouse. "Now, mind telling me where Peter Firth's at?"

"Ain't seen him all day."

Branigan blocked Eastman's path and stood in front of the door. "Like I said, this is private property."

"Seems to me your bar's due for an inspection real soon, Barney boy? Fire regulations, noise pollution; all that kinda thing can be a royal pain in the ass. It's so easy these days for a guy to lose his licence. You agree?"

Branigan lowered his eyes and moved aside, allowing Eastman access to building.

"Now you boys go about your lawful business, 'cause I gonna have a chat with your boss. I don't want any interruptions."

Eastman pushed the door open with his foot and went inside. A single striplight illuminated the rows of neatly stacked boxes that filled the deceptively large structure. Although the light was poor, it was enough for him to make out Peter Firth, standing with a clipboard, with his back to the door. Eastman walked a few short feet and then abruptly stopped.

"I'm kinda busy right now Sheriff. Mind calling back later? Unless of course, it's a social call?"

"My Granddaddy always said never mix business with pleasure. So I reckon this isn't a social call."

Eastman was finding it hard to keep up his professional attitude. His behaviour hid the fact that he wanted to take this bum apart at the seams. He stepped up to face the other man. Firth waved a bundle of receipts at Eastman. "I got legal purchase ledgers for all this stuff." He swung his arms, indicating the rows of boxes.

"What is it today, everyone's an accountant? Look I got a deal for you."

"Ah, now why didn't you just say that before? I can give you a good discount..."

"Not that kinda deal. You hear what happened at Wal-Mart this morning?"

"Can't say as I did."

"Lot of people turned up and then things got ugly when they found half the stuff they needed had gone..." Eastman tapped the nearest box to him with his stick, "...this stuff, in fact."

"And I'm to blame for that?"

"At a time like this, if people can't get what they want, they gonna panic."

"Sure, and then they gonna come to me, cause I got what they want."

"At hell knows what price tag, that it?"

"I'm a businessman. This is a business venture."

Eastman clenched his fists at his sides. There was no reasoning with the man.

"I call it making a quick buck off your neighbour's back."

"Free enterprise. Ain't you heard? It's the American way."

"This is the deal and it's the best you gonna get. You got two hours to take all this... stuff, back to Benny Arnold. Then you get every penny back; just call it a refund."

"And why would I want to do that?"

"Well maybe, cause it's the right thing to do. Or maybe because if you don't then I'll bust your sorry ass and confiscate everything. Then you don't get a cent, Mr Firth."

Eastman watched Firth's reaction as he changed from red to purple. He doubted his Grandfather's philosophy about no business with pleasure, because right now Eastman was enjoying every single moment.

"You can't do that! It's all legal. I already told you."

Eastman walked over to Firth, placing his face inches away from Firth's. "You'd be surprised just what I can do. Two hours, that's all you got."

"Arrest me! For what?"

"I'm sure I can come up with something in the next twenty eight days that'll cover it. You want to see if I can? You'll have enough time to reflect with that crazy nut in the next cell."

"You got nothing on me Eastman, nothing!"

"Two hours."

Eastman shot Firth a scowl, turned on his heels and left the room.

Of course there was always the possibility that Firth would find another location in the time but Eastman was a man of his word. The ball was in Firth's court now; it was up to him. Besides, it might be enjoyable if Firth decided to do just that and a faint smile crept onto his face as he got into his patrol car.

****

The cool evening breeze drifted through the door as Sam Cortez walked into the general store. Tom Price and Rudy Goldsmith stood with Oscar Majors, discussing the events of the press conference not more than an hour ago.

"I find it sort of hard to believe that Brad Eastman could have killed Erin and Zoë like that."

Tom Price shook his head, sadly. "It's like it's not real."

"Real enough though." Majors stopped to serve Cortez. "What I don't get is why the need to shoot them? I mean what about cuffs, that kinda thing?"

As Majors handed Cortez his change, Cortez grasped the shopkeeper's hand.

"Oscar, Erin Burke darn near bit her husband's head off then she took a chunk outta Zoë. Any one of us could have been next. I was ready to put an axe though Erin's head myself. Thank God them boys showed up when they did."

He looked at Tom Price. "That real enough for you Tom?"

"Hey sorry man." It was the best Majors could offer up, averting his eyes. Cortez stared at the trio, ruefully shaking his head; they watched in silence as he left the store. The ringing of the shop doorbell sounded like a starting pistol and the men resumed talking.

"Geez, some people." Majors shut his till with a self satisfied look on his face.

"I heard it took them hours to clean the blood up."

"I said I was sorry. Hell, Rudy I don't know what else I can say."

Price grinned at them. "Say Rudy, how'd it go up there today?"

"The truth is we spent half the day chasing our tails." Goldsmith winced. "And I got blisters on my blisters to prove it boys."

"Yep, it was like that yesterday," mused Majors. "We covered miles of nothing."

"I think folks gotta start looking to their own affairs," Goldsmith cautioned. "Any news on Nancy Jorgan yet?"

"Will Yardman said she'd been dragged out of the house; the place is in a hell of a mess."

Majors shot his eyes skywards in desperation and let out a loud sigh. "Then Tom, it gotta be true."

"Reckon they gonna go up again tomorrow?"

Majors looked at the other two. "I can't take time for another search. Besides like Rudy said, we gotta start looking to ourselves."

"Right now, all Rudy wants is some cream for his feet. Give me some of that stuff you sold Pal Yantos, yesterday."

Majors looked thoughtfully at the foot care section, sucked his lips and selected a small blue box. Triumphantly he passed the box to Goldsmith.

"Try this. It's as good as anything you'll get from the pharmacy."

Goldsmith fished in his wallet for some money then noted the price on the box.

"Hold up there, *three dollars fifty*? This was two dollars yesterday, I saw the box."

Majors shrugged his shoulders.

"Yeah I know, call it 'a change in economical status' buddy," he gave a mischievous smile and held out his open palm.

****

For the second time that day Luke was doing all the work while Zach sat back in 'the beast' giving orders. But hadn't it always been like that anyways? Since the old man had taken off and left them, Zach had done all the thinking and the sorting out. Hell, it was easier that way, too much thinking hurt the brain. Luke had tried doing things for himself, like the time he'd almost joined the army.

Luke had waited until Zach was out, then he'd caught the Greyhound to the army place barracks and sat the test. The sergeant guy was real nice to him; he even said that Luke had some of the personal details kinda right, like his name and address, even his telephone number. But the guy had said he'd failed the test. They wanted someone with a better H.Q. or I.Q. – some kinda military thing. Anyways, it never come to nothing because after the White House and the Nimitz going down, they went and dropped the bomb and the war came to an end. Maybe it was best to leave Zach do the thinking after all.

He made his way down the winding track towards the Woodridges' farm; the full moon bathed the area like an oversized flashlight. He could make out the house and outbuildings nestled between the woods and the hills. The farm stretched out for over two hundred acres and grew some of the best produce in the county.

He was still a little way off, so Luke decided it was a good time to go over some of the things Zach had set him. He needed to find if there was anybody in the house before Zach could hotwire the four-by-four. It was unlikely that either Mike or Susan Woodridge would be impressed at finding one of the Clayton brothers on their property in the dead of night. After several uneventful minutes he decided the place was empty and climbed over the heavy metal gate.

He made his way towards the four-by-four; as he drew near he noted the brand new plates. This had to be one of the best finds they'd ever made; the truck was worth at least thirty, maybe forty grand. After a paint job and new plates, it would be ready in a few hours. He could barely resist the temptation to touch the shiny blue babe. But Zach would tear him apart if he set the car alarm off.

He was only a few yards from the house. As the full moon lit up the ground between the shelter of the vehicle and the house, his heart beat faster. He could feel the sweat under his arms begin to soak through his shirt. Woodridge owned a combat pump action shotgun, a monster that could drop a bear. And here he was on the guy's land, about to steal his car. Damn Zach! Was this worth it? *Yeah, sure it was, now get on with it.* It wasn't too late to turn back. Even now he could still do it. *Oh yeah, great plan. Forwards and backwards: that would sure confuse them. Idiot!*

He was inches away from the back door; his heart was pounding so fast, he hardly registered the buzz of flies from the open top window. What *was* that stink? *Quit whining, just knock on the damn door and get outa here.* He knocked on the dark timber door and called out uneasily, his voice little more than a whisper. Then before he could stop himself, his hand was on the door handle. He pushed the door and it swung open. *That's not in the plan, dummy. Don't go in!*

He called again, pushing the door open wider. Something was blocking the door, so he pushed harder; to his surprise an arm flopped down from behind the door. Moonlight flooded into the room through the large window. A body was lying a few feet away in the space between the kitchen worktops and table. Luke's limbs went cold and he began to shake.

Without warning the door wrenched backwards and Mike Woodridge filled the doorway. Only it wasn't Mike Woodridge anymore. The lower section of his jaw had been torn away, exposing his gums and teeth and three fingers from the left hand were missing. Perhaps the most disturbing aspect of his appearance was the large kitchen knife sticking out of his chest.

His senses reeling, Luke stumbled backward and fell to the ground, striking his head hard. He shook his head to clear the ringing in his ears, but when he tried to get up; his legs went from under him. Woodridge let out a godless howl and lurched towards him. Luke scuttled backwards, like a frantic four-legged crab. He out-paced Woodridge and managed to get to his feet, trying to find his balance. Turning to check on his pursuer he staggered into the four-by-four and set the high-pitched alarm off. The combination of flashing lights and electronic screech was surely enough to wake the dead, he thought.

At last he found the gate but he was too dazed to clamber over, so he desperately struggled to open the bolt. Just as he succeeded he felt grasping fingers clutch at his collar. He tore himself free and frantically made off through the gate.

There it was: 'The Beast'. Although his head still hurt he felt a lot better and managed to race the last few yards. He flung the front passenger door open and jumped in.

"What the hell have you been up to you...?"

Luke slammed the door shut.

"They all dead!"

"What?"

"They all dead."

"Who you talking about, who's dead?"

"The whole family. All gone."

"*Dead*? God! What you done Luke?"

Zach grabbed his brother's shoulders and shook him violently. Luke pushed Zach away. "Nothing, I never done nothing! It was Mike Woodridge that must've done it."

Zach rubbed his fingers roughly over the side of his head then looked at his brother. "Luke, I want you to tell me what happened."

"I got to the farm and the door was open, I looked inside and saw the bodies. I reckon it was Susan and Mike Junior. Then Mike Woodridge come at me and..."

Luke buried his face in his hands and started to whimper.

"And what?"

"Zach, he was all torn up, I mean he got a carving knife stuck in him, dude!"

"Where'd he go?"

"He chased me but I lost him."

Luke caught Zach's arm, "We gotta tell the cops about this. Come on!"

"Now I know you're crazy."

"We gotta tell about this, they..."

"How'd you reckon that's gonna go little brother? Excuse me there, Mr Sheriff Sir, but we done found some dead bodies. Say what there, boys. Well looky here, the Clayton boys found some dead folks. Our damn feet wouldn't touch the ground. We only gotta fart too loudly and Eastman's looking for a jail key. We say squat."

"It ain't right, them people just lying there like that. *It ain't right!*"

"I know but..."

Mike Woodridge's snarling face slammed up against the driver's side window. Zach recoiled in horror at the grotesque face inches away from him. He started the engine just as the fiend opened the door. Zach sped forward with the unwanted hitchhiker still clinging on, until it lost its grip and bounced off into the trees.

CHAPTER - SIXTEEN

"Tony, he's burning up. We gotta take him to the hospital."

"Look I know. We've been through all that. It just isn't safe."

"Is that all you gonna say?"

Bridget banged her hand on the counter and rounded on him. "For all we know, that boy's dying up there!"

"Think that ain't crossed my mind? Of course I'd like to take him for treatment but..."

"You think he's got it. That's it?"

He looked at his wife, long and hard. "Sure he's got all the symptoms; what if it's just the flu? What if this is some kinda cover up? What if they just write him off?"

"What if we've written him off?"

He walked up to the French windows and looked out at the early morning sunshine, the grass still damp with dew, and then he turned to face Bridget.

"Lenski said this thing could be... may be curable if she caught it early enough. If we got hold of some kinda medicine we could treat him ourselves."

"Where we gonna get something like that from and how the hell would we know how to use it?"

"Peter can help us. I'll ask him."

"He ain't no doctor." She rolled her eyes and tutted loudly. "How's he to know?"

"He's got contacts. That's how."

"Eastman made him take all that Wal-Mart stuff back and even if he still had some medicine we'd need someone who knew what to use."

"He got someone."

"Oh bull. We need a doctor or a nurse, your brother don't know them kinda people."

"Yeah, he does."

He stared at her, his eyes serious and troubled, "and he can get whatever we need."

"How come? I don't believe you. Who'd be dumb enough to get mixed up with him?"

"He's got someone on the inside at the hospital and that's all you need to know."

"Don't give me that 'hush hush' crap; you're talking about my son. I damn well need to know! And you sure as hell are gonna tell me."

"I said no." He paced over to the breakfast bar.

"You expect me to go along with this, then spill or I damn will."

"You wouldn't dare!"

"Right now, you've given me nothing 'cept this crackpot trash. Make some sense!"

"Okay, okay damn it! It's Judy Garcia, she owes him."

"No way! She ain't gonna get involved with him."

"Her brother's been working for us for months; the problem is he ain't got a green card. Peter found out, so every now and again she gets the key to the drugs cabinet and hey what do you know, things go missing."

"I never knew she had a brother."

"Well you ain't supposed to. Who the hell do you think's been building that stone wall for us, eh?"

"So you reckon they'd help us?"

"He's gotta help and she can't say no, in fact she'll tell us what to use and how to use it. I'll go right now and find him."

"Tony, how long can we keep this up? I mean, somebody's gonna find out."

"Look there's no search today because of that bad weather Merka says is coming in.

Conrad will be up and about in a few days. We'll just say he's come back, all done in."

She reached out and caught his hand. "Tony, do this right."

"I'll fix it. Don't worry, it'll be all right." He kissed her and left the house.

****

Frank and his boys had resumed their search, only now the wind had picked up. He watched the tips of the tall pines bending. Looked as if Merka had been right after all; still, they had to get on with the job.

Shortly after first light, Iris had made them a good breakfast and a packed lunch to get on with. Jedrey Bodien had called up to the farm and said the search was off on account of the bad weather; it was too dangerous for Eastman to risk anybody in the hills, except for volunteers. So far only Bodien had turned up. Frank and Kurt were searching one side of the riverbank; Bodien and Larry were searching along the other side.

Frank yawned and stretched, he'd spent a restless night. He just couldn't get Eastman's remarks out of his head. He'd already pushed the notion of his wife being a monster from his mind. But that little seed had stuck with him and grown into gut-gnawing uncertainty, aided by what the man in the jail had said to Kurt up at Hinckle Point.

"Hey Pa, what's with all this wind up around here?"

"It's on account of them meteorites, nothing to get worried about."

"Pa."

"Yes boy?"

"How come no one's turned out to look for Ma and they looking for that Firth kid?"

Frank stopped and looked at his son.

"They ain't looking. The Sheriff done called the search off. It's not safe up here 'cause of the wind. Besides Jedrey ain't exactly no one now is he?"

Frank surveyed the rough ground about them; the odds of somebody sick with no footwear making it this far was pretty unlikely. Yet he had to find her and with weather changing it needed to be fast.

"Hey Pa!"

Kurt's voice brought him back to present.

"Take a look at this."

Frank had missed the light blue shred of cloth fluttering in the wind. He walked forward and took the item from the small bush. It was from Nancy's night-dress, the one he'd bought from Fosters at Christmas time.

"Is it Ma's?"

Frank turned the fragment around in his hands and then gave the boy a triumphant look.

"Yep, it sure is, best give the others a call."

Kurt called across to the others and soon they were joined by his brother and Jedrey.

"You sure this is from Nancy?"

"I got this colour one but she wanted a green one, I thought she'd hate it but she said it reminded her of the sky." He placed the remnant into his pocket. "I'm sure enough."

"Well at least we know she come this far."

Bodien stopped talking; pointing to a small shed a way off.

"Frank, what's that up ahead?"

"That's the old powder shed they used to keep dynamite in when there was a mine here abouts. It's been closed up since ever I can recall."

"I reckon we need to take a look; it's the only shelter till your place."

"Mr Bodien, you reckon we gonna find Ma in there, Sir?"

"Well, we just may there Larry boy, let's take a look."

Bodien led the other three over to the small derelict stone structure. Its door long rotted away, the heavy roof cast an impenetrable blackness within. Tall grass hid the base of the walls and partly obscured the doorway. These last remnants of the once busy mining industry were gradually fading away to nothing.

"Hey Ma you in there?"

Larry ran excitedly towards the doorway and began calling. Bodien called to the boy, as he reached in his daypack for the flashlight. "Hold up there now son, watch for snakes."

The boy disappeared into the gloom only to re-appear almost instantly. A huge smile spread across his face.

"I found her, I done found Ma." With that, he dashed back into the powder shed. Frank felt every fibre in his body tingle; the Lord had returned her to them just as he'd prayed. He felt like shouting for joy and weeping at the same time, then he looked at Bodien. The man's face was a mask of apprehension; suddenly Frank was gripped by a feeling of panic. What if Eastman was right? What if...?

"Larry, wait, wait!"

He shot ahead of the others and crashed into the tiny space. He could make out a figure crouching in the corner of the room. Larry was calling to his mother and as he reached at the figure the glare of the flashlight lit up the figure's face. The hideous features that looked back at them were no longer Nancy Jorgan. The creature caught Larry's arm, sinking its teeth into the soft flesh of the back of his hand. The boy let out an agonised cry of pain and fell against the wall. This nightmare seemed far from content at the paltry mouthful of flesh and reached out to grab him again. Frank sprang forward and pushed the creature back, pulling his son into the outside sunlight.Larry stumbled backwards onto the hard ground, holding his hand in front of his stunned face, the blood soaking his sleeve.

"She bit me Pa, why'd she do that?"

He looked into his son's tearful eyes and saw shocked betrayal staring back at him. What had she done?

"Pa, look up, she's a coming outside!"

Frank looked up and saw Kurt's trembling hand pointing back at the doorway. The apparition was standing just outside of the doorway in the grubby pale blue nightdress, now stained with Larry's blood. Frank gasped, stifling back tears as he saw the sunshine reflect on the wedding ring. Was *this* his wife, his Nancy? Out of the corner of his left eye, he could see Bodien draw his pistol and aim at Nancy.

"Put that thing down Jedrey." Frank pointed his shotgun at the other man.

"Frank, that ain't Nancy no more, that's a killer now!"

"I ain't telling you again."

Bodien slowly lowered his automatic but kept his finger on the trigger then backed away. "Okay, it's your call, what you gonna do next?"

Frank watched as she stalked closer, he would have to act fast; otherwise somebody else could get hurt. The truth was he didn't have a clue. Desperately he tried to work out the next move.

"Jedrey, I need your rope."

****

Eastman was troubled. He drummed his fingers on his desk rhythmically and looked over at Benteen, sitting in front of him.

"How's Kate?"

Benteen pushed the small of his back up against the chair, and widened his eyes looking back at Eastman.

"It was all pretty damn gruesome, buddy. Hell of a thing for her to see, but she's a tough girl. She'll get over it."

"Still no sign of Mike Woodridge?"

"Nope."

"All wiped out, the whole bunch. No sign of any guns being used; Mike would use his last shell to protect his family. We gotta be looking at him being infected."

Benteen flicked through the statement. "Yeah, I reckon so. All the bodies were well chewed. Kate reckoned they'd shut the inside door, but Mike got in through the outside one. What a mess. When can we get some people back up there? We gotta find him."

"Bill says the weather front could last a few days. Gerard, we got too much going on to think about another search party. We still got Conrad and Nancy to find yet."

Benteen nodded and raised his eyebrows.

"Tall order then? Beats me how Bill can tell all that, without the computers?"

"It's only if you want stuff online. He uses all those aerials and such to take the readings. I gotta call him soon, any case. You can ask, if you want."

"I guess it ain't no rocket science. What you make of this search and Tony Firth?"

"I was gonna ask you what you made of it, since you were up there with him?"

Benteen shifted in his chair. "A day back and he's banging my door down to look for his kid. Yesterday and he's more taken by some guy that 'might' have been there. Now today, we ain't seen his hide for jack. That's some real odd dealings."

"He's been sort of weird since the health center; reckon I'll pay him a visit later?"

Benteen punched the air. "I'd have loved to seen his brother's face when he took all that crap back to Wal-Mart."

"Though I'd have preferred it better if we'd had to take it back from him."

Eastman's radio set burst into life. "Bill Merka calling Brad Eastman. Over."

"Yeah, Eastman here. Your ears gotta be on fire, I was just about to call you. Over."

The voice on the other side of the call sounded agitated.

"Brad, I got activity up at Murray Ridge, there's a bunch of guys putting up some kinda equipment. Over."

Eastman sat forward in his seat and stared at the radio set intently. "What kinda equipment Bill. Over?"

"Can't tell. It could be some type of radio mast, not sure. Over."

"Okay Bill, keep an eye on them, I'll send Gerard and some of the guys up there. Out."

Eastman replaced the handset and looked at Benteen. "Take some boys up with you, have a look what those bozos are up to. Be real careful, they could get hostile."

"They want hostile," Benteen's lips curled in a sneer, "I'll give 'em damn hostile. Now where's Sarge and his rocket launchers when you need him, hey?"

"Oh, he's up there all right."

"How come? I thought you'd pulled the plug on any searches, cause of the weather?"

"I have, but Sarge is on a 'Sarge mission' looking for Conrad. He's got a theory."

"Sarge on a mission with a theory; that ain't never a good thing."

"Never mind all that. I don't want any fire fights up there. You gonna have civilians with you. Take care."

"You know me, Boss." He got to his feet and grinned. "The soul of tact."

Eastman looked back at him, open mouthed, then pointed to the door. "Vamoose!"

****

Anne Lenski was sitting in her office with Vinnie and Leona Arcado; the look of worry on their faces cut her to the bone. She detested this aspect of her job; the anguish mixed in with that little slice of hope was a heart-rending cocktail. Before calling them to discuss Tony, she'd wracked her brains on what to say. However, with them sat directly in front of her, she found it near impossible even to find the opening line.

"I ran tests on Tony," she began. "I'm afraid they all came back positive ..."

"But that's good right? Positive is always good, right Doc?"

"No, Vinnie, no. In this kinda thing, she means it's bad."

"Your wife's right, in this case it means Tony is infected with the virus."

Anne saw the awful recognition dawn on Vinnie Arcado's face as he finally grasped the implications. His eyes shot open wide and his breathing became heavier as he placed his hand over his mouth. Anne desperately tried to recount the response she'd rehearsed for this part of the dialogue however, her mind was blank. She looked at Leona, the woman's eyes had welled up with tears but she was putting on a brave face.

"Doctor, what are his chances?"

"Well Mrs Arcado, I'm giving him broad spectrums of shots. Antibiotics aren't a good treatment for a virus. I just don't have anything else."

Anne doubted even with the resources of a hospital, there was any hope of redressing the condition. The X-ray of the boy's internal organs had shown severe damage. This could only mean that they were in the process of liquefying. This was beyond repair, she couldn't hazard a guess but the boy didn't have long.

"So what, you just gonna give up on him?"

Vinnie Arcado leant angrily over the desk to Anne.

"Can't you try something else?"

"There's no question of giving up. I'll try everything on the shelf and I'll do everything I can. But he's just one very ill boy."

Vinnie sat back down with a heavy thump and rubbed the tears from his eyes. Leona reached over and tightly held his hand. It amazed Anne at just how strong this woman was.

"Are you sure Tony's got this infection? I don't understand; he wasn't bitten. I thought that was how you caught it?"

"No. It only has to get into the bloodstream for someone to become infected. A bite seems the most common way but contact with any body fluid is enough. I'm so sorry, there's no question. *He is infected.*"

"I know he's ill but you can cure it, right?"

"I'll try my best."

She hoped she'd concealed her fears well enough from him to take some tiny speck of optimism.

"Can we see him?"

"Yes of course, but we've had to move him to the isolation section, we can't risk infection. I'll fix you both with protective clothing. I won't be long."

She was glad of the break to leave the room and she stepped into the corridor. As luck would have it, Elle-May was coming towards her.

"Jeez honey, you look as if you just got outta the ring. You okay?"

"I feel like it too. I just told Tony's Mom and Dad he's got the virus. What I didn't tell them was that he's dying and I don't have a damn clue how to stop it."

"You can only do the best you can for him. That's only thing anybody can do."

She caught Anne's arm.

"Yeah, so I keep telling myself, only I don't think it's going to be enough? Elle-May, can you find two suits for Tony's parents? They want to see him."

"Sure thing, Norris will go dig some up for you. You need anything else?"

"Has Jill turned up yet?"

Anne had not seen Jill Paxmore for days, she'd tried to contact her using the CB radio but Jill and Al had gone to stay with her brother Edge Biggs, in town without the radio. Anne had meant to call around but there'd been no chance. Now she was concerned.

"No, she should've been here this morning. Why don't you get someone to call over?"

"Elle-May your talent is wasted here. Can you sit with Tony's folks while I call Brad?"

"Yeah sure, what about the suits though?"

"I won't be that long."

Elle-May nodded and Anne left for the reception area. Within a few short moments she'd rounded the corner and sat down at the desk, operating the radio set. She pressed the handset call button and was through to Clara.

"Dr Lenski calling Sheriff Eastman. Over."

"Clara here, go ahead Doctor. Over."

"Can you ask Brad to send someone over to Jill Paxmore's brother's place. Over?"

"Sorry Brad's off site. How can I help? Over."

"She hasn't turned up for work. In fact, no one's seen her or Al for a few days. Over."

"Yeah, that's kinda funny, Edge was supposed to be on patrol last night and he didn't show. No one's seen Al either in a while. Over."

"I'd appreciate if you could look into it for me Clara. Over."

"No problem, I'll try send someone as soon as I can. Is there anything else? Over."

"No thanks. Call me when you can. Out."

****

Bridget looked in amazement at the collection of medicines on the living room table. Tony had brought everything from simple pain-killers to antibiotics. The medicines were grouped into categories with a set of typed instructions on how to use each of them. She shook her head in bewilderment. Tony would be the one to use these, it was difficult enough for to manage her vitamin supplements. She looked at her husband as he came back into the room.

"You figured out how to use any of this?"

"I gave him some of the pain-killers and started the other stuff."

He looked at his Seiko watch. "We gotta dose him up very four hours. We gotta be on the ball with this."

"Think any of this is gonna work Tony?"

"It's gotta work." He walked to the drinks cabinet and poured himself a large brandy. "Any news from outside?"

"No, only they're still looking for Nancy Jorgan but..."

"How come they're looking for her and ain't looking for Conrad?"

"What? *Cause he's upstairs* or you forgotten, jeez."

"I ain't stupid," he rounded on her. "I know that, but *they* don't do they?"

Bridget came right up to Firth's face. "That so, well maybe you ought to be up there looking for our boy!"

"Yeah well, you don't have to be up there to be up there if you take my meaning?" He gave her a sly wink as he took a large sip of brandy.

She pointed to the medical supplies. "What he ask for this lot? What's he want from us?"

"Nothing. He's my brother."

"Yeah, that's what worries me. He don't do anything for *nothing*; he's gonna want something."

"Look, he..."

Firth was cut short by the sudden knocking at the front door. Bridget moved swiftly to the window and peeked through the net curtains.

"Who the hell's that?" hissed Firth.

She held her finger to her lips and bid him silence. "Well it sure ain't the AVON lady. It's Brad Eastman!"

"What!"

She sprang back from the window. "What we gonna do?"

Firth jumped up from his seat and blew loudly into his cupped hands.

"He's come about the meeting. Quick, get all that crap hidden away."

"Are you nuts? Just don't answer the door!"

"Car's still out front, he may have seen you at the window. We can't risk it. Take that into the other room. Damn it!"

This was no time to argue; Bridget scooped the medication up in the table-cloth and dashed into the other room. Firth steadied himself, walked to the door and opened it. Eastman was standing on the doorstep, with a smile.

"What took you so long; you think I was the repo guy or something?"

"Sorry I must have been dozing."

"I wiped my feet, Tony." Eastman gestured towards the hallway.

"Oh yeah, sorry." Firth moved aside and showed the other man into the hallway. He led Eastman into the living room and frantically scanned the area for anything incriminating left behind but he could see nothing out of place. Firth sat in his armchair and Eastman sat on the sofa and placed his hat on the small coffee table.

"You come about the meeting?"

"Well, that also, but I wanted to see if you were all right after the search yesterday?"

"All right? Sure I'm all right. My town's falling to bits and my boy is still missing. Everything's just dandy."

"I'm sorry about calling the search off." Eastman shifted awkwardly on the sofa, "but I gotta think about the search teams."

"Frank's up there looking for Nancy, maybe I should go look for Conrad?"

Eastman averted his gaze then looked directly at Firth.

"Frank found Nancy. She took a chunk outta Larry."

"Oh my God! She's, she's..."

"Yep. And so is Larry now."

"Poor Frank, what lousy luck."

"That's not all. Kate found what was left of the Woodridges all over their kitchen earlier."

Firth held his head in his hands. "What the hell did we deserve to have all this happen?"

"Mike Woodridge's gone missing so I put an APB on him. Looks like he may have 'turned.' I don't think we can take chances anymore. Anybody that's infected has gotta be brought in for treatment."

"You want 'people bonfires' like a year back Brad?"

"Let's hope it never gets that bad, but I'll do whatever it takes to keep us safe. I'd best be off, I gotta lot to do."

Firth suddenly caught sight of a small pack of tablets just behind Eastman's left boot as the man rose to leave.

"You okay there Tony? You look a bit odd."

Firth recovered his self-control and caught Eastman's arm and led him to the door, away from the tablets.

"I'm sorry Brad; it's all been a dreadful shock for me. I'll see you at the meeting."

He ushered Eastman outside and still smiling closed the door. That had been too close. If they wanted to keep Conrad safe they'd both have to be more careful. He reached down and picked up the box and held it firmly with both hands.

Bridget opened the kitchen door and walked into the living room.

"Has he gone?"

"Yeah, put these away."

He tossed the box at her.

"We may not be that lucky again."

"God, what we gonna do about Conrad?"

Firth poured himself another brandy and took a set of small keys from the French *bureau* and turned to Bridget.

"Now on, we keep his door locked."

****

Eastman was a few blocks from the station house. He was using the walk to sift through his thoughts. Murray Ridge had drawn a big fat blank. By the time Benteen had arrived whoever had been there had cleared off. Apart from a few boot prints and tyre tracks, he'd found nothing. The trip to Firth's home had also been largely fruitless. Even so, Eastman was convinced the man was behaving strangely. Maybe the guy was just cracking under the pressure or maybe Eastman was just reading too much into the situation.

Turning onto Jenkins Street, Eastman was struck by the recent home improvements people had made on this row of semis. The once neatly manicured lawns had all been replaced with a series of ugly, makeshift barricades. Some householders had placed rails or mesh around the windows. The whole street resembled a town under siege.

The other stark thing he noted was that there were no kids about: even the front yards and drives were devoid of toys. Travelling past Keegan Avenue, he could see one of the Jeep patrols' two four-by-fours, crammed with armed men. A necessary evil he mused, shaking his head as he pulled up outside the station house.

Walking out to meet him was the unmistakable figure of Sarge. With his pack on his back and from his general appearance, it looked as though he'd just come back from the hills.

"Sheriff, I heard about Frank and the Woodridges – a real shame."

Eastman bowed his head.

"I know you're up to your eyes in it, but we've got to talk right now."

Eastman groaned inwardly, he really was not in the frame of mind to listen to anybody at the moment, least of all Sarge. But then again, if Sarge thought something was important, then it probably was.

"Sarge I got a meeting in…" he looked at his watch, "…just over forty minutes time. Whatever it is make it quick?"

"Affirmative. I found some tracks up at the murder scene. They were Conrad's prints. I followed them about two clicks leading into the hills, then he did a U-turn and headed back to town. I lost the scent by that marsh ground up the top of town. I'm damn certain he made it back here, someplace."

"There's nothing up there other than that deserted brick works."

He stopped as an idea flashed into his head. "It's also near his home."

"Say again?"

"About half a mile from the brick works is Tony Firth's house. Did you cover any ground the other side of the marsh?"

"I started, but the area's too big for one man and besides I got something else."

"It'll have to wait; I'd better get a search ready and…"

"You gonna want to see this and in any case, you got about two hours of light, max."

Sarge was right; by the time he got a search team together it would be too dark to follow the tracks. Years of sand and brick had reduced the area to dust – if they were to find any prints they'd need good light to do it. A thought nagged at the corner of his mind Firth had almost fallen over himself to get him out of that door. Could it be…?

"Sheriff, know what this is?"

In the palm of his hand, Sarge held a spent M16 case.

"Wanna see some more?"

Sarge held up a small grocery bag up and shook it with a distinct metal jingling sound. Eastman took the bag from him. The bag was full of shiny brass M16 cases.

"Where'd you get these from?"

"Off the track from the air base at the bottom of the ravine. See the dents and scratches on some? It means they were fired a-ways up, then ejected on to the rocks below. I found the place just above the shell cases. I think we found us an execution site!"

Eastman watched the expression on the other man's face; it was deadly serious. "What makes you think that?"

"I seen this kinda thing before. To hide the evidence they need to clear the killing area; everything has to be sanitised. Sometimes they use chemicals to dissolve the blood. This place stank of chemicals."

"Sarge, we need to be real sure about this, you understand?"

"Roger that. I can take you to the exact spot."

"Tomorrow I want you to help with the search around the brick works. Then you can show me that site, you okay with that?"

"Yeah, just give me the nod." Sarge handed Eastman the bag and started home.Eastman watched as he turned the corner and then dragged his own weary frame up the steps. This was going to be a darn long night.

****

Judge Carmille brought the meeting to order with the sharp bang from his gavel. This was a closed meeting, on the strictest need-to-know basis. The meeting would in all probability cover matters not suitable for the public. As such, only a select few had been invited to contribute. Carmille had elected himself to preside over the gathering, with Tony Firth as the civic leader. Sheriff Eastman, Anne Lenski and Ron Virdon were the heads of the town's emergency services and Benny Arnold was head of the Commerce Committee.

"I call this meeting to order. As a closed meeting, nothing leaves this room unless I say so. Tony, is there anything you'd like to say to kick this session off?"

"Thank you Judge. The town is in a tight spot and our people are looking to us to pull them out. We've made some tough calls and looks to me, as we gonna make a sight more before we're done. The only way we gonna get through this is by strong leadership. But for that I need your backing. We each gonna have our say on this, but I'd like to start with Brad."

He pointed to Eastman.

"Well, we're all aware of the recent tragedies, so I don't need to go over them, but as a result of this, I'm calling in everybody living outside town. I think it's a safe move, it may not be popular, but it's what we need."

The other members of the group murmured their approval; now was the time to circle the wagons. Virdon cast his gaze at Firth; they had a strained relationship to say the least. It was widely regarded that since Virdon had become the Fire Chief some three years ago, he'd turned the department into a professional organisation. He'd increased the size and capability and for a time, it had been up with the best in the area. Then Firth had been elected Mayor and things had changed overnight. He'd slashed the budget and made half the fire fighters part-timers. He'd maintained that Armstrong did not require such a large Fire Department. But Virdon knew it ran deeper than that.

"When do you suggest starting that up?"

Eastman looked at Firth. "As soon as. I'd also like to double the patrols, I know it's not good for armed people in town, but we got to be ready. In view of those tracks Sarge found, I want to set up a search of that location first thing tomorrow."

"I appreciate that Brad just don't forget about that front coming in. I don't want anybody at risk looking for my boy?"

"Bill was concerned about operating in the hills; I don't think we're gonna get problems this far down. But I'll call it off if we do. I think this is the best chance we've got of finding your boy. Okay, now is there anything you want to know concerning my side?"

Ron Virdon voiced his unease.

"Brad, I heard a lot of people talk about 'outsiders' being mixed up in all this. What you got on that?"

Eastman looked at Carmille who nodded.

"We've strong evidence that's the case. People and vehicles, even a helicopter and drones have been seen about. What we don't know is what they want."

"Do you reckon they're hostile to us?"

"So far Ron, they've given us no cause for any concern in that direction."

Eastman stopped and looked at the Judge who again nodded. "But we need to treat them with suspicion."

"Brad, I know it's not my turn, I've never been to a meeting like this. If the town is in danger shouldn't we think of moving out?"

"What the hell for? It's *our* town – we don't run. Look, what if this is not just us? What if it's all over? Right now we got a good base to defend, if need be. Now, if this is everywhere, then I don't want to get caught out there with our people in the open."

"I'm with you on that, Brad," Virdon cautioned, looking at Firth. "It's darn well over a hundred miles to Burnsville. That's a long way to go, especially if we don't know what's out there."

"I think that's all settled. We all gonna stay right here. But we do need some kinda evacuation plan."

"I've already drawn one up Tony. If the time comes, I'll send out small parties before we go committing the whole town."

Firth nodded his agreement then indicated Dr Lenski to speak.

"There's not a lot I can add to what I've already said. This virus is not airborne, so you can't catch it like the common cold. You have to have contact with the victim and even then, it's only through bodily fluid that you become infected. However, when you or someone you know contracts this virus, you must seek medical assistance immediately. You can't treat it with aspirin and it won't go away. The longer you leave it the worse it will get. We're doing our best but we need the town to cooperate."

The small group sat in thoughtful silence each avoiding the others eyes, then Carmille pointed his gavel at the Fire Chief and tipped his head forward. Virdon was an impressively built man, his handsome face, fair hair and blue eyes gave him a film star look. Some time ago he'd been a quarter-back for the *Burnsville Bears*. He'd had a riot of a time but never really taken any of it seriously. The girls, the parties and the lifestyle had just been fun. All that had changed when J.J. Eastman died. J.J. had lived the life a little too hard; it had been like a drug, he just hadn't been able to get enough.

J.J.'s death had acted like a wakeup call; Virdon had decided that he needed something else. When he got back to Armstrong his father was madder than hell. He'd always wanted his boy to be a big star. It had taken a while for him to come around but eventually he'd even helped him apply to the Fire Department.

"Since the start of this hullabaloo we've had less callouts than I can remember. Not saying that's a bad thing, but we're not exactly stretched."

He shot a fleeting glance at Firth.

"Since my guys are nearly all part time now, I got more trouble in them joining Brad's little outfit. But my guys know their duty and we're ready for anything that comes our way."

"That's reassuring, but I think Brad's got enough people for the time being."

Firth nodded towards Benny Arnold.

"We asked Benny along because he represents the store holders; he's got an eye on the supplies we got here in town. So Benny how we doing?"

Benny loudly cleared his throat. "I just come from a Commerce meeting as it happens. Most of us agreed to keep the price of things at the current cost. We kinda thought it would help calm things down a mite. We also think rationing things is a good idea."

"So no more repeats of the other day then I hope eh, Mayor?"

Firth rose out of his seat, shoulders bowed; a humbled man. "Ron, everybody, I can't begin to say how sorry I am about all that. What that clown did was inexcusable and I gotta tell you all, I'm ashamed of him and I told him so. But what's done is done. Greed got the better of him. Let it be a lesson to all of us. Now if we spend our time just pecking at each other, we ain't gonna get a whole lot done."

"Here, here. Now, no more back-biting, and that comes from me! Armstrong is looking to us."

Carmille looked around the group with a look that would sour milk, daring them to disagree. "Benny back to you. What's the situation?"

Benny Arnold timidly loosened his tie and gave a weak smile.

"Um, well, regarding foodstuffs we got about enough to last a month, maybe more? But of course, the perishables only gonna keep to their sell by dates. Now we got farms out there that supply us in any case, but if we bring those folks in, then who's gonna tend the produce?"

Eastman rapped his finger on the table-top. "Good point. We'd have to provide an escort for that. What about non food stuffs?"

"I don't think there's a plank of wood left in the whole town. It's the same for most of the building bits and pieces. We just gotta keep things limited from now on."

"Okay, I appreciate everyone's efforts on this. Now Tony's got his work cut out putting some type of plan together. If no one's got anything to add, I'm calling time."

With that Carmille brought the meeting to an end. The group headed for the exit but Eastman stopped Firth.

"Tony I got some news for you about Conrad."

Firth gave him a blank stare. "Yeah, what is it?"

"Those prints Sarge found are headed towards the marsh area near the brick works. We're pretty sure they're Conrad's."

"How come? I mean I thought we were looking at the hill?"

"Looks like he may – and I gotta stress 'may' – have doubled back and tried for home. I'm calling a search of that whole location first thing."

"Well... I... what... I mean what makes you so sure?"

"Sarge followed them from the murder site and..."

"Hold on there, *Sarge*?"

"Yeah I know, but it's worth a try."

"I think it's gonna waste our time, when we could be doing real searching and..."

Mitch Chattman suddenly appeared in front of the two men.

"Brad, I got some bad news." He paused and gave Firth an awkward glance. Eastman caught the brief look. "Tony, maybe you should sit this one out, eh?"

Firth gave Eastman a puzzled expression. "What?"

"It could be Conrad, you'd better..."

"No, Brad it's nothing to do with him. I just come back from Edge's place."

The group of people had now gathered by the doorway, awaiting Chattman's news. From the grim look on his face, it was plain something had happened. Anne Lenski moved to stand next to Eastman, eager to learn where her nurse had been the past few days. When Eastman spoke, his tone was grave. "What you got then, Mitch?"

"They've both been murdered, torn apart more like."

He looked at Anne, "Sorry Doc."

"You said Jill and Edge, what about Al?"

"No sign of him Brad. We searched all around. Nothing. I left Max in charge and we sent for Jack Larson."

"When did all this go down?"

"About ten minutes ago but..."

"*Ten minutes* and now you're telling me." Eastman glared at Chattman.

"I knew you had the meeting, besides we couldn't raise you on the radio."

Eastman checked his radio. "Damn! Knocked it off. Come on, we gotta find Al, while there's some light left." He walked towards the door.

"Same as Mike Woodridge."

Ron shook his head. "Why'd they kill their own, like that?"

Eastman halted and turned back at the group. "It's like Anne just said. People think this thing is like a cold; it'll just go away. They don't want to hand over their folks, 'cause they're too damn scared. By then it's too late. We gotta make people hand them over."

"What would you do if it were one of your family?" Anne looked deep into his eyes.

"I don't have any family." With that, he strode out of the room.

CHAPTER - SEVENTEEN

"No! Although I detest that little creep, you can forget me issuing a search warrant on Sarge's say-so. The man has a bruised brain for God's sake!"

"He was an Army scout in Syria; he followed the tracks to a mile of Firth's house. I think that Conrad could be in the area and I'd like to search the house..."

"Forget it Brad. We already did that. Those tracks are days old by now, it'd be a waste of time."

Eastman felt like a school-boy in Judge Carmille's study. He'd been there on many occasions but the grand wooden interior still filled him with awe. The whole room emanated history. The shelves were stacked with law books as old as the town. But Eastman was determined to have his say.

"It's the best lead we've had so far. I can't see the harm in searching that house to make sure."

"You can't see the harm in searching the Mayor's house? The people of this town need to see that they have strong leadership or they're gonna start falling apart. You do a search right now and morale is out the door. Firth is the Mayor damn it!"

"All I can see is upholding the law not some PR stunt."

Carmille shot to his feet, his face a dark shade of purple.

"Don't you dare come into this room and tell me about the law! I was serving the law while you were in short pants. There's gonna be no more about searching Tony Firth's house or so help me' I'll damn well suspend you!"

Eastman rose silently from his seat and left the room. It wasn't that he felt subdued, he just felt enormous disappointment. His hero the great Judge Carmille had lost all sense of the true meaning of the law. The law was to be upheld at all costs, with no favouritism or discrimination. He walked out from the court house and stepped into the cool night air. It seemed to him it wasn't just the creatures in Armstrong that were rotten. He was going home to take a long hot shower.

****

The rain poured down onto Parish Road, adding further gloom to the murky night. The windshield wipers chased across the glass, back and forth like the hands of a demented clock. The headlights barely pierced the black void of the night as the blue Dodge four-by-four charged on. A constant stream of Freddy Mercury hits belted out from the CD as Luke Clayton drove the truck at break-neck speed. At last Zach could take it no longer.

"Luke. Turn that freaking thing down!"

"Huh?"

"I said turn it down!"

Luke turned his head to look at his brother. "Say what? I can't hear you."

"Watch the damn road!" Zach angrily jabbed his finger at the windshield.

"Yeah, yeah. No need to shout."

His thumb eased down the volume button on the steering wheel.

"If this arrives with so much as a scratch on it, then... just take it easy will you?"

"Sure, I know that. We use this road all the time. What do you take me for?"

Zach rolled his eyes skywards and shook his head. Luke was right, the road was well known to them and that was the reason he'd allowed his brother to drive. The road was hardly used by anyone now, since they'd built the new one. Why mess with something that already works? They were nearing the intersection where they needed to turn off and just a few miles further, they could hand the vehicle over.

"Zach, am I gonna meet this guy, am I?"

"Yeah and you'll never guess who he is."

"Aw, come on tell me who?"

Luke had never met the guy who they sold the cars to. Zach had always carried out this part of the operation himself. Luke's imagination had run wild over the years, with everyone from the Mafia to Brad Eastman. But it was probably just dumb old Peter Firth.

"Nope. You just gonna have to see."

"Reckon he gonna have the money for this baby?"

"Well duh. Why else you think we're meeting with him?"

Luke flicked up the volume on the radio in excitement and the sound boomed out. He started flinging his head wildly to the music. His brother's hand flew at the radio and hit the eject button, throwing the disk into Luke's lap.

"You gonna scratch the CD, man!"

Luke fumbled with the disk as he rounded the bend.

"Sorry, I... Hey, watch the road!"

The cab of the four-by-four was flooded by a blinding light. Zach threw his hands in front of himself and Luke screeched to a halt. Just a few yards ahead, Zach could make out a line of vehicles. Men with torches were running towards them, shouting and yelling. "What in hell's going on Zach?"

"Get us outta here; it's a God damn road-block. Move!"

Luke reversed a short distance then spun the Dodge around facing the other direction, showering the pursuers in clouds of loose rocks. Then all hell was let loose. The distinctive chatter of M16's on three-round bursts, shattered the night air.

"Crazy son of a... they're shooting at us! Drive, brother. Drive!"

Luke put his foot down as bullets ripped into the rear of the vehicle. Suddenly, the rear window disintegrated; jagged fragments of glass peppered the interior.

"Jeez, Eastman's got no cause to do this."

"It ain't him, they're soldiers!"

Receding into the distance, Zach could see soldiers with respirators and weapons chasing after them, stopping to shoot at them intermittently. Worse still, now he could see several sets of high-energy headlights joining the hunt; explosions erupted around the speeding car.

"What the hell's up with these people? They're shooting freaking bombs at us!"

"I don't rightly know! But whatever it is, they're sure mad as hell!"

Zach could see the lead vehicle had a roof-mounted grenade launcher – it would only be a matter of time before it hit them. If they could just out run them, then Luke could lose them in the woods. Dozens of tracks ran through there. These army guys wouldn't have a clue. They just needed a bit of luck. Then one of the 40mm grenades hit its mark, tearing the left rear wheel off and flipping the four-by-four. The vehicle rolled over and over in a grinding, sparking lightshow before coming to a rest on its side in a gully. With the rain and wind now abated, the only sound that could be heard was the sound of the approaching military vehicles, speeding towards the smouldering wreck.

****

Eastman watched as the rain ran down his office window. It was just after eight in the morning and it had rained all night. Downhearted, he knew there was no chance of finding any tracks.

"I guess we're screwed now eh, Boss? Even without all this rain that wind last night just about blown any tracks half way to Canada."

"Gerard, I felt sure we were onto something with these tracks. I could always search Firth's place and..."

"That *is* a joke right? The Judge would have your hide. You know that yeah?"

Benteen was right of course, after last night's 'friendly' advice, any idea of a house search was out of the question. From now on they had to play at happy families.

"We can't do much today out of town with this rain, but I reckon we'd best up the man-power on Al's search."

"Sure, I'll get some more guys on it. Brad, if he's *changed* and all that, some of the boys are getting edgy. I got to thinking, well...what do we do?"

"We've known Al for a long time, but I'm not taking chances. If you've cause to, then take him down."

Benteen nodded silently then got up to leave as they heard a loud tapping on the door. Benteen opened the door; it was Anne Lenski.

"A bit early for a social call Doc?"

Benteen smiled at her, ushering her in before leaving the room. She looked drained, as if she hadn't slept all night. Eastman offered her a chair and poured two coffees.

"You all right Anne?"

She sat down and sighed deeply. "I don't know. I've lost more people here in two days than I lost in the war. I spent half the night trying to figure this damn bug out."

Eastman scratched the back of his head, slowly bringing his hand to rest on his jaw. "I'm sorry about your girls. I got people out looking for Al. You gonna find a way to treat this thing. Don't get down."

"Brad I'm sick of telling people the same thing, 'I'll do the best I can' then moving the infected into isolation. Infected! What do you call them – 'dead 'eds?"

He knew just how she felt. They were stumbling about in the dark looking for answers and all the time people were dying. There had to be some way forward. Eastman stood up.

"Come on. Let's go see a man about a bug."

****

"Look, if you want my help and I guess you do, then you got to work with me on this."

Eastman viewed the man through the cell bars with deep mistrust and yet...

"Okay, what do you need from me?"

"Well, apart from the evil dead chomping through half your town and the comms black out, notice anything else that's out of the ordinary?"

"Explain."

If this guy wanted information, Eastman would make him work for it.

"Any strangers, any building works. Anything just... *out of the ordinary.*"

"Anne and me caught two of those things a day or so back. We locked them in a barn. When we went back for them, someone had let them out from the *outside.* There were military tracks all about."

"Military? Anything else?"

Anne looked at Eastman. "Brad, tell him about the chopper and the four-by-four."

Eastman began slowly, carefully observing the other man for any reaction.

"While we were up at Ben's barn we saw a blacked out helicopter. This thing had more cameras than a Japanese tourist. As soon as we eyeballed him, he just took off."

"And..."

"Some folk seen that and a black four-by-four with no plates buzzing about town. The car just about mowed some kids down. And there've been sightings of small drones thereabouts. We also found a whole bunch of spent cases at various sites, M16 and 9mil."

Taylor sat bolt upright on his bed. Eastman had struck a nerve; he could almost see the cogs turning in Taylor's head. But it was Anne who spoke out.

"Looks like you've seen a ghost Mr Taylor. Anything wrong?"

"That's quite a grocery list. If you two are right, then you got more trouble than some homicidal bone bags."

"You ain't going nowhere until I hear something I can act on."

"You're not going to believe a word."

"Maybe, but you're staying right there until I do."

*

Taylor had breached the ZerTon perimeter with experienced ease, dodging the K9 teams and foot patrols. Now he was in the main building, he needed to find Aaron Lenox fast. Looking about the plain hallway he couldn't detect any security systems. According to the info, Lenox's office was around the next corner. Taylor rounded the corner and found himself outside Dr Lenox's office.

Taylor cautiously tapped the door. Seconds later a desperate looking man ushered him into the room. Taylor looked at the man in front of him. The guy was a mess. It wasn't his appearance or dress; he was smartly turned out in a suit and tie: it was his eyes. Taylor knew this look all too well from people who'd suffered trauma. This man had been through the mill.

"You Lenox?"

"Are you Taylor?" The man countered nervously.

"Yeah, I'm Taylor. I need you to show me where the info's kept."

"Ah, the wonder cure you mean. NB33. You know, I've had days to think about what I should do about this. And..."

"I don't have time for a speech. Just show me what I need."

Taylor had come across informants like him on operations. They were prepared to sell their own out, but they often had the need for some kinda self-vindication. He hadn't time for long speeches.

Lenox continued. "No. Do you know why? Because it doesn't work. It's totally useless. There, what you make of that?" The man gave a look of satisfaction.

"Oh, I get it. You want more money. You can sort the price tag out later."

"It's not about the money. NB33 is not just a failure, it's dangerous."

"I don't think that's up to you. Now if..."

Lenox pulled up a chair and sat down heavily in a state of exhaustion. He buried his face in his hands massaging his temples with his fingertips. Against his better judgement, Taylor decided to let the man continue.

"Do you know what we were working on here? The cure for diabetes. Imagine how many diabetics out there don't want to be diabetic? When we used NB33 for the first time it worked. The diabetes had been destroyed and then something went wrong. Somehow the medication attacked the infected cells and altered them. Then we noticed that some of the test subjects started to fall ill. Within days, they died. Well, perhaps not exactly died. The first one got up and attacked some of the medical people. Within days the same happened to the victims."

"Why not help them? They should have gone to hospital."

"Hospital? Have you seen them? Would you like to see them Mr Taylor?"

Lenox's voice began to take on a strange edge that unsettled Taylor. But he thought if people needed help then he needed to get them out of this madhouse.

"I want you to take me to these people right now."

****

Standing before a locked door in a dimly lit basement, Lenox slowly pulled down the metal bolt. Both Taylor and Lenox stepped into the darkened room. The stench of decay caused him to put his hand to his face. It was the smell of death. Then he heard the groans and moans of people.

"Turn the God-damned light on!" Taylor ordered.

Strip lights erupted into life across a large hall. At the far side of the hall were animal cages. Rows of deathly grey faces stared into space with colourless eyes. Dried blood and other stains covered their clothes. Most of them seemed to be wearing hospital gowns but a few were dressed in ordinary clothing. The only people he'd ever seen in this state were dead ones. What had happed to these people? Taylor spun around and grabbed Lenox by his lapels.

"What the hell have you done to these people?"

"You still want to take these creatures to hospital? What do you think would happen if I let them out?"

"They need help! Why are they in this state?"

"The government partly funded this establishment, what do you think would happen if they could see this?"

As Lenox walked closer to the caged creatures, the moans and groans started to turn into wails like the screeching of demented souls. Taylor could see the creatures were becoming aggressive as they beat themselves against the bars. But Lenox went even closer.

"Lenox, you're freaking them out. Come away you fool!"

Taylor had the feeling that this was not going down well and he caught the other man's arm. But Lenox pulled free and went ever closer to the cage, producing a small key card from his pocket.

"You wanted to let them out. I should have months ago but it's not too late!"

There was a certain tone in his voice that went beyond hysteria. Lenox unlocked the padlock on the cage. With inhuman howls the creatures tore into him. Biting and tearing, gauging handfuls of flesh until he hit the concrete floor with a lifeless soggy thud, like a wet bath sponge thrown at a wall. The creatures continued their fearful attack and more of them began to leave the holding pen. In front of Taylor's horrified eyes, dozens of them ripped and pulled at the lifeless body, until all that remained was a bloodied mess.

He'd seen many things during his military service, some which he still had to come to terms with, but he'd never seen someone eaten alive. Whatever the hell was wrong with these 'people' he wanted out. For the moment they seemed almost oblivious to Taylor. Taking advantage, he started to back away moving to the door. Then he noted the door could only be opened from the outside. He was trapped. Suddenly one of the creatures looked up at Taylor and let out a piercing shriek. This attracted the attention of several others and they started to lumber forwards with outstretched decaying hands and snapping jaws.

Then with a sudden force the door hit him across the back; there were voices and a flurry of activity. Security guards burst into the hall. Taylor took full advantage of the timely distraction and brushed past the guards and ran into the corridor. As he escaped he heard a short burst of sporadic gunfire followed by screams of fear and pain.

****

"That's one hell of a yarn Taylor."

Eastman paused briefly.

"You mentioned there were things worse than those creatures. What exactly?"

"At the height of the Ebola outbreak, the British devised a tactic to cut the spread. They got such a small island; you only gotta sneeze to land in the next county. It was brutal but effective and it worked like a kinda 'scorched earth' policy. They got it under control a damn sight sooner than anybody else."

"Yeah, we know all that, but this isn't England..."

"Don't tell me you think the good old US of A hasn't got something similar. Especially you Doc."

"What's he talking about, Anne?"

"Come on now, as an army medic you of all people should be aware of *Bushfire*."

"What makes you think I've anything to do with the Army Mr Taylor?"

"I saw your key ring. 477. The 477 was a MASH unit in Syria. Why don't you tell him about *Bushfire*? He likes good stories."

"Anne if you know something about..."

"I don't know anything about this. I'm in the dark just like you."

"What the hell is *Bushfire*?"

"It's nothing it's... its just theoretical."

"Anne?"

"It was just some crazy plan to burn out any type of contagion. Thank God they saw sense and shelved it as being too extreme."

"When you say 'burn' you mean...?"

"She means fuel air bombs. It's a thermobaric weapon."

"A what?"

"It uses the very oxygen to burn you to a crisp. The most powerful non-nuke we got. Reassuring isn't it?"

"Oh bull! Goddamn rubbish."

"You both forgotten about Mercy Creek? Plane crash, high winds. Heat so bad they had to send in special fire units. The whole town burned down. Now whatever they were pumping on that town, sure as hell was not CO^2."

"Taylor, you got rocks in your head."

Taylor landed a savage kick at his bed. "What is the damn point of me telling all this, if all you do is stick your fingers in your ears and shout *I'm not listening?*"

"Because all you do is give me conspiracies and fantastic tales. You're like Emmett on a bad day. You give me nothing concrete."

"You don't believe me?"

"No. Not everything. How can I?"

"Blood test."

Eastman and Anne exchanged confused glances.

"Yeah, what about it?"

"I'm not saying one more damn word until she does a blood test."

Taylor sat down and folded his arms like a petulant child.

"And what will that prove Mr Taylor?"

"For God's sake don't humour the guy."

"It'll prove that I'm telling the truth. Then you Clint – freaking – Eastwood can let me the hell out this madhouse!"

"Brad, maybe we should..."

Eastman looked at her in disbelief. "You gotta be kidding me, right?"

"I know it sounds crazy but what have we to lose?"

"Crazy' about sums it up. You think I'm letting you in there with that butt head? He's a killer. It's not worth the risk."

"Brad, you and I are working in the dark here; we owe it to the others to try something. I think..."

"I think you're as mad as he is. It's way too dangerous. Forget it."

"Gag him, chain him up. Do whatever you need, but I want that test."

"Eastman, as soon as you see that result we can work on this. You'll have all the evidence you want. You can't afford to sit about with your finger up your butt any longer."

"Brad, we're clueless here. If he's talking garbage then that's that... but what if he *is* telling the truth?"

Eastman rubbed his fingers roughly through his thick black hair. Every fibre in his body cried out warnings. It went fully against his better judgement, but it was worth a try.

"All right, you win! We do this my way. No compromise. I'll pull the plug if need be."

"Thanks Brad. I'll get my gear." With that she smiled at Eastman and left the room.

"Taylor, you even so much as look as if you gonna give me a problem, I'll shoot you down like a dog!"

****

"He's no better."

Bridget quietly closed the living room door and walked to her husband.

"We gotta give these things time to work."

Firth put his arm around his wife. "Maybe it's time to take him to hospital..."

"Aw, I told you what Sam Cortez said everyone who's been infected or looks as if they got flu are in isolation. Now that's what he said."

"Yeah, I know but..."

"He also said Lenski has stopped all visitors. Why you reckon?"

"I don't know." Bridget pushed away from him and stood by the kitchen door.

"Cause they ain't there anymore. They've been handed over to whoever the hell knows."

"Tony, how come you're so sure about all this stuff?"

"Eastman was the one who didn't want anybody leaving town and he's the only one with radios that work. If something's going down, then the cops and medical people are the ones who gonna cover things up."

"What if you're wrong? What if there is no cover and people are just getting sick?" "He's not going anywhere. I never been a fantastic father to him, I admit that.

But I gotta do right by him now. I got a gut feeling on this; I spent my whole life around two-faced liars. I know when something stinks and this stinks."

"I hope to God you're right on this, 'cause heaven help you if you ain't."

152

"We just gotta give these things time to take effect. I'm gonna start loading up the Jeep. I want you to start getting things ready."

"We going someplace?"

"If this thing gets any worse then I want us ready to roll. We head for Burnsville and take our chances."

"Can it get worse?"

"I don't know. I just don't know."

****

"Okay Jim, run that by me again will you?" Eastman was sitting opposite Emmett.

"I was up near the 'old base' when I heard the shots. Two shots, then an engine. By the time I got there, these guys were loading a body into the back of a truck."

"And they were wearing yellow suits. Now you sure about that?"

"Jeez Sheriff, you ain't about to forget something like that. They was wearing full all over bio – suits, but the ones in the Jeep had ordinary Army chem suits on. I know about these things."

Emmett always knew about everything. Most of the time it was baloney, plain and simple; stuff he'd got out of books or The Discovery Channel. But this time it was highly possible he was right.

"What about the body? Did you get a look?"

"Nope not real close, but he looked as if he'd fallen out of a dumpster that I can say."

"Where exactly did this take place?"

"Right about near that old rusted up Dodge."

"I know the spot. Which way they take the vehicles?"

"Back down the road then they went left."

Eastman got up from his chair and collected his hat. "Well we'd best take a look."

Emmett gave him an incredulous look. "You mean you gonna take a look... *you actually believe me?*"

"With everything that's happened over the last few days, I believe in the Tooth Fairy."

"Damn! After all these years I finally got someone to listen, I'm gonna have to give it a miss."

"Hey, Jimmy this is your big chance. What gives?"

"Yeah, yeah you don't have to tell me. I reckon I got the flu. I feel kinda washed out."

"Are you sure about this now?"

Emmett did look as though he'd seen a better week. Eastman would have to do without him, although the area wasn't too difficult to find.

"Yeah, I'd best get off home, put my feet up awhile."

Emmett rose and left the office only to be replaced by Anne Lenski.

"Hey Jimmy you all right?"

"Nope. I got a mother of a headache and I'm going home. See you doc."

She watched as Emmett disappeared down the corridor.

"Something I said?"

"Take no notice. Say, you got the test results then?"

He motioned her to Emmet's now vacant chair.

"Hold on, not yet. I just got back from Mandy Galway's. She's taken an overdose."

"Hell no! Is she...?"

"No, she'll pull through."

Eastman breathed a sigh of relief. That family had already been through enough. "You fancy a trip into the hills?"

"Why you old romantic, what's a lady to say? But I'm needed elsewhere."

She looked at him and then flashed her eyes in mock surprise.

"You and Emmett both. Reckon I'm gonna have to change my cologne."

"What'd he want anyway?"

She knew Emmett was largely regarded as a crank to be avoided. He'd kept away from the Station since Benteen threatened him so he was about the last person she'd have expected to see sitting in Eastman's office.

"Long story. You headed back to the hospital?"

"No. I've got to take Jane Opel's cast off." She shook her head and got up from the seat and headed for the door.

"You gonna make a house-call for that? Send one of the girls."

"I can't spare anyone and Jane won't come to town."

"Why the hell not?"

"After the other night she thinks it's not safe in town. And she's not the only one."

"Can't say as I blame them."

Eastman averted his eyes and got to his feet then headed for the door. A lot of folks seemed to be thinking along the same lines.

"Now what's the deal with Emmett?"

"Come on. I'll walk you to your car."

****

Elle-May sat at the nurses' station leafing through her patients' drugs charts. Things just did not add up. The problem had been going on for some weeks and she'd narrowed the range of suspects to just the one. Zoë and Jill were now both dead so that left Judy Garcia. But even before this cruel process of elimination had ruled out the other two, she'd worked out it had to be Judy. It had been Zoë who'd first noticed the books did not add up but there'd never been any evidence. She'd insisted they confront her, but Elle-May had wanted real proof before making any sort of allegations.

The last thing she needed was to get dragged into any legal wrangling. Then one day it had stopped. Judy had worked a full shift on her own and nothing had gone missing. Then this morning after Judy had worked nights, Elle-May had discovered a whole range of medical supplies missing; antibiotics, opiates and even bandages. This was the last straw.

Judy had agreed to cover an extra shift in the afternoon. This would give Elle-May time to let Anne in on her suspicions and then she could handle the whole thing. She knew Anne had taken the deaths of the two girls hard and she'd also conducted Jill's autopsy, with Jack Larson being off sick.

The thought of having to do that to one of your own made her feel sick. Drinking coffee one minute with them and the next, up to your elbows in their gut. Two friends gone in as many days, Armstrong had turned into a war-zone.

She looked up at the sound of heavy footsteps, only to see Frank and Kurt striding towards her. The older man's face was a vacant mask, except for the wide staring eyes. This together with the sight of their guns gave her an uncomfortable feeling.

"Where're Nancy and Larry?" Frank's tone was flat and bland.

"We put them in isolation. Tell you what, come back in a while and I'll fix you up with some suits."

"No need. Just show me where they're at."

She studied Frank's face. There was something very wrong about this picture. It was as if he'd detached himself from what was going on; just going through the motions in his own little bubble. Kurt was another matter. He was the exact opposite of his father. Like a cat on a hot tin roof, his eyes darted around the place, his chest rising and falling rapidly.

The radio crackled into life. In one fast and furious moment, Frank wrenched the device from the desk hurtling it onto the hard floor. Bits of electronic parts flew across the room.

"What the hell's up with you?" raged Elle-May, stepping forward past the desk.

Frank poked the barrel of his shotgun hard into her ribs.

"I never killed anyone in my life, much less a woman. But I swear if you don't show us our folks, I'm gonna damn well start with you!"

"Pa! What you doing?"

"Shut up! We come for our people and we ain't going no place without them."

Elle-May heard the sound of the hammer creaking back on the ancient weapon. She shut her eyes and waited. Time slowed to a crawl and she was surprised just how quiet everything had become. Soon the only thing she could hear was the sound of her own breathing. She opened her eyes as she felt the pressure of the gun ease off. She had no choice other than to help Frank.

"Okay. But you keep that thing outta my face. You hear me!"

He lowered the gun and nodded.

"Fair. But don't sass me none. Now I want the strongest sleeping pills you got and lots of them."

She didn't like the sound of this one bit. But she wasn't prepared to argue, she wanted them gone. The longer they stayed the more likely someone was going to get hurt. She took a long look at Frank and then led them off down the corridor.

****

Eastman stood in front of the old Airbase, its sharp concrete lines in stark contrast to the green lush vegetation surrounding it. Apart from green moss growing about the building, the base had remained largely unchanged for over a half a century. How many carefree hours had he spent here? As a kid he'd hidden from Ben Burke with Benteen so many times after raiding the apple trees, he'd even stolen his first kiss from Helen here. Happy days.

The sky had darkened and the tips of the trees moved uneasily against the wind. He hitched his shirt collar up, felt ill at ease and tense, but he was here to investigate. He'd searched for the area where Emmett claimed he'd seen the killing but he'd drawn a blank. There'd been a strong smell of some kind of chemical but nothing else. Something Taylor said about the base had plagued him. He needed to look over the area to satisfy his own curiosity.

The structure was a two-story box, designed to house about thirty people, jammed full of electronic equipment. It was hard to think that in its day the base was considered a vital part of NORAD. He could just about remember the wooden buildings dotted about the area. Now the undergrowth covered cinder block foundations were the only clue to anything ever having been there. The windows had long since been boarded up but the main doorway was still accessible.

Moving about the ground floor he struggled to see in the partial gloom. He shone his flashlight around the room, only to reveal a lifetime of faded graffiti scrolled on the walls. If he looked hard enough he'd probably find his name too. As he moved from room to room he wasn't even sure he knew what he was looking for. Was it the boy? Evidence of something else? Or was he there just to satisfy his curiosity?

As his eyes adjusted to the dark he found the entrance to the upper floor stairwell. He pushed hard against the blocked door but it was stuck fast. He swept his light across the floor only to discover an array of used condoms, syringes and beer cans. Any further fond memories of the place were now pushed from his mind.

Then a strange feeling overwhelmed him, like being in an old attic or basement. That sudden unreasonable fear, that same fear that makes you snap the light on in the middle of the night. Eastman had the sensation that someone was standing behind him. It was as if he could feel eyes watching him. His heart beat out a Samba and his hands became cold and damp lumps of meat. The dank smell of damp and a sudden coldness made him turn on his heel and race outside.

He lent up against the outside wall and brought himself under control. In the cold light of day it was impossible for Eastman to see why he'd reacted in panic. It was just an old empty building and yet... He took one last look at the base; he never wanted to come here again. He started back down the track and headed for town, unaware of the sudden movement in the foliage behind him.

****

PFC Alan Harper rested his finger on the trigger of his M16. The cross hairs of the weapon's sight sat on the back of the lawman's head. At this short range the powerful 223mm round would smash through his head like an over-ripe melon. He'd watched as the man had made his way from the incident site to the base. The exact location where only a few hours earlier, Corporal Wyllie had blasted the crap out of one of those creeps.

The whole unit knew the importance of holding the line and not letting anything out. The thought of any of these things getting into a major town was enough to keep him sharp. This guy was near that line right now. Harper knew that the images from his head-cam were being relayed to the command post and now all he was waiting for was the order to engage.

Although he was well acclimatized to heat, this temperature was almost unbearable in his protective suit and heavy rubber respirator. He could feel the sweat run into his eyes but he had to hold the shot. It was with immense relief that the order came to stand down'. He eased his finger away from the trigger and flicked the safety catch on and watched as the 'potential' moved down the track, out of sight.

Harper left his position and moved swiftly through the dense tree line to rejoin his unit. This place gave him the creeps and he was glad to be away. Since the mission had started no one in his unit had killed any of the 'potentials' and he was happy not to be the first. He'd killed several of the infected and that was okay; they were beyond help anyway. It was the best thing for them. The medics had made it clear that there was no cure for these SOB's. He sure as hell didn't want to end up like that, and that meant they had to keep them in the containment area.

Wyllie said the whole town had gone bad and this was God's way of punishing them. Growing up in the Bronx, Harper hadn't had much time for religion. In his book, the guy was cause for concern. He was wrapped too tight for this crap and guys like that come unstuck. But he was the squad leader and you'd have to be some kinda nut to squawk about him. Besides, this unit was far from ordinary and the things they'd had to deal with made people a bit odd. During the Ebola emergency, they'd got involved in some pretty heavy stuff and now this was going along the same lines.

As he headed toward the small group of soldiers he could see another two infected in the back of the truck. Things were getting pretty heavy after all. The guys in the yellow suits bustled about giving instructions but they just seemed clueless. The way he saw it was that they'd been sent here too late. By the time they'd set up the containment area, hell knows how many of the things had got out. They didn't have enough guys on the ground in any case. Somebody had messed up and that kinda 'mess up' usually meant bad news all around.

Drawing near the others he couldn't help but wonder if it would have been kinder to have shot the guy. At least it would've been quick and over. What the brass had planned for this hick town was far from that. But that was the best part of being on the bottom of the chain of command. He was just following orders.

CHAPTER - EIGHTEEN

Hardly a sound disturbed the quiet of the house, except for the ticking of the old clock resting on the dresser. Nobody could remember just how old the thing was for sure, but they knew it was old. It had been in the family since Grandpa Joe had been a boy and still kept the right time.

The sitting room was neat as a new pin with nothing out of place. The clutter of the last few days had been banished; the ornaments on the mantelpiece and the many picture frames dusted. Things were back in order, just as Nancy liked it.

Frank, sitting at the large wooden table in his Sunday best, looked about the room thinking how pleased she'd be at his efforts. The suit was the stylish blue one he'd bought for his cousin's wedding the previous month; Nancy had said that looking smart made him appear years younger.

Frank looked over at Kurt and Larry who were slumped in the two armchairs, heavily sedated. Kurt had been easy to drug; Frank had just crushed some of the tablets into his food and Larry was already out cold anyway. They looked peaceful, at rest with no fear, safe from the world. It reminded him of when they'd been babies and he'd used to hold them tightly. That was over twenty years ago; he was proud of the way they'd both turned out, honest hard working men.

He'd tried to put Nancy out too, but even the strongest knock-out drugs had been of no use. He'd hated doing it, but the only way to stop that awful noise had been to gag her and put a pillow-case over her head. He just couldn't look at her eyes. The eyes were the worst part. They just didn't belong to her anymore, not his Nancy. It had been a mistake to try to get her to sit down without the rope but it had felt wrong. He looked at the bite on his hand; it was only a small wound but it had bled like anything. Still, she was safe with them. They were all safe now.

Frank tried to get up to draw the curtains but his legs felt like jello and he slumped back into his seat. The sleeping tablets were taking effect sooner than he'd thought. He picked up the letter from the bank but couldn't make out the print, so he folded it and placed it into his suit pocket. The last thing he wanted was to litter the room. He tried to force his eyes wide open but his eyelids felt like lead bars.

If only it could've been different, if only it had all worked out. There was nothing left for any of them now; this was the only thing he had the power to do. He clutched his wedding photo to his chest and sighed deeply. Frank was vaguely aware of the smell of smoke replacing that of the gasoline. As he closed his weary eyes, thick black smoke seeped under the door and into the room.

****

Benteen cursed his luck at missing out on some action yet again. Here he was stuck playing baby sitter to that scum-bag drifter when he should've been with Brad up at the Jorgans' place. Not that he had any beef with Frank, but the guy had lost it; he was armed and dangerous. Elle-May was still shaken up by it all and she didn't spook easily.

Brad had gotten the call from the hospital as soon as he'd got back from the airbase. He'd taken off out of the door with Mitch and Kate. They were both good peace officers although maybe not the best suited for the task. It should've been him standing with Brad, like the old days. Still Brad had left him in charge so he'd best take a look at that lousy punk. Was he now just the nursemaid or something? Angrily he shook his head and walked up to the cell and went inside.

Taylor was writhing about on the floor, clutching at his throat and gasping for air. Benteen started forward then stopped. It was obvious this guy was choking and he needed aid. But then again, this bum was the cause of all the problems. This was the perfect way to get rid of him and all Benteen had to do was sit back and wait for him to die.

Taylor stopped convulsing and crashed back onto the floor in a heap. Somehow this was less enjoyable than Benteen had imagined. Sure he wanted this bum dead, but he wanted to do it himself. In any case, Brad would be almighty mad at him for losing his star prisoner. Cursing loudly, Benteen undid his pistol belt and placed it on the desk. Taking the cell keys, he opened the door and went in.

Taylor lay perfectly still, controlling his breathing to the point where his chest hardly moved. His plan depended upon this creep getting in very close. Benteen was all that stood between Taylor and freedom. Taylor heard the metal door ease open and waited.

"Okay, I'm gonna help you, but don't you get any dumb ideas now."

Taylor waited until he felt Benteen's hands on his arm and then sent a lightning blow to the other man's head. The strike hit Benteen on the left temple, sending him crashing to the hard ground, unconscious. Taylor sprang to his feet and surveyed the downed man. Such a blow could be used to kill or stun: the last thing Taylor needed was a dead cop. He took Benteen's radio and dashed out of the cell, locking the door behind him.

Heading towards the outer door his eyes caught sight of the automatic jutting out from Benteen's pistol rig. His hand snaked out towards the belt... it was bad enough they'd be looking for a guy who'd just broken out of jail, let alone one armed with a gun and a cop's gun at that. Any excuse for Billy Bob or Billy boy or Billy whatever the hell, to hunt him down with the hounds.

Glancing over at Benteen's prone body he made his way to the cell room door and carefully opened it. Checking both ways were clear he made towards the reception area and his long overdue freedom. His objective was to put as much distance between him and the town; beyond that he'd just have to make it up as he went along. His nose twitched as he picked up the aroma of Clara's home cooking. His escape had come at the right time.

****

The flames shot up way above the house as if the fire wanted to engulf the very sky. The shattering window-panes could just be heard over the roaring inferno. Virdon looked over at the nearby tree line. It was obvious his team could get no closer to the house; even if they'd still got the fire suits, it was just too hot.

What worried him was the real possibility of the fire leaping onto the trees. Despite the recent rain this kind of heat could set the mountain ablaze. The best they could hope for was to dampen the area and wait until the fire burned low enough for them to put it out. The only saving grace was the two fire tenders could use the nearby river to fight the fire.

Javier Martinez walked over to Virdon. As he removed his helmet it looked as if he'd just stepped out of the sauna. He wiped the sweat from his face.

"Ron, she's just too hot for us to get in close. You want I should try getting one of the engines in nearer?"

"Nope. We still ain't sure if Frank had propane tanks in there. We gotta keep our distance, Javier. I want you to get some more water on those trees over there."

He pointed to the closest of the trees.

"What you reckon happened in there with Frank. He just gone loco or something?"

Virdon wasn't even sure if Frank was in the house. Just before he'd arrived at the scene Eastman had radioed him about the situation at the health center and how Frank and Kurt were to be regarded as 'dangerous'. If anybody other than Brad had said that he'd have told them where the hell to go, but Virdon had the safety of his crew to consider. Things were going on in the town that just made no damn sense.

The thought that Frank or Kurt could have a bead on them right now made the situation a whole lot worse. The shrill wail of police sirens made him turn to look back down the road to Jorgan's farm. Eastman's white Ford pulled up just behind Virdon's car swiftly followed by the second car, containing Mitch Chapman and Kate Black. Eastman got out of the car and walked up to the Fire Chief.

"Frank and his people still in there?"

"You tell me. This is the closest we can get. Besides I don't know for sure if there's propane in there?"

"Propane! Hell Ron, you need a safety line here someplace buddy."

"You're looking at it. We can't stay too far back; the hoses don't reach the trees." Virdon indicated to Eastman the now steaming tree line.

"If this jumps over there we gonna have us one hell of a forest fire. We just don't have enough manpower to cope with this."

"Yeah, didn't help Firth giving all the fire suits away!"

"As much as I never thought I'd live to say it, but it ain't all his doing. Frank just about covered the whole darn house in gasoline. It's just too hot."

"So we just gotta sit this one out, eh?"

"What makes a man like Frank Jorgan do something like this? I just don't get it."

"Desperation."

With an ear splitting bang, the centre of the house erupted into a blinding flash of orange and red. Burning debris spiralled into the sky and shockwaves struck the surrounding trees, like the ripples on a pond. The force of the explosion levelled the house, completely destroying the roof but in doing so, substantially reduced the size of the blaze.

"Guess that accounts for the propane then."

"Yep."

Eastman adjusted his hat and gently patted his ears with the palms of his hands.

"Look on the bright side – that bang just did the work for us."

"How long till you start sifting through that bonfire?"

"It'll be some time before we can get into that and a while later before we can start looking. We gonna be here a while."

With that, Virdon ordered his crew in closer. But he knew it would still be some time before he'd be in a position to search for bodies. There wasn't much point in Brad hanging about. Virdon walked Eastman towards the cars.

"I'll let you know as soon as we find any bodies. I know it sounds kinda bad, but I almost hope we got us four bodies in there."

"Yeah, I don't want any more crazy people running about either."

Mitch Chapman called over from his squad car holding the radio mic up, his face grave. "Brad that was Clara."

"What's up Mitch?"

Virdon watched as the Deputy handed Eastman the mic. He spoke a few short words then cursed, slamming his fist on the roof of the car before lowering his head.

"Problems there dude?"

Eastman slowly turned to face Virdon and nodded. "That guy Taylor, he's escaped."

****

Eastman pounded along the hospital corridor from Benteen's room. He was beyond furious. He couldn't believe his best lead to solving this fiasco had escaped and had done so by using one of the oldest tricks in the book. For two pins, Eastman had thought on giving Benteen a crack around the other side of his thick head. Still, he was thankful that Taylor had only floored Gerard, it could have been worse: a lot worse. Taylor could have easily killed Gerard but chose not to; he'd even left the man's gun behind. Neither of these were the actions you'd expect from a cold-blooded murderer. But this did not alter the hard reality that he was a highly dangerous man, and now a man on the run.

Eastman rounded the corner and saw Anne and Elle-May standing by the drinks dispenser. Anne had left Eastman alone with Benteen after she'd completed his examination, which was just as well, because Eastman didn't hold with swearing in front of women."How'd you feel now, Elle-May?"

"Oh you know me. It's gonna take more than a scattergun to put me off."

"Well any time you want to trade those scrubs for a star, you come and find me.""Funny you should say that, but Elle-May's already turned detective."

"How so?"

Anne looked at Elle-May. "Now's your chance, I'll let you do the talking."

"Thanks a bunch, you're a real pal." Elle-May raised her eyebrows.

"Well one of you better tell me."

"We've been losing drugs for some time. More being taken than we got signatures for. It took me a time but I'm damn sure it's Judy Garcia."

"Serious allegations. You got any kinda proof?"

"'Most every time Judy was on a shift a bunch of stuff went missing. Now I don't want to point fingers at no one, especially right now, though as far as I can tell it just gotta be her."

With everything that had gone on, the possibility of losing trust in a nurse wasn't good. However, it was apparent that both Elle-May and Anne had cause for concern and he'd have little choice other than to support their judgement. Although the last thing he wanted was to arrest Judy Garcia at this time.

"Like me to have a word with her?"

"No, that's up to us. It's still an internal matter. But it could go that way."

"Okay, that's fine by me. I'll be about if you need me."

Anne was right of course, they had to stick to protocol and it had to come from her. He'd reached the end of his tether and right now all he wanted was to get back to his ranch. He smiled at the two women and headed home.

****

From his vantage point high above the valley, Taylor watched the buzz of activity behind the rows of razor wire. Squads of soldiers dashed about and military vehicles were everywhere. It reminded him of an ants' nest, everything with a purpose and a purpose for everything. A number of small pre-fabricated huts made up the bulk of the base and sand bag positions ringed the well defended area. Arc lights stood like huge metal trees around the perimeter waiting for the onset of the dark.

Although well equipped and heavily armed, he figured there were probably no more than a hundred men. Not nearly enough to secure the whole area. This was a small, low key operation. That could only mean one thing; they had to have another way of containing this situation. The possibility filled him with dread. Somebody wanted this off the books and away from the media. That meant whoever was running the show could pretty much do whatever the hell they wanted.

An operation to contain a town even of this size would require a huge amount of military resources and forests of razor wire. That kinda high profile activity would in turn produce an equal army of news hounds and be front page headlines before you could yell 'cover up'.

The Government had tried to keep the early Ebola containments as quiet as they could, to minimize panic, but it had proven an impossible endeavour. You just couldn't keep that much manpower and hardware in one place without someone noticing, not to mention of course, sealing off whole communities. But somewhere this far out and with such a small force, you could just about get away with it. The only reason he'd found the camp, was he knew it had to be there someplace.

His attention was drawn to the group of soldiers he'd followed from the road. In the back of their vehicle were three bodies in black plastic body bags.

The men threw them unceremoniously from the back of the truck, whilst another group in yellow bio-hazard suits, lifted them onto a small cart.

Unexpectedly, one of the bodies forced an arm out from the bag and grasped one of the 'yellow suits'. The man clubbed at the arm and broke free. The two nearest soldiers poured the contents of their thirty round magazines into the body bag. Two of the yellow suited individuals dragged the shattered remains of the body onto the ground, while a third blasted it with a flamethrower.

It was only then that Taylor noticed the two six wheel rigs with the jamming equipment on the back. The jammers resembled oversized ghetto blasters and were about as big as a station wagon. The type he'd seen used in Syria had been a fraction of the size and they'd devastated the opposition's communications for miles. He was no electronics warfare expert, but these monsters looked big enough to block the whole of Montana. No wonder the town had blacked out. He took a mental step backwards; that wretched town's problems were no concern of his.

He shifted his position as he reminded himself of why he was here. He had to find information on the location of Dr Tellermine's new base. He wanted to give this guy a whole bucket load of payback. But this was a hell of an expanse to search and without even the most basic map he was near clueless.

Eastman had been less help than a New York cab driver with double the attitude. According to his views, there was nothing in the vicinity that would fit Taylor's ideas. But then, it was hardly surprising, since it was supposed to be a secret base. The first base had been a huge complex with an even larger budget. No need of secret locations.

What if this new base was not hidden, what if the base was in plain sight? A disturbing question hit him, could *this* camp be what he was looking for? Were these guys here to stop the hicks from getting out or getting in? There was only one way to find out; he'd have to go and take a look.

This was the last thing he wanted to do but he was running low on options. He'd need to wait for nightfall before it would be safe enough to infiltrate the camp. Taylor settled himself down and prepared for the long wait for sundown.

****

Eastman had his back to Anne, with his arms resting on the corral fence. He looked different in his jeans and shirt: during the last few days she'd hardly seen him out of his uniform. However, he was still wearing his gun belt so she decided against any untoward surprises. After the recent events, the town's nerves were in tatters, it was best to avoid accidents. She announced herself well before she reached him.

"Sorry Brad, but I tried the house first. Gerard said I'd find you here."

Eastman spoke without turning around.

"I used to spend hours here with Helen putting the world to rights. Guess you could say it was kinda our spot."

"I didn't mean to intrude. I'll call you later. Sorry." She turned on her heel and started back down the long track.

"Anne, wait on there. How'd all that go with Judy?" He turned about to face her, placing his elbows on the barrier and leaning backwards.

She smiled and moved to stand next to him. "Elle-May was right. Judy confessed under our 'good cop / good cop' interrogation."

"Hate to correct you, it's meant to be 'good cop / bad cop…' "

"I know, but neither of us wanted to be the bad cop."

He raised his eyebrow. "Well that's new. What you get?"

"Judy was supplying Peter Firth with the medication."

"Now why aren't I surprised at that? Bum's been running a black market. I knew it."

"Maybe not."

A look of puzzlement spread across his face. "Okay, so you got me hooked. Carry on."

She pushed her sunglasses back on top of her head. "Firth had a hold over her and she stole to order."

"Why'd a good Catholic girl like that get mixed up with him?"

"Brad, if I tell, you've got to promise not to go all legal on me. Will you do that?"

"Oh, I hate these." He sent a heavy scowl at her. "That kinda depends on…"

"No. No conditions."

"Is there any point in arguing this?"

"What do you think?"

"Okay, like what I think matters already. But this had better be good."

"Did you know Judy had her brother staying with her?"

"Brother? Say where'd he come from?"

"Across the border and he forgot to bring his Green Card."

"Oh boy."

Eastman moved away from the fence and cupped his hand over his mouth.

"Firth got to know about him and said he'd report him if she didn't help out."

"So it *is* the black market then."

She held her finger up and shook her head. "She said something about Peter wanting to *help* his family. Now she gave him a lot of antibiotics and strong pain-killers but not enough to sell wholesale. I think your idea about Conrad may be right."

"You think Peter was giving them to his brother?"

"Could be. Tony was very interested in how to treat this virus. The antibiotics would be used to fight the infection but when that failed, he'd try the pain killers."

"Yeah, but it's been over three days by now. That's how long it takes you to turn, that's what you said."

She placed her hands out in front of her.

"The incubation period is not set in stone; there could be all types of variations."

"Reckon I'd best pay Tony another visit."

"I'd like to tag along too, if that's okay with you?"

Eastman nodded, then took her arm as they walked down the track. "Anne, I know I seemed kinda hard on Gerard... How is he?"

She narrowed her eyes at him before replying.

"Yes you were. He's lucky Taylor knew what he was doing. If that blow had been harder, Gerard could well be dead."

"I guess I was too heavy handed."

"You two go back a long way, don't you?"

"I know he's a brute and damn infuriating one at that, but after Helen was killed he stuck to me like glue."

"Helen was a big part of you but you never talk about her. I have to ask other people to find out about her."

"Sometimes when the light is right or certain times of day, I swear I can see her across the other side of the corral. I try my darndest not to blink, 'cause when I do she's gone."

He looked at Anne with an almost apologetic look. "It must sound kinda crazy to you."

She looked deep into Eastman's eyes. "After Paul was murdered, I had to take some R and R and I went home. For weeks I could smell his cologne in every room. Brad, as long as we remember them they're not really dead. It's when we forget them, they're gone."

Eastman smiled at her. "Come on Doc. We got us an appointment with the Mayor."

※ ※ ※ ※

Taylor felt dejected. His search of the camp had proven fruitless. He'd spent hours dodging grunts only to reach the conclusion the camp was just that: a camp? The prefabs had turned out to be accommodation and supply rooms. There'd been a medical unit but this had no more devious purpose than to serve the medical needs of the containment force. Even the dead bodies he'd found had been stored in refrigerated storage. There'd been no sign of any holding pens for the infected or gruesome experiment labs. Damn, what a waste of time!

As he walked around the old airbase he was thankful for the Army jacket he'd 'liberated' from the camp, as the chill night air rustled through the trees. He zipped up the front and studied the map with the torch, two more 'liberated' items. Eastman had been right; this old relic was nowhere near the size of the structure he'd imagined.

Taylor knew a lot of these places had shelters below ground and some were vast, but this was way too rural to warrant that kinda expenditure. Then a small patch of concrete took his eye. Nothing special but why would anybody want to patch up this dump and with *new* concrete? The beam from his flash-light danced about the desolate shell as he went inside.

The smell of damp hit him as he cast his eyes over the walls and the rubble-strewn interior. This had once been a magnet for low lifes judging by the beer cans and other rubbish lying around. However, that had been some time ago, the cans had rusted and his gut feeling told him the place was a dead house. Just as he was about to leave, his probing gaze picked up a bright glint of polished metal amongst the filth and grime.

On the countless military operations he'd endured, the ability to detect and process information could be the difference between setting an IED off, or walking home on both your legs. The position of rocks and objects on a sidewalk, even plain old trash that just looked out of place spoke reams of information. If something didn't look right then it probably wasn't.

Taylor walked over to the object and bent down to retrieve silver eight inch long bolt. Turning the object between his fore finger and thumb as he scrutinised it in the bright beam, it was the type of bolt used to secure something to masonry or concrete. Directly in front of him was a section of dirty wall that looked plain wrong.

There was something not right about this section, but what? It looked every inch as grubby as the rest of the dump and had as much graffiti, but... The drawings and scribbles were way too new. They were meant to blend in but looked too sharp, too clear. He looked around for a heavy object and quickly found half a cinder block. He struck the wall hard and wasn't surprised to find it hollow.

He hammered away at the wall revealing a section of metal. He continued his work until he uncovered a complete segment. This was a door. The metal displayed no evidence of corrosion; in fact the metal door and its frame were very recent additions to the structure. Someone had gone to a lot of trouble to hide this away.

As Taylor stood back to admire his handy work he heard an M16 bolt being drawn back. Following the muffled instructions from behind him, Taylor placed his hands in the air and slowly turned to face the threat. High energy Mag-lights blinded him while dozens of small red target lights darted around his body.

"Check his eyes. Check his eyes!" barked out a disembodied voice from the darkness somewhere in front of him.

"Affirmative. All clear," came the reply from the other side of the room.

"Okay take him down," ordered a third voice from the doorway.

Suddenly Taylor shot backwards as the intense pain of a Taser racked through his body, throwing him against the wall. Taylor pitched forward and fell to his knees as he felt plastic restraints securing his wrists. Before passing out he could now clearly make out the skull like shapes of Army respirators above him.

****

Eastman looked over his desk at Robert Pool. It had been a long time since he'd seen the guy anywhere near sober, but here he was as nifty as a judge. His clothes were clean and he didn't smell of booze, or worse. The guy had been hit hard after his boy had been killed. Eastman knew all too well that feeling, but Pool had come apart at the seams. There was only so much sympathy people would give; as his behaviour had gotten worse, so people had stopped caring.

"Look Robert, I appreciate what you've just told me but why now?"

"If I'd come in with a story like that before would you have believed me Sheriff? I mean really."

"Emmet gave me a similar story and I went up to look at the base. There was nothing there. I'm not saying that I don't..."

"Tony didn't believe me either until I showed him the spot and the shell cases."

"Tony. Tony Firth?" Eastman lent over his desk and looked at Pool.

"Yeah? I thought he'd have told you by now?"

"So Tony was aware about this days ago, is that right?"

"Sure. He said not to say anything about it. But I figured with all this going on I'd better tell you. He's not himself anymore."

"How come?"

Pool shifted awkwardly in his seat clearly anxious: flushed and sweaty. "I called there the other day and he damn near threw me out."

"Well that's nothing to go by. He treats me the same."

"Tony was the only one to give a crap about me after Robert Junior was killed. Oh yeah, people were sorry, but it was Tony who sat with me night after night. After you took my gun and then my truck, it was him who cut me down from my apple tree."

Eastman sat back in his chair. "I didn't know about that. Why in hell didn't you come to me or Anne Lenski about all this?"

"After a while I stopped caring. But Tony kept me alive and that's why I feel like I've done him down. But you had to know what's been going on."

"Robert, I believe you. So you say these guys in the chemical suits were up at the Old base, but like I said there is *nothing* up there."

"And I'm telling you somebody's been doing work up there. I saw a whole bunch of lights up a while back. There are concrete slabs up there that ought not to be. Like someone trying to block up the ground."

Eastman brushed his fingers over his eyes. Both Emmet and Pool had implicated the base in their stories, yet his own investigations had proved fruitless. He'd taken no notice of the concrete slabs, that was something he could look at later; right now he needed a long overdue word with Firth.

****

Eastman rapped at Tony Firth's large wooden door and looked impatiently over at Anne. She was peering through the front window. He was in no mood to be kept waiting; there were things that needed sorting. The fact that Firth had known about some kind of military involvement was unacceptable. He banged the door and called out. It was plain that someone was in; apart from the interior house light burning away, Firth's BMW was in the drive and his four-by-four was outside the garage.

"Hey, come and look at this."

Anne was pointing through the window. Eastman walked over to join her and he too looked through the small space between the partly drawn curtains. The room was a mess. The small table was on its side and various objects were scattered across the floor. If Bridget Firth was nothing else, she was house proud to a fault; she'd never allow this chaos.

"Front door's shut, I'll try round back."

They walked around the unlit side entrance to the back door and Eastman banged on the door and then tried the handle. It swung open and he looked at Anne.

"Shall we?"

He called out once more and then entered the house. The overpowering reek of disinfectant reminded him of hospitals. Littered across the work surface were packs of medical supplies, used and unused. The trash-can was over-flowing with blood-stained dressings.

"Looks like Judy was right after all."

"Unless someone's cut themselves on a can of caviar, I think we'd better be careful."

Eastman nodded his head: things weren't looking too good. Then he saw the blood on the floor. A small patch of dried blood lay just behind the inner door, with further stains on the bottom of the door. He turned to Anne.

"I want you to stay in the car until I find out what's happened here."

"Why don't you just call for backup?"

"There isn't any backup. Everybody's out."

"Just call up and wait then."

"This *ain't* a debate here. I don't want to be worrying about you if I gotta search this place. I want you out and in that car. Now!"

"Just be careful. I'll call it in for you shall I? I've watched plenty of cop shows."

She was not happy at the prospect of leaving him alone, not at all. Nevertheless, she gave a nervous smile and left for the squad car. Eastman knew she was right; however, the bottom line was that someone was hurt or worse. He did not have the time to wait. He called out loudly before opening the living room door. The place looked as though there'd been a twister through it. Medical packs were dotted all around; up-turned furniture and left over food littered the floor. He tried to put a picture together, but there was no evidence of any violence and no blood. He carefully pushed open the hall door and walked in.

The hall was in darkness and he fumbled for a light switch. As far as he could recall from a visit some years back, the hall led to the upstairs and the rest of the house. There was also a basement that Firth had converted into a games room. At last Eastman's fingers found the switch and he flicked the light on. Gradually his eyes adjusted to the sudden glare and he noticed that the plush cream carpet was saturated with blood.

Bloody handprints drew his attention to the basement door. The scuffed carpet and marks on the textured wallpaper told him that this was the violent struggle he'd hoped not to find. It looked as though someone had been forced through the doorway into the basement. Cautiously he moved toward the door, unclipping his holster as he did so. He felt his heart rate speed up a fraction and the palms of his hand began to sweat. He reached out to the door-knob, preparing himself for the worst. There was no telling what he'd find the other side of the door.

"Don't go in there!"

Eastman turned to see Tony Firth; in his trembling hands he held his pistol aimed at Eastman's chest. His face was badly clawed, with blood running down onto his shirt collar. His eyes were red with tears and he looked like a wild man. Eastman squared up, keeping his hands well away from his own pistol. There was still room for negotiation... he hoped.

"Okay, let's talk about this."

"Talk? I'm through taking. I done too much talking already."

"I saw all the medical stuff. Where's Conrad?"

Firth silently nodded to the basement. "That who you come for Brad? You want to put him with the rest?"

"I'm here to help you and..."

"You're here for my boy. Well you ain't getting him."

"Tony, all I want is to talk this over without you waving that thing at me. If he's ill then let Anne take a look at him."

"I never knew you did a line in comedy. She can't cure them. When they get as bad as this, then that's it. You just put them down or hand them over to your friends."

"That's a crock, Tony and you know damn well. There's a whole bunch of folk trying to figure this out, and you're one of them. I'm not your enemy. But somebody's playing us for sure. Think about it."

Firth lowered his gun and lent up against the wall. "I should have listened to Bridget, should have taken him to the hospital. I thought it would be all right."

Eastman took a step towards him and held out his hand. "Give me the gun and let me help you. Please."

Firth stood bolt upright and aimed the pistol at Eastman. "No, that's far enough. You'd best leave now."

"Where's Bridget?"

"What?" Firth's eyes had a glazed look to them as he looked at Eastman.

"Where *is* Bridget?"

"In there."

"She's in there with Conrad? Tony, that's kinda dangerous man."

Firth looked at Eastman and laughed loudly and moved across to the basement door. "What could be dangerous about a mother with her son?"

He swung his head around as a loud crash came from the basement followed by shuffling footsteps coming up the steps. Horrified, Firth put his hand over his mouth, his eyes now wild with terror.

"They got free."

"Tony, let me help you."

Almost on cue, there came a loud pounding from the other side of the door followed by inhuman wails.

"Too late for that. I was never a good father and a poor excuse for a husband. I need to take care of this my way."

Firth flung open the door and pushed his way in. Eastman saw briefly the snarling faces of Conrad and Bridget Firth, before Tony Firth slammed the door.

"What the hell's he doing?"

Eastman spun around at Anne's voice directly behind him.

"More like what the hell are you doing? I told you to stay..."

The sound of a gunshot ended his sentence, followed by a second and third. Eastman's shoulders fell heavily and he briefly shut his eyes. Would this thing never end?

CHAPTER - NINETEEN

Mitch Chattman turned his squad car towards Spencer Street. The mid morning sun glinted off his windshield as he drove along Sherman Avenue. Just another average day in Armstrong, except he'd difficulty in working out what 'average' meant these days. Time was, when all he had to worry about was pulling Robert Pool out of the traffic or chasing after the Clayton boys. Now things had changed.

More people had died of 'unnatural causes' in the last week than the past hundred years. And there seemed no end to it. These were people that Chattman had known and grown up with. He was thankful his parents had moved to Burnsville three years back; at least they were safe. However, Emmet and his crazy talk had started people thinking and Chattman was one of them. What if these events were not isolated to Armstrong?

Another three people had added to the growing list of losses after the previous night's events. Eastman had called in from Tony Firth's place and, even now in the safety of the warm day; it was difficult to process. Tony Firth, his wife and the kid, all dead. Chattman had overheard Eastman talking to Benteen about how Firth had shot them just because they'd been infected by this terrible virus. To kill your own family like that was beyond him. But then again, wasn't that what had happened with Frank and his family?

Manny Hardbuckle was struggling across the road with an impossible armload of groceries, it amazed Chattman just how Mrs Hardbuckle could have produced such a monster. She was the sort of woman who looked as if she'd go airborne on a summer breeze.Chattman grimaced as he watched the guy waddle up the sidewalk. Manny always wore pants that were too tight for him, producing unsightly bulges in all the wrong places. With these images ironed into his mind, Chattman swung left onto Reno Boulevard. He'd travelled a short distance when he noticed a commotion outside Amoco's Delicatessen.

Several people had rushed out of the shop and were standing outside. Although there seemed to be a sense of urgency he was unable to tell what had happened. As Chattman headed towards the scene, another surge of people charged from the shop, pushing through onto the sidewalk. They had a look of blind panic and at least two appeared to have injuries. He stopped his car and walked over to the crowd. As he got closer he could hear the sound of smashing glass from within the delicatessen. Ned Horvitz had lost a finger and was standing on the corner, blood dripping onto the road. It was Joe Levine the Wall- Mart Security Guard who spoke first.

"Thank God you turned up Mitch, he's gone berserk in there."

Joe's face was bloodied and bruised, his white security shirt heavily stained with blood. He had what looked to be a bite mark on his right cheek. The rest of the group were badly shaken; James Burke was using his inhaler. Chattman walked up to the doorway and peered in. The hubbub had all but stopped, bar for a sound that made him think of a pig eating. Stepping into the doorway he could see what was left of Sam Lock.

The man's stomach had been ripped open with most of its contents slopped onto the black and white tiled floor. However, before Chattman could fully take the terrible scene in, two powerful hands grasped his arm and he felt someone bite down onto his coat. The force of the assault pushed him backwards, landing him on the sidewalk with a crash. Chattman looked up into the lifeless eyes of Al Paxmore.

The weight of the creature pressed Chattman against the hard ground, making it impossible to move. Chattman stared at the misshapen parody of a human face snarling and dripping slime inches away from him. This thing didn't even have to bite him: one drop, just one drop of that foul smelling ooze would be enough to contaminate him. At all costs he had to keep the snapping, drooling head away, but the thing was too heavy. Chattman began to think it would only be a matter of time before he lost the struggle, when suddenly Al Paxmore flew off him.

"Well I ain't about to do all the work for you, son."

Chattman took hold of the extended hand reaching out to him and was surprised to find Robert Pool smiling down at him.

"Jeez Rob, thank you buddy," was all he could manage.

"Yeah well, it ain't over just yet."

He pointed to the creature getting slowly to its feet. Having lost interest in Chattman the thing was now seeking prey far closer. It made a lunge at James Burke, who dodged out of the way, accidentally lining up the next kill. The little girl stood transfixed by the danger shambling towards her. She clutched at her rag doll as her yellow spotted dress fluttered in the gentle wind.

The bullet entered just under Al's right eye and exited through the back of his head in a crimson mist of bone and flesh. Paxmore fell to his knees then dropped sideways hitting the floor with an audible thump. The girl's mother raced across the road, cradling the child in her arms. It was a family reunion that none of the relieved onlookers could have imagined seconds ago. Chattman walked over to the body, oblivious to the congratulations of the crowd. Then he realised he had the answer to his earlier question. Death, terror and blood were all part of the average day in Armstrong.

****

Taylor eyed up his captors as they led him into one of the many pre-fab buildings dotted about the camp. The men wore standard US Army fatigues and light order equipment, with black woollen watch caps. They had no divisional flashes or insignia of any type, except rank badges. It was clear this was no regular outfit; perhaps they followed another rule-book and perhaps that extended to prisoners. It would be a good idea if he played it smart until he could find what was going on.

They marched him through a set of doors and stood silently as if on parade. Taylor looked about the plain wooden hut. A long table covered with a variety of maps and three plastic chairs occupied the area to his front. To his immediate left lay a second door. Apart from the two doors and small shuttered windows, there was no escape. One of the guards touched his earpiece, walked to the second door and beckoned Taylor to him. The guard pushed open the door, stepped back and ushered Taylor into a tiny room. A man dressed in Army fatigues stood with his back to Taylor looking at some papers on a desk.

"Well, well, well. Look what the cat's dragged in."

"J.J. King. I wasn't expecting that."

The man turned to face Taylor and gave a wry smile. He was a tall man with dark, almost black eyes. "How long's it been old sport? Two, three years?"

"Just after Damascus, *sport*."

"That sure was a hell of a dust off."

King motioned to the guards. "I'll call if I need you. Wait outside."

The soldiers left the room leaving the two men alone. King pointed to a vacant seat then pulling up a chair he sat down. Taylor looked at the chair for a moment then sat down.

"So who you working for now; some kinda black ops CIA, NSA?"

"Let's just say I work for a government department."

"You running this then?"

Taylor sat with his hands resting on his knees. It had been a long time since he'd last seen J.J King.

"No. General Stone is the CO."

"Wasn't he the guy at Mercy Creek?"

King nodded and sat forward in his chair. "So how'd you enjoy Hill Billy land? Looks as if it was getting kinda rough down there."

"You left the cop channel open?"

King smirked at Taylor. "We had to have some way of keeping an eye on them. The net is so slow up here it damn near runs in reverse. The rest was easy. Those idiots haven't the faintest clue what the hell's going on up here do they?"

Taylor smiled. "This outfit's kinda on the small side for an operation of this size, and that worries me."

"How come?"

"Means if you lost control of the situation, then you don't have enough manpower to deal with it. So you gotta have a plan 'B', right?"

King gave a dry smile, slowly clapping his hands in mock applause.

"Well you're still as sharp as cheese wire old sport, but you'd have to ask the General about that. I'm just here to advise. However, I can tell you this; we're now at Level Three Containment."

"Where's Tellermine?"

King shook his head and waved his finger at Taylor like a teacher.

"Now that's a mark off your score board. You already know where he is."

"Damn! It was the airbase after all. But it's way too small I..."

"What you expect, shiny windows and a ten foot sign? Armstrong was one of the backup bases if NORAD ever fell. That place goes down ninety foot and out for half a mile. There's room for a whole regiment. Tellermine's been down there for weeks."

"I thought he was closed down."

"Look you know how it is; things are never that simple. People had their eyes on ZerTon and when it imploded they had to shut that operation down. There's so much tied up in all this, they gave him another chance."

Taylor's face flushed with anger and he jabbed his finger at King.

"He's being bankrolled by the government?"

"Not exactly. There are, shall we say, 'interested parties'. They deemed the risk worthwhile but something happened down there and those things started popping up outside. People got nervous and, well you can guess the rest."

"What caused the breach down there?"

"Not sure. We had a guy on the inside, said there'd been a fire and then we lost contact."

"Then you turned up and sealed the place. Why not just wipe the place out?"

King got up from his chair, walked over to the map table, then turned back and sighed.

"Things were done during Ebola that freaked people out. The last thing those up top wanted was a media circus here. So we isolated the town and sealed the base and reckoned that everybody down there would just die. What we didn't reckon on was that they'd start showing up in town."

Taylor sat forward and dipped his head. "Yeah, real inconsiderate of them and so embarrassing too. But you got that covered right? What is it some low yield nuke?"

"Oh come on Brent, give us some credit here. A nuke even up here is going to draw attention like a God damn smoky bonfire."

"Operation Bushfire. Sweet Lord." Taylor brought his fingertips to his mouth. "I never really thought anyone would use that. *On our own people*."

King pointed to the map showing Armstrong encircled by a thick red ring.

"The M900 is the latest thermobaric killing machine to roll off the conveyer. The press of a button and all our problems become dust in the wind. Simple as."

"What's the trigger?"

"Well sport, we're there about now, I should think. If there were any cases from within the town, then Stone's authorised to use the weapons. But thanks to the good Colonel Steedman, Stone decided to let it play out a while longer. See if the hillbillies can stop it themselves."

"Who's Colonel Steedman?"

"The second in command. A real pain in the ass. He's got 'principles' and he's gonna let that thing out if we ain't careful."

"The ever compassionate Major King, I see."

"Nobody will thank us if that virus reaches a populated area. You ought to know that."

"You've turned over a new leaf or something. The last time we met, you were throwing people off buildings."

King walked over to Taylor. "And how many people did I save by doing that? Including you as I recall?" He relaxed his attitude and continued. "And I'm going to do just the same this time too."

"Yeah, and how you gonna do that?"

"Brent, they want to pull you in for some tests. Just a few, to make sure you're okay. No need to worry. They just want to check you over, that's all."

Taylor could feel the sweat form at the back of his neck.

"Kinda nice of you."

"Some medical boys want to take a look at you."

"Well, as much as I appreciate your concern there JJ, I've already had my fill of medical tests..."

"It's out of my hands. Stone has a helio on a pad waiting. You're leaving right now. I'm sorry there's nothing *I can do.*"

He lent forward and spoke softly, looking anxiously at the closed door.

"It's all up to you."

Then he shouted out to the escort in the next room.

"Okay, Mr Taylor is ready to leave now."

The two guards entered the room and awaited orders.

"Brent these guys will take you to the pad and then you get a free ride."

Taylor got up and walked towards the two other men then stopped and looked back at King.

"You know what they're going to do to me, right?"

"Like I said, it's all up to you."

Taylor and his escort left the room and walked down the short duckboard path into the fresh air. He drew in a long breath and surveyed the scene, then started moving forward with the two men. They placed themselves to his left and right. Taylor surmised from their relaxed manner and from the fact that their weapons were in safety mode, they weren't expecting any trouble. The immediate vicinity was deserted expect for a cook throwing some food into a garbage bin.

Taylor waited until the man had gone back inside the de-mountable and then made his move. He stopped abruptly, allowing the two men to draw parallel with each other, and then grabbed the men by their collars, violently cracking their heads together. Both men collapsed in a heap and Taylor ran for his life towards the fence. He jumped onto a Humvee parked nearby, clambered on the roof and leapt over the fence. He sprinted for the tree line and within seconds had disappeared from sight.

****

Anne Lenski took a long hard look at herself in the station house rest room mirror. It seemed that whatever she tried with this virus, failed: people died... or worse. The only thing she could do was to make the victims comfortable and then watch them change. It was a cruel process; those infected went through great pain as the virus altered their bodies. Even when the transformation was completed the victim's suffering was far from ended. They entered into living a nightmare. She didn't even know if they were dead or alive. She closed the door and went out into the corridor.

"Anne, Anne you alright?"

She looked up through tear-blurred vision at Brad walking towards her. The last thing she wanted was for anybody to see her in this state, but she just couldn't help it.

"Brad I'm so sorry I just..."

"Take it easy. What's wrong here?" He held her head with both his hands and looked into her face.

"Don't look at me, I'm a damn mess." She pulled her head to one side and brushed the tears from her cheek.

"We've got to stay together in this..."

"I'm not strong enough to cope with this. I can't do it anymore."

Eastman fixed her with a firm stare. "Anne Lenski. You are one of the strongest people I ever knew. Sure this is tough and it's likely to get a whole damn sight tougher. But people are looking to us to hold them together."

"Brad, I can't fix this. I just can't."

"But you can give them hope. And that's all these people need right now."

"I can't lie to them anymore. There is no cure for this!"

Eastman took her arm. "Right now we got us a trickle of panic. If they think there's no hope left, then we got us a tidal wave. Something got to give somewhere."

"Brad, I wish I had your confidence. But it's going to take more than that."

"We will. Now what's got all this started?"

"I just got back from telling the Arcados their boy's 'turned'."

"Damn!"

"That's not all. We've another three confirmed infections. Things are getting out of hand."

Eastman briefly closed his eyes and gently shook his head. "Come on, we got a meeting with the Judge in my office. He doesn't like to be kept waiting."

He took her arm and led her the short distance to his office. She dried her eyes, looked at Eastman and smiled.

"Let's go kick his ass." Eastman pushed his office door open. Judge Carmille was sitting behind Eastman's desk, his glasses perched on the end of his nose and his hands clasped together. He had a look on his face that could have turned milk sour. Eastman touched the brim of his Stetson and looked at Carmille. "Judge."

"Sheriff, what in the hell happened out there today?"

"We found Al Paxmore and..."

"Tony Firth I'm talking about. What the hell were you doing up there in the first place?"

Carmille's face had turned crimson as he spat the words out.

"It's lucky he was up there or we might have had three Al Paxmores to deal with."

"I didn't ask for your opinion, Doctor. This is police business."

"It's not an opinion Judge, it's an obvious fact." Anne spoke in precise and deliberate tones as she addressed the Judge.

"I believe you're being impertinent madam, and I don't much care for it."

"And I believe you are being chauvinistic and rude. And I don't much care for that."

Carmille rose to his feet, his eyes narrowing into slits as he spoke from the side of his mouth.

"I think it's high time you left us."

"Doctor Lenski is a vital member of this town and I say who leaves my office or not, Judge."

Eastman's tone was direct and demanding as he looked squarely at the other man.

Carmille cleared his throat and moved to the other side of the desk, gesturing to the empty seat. Eastman looked at him and without a word, walked over to his chair and sat down.

"We were up at Firth's house because I received evidence that Peter Firth was supplying his brother medication. When we looked at the type, they were antibiotics and painkillers. The kinda DIY thing you'd expect someone to be treating individuals who didn't want to go to hospital."

"What happened?"

"Bridget and Conrad had already 'turned', Tony had them secured in the basement. They escaped – he didn't have a choice."

"Why didn't you stop him?"

"Because he had the drop on me."

"And that's what happened. You *did not* fire your gun?"

Carmille leant forward in his chair as if to emphasise the urgency in his voice.

"Who said other?"

"Peter Firth's been telling how you shot them all down."

"That's a lie! I saw what happened, I was there."

"Doctor, you think I'm gonna take that low life's word over Brad's? But now there has to be an investigation. We have to follow due process."

"I don't believe what I'm hearing. You want to investigate Brad over what that deadbeat says?"

"It's the law. Three people have been killed, there has to be an investigation. Brad knows the rules."

"Well damn the rules. We need him, now more than ever."

"I don't come into your surgery and tell you how to give out pills. I don't want you telling me how to do my job."

He pushed his glasses on top of his head and continued, "I said there has to be an investigation; I did not say right now."

"I..." Anne sat back, her embarrassment plain to see as her face coloured.

"Okay. We need someone to lead the town."

The Judge scratched his head in thought. "Ed's still on vacation. There isn't anybody else."

"Great, where's the Deputy Mayor when you need him? Still in Honolulu? There has to be someone in line."

"What about Veronica Redman, she's on the Town Council? And she's not one to sit about. She could do it."

"Yeah, Anne that's a good idea and I..."

Carmille raised his hands in the air, the look of exasperation clear on his face.

"Hold up you two. We don't want one of her kind running this town."

"When you say *her kind* do you mean female or gay?"

"Doctor, all 'that' may be fine and dandy in the big towns but it's got no place out here. You'd do well to remember that."

Eastman stood up making a 'time out' gesture and raised his voice above the other two. "Alright, alright! I don't care if it's a she, a he or she who thinks she's a him or a him who thinks he's a she. We gotta have somebody steering the damn canoe!"

"Agreed. What's your next move Brad?"

Eastman looked over at Carmille relieved to have averted yet another argument.

"It's time to circle the wagons. We need to get all the homesteaders into town. All but two farms have agreed to come in. They're the only people we've failed to get hold of."

"You think it could be trouble?"

"I've sent Jed and some of the boys to look. I'm hoping they've got radio problems or they've just taken off. We need to barricade the town and stop those things getting in."

"Al Paxmore was already in town and look at the damage he did."

"Anne, everybody who's been infected is accounted for. Al was already here."

"Brad, when you say 'everybody who's been infected,' just how many people are we dealing with?"

"Anne, do you want to take this?"

"On top of the cases I already have, after this morning I've got an additional three confirmed positive results. That's not including Tony Arcado; he 'turned' this morning."

Carmille stared at the desk top.

"Poor kid. What about the infected people from today, are they gonna change? Can you answer that, doctor?" His tone was terse as he looked directly at her.

"Judge, she's doing her best. We just need to let her get on with it."

Eastman walked over to the door and looked back at Carmille.

"We all got a lot to get on with."

Carmille rose from his seat and moved to the door.

"I'd best leave you to it then. I'll find somebody suitable for the vacancy. If not then it might have to be me."

Eastman looked at Carmille. "That's not how it works and you know it."

"We'll see about that. Brad, Doctor." He nodded towards them and left the room.

"That man is a dinosaur. He's wrong on so many levels. Sorry Brad, I know he's your hero but..."

Eastman looked at the door then looked at Anne, a deep frown cut into his face. "There was a time when I'd have said yes: now I'm not so sure."

****

The night was drawing in. Taylor turned the plastic key card over in his hand and studied the I.D. The small photo card displayed a picture of a pretty dark haired woman, about twenty-five or so: Mary Bakewell - Assistant Researcher. Then he dropped his gaze to look at the putrefying mess sprawled out in front of him.

It was almost impossible to imagine that this 'thing' was the girl on the card and yet he knew it was. He'd taken the damn thing off her. *Her*? In all this time he'd never really thought of them as people. He never regarded them as being someone's loved one or friend, with all the aspirations and hopes of the living. She had an engagement ring on her finger but that's all he knew about her.

The body was dressed in a filthy lab coat, so he guessed she must have worked on the project at some point. Just how she'd come to be here on the surface was beyond him. She'd been dead only a few hours, judging from the way her blood was still soaking into the ground.

Three neat bullet holes in her chest with a fourth just below her right eye, told him how she'd died. He'd never seen one like this before; sure he'd seen dead ones but never had the time to 'really' look at them. Mary Bakewell seemed at rest now. Hell, was he going soft?

He put the card into his pocket. There were other things he needed to look at. JJ. King for a start. He'd been the last person Taylor had imagined to have been here. It mystified Taylor as to why King had been so damn slack in allowing the escape.

Taylor had re-worked his time in the base over and over. It was almost as if King had wanted him to get away. King was well aware of Taylor's abilities and yet the guards seemed oblivious as to whom they were escorting. As soon as they'd left the room Taylor had sought the opening to escape. Was it that King had compassion for his old army buddy? Fat chance! King's people skills consisted of 'interviewing' while using a power drill on people. The guy was a certified nut. Whatever the reason, he was free and he wanted to stay that way.

A few hundred yards away, reaching high into the sunset was the Ranger tower. There was no way he was going to risk being spotted by that parks guy. Taylor was well aware that these people had the experience and resources to spot anything. That would put him a short radio call away from Eastman and his mob but even closer was good old JJ. He was someone Taylor wanted to keep well away from.

Taylor studied his options: Complete his mission? Escape to Canada? Find out what King was up to? Warn the town?

He had no resources to access the underground base and it would be suicide to do so on his lonesome. He'd only just escaped from the camp and in all probability he would either get captured or killed. As for the town, they'd done him no favours and he was not about to do them any. With the Level Three Containment situation, Stone could vaporise the whole damn place at any moment. Yeah, he could definitely hear Canada calling out his name.

CHAPTER - TWENTY

General Marcus Stone marched into the small command room flanked by Colonel Steedman. Stone was a large impressive man with grey cropped hair. He glowered at the arrogant man standing before him. Stone had seen his type so many times during his long military career. King was a damn black ops spook, and he hated them. They got involved in all sorts of situations, most of which had nothing to do with them. The field operatives regarded themselves as soldiers and that was the part he hated the most. Real soldiers had to follow a code of conduct, with strict rules; these individuals just made it up as they went along. It was a kind of cheating.

"Mr King, to say I'm unhappy at your efforts would be an understatement. If I thought you'd anything to do with this man's escape, you'd be in the brig."

He scowled at the other man, finding it hard to control his anger. But people like this sack of pus were always well connected and after all, Stone was a little under a year off retirement.

"Now hold up there General. I can't be held responsible if your goons lost him."

If you were one of my men, your ass wouldn't touch the ground.

"You knew this man and you fought alongside him. That creates a bond. Could it be you were looking out for him?"

King gave the General a disagreeable sneer. "I don't do friends. I look after my own interests."

Where the hell do they make you damn people?

"Never the less, if you look as though you're going to compromise this operation, I'll throw you on the next chopper out of here. Are we clear on that?"

King snapped him a drill book salute. "Sir yes sir. General Sir!"

Insubordinate punk!

Steedman moved forward and spoke to King.

"Where's he likely to go now?"

Steedman was a tall athletic man with blonde hair. The decorations on his chest and his Airborne shoulder flash told their own story.

"He's unpredictable, there's no telling what he'd do next. But I'll say this; he's like a dog with a stick. He'll do everything possible to bring Tellermine down."

"Is he likely to try getting into that base?"

"He has no resources and he's out of time. I hardly think that's a possibility."

King scratched his head and looked back at Stone. "Crap like that never deterred a Ranger before. If he wants that creep, he'll get him. But like I said, he's not dumb."

And you're up to no damn good, I just don't know what.

"Colonel, what's Lieutenant Baker got for me?"

Steedman walked over to the table and switched on the laptop. A schematic of the base appeared on the Whiteboard and he pointed to a highlighted section.

"This is a thermal map of the base, Baker's detected 'hot spots' all along this area. He believes they're fires."

Steedman looked at the other two before pressing on. "These hot spots or fires are headed to this point here." He jabbed his finger at a yellow box on the plan.

"And what's so important about that?"

"That, Mr King is where the fuel cell for the whole base is located."

King clicked his fingers and let out a loud laugh.

"That's good news. It'll save us having to do the job."

Stone looked at King and nodded in agreement. "He has a point. What's the proximity to the infected zone Colonel?"

"It's too far to cause any direct damage to the town, but right above that cell is one of the town's electrical sub – stations."

"What effect would that have on the infected zone?"

Steedman shook his head. "Minimal. It'd knock the power off, but they'd re – boot in hours."

Stone brought up a satellite map of the area and highlighted the base and Armstrong. They could use this as a diversion and fire the missile in the confusion. If the town had to go then perhaps this would be the best way to do it. They'd never know what hit them. It was decision time and there was no easy option for anybody.

"Colonel, start preparation for missile firing!"

Stone watched as Steedman's face dropped. The guy was a good soldier, one of the best he'd ever met. But he had a massive problem. He was too compassionate and this was a downright liability. The events of Mercy Creek had taught Stone all about the drawbacks of compassion. That situation had deteriorated so fast there'd been precious little time for hand- holding. It had needed fast and decisive action. He drew solace from the fact that he'd followed protocol and done what was needed. But that notion did nothing for the nightmares he'd endured ever since.

"I'll get on it ASAP, Sir."

King circled his finger on the map and nodded his head as if in answer to an unspoken question. "As a point of interest here, is this firework display going to work?"

Firework display! Arrogant little creep for half a dime, I'd...

"The M900 is state of the art weapons tech Mr King."

"Yeah, I knew the guy who stole the firing system. I just want to know how you plan to use the damn thing."

"Colonel perhaps you'd like to fill Mr King in on that?"

"Since you obviously know so much about the system I'll skip to the deployment."

King sat on the edge of the desk and peering at his watch briefly shut his eyes. "Oh yes Colonel, please do."

"The device will airburst at five hundred feet above the town. The heat wave will incinerate everything in a three-click kill radius. It'll wipe out the town, the base and all the surrounding farms."

Stone looked at Steedman: it was a tough call but it wasn't Steedman who needed to make it.

"See Mr King, all our problems taken care of in one go. End of emergency."

"No it won't."

King rose from the desk and quietly walked to the centre of the small room. He stared at the other men, almost daring them to challenge him.

What else are you keeping from us?

"It would seem Mr King has some information that we don't. Well the floor is yours."

"This base," said King pointing at the airbase "was part of the NORAD defence system. It's over ninety foot down through rock, reinforced concrete and steel. The place was built to withstand an over burst by a ten megaton bomb. Your Molotov is barely going to warm a Hershey Bar down there."

"Steedman, what's he talking about here?"

Steedman clasped his hands behind his neck and nodded at King in agreement.

"I'm afraid I have to agree with him, Sir. The M900 uses the oxygen to burn its target. It's a surface weapon. It would be impossible to penetrate to such a depth."

Stone could not believe his ears. It was as if everything was conspiring against him. This damn bomb was supposed to be the best invention since the wheel, yet in all reality the device was useless against the underground defence. He'd have to find something else.

"Colonel, we'll use the second device on the base after we take out the infected zone."

"You got two bombs? Now that's where my tax goes." King whistled loudly. "You need to take out the base first then the town."

And you need to watch your step boy. You're living on borrowed time!

"Are you telling me how to run this operation?"

"General, that warhead may not be powerful enough to reach the underside of that base, but it's going to level the topside. You'd need to dig through tons of crap to get at the door."

"We have enough manpower to shift a few cinder blocks," replied Steedman with contempt.

King looked from one man to the other. "What you don't have is time. As soon as people notice that thing busting up the atmosphere, you're going to be knee deep in media and eggheads. So we nuke that after the town, right!"

Stone looked at King. As much as this irritating pile of dog vomit needed to be taken down, he was right. An explosion of that size would be picked up in China. That much attention, Stone could do without. They'd have to play it King's way. Stone was more than aware that he had to cooperate with this idiot but it was a military operation.

"We'll set off the second device after the first. I don't want a moment's delay in this. That town must be eradicated. Colonel, prepare both missiles for use. Get a detail to open that door as soon as the first missile is ready."

"The missile will need to be transported into the base for maximum effect. That means exposing the men to whatever is in there, Sir."

Stone didn't want to put his men in that kind of danger but there was no option. The M900 had to be placed in the best possible spot before it was exploded, and that meant going down into that hell-hole.

"I'll lead the team myself and you blow that thing when I say so."

Steedman shook his head. "Sir, with respect you're needed up here. I'll do it."

"If you're done with all this hero bull, I'm best suited for this mission."

Stone raised his eyebrow and shot King a cynical look. This kind of guy never put others before themselves unless of course, there was something in it for them. What could be down there?

"That's very civic of you, yeah okay. But I'll pick the team and you follow my orders to the letter. Are we clear on that?" King nodded his agreement.

"You don't need the whole missile for that. I'll get weapons tech to remove the warhead. It'll be easier to lug about."

King looked at Steedman. "Thanks. You got some kind of trolley I can use for this?"

"I'm sure we can find something for you even if I have to tie it to your back."

There was no humour in Stone's remark, in fact that seemed a fair idea to him. This guy was certainly up to something. Stone was uneasy at the prospect of placing his troops under him.

"How long till the devices are ready for use?"

"We'll get on it ASAP. But this will take some time to put together. Why don't you have a coffee and finish your book."

"Can't stand coffee and I finished the book. The General did it with a big red button." King took a last look at the map, nodded to the others and left the room.

"Sir, can that man be trusted with this? I'm getting a bad feeling about him."

"That individual gave me a bad feeling the minute I met him. The team will have eyes on him all the time. If he tries anything they can blow his pecker neck head off. Colonel, I want everybody withdrawn to the safety zone. Pull all surveillance and patrols back to the camp. If we got to fire those things I don't want any of our people in the way."

"Yes Sir."

Steedman saluted and left Stone gazing at the map on the whiteboard deep in thought.

Stone had been around long enough to smell trouble and this Spook gave off a stench to rival the dirtiest latrine. They'd have to keep an eye on him. This operation was top-level stuff with no margin for error; everything had to fit together. This contamination had to be contained; there was no time to waste on this guy.

****

Something was happening and it sounded ugly. Mary Firth stood uneasily in the kitchen. Her husband was in the other room on the phone. It was difficult to hear the exact words because he'd slammed the door shut. She could tell it wasn't good. He'd arrived about half an hour ago, in a foul mood. He'd ranted on about how Carmille was supporting Brad over the killings. Peter still blamed him, but it had got worse and she feared he'd do something dumb.

She needed to find out what was going on, but she knew from past experience that poking her nose in was both unwise and painful. However, she had to know. Mary selected a yellow duster from the drawer, tipping even more junk onto the cluttered floor as she moved warily into the hallway. At least the duster would help mask her mission, even if she rarely ever used one. As she edged nearer the scuffed old door, her heart beat so loudly she feared he'd hear it. She licked at her dry lips and moved ever closer to the door.

He was talking to Barney Branigan. How she hated that man. After the collapse of their marriage Branigan had taken to calling over when Peter had been out. Then one night he'd called drunk and things had gotten out of hand. He'd tried to kiss her but she'd warned him off with Peter. Thankfully it had been enough and he never tried that again.

"Look Barney, I already told you I'm positive Eastman and the others are in on this whole thing... because they're helping to cover it up. Who's gonna argue with the cops and Lenski? It's all a cover up."

This was utter nonsense! Brad and Anne would never be a party to such a thing. She'd known Brad since forever and he didn't work that way.

"What? Because Tony found out and that's the only way they could shut him up... Well it's obvious Bridget and Conrad knew too much... Look when you're in charge like that, you can make up what the hell you want to... Do you think I'm about to let this go? That shmuck killed my brother...Well all I want is a bit of extra muscle...Yeah, that's right... Well, I kinda thought you, Kolp and maybe Don Breck and Murray Scott... He's out of town, up at the tower right now...Yeah, of course we gotta be careful but I know what I've got in mind... Don't talk crap! How the hell would it look like an accident? It's more like a dreadful case of mistaken identity...Well yeah; of course someone obviously thought he was one of them creatures."

Mary drew back, sick to her stomach. Had Peter finally gone mad?

"Yeah, I know it's risky. But with him outta the way you and me can run this damn town... I take it you like that then? Trust me, nothing can go wrong if we do this right..."

Suddenly Peter Firth's sneering face replaced the section of battered door she'd been staring at. She shrank away from him in utter terror.

"What you hear, baby?" His lips curled upwards in a cruel smile.

"Nothing, I never heard nothing. I was just dusting that's all."

He reached out and closed his fist over the yellow duster in her hand and squeezed until she let out a painful scream.

"Peter, you're hurting me!"

"I've never seen you use one of these, you lazy sow."

He snatched the material from her hand, held it between his fingers, then let it slowly drift to the floor. She backed away as he moved out from the room and walked towards her.

"Honest, I didn't hear a thing. I swear to you."

"Oh, you heard all right. But what can I do to stop you blabbing?"

"I'm not going to say a thing – please, you gotta believe me."

There was no point in playing dumb any longer. All she could do was plead for her life.

"How dumb do you think I am, you lying broad? I know you got the hots for Eastman. If 'goody two shoes' Helen hadn't come along, you'd have been right in there."

As he advanced she stumbled back into the bedroom and tripped onto the hard wooden flooring, hitting her head. He reached down and clasped his fingers tightly around her throat and started to squeeze.

"You ain't never gonna tell anyone about this. Do you hear me? Never!"

As she started to black out, unexpectedly, he let her go and she slid to the floor like a rag doll. She lay on the patchy blue carpet, barely conscious as he bent down and grabbed her by the jaw and looked right into her face.

"You ever mention this and I'll feed you to the pigs." He let her go and made for the bedroom door. "After today there ain't no place for you anymore."

Several seconds later she heard the front door slam and he was gone.

****

Eastman looked up fleetingly at the ladder leading to the 'fishbowl' then began his ascent. It wasn't that heights bothered him; he just preferred to keep away from them. Climbing this far in the near dark and with the wind picking up was nowhere near his idea of fun. But his purpose for seeing Merka had taken on a different slant now. Why hadn't he responded to Eastman's calls? It was unlike the guy to cut himself off like that.

As Eastman reached the top of the ladder he pulled himself onto the balcony and looked out over the darkened landscape. Feeling the evening breeze on his face, Eastman could see why Bill spent so many hours up here. Peace and solitude meant a lot to him also. But it was Bill he'd come to see and so he pushed the reinforced door open and stepped inside.

Walking into the room he gazed around the space although there was no sign of Bill. Eastman headed for the crew area, calling out to Merka. As he pushed the door open, the room was lit by the screen of a solitary computer on the desk.

"Don't you ever lock your front door? Hey Bill."

Eastman walked forward and his blood ran cold as the figure in the chair slowly turned to face him. The blank eyes looked right through Eastman, then the familiar growling sound he heard so often filled the room.

Gradually Merka rose from the chair and edged forward. Even in this light Eastman could see the cause of the transformation. A huge jagged hole had been ripped out of the side of Merka's neck and part of his scalp had been torn away. Looking at his empty holster, Eastman hoped that at least Bill had put up a fight.

Eastman drew his weapon. He looked at the shambling monster before him and faltered. What if Anne was right and there was a way back? Could there be a bit of Bill left in all that mess? He was brought back to reality with a howl as the thing sped up and lunged at him. The deafening roar of the 357 Magnum in the enclosed space rang in his ears. At such close range the impact threw the thing backwards crashing into the desk. Eastman looked over at the near decapitated body and replaced his pistol. After what seemed an age he collected his thoughts and went into the other room.

Apart from Benteen, Merka had been the closest thing to a friend he'd got in the whole town. Merka had been a good man. If Taylor was in anyway responsible for any of this, Eastman would take delight in hunting him down.

As he opened the door to the balcony he heard the first of several distant explosions. Even a way off, the bangs were strong enough to rattle the windows. Then the night sky near Sam's place lit up with a kaleidoscope of colour; red, orange and even green and blue flames flying into the night sky. Then abruptly the tower was plunged into darkness, as if someone had hit the light switch. Eastman looked towards the town, but Armstrong was nowhere to be seen.

****

Harper opened the last can of beef from his ration pack. It was close to 21:00 hours and he could hardly wait to stand down. It had been a long watch with zilch to report, which was probably just as well. It was still mind-numbing. He looked at the other members of the team: Dodge, Smithy and the new kid, Ford. They were covering the road approaching the camp. There were two other checkpoints but Harper's team were the furthest from the camp. Apart from the green phantom-like images produced from their night vision, they were surrounded by the black velvet shroud of night. They had a ton of firepower but that only worked if you could see the target.

Dodge was resting his elbows on the hood of the Humvee, scanning the area in front of them with his binoculars. Dodge was from back East, they all were, even the new kid. Harper had known Dodge and Smithy from the start, they'd gone through the unit selection and been thrown into the same squad. He was smart for a big guy, no Einstein, but he got by. Then there was Smithy. What could you say about him? He was the kinda guy that only a mother could love and now he was doing that thing with his nose again.

"Hey Smithy, you want to eat something green, then eat the damn peas," Harper called crossly.

Dodge swung around. "He ain't doing that thing again? Oh, gross man."

"Hey you, face the God damn front. You're supposed to be watching for them, not me."

Smithy got to his feet and switched on his night vision. "Hold the fort you bums, I'm gonna take a leak." He started down the road to a nearby cluster of trees. Harper could not resist the temptation. "Mind they don't bite it off Smithy."

"All right, already!" He stormed back to the group and sat away from the others.

"Aw, you done it now Harper. He'll sit like that all damn night now."

"Do you think there's any of them out there?"

Harper looked at Ford. He'd seen kids like this before; hell he wasn't too different from him. Except at his age Harper had been doing his best to keep from getting wasted or serving time. This kid was far from dumb.

"Who knows? But that's how Landon got it."

"I heard about that. What happened?" Ford clutched his M16 and looked at Harper.

"One minute everything was clear then the next, two zombies come outta nowhere and bit his fingers off."

"Okay, enough of the spooky stories already." Smithy moved and sat in the middle of the group. "But you can't die from that, right?"

Dodge called over his shoulder. "It's enough. That's all it takes, kid. You get the bug and it's no more PX for you."

"See, what I don't get is why these dummies just don't take off?"

Remarks like this were why Smithy was regarded as a klutz. Harper viewed the other man with despair.

"The only way outta of this hole is blocked by that pile of rock we made the other day."

"Sure, but these kinda people always got four-by-fours. So why don't they just use them?"

Harper had also thought about that, but fair play to the kid, that was one hell of a good point. After they'd brought the hill down and shut the road he'd imagined the potentials taking off through the mountain tracks. But they hadn't.

"Who knows kid?" Dodge shrugged his shoulders and rasied his eyebrows.

"It's their town, why should they run? We'd stay and fight."

Harper looked at Dodge; was it just about turf? Back in his 'hood,' Harper had fought to keep the gang's turf clear. He'd never thought about what others felt about their turf. That made sense.

"Whatever. But why aren't people trying to get into that town?"

"Cause kid, Labrinski and his crew got a ten-ton road-roller and a stop sign."

Exasperated, Ford flung his arms into the night air. "Which means?"

Harper put his empty can into a bag and looked at Ford.

"How many times you come across a bunch of dudes in hard hats and a stop sign with the road up? And who the hell would argue with them?"

It was the perfect cover, some guys with a hole in the road. It was the kind of thing people were used to seeing; who would take the slightest bit of notice? A tank made for a persuasive roadblock, but it came low down in the stealth stakes. This type of mission wasn't about flags or medals, nor was it the sort of thing you told your grandchildren about. They all knew that heroic deeds would not be written about Operation Viking.

"Okay, what we gonna do with this place now we got it?"

Harper sat on his pack and opened an energy drink before answering Ford.

"Nothing. We don't want it. The place is about to be overrun by a herd of cannibal freaks. All we gotta do is stop them escaping."

"Yeah, I managed to work that out all on my own. But what happens *now*?"

"They're just as likely to nuke the whole damn lot."

Smithy got up and walked over to Dodge and took his place on watch. "Yeah right, sure they will."

Harper got up, let out a huge yawn, stretched his arms and moved over to Ford.

"If any of them potentials get out and they're infected, they could eat their way through New Jersey."

"Well that's not any great loss."

"Hey, watch your mouth, you bum. I got people in New Jersey."

Dodge waved his finger at Smithy and scowled.

"Whoever said potentials were smart?" Harper laughed, shaking his head.

"What in hell's a potential, anyways?"

"If there's an infection or something like Ebola, that kinda thing, then individuals have the 'potential' to become infected."

Ford took a long look at Harper.

"So what about us are we potentials?"

Harper frowned and rubbed his eyebrow. This kid was getting too smart; soon he'd be able to wipe his own butt.

"That's why we got M16's and razor wire."

Dodge nodded his support. "Not to mention the nukes of course."

"Wyllie says the whole town's gone nuts. Nuke the freaking lot, I say."

The brass had withdrawn them for a reason. That reason looked to be pretty damn obvious and it worried Harper.

"You don't want to listen to him. Sergeant Rai says the town's fighting back."

"Wyllie's done alright by us and he's..."

"Come off it Smithy, those people in that barn. That was freaking murder."

"What happened?" Ford looked at Harper for an explanation but Dodge interrupted.

"Hey guys, I heard that Stone was spitting blood at losing that prisoner. Who'd you think he was, Harper?"

Harper had been up close to the guy and he'd had military written all over his mug. Perhaps he was some type of rogue Black Ops or something. Who could tell? But the General had gone ape. This dude was important but Harper couldn't fit him into a picture.

"Okay, so if they want to zap the town, how the hell you gonna cover something like that up? It's too big."

"You still on about that crap kid." Smithy shook his head.

"Damn right I am. You're on about killing hundreds, maybe thousands. Or didn't you bunch work that out yet?"

"Look kid, they can write a cover story better than any Hollywood movie."

Harper swatted an insect on his face before continuing.

"They don't use nukes, they use a kinda firebomb. You can bet your bottom dollar that some PR team has already written the 'day after' headlines. Something like; a terrorist attack, plane crash or red neck's moonshine factory explodes. You get the picture."

Once it was done it was done, too late to cry about it then. Harper knew that was the way it operated. The cops were always pulling stuff like that; they'd bust you and then think something up later. This whole thing was being run by the US Army; they could do what they wanted and get away with it. Harper looked at Ford, even with the limits of night vision he could tell the kid was shaken. "Cheer up kid. At least we don't have to push the button."

"Yeah we're just doing as we're told, ain't that it guys?"

Ford looked at Smithy and slowly shook his head.

"Yeah, we're just doing as we're told, right. Reminds me of what those Syrians said when the SEALs took out that torture place."

Dodge pointed at Ford and waved his finger at him. "We're doing it to save lives."

"Why don't you tell that to the people down there?" Ford got up and moved towards Smithy to take up his turn at watch.

****

Eastman's headlights sliced through the inky black night as his police lights bounced about the deserted streets. The sound of Benteen's voice sounded distorted as it drifted through the open window of the car. He was warning people to remain calm and stay indoors. Eastman let a faint smile cross his face as he recalled the last time they'd used the PA system. Someone had forgotten to switch the thing off, subjecting half the town to Benteen singing 'Silent Night.' With all that had gone on that week Eastman knew all too well that the town was sitting on a powder keg.

In the distance he could make out the headlights of the mobile patrols as they prowled around the town. Luckily Clara had kept him posted on the developments after the explosions; he knew what to expect. He was thankful the curfew had kept people safely indoors, and the tannoy had further discouraged any sightseers. The town needed lights and fast if they wanted to keep a lid on things. Langley and O'Brien had joined forces with some of the power company guys to get things up and running.

The tyres of his car ground nosily on the tarmac, as he turned into McNally's Drive only two blocks away from the station house. Eastman could make out the homely glow from the emergency lighting. The health center also had power, thanks to Anne spending money on over-hauling the ancient generators.

He switched the annoying static of his radio down then braked hard. Parked across the single lane was Murray Scott's truck, the driver's door wide open. The vehicle was left in such a way, it was impossible to pass. Eastman cursed loudly and gave a blast of his siren. Of all the times to block the damn road, he thought. What a moron. He gave another blast, then angrily got out and walked towards the truck.

As he drew level with the driver's door, Eastman warily looked inside the cab. Suddenly he heard the crack of a pistol shot followed by a high pitch whine. The side window disintegrated into showers of glass. Eastman threw himself against the side of the vehicle and drew his sidearm. The shot had come from the other side of the street and judging by the angle, from the roof-tops. Fortunately, the shooter was the other side of the vehicle.

"Ceasefire you mutton heads! It's me, Eastman."

He waited for the awkward apology but two more shots ripped into the driver's side of the truck.

"Alright, I said it's me, you dumb son of a..."

Two more bullets hit the truck and this time they were thirty eights. Now there was a second shooter. What the hell was wrong with these guys? They must have heard him yell out. Then it dawned on him. They weren't shooting at him because they didn't know who it was; they were shooting because they *did* know. This was now a whole new ballgame and there was only one man who'd be fired up to try this.

"Peter Firth. I'm gonna give you the opportunity to lay down your weapons and after that I'm gonna come and take them. You hear me?"

Although the muzzle flashes had shown him roughly where the gunmen were, it was impossible to target the exact position in the dark. Two more shots from the thirty-eight signalled to Eastman that this gunman was working his way around the rear of the truck. If Eastman wasn't careful they'd catch him in a cross-fire. He still had the option to move to the front of the truck if the thirty-eight guy got around the back. Or take his chances in the gloomy streets.

The main problem was that the squad car's headlights lit Eastman up like a rabbit. Any movement beyond the darkened side of the truck could well be his last. He heard someone scuttle across roof tiles somewhere to the rear of the truck, but they weren't in place to take a shot at him, or he them. The last thing Eastman wanted was a gun battle in the street. Looking into the dazzling lights of his car made it impossible for accurate fire. Damn!

Then the sound of a large bore rifle ripped through the still night air and smashed through the truck's windshield. That was it; he was now surrounded by three assailants and no place to run. Two rounds in quick succession followed by a cry of pain evened the score, as one of the gunmen fell to the sidewalk. The shots had come from a 9mm, somewhere to the left of the truck. It had to be Benteen.

"What took you so long you great lump?" Eastman called, relieved.

The unfortunate rifleman sent another round into the night only to meet the same fate. Eastman heard the weapon clatter down the roof until it smashed onto a parked car. That left the guy with the thirty-eight to deal with. At that moment Eastman got lucky; he caught sight of a shadowy figure on Alec Bushes' roof. It was a long shot, but he took careful aim and sent a 357 round crashing into his target. The man yelled in agony as the heavy round tore into his shoulder and sent him flying off the roof.

Eastman heard the sound of trash-cans being up-skittled as the man hit the ground, followed by receding footsteps as he made his getaway. Eastman scanned the area for Benteen then detected a figure walking towards him, silhouetted in the squad car's beams. He shielded his eyes and squinted in the harsh light as the figure got closer.

"We just gotta stop meeting like this Eastman."

It was Brent Taylor. Eastman looked down to see a 9mm pistol aimed at his chest.

CHAPTER – TWENTY-ONE

Mary Firth was sitting in the total darkness of her front room. It wasn't the first time she'd found herself without electricity; the Power Company got pretty mad when you didn't pay the bill. However, this time things were different. This time the whole town was off. Perhaps she should've been scared, being on her own at a time like this, but she wasn't. It was almost as if the darkness gave her protection, a form of anonymity. She could watch the town but the town couldn't see her. She brought her knees up to her chest and took another sip of beer. Booze was something she never did; too many years of seeing the effect it had on Peter was enough. Tonight was an exception. She'd a feeling that something was about to happen.

She looked up as she heard one of the patrols approaching the house, then the sound trailed off as the men moved away. Maybe it was connected to the gunshots from earlier on; there'd been a lot of activity. Benteen had warned people to keep off the streets. What if it had been something to do with those things? What if some of them had wandered into town? She hoped that it had nothing to do with Brad.

Mary was confused but it wasn't the beer talking. These past few weeks she'd been aware of feelings for Brad, deeper than feelings. After his last visit she'd thought of nothing but him. He'd never give her a second glance with Anne Lenski on the scene. They had a kind of chemistry about them and even if they hadn't noticed, everybody else had.

Mary threw the empty can onto the worn carpet; she wasn't much for household chores. She reached into the little camping chiller and opened another can. She sighed then and shut her eyes tightly. Everything had been fine up until the end of High School and then Helen had shown up. It wasn't even as if Brad and Mary had been an item; they'd not so much as even held hands. But Helen had put paid to anything they might have had.

After Helen died, Brad had been in a mess, the kind of thing that few people would have got through. Even though Mary had been with Peter, it had crossed her mind to make a play for Brad. She knew it was wrong trying to hit on him, but she'd been desperate for affection. She cringed at the memory; how she'd hated herself back then. She pushed it from her mind and tried to read the time from the clock on the wall.

The flashlight barely lit the back of her hand. She fumbled for the replacement batteries but dropped them into the void. It had to be after ten by now. She'd been watching the DVD and the LED had read almost eight, then some time after, the explosions had knocked the power off. Peter had been gone hours before that and when she'd heard the guns she'd expected him home. If it had been something to do with his plan from earlier on, she hoped with all her heart that Brad had killed him. Mary reached under the cushion and brought out her father's old 22 caliber pistol.

****

Mary's eyes shot open like a startled deer and she awoke with a jolt at the sudden noise outside the house. Fearfully she made her way to the doorway. Scarcely breathing, she pressed her head against the door and listened hard. She could hear the groans and moans as someone or something got closer. What if it was one of those creatures? She'd seen Al Paxmore raving and attacking people the other day at the deli. Mitch had been forced to kill him. The people he'd attacked had gone to hospital and some hadn't come out.

The racket got ever closer and she drew back wondering what to do. They'd said in the meeting, the best thing to do was to strike at the head. She didn't care for that notion one bit. What if she kept quiet and did nothing? How would it even know someone was in? Yes. That was the best thing. Then it would have to go someplace else. Her heart sank as she heard her husband's voice.

"Open up you dumb broad! I'm hurt out here!"

In blind panic she rushed forward to open the door then stopped dead. She held her hand to her mouth and darted back a few steps and waited. If she didn't answer then perhaps he'd go away? She stood riveted to the spot and stared at the door in the vain hope he'd do exactly that.

"Are you in there you lazy witch? My Goddamn arm's hanging off out here!"

She tightly shut her eyes. It'd have been better if it had been one of those things. If he was standing out there hurt, then it could only mean one thing. Brad had come off worse. Tears ran down her face. This foul man had taken everything from her – her dignity, her self-respect and now even Brad Eastman. Mary levelled the tiny handgun at the door as she heard the hinges tear out of the frame, and Peter forced his way in. She remembered to pull the hammer all the way back and then aimed at the figure in the doorway.

"Well don't just stand there, I'm bleeding to death, you cheap slut!"

She squeezed the trigger and emptied all six bullets into her husband. The flash from the pistol was enough to see the look of surprise on his face as he fell to the ground. She walked over to the lifeless body and used the remaining battery power to gaze at him. The time she'd spent with her father shooting at old tins had paid off. All six deadly bullets had found their mark. Peter Firth was no more. Mary walked over to her seat and calmly sat down. She felt no remorse, no regrets, only a sense of immense relief. She placed the pistol on the seat next to her and wondered how long it would be before someone came to investigate.

****

"You carry a good tale Taylor, I'll give you that."

"What's it with you, you always been this way or you had some life changing experience?"

Eastman pointed to the 9mm in Taylor's hand. "Stop waving that thing about and maybe I'll listen."

Taylor patted the pistol and shook his head. "As I recall the last time we met *you* never had any difficulties with that."

Eastman reclined in his chair and looked up at the ceiling then back at Taylor.

"Let's see. So as well as a secret military unit holding my town hostage with a bomb, you just happen to turn up and save the day. I mean what's not to believe about that?"

"Who'd you expect, a bunch of meddling kids in a VW van and damn dog? I could've been half way to Canada by now."

Eastman averted his eyes momentarily and dipped his head sideways.

"Yeah well, you did pull my fat out of the fire back then. I owe you that."

"I'm thinking the 'good doctor' didn't run that blood test. Am I right?"

Eastman shifted uneasily and gave the other man an embarrassed look.

"Well we've been kinda busy since your last visit."

"How busy?"

"There was an incident." Eastman paused and tapped his chin thoughtfully before continuing. "Now more people are infected."

"That's not good. There's a guy itching to exercise his trigger finger on a big red button out there."

"What'd you mean?"

"This is now a Level Three Containment operation. If Stone even so much as thinks you hillbillies have lost control, you and this whole town are gonna be so much dust blowing in the wind."

A look of shock was etched over Eastman's face. "Okay, okay. What'd you want me to do?"

Taylor pushed the radio handset towards the lawman. "Call that doctor of yours and tell her you want those results."

Eastman studied the mic then looked over at the other man.

"What's so damn important about that test? What you trying to prove to us?"

"Cops don't like gaps in things. That result is a whole truck-load of cement. Now make that call."

Eastman lifted the mic to his mouth and pressed the button. "This is Brad Eastman calling Anne Lenski. Are you there Anne? Over."

Seconds later Anne's voice rang across the room.

"Hello Brad, I was just about to call you. What was all that shooting? I've got Aldo Kolp and Don Breck on my slabs here. Over."

"Yeah, I'll tell you later. Out of the blue I know, but have you got that hobo's blood tests? Over."

"Sorry, did you say hobo? Over."

"That's right, the hobo. Over."

"Hobo? Oh, you mean...."

Eastman keyed the mic, deliberately drowning out her message. "I mean the hobo. Yes. Over."

"Well to be honest, it's not on my 'things to do' list. Why? Over."

"Let's say something's come up. Over."

There was a long silence before the reply came. "Give me half an hour. Brad, is everything all right? Over."

Taylor put his finger on his lips and shot Eastman an anguished look. "Call me when you got something. Out."

Eastman sat back in his chair and looked at Taylor. "Now what?"

"I guess you'd best take this. I found it up by the tower near one of those things."

He extracted the ammo clip, slid the breech open then placed the pistol on the desk in front of the astonished lawman. Before Eastman could respond, the office door crashed open. Taylor spun around only to see Benteen's burly figure framing the doorway, shotgun aimed directly at his head.

"Well, now look what we got us here." Benteen gave Taylor a cruel grin.

****

Sam Cortez looked out across the health center parking lot into the darkness. The only light radiated from Henry Chan's solar-powered lawn lamps across the way. The health center, station house and the fire department were the only places in town that had emergency power. He walked to the end of the corridor, pulled the outer door shut and activated the security alarm. Elle-May had placed him in charge of things for now. Conrad Brown had gone home before the power cut and Norris Zillman may as well have gone, for all the use he was. Cortez couldn't get the guy; it wasn't that he was lazy or unlikeable, he was just awkward. He had to be told two or maybe even three times before he got it right. Nobody knew where he'd come from, he'd just turned up one day. Of course, all that slaughter the other night was enough to stop a guy working nights.

Cortez stopped by the vending machine and viewed the selection behind the glass with relish. He fumbled in his pants pockets for the correct change, selected the candy bar and punched in the product code. His smile was short lived as the machine emitted a grinding noise and then suddenly stopped.

"Oh, you little... Damn!"

He banged his palms on the glass and then tugged repeatedly at the selector lever. Nothing happened. He tried once more before residing himself to his fate then moved away. He still had to check stuff off his list before he could put his feet up. Though things weren't all bad and he smiled at the prospect of a nice fat overtime cheque. The medical staff had been hit hard and Elle-May needed extra people. It worked out well for him after all; a little extra cash was never a bad thing.

He keyed the locking code and opened the heavy door to the morgue and stepped in. He cursed the janitor for not having fixed the lights as the neon beam danced about the room. Cortez shielded his eyes from the annoying flashes and switched the broken set off. He only needed enough light to check the room temperature and the chillers.

Next to the rest areas, this was his favourite place to be. Except for a handful of people, he was about the only one to come into this room and he was almost certainly the only one after dark. It was a great scam for quiet time. He looked over at the latest three occupants; they sure as hell weren't gonna let on. Bodien had brought in Kolp and Breck a while back and now Peter Firth had joined them.

He dragged the two plastic chairs over to the storeroom; he sat down on one and stretched his legs out on the other. He'd almost completed his work so a few moments weren't going to harm. As he started to drift into a slumber, a sudden clatter from outside ejected him from his seat. Cortez opened the door and stepped into the corridor.

He looked all around, but the area was completely deserted, then he heard another clang. It sounded like one of the fire buckets; cautiously he rounded the corner and stopped dead. Three creatures were feasting on the body of Adrian Gates, one of the patients. As Cortez turned to run he screamed at the rotting face directly behind him.

****

"So why'd they go and arrest her?"

Elle-May popped another piece of cherry pie into her mouth. The nurse post was deserted apart from she and Jedrey Bodien; their shadows cast long shapes down the dimly lit corridors.

"Well she ain't been exactly arrested. She come in voluntary. Gerard still gotta question her."

He put his hand up to ward off another helping of pie.

"What's to question? She killed that no account creep and that's all there is. Sure you don't want another slice?"

Bodien gave a half smile and shook his head patting his stomach.

"Ain't as simple as that. She never admitted to killing him. What Gerard said was: she told him she thought it was one of them things."

"Well that's gotta be all right. She was scared. Anyone would have done the same."

"That's why we brought her in because we don't know what happened."

"Take it from her side; a lone woman in a blackout with a possible monster at the door. Listen, I'd have done the exact same."

"I take the point, but how many of them critters you seen walking about out there tonight? None. We gotta be sure it happened the way she said, that's all."

"Do you reckon they gonna get the power on tonight?"

Bodien rubbed the back of his neck and sighed.

"Don't rightly know, but the power guys said it was a fine mess. Darndest thing was they reckon the blast come from beneath the station. Like something blew up from underground."

"Well there's no works around there. What'd Brad think?"

"Don't know – nobody's seen him since the shooting."

"Oh sugar, he's back at the station."

She pointed in the direction of Anne Lenski's office. "Anne's talking to him."

He grunted and frowned at her. "Nice someone knows what going on here. I'm about run off my feet."

"I hear you on that. We've been chasing our tails all week and it's worse now."

"How you managing to keep this place running anyway, without the rest of the... well you know?"

She nodded her head sadly. "Anne roped some of the military in and I got a bunch of ex-nurses to help out but it sure ain't no picnic in here."

"I bet. Don't think I've had time for real chow for days."

"Tell you what, how about you come over to mine and I'll cook some of that pot roast we had us in the summer fair?"

He shifted uncomfortably, flicking his hat nervously. "Ah well, you know..."

"You're a fine figure of a man. It's about time someone spoiled you. Now what you say?"

"Well I... I suppose I could do, if it ain't too much trouble and I'm not working of course."

Elle-May beamed at him. "That's a done deal then. I'll expect you about noon."

He shot her a hesitant grin. "So apart from you three who else is on tonight?"

"There's two girls up on ward one and Norris is about someplace, why d'you ask?"

"I got to be off soon, but I don't like the notion of leaving you on your own."

"Oh honey don't mind that none. Sam's shut all the doors; we're as safe as houses in here, you get off. At least we got us light."

They both looked up as the corridor lit up with a crackle as the strip light blinked on. Anne Lenski walked towards them with a look of confusion on her face. She held up her hand to greet them and then turned to Bodien.

"Jedrey, not that I want to get rid of you, but are you going back to the station?"

"Yeah, I was about to leave now. Anything up doc?"

She glanced at him thoughtfully. "Just spoke to Brad, I got the impression something was up, not sure what."

Elle-May looked at her with concern. "It's what's been going on that's all. He's had a lot to deal with tonight."

Anne smiled at her but it was difficult to hide her unease. "You're probably right, but I'd like to check."

"I'll go right away Doc. Don't worry." Bodien gave her a reassuring smile then looked at Elle-May. "I'll be sure to set that date in my book." He tipped the brim of his hat to them and walked towards the doors to leave. Anne bent forward and whispered excitedly into Elle-May's ear. "Date, did he just say date?"

"No, what he meant was he's coming to dinner with me tomorrow and..." Anne smiled at Elle-May and spoke in her best Sothern accent.

"Oh well sugar, I do declare that's almost a date." Elle-May blushed a deep shade of red and tidied her notes.

"Oh hush now!"

Sam Cortez burst through the door, blind panic on his face and terror in his voice as he clutched at Bodien. "They're in the building. They're in the building!"

Bodien prised the other man's hands away shaking him roughly. "Who's in the building?"

The terrified man pointed behind the two women and hissed in a low tone at Bodien. "They are!"

All three followed in the direction only to see four of the creatures lumbering towards them. Both women raced to Bodien and Anne called out a warning and gestured to the corridor that Cortez had emerged from. Shuffling towards them was another group of ghouls; one of them was dragging a severed arm behind it. Bodien drew his pistol and aimed at first one group and then the second, unsure which to engage first.

"Doc, is there another way outta here?"

"Follow me."

She pushed him along the only safe corridor open to them, the other two following on their heels. Cortez shut the fire doors as the creatures gave pursuit.

"Sam lock these doors. We have to get to ward one, Jedrey."

"Okay Doc what's up at ward one?"

"It's the overnight ward and the isolation room; the only areas occupied at night. We have to secure them."

Bodien spoke urgently. "Doc is everybody accounted for?"

"Yes, wait a second. Has anybody seen Norris anywhere? Where's Norris?"

Cortez shrugged his shoulders. "The last time I saw him he was on break up at L12."

The exchange was interrupted by a sudden pounding on the double doors as the creatures discovered their way blocked. Anne pointed to the other end of the corridor.

"I think we'd better get out of the way. They hunt on sight, if they can't see us they may calm down."

The group moved away up the corridor and out of view.

"This is Bodien to all units. We have a situation at the health center. Send help. Over."

The radio let out a crackle and he pushed his ear piece in to get a better reception. "Yeah Brad, we got them things all over the place... Everybody bar Norris

Zillman...We ain't sure...We gonna secure ward one, that's were all the folks are...Yeah well don't spare the horses...See you then. Over and out."

He looked at the worried faces of the others.

"They're on the way now. That's all we need to do is hold them off until the guys arrive. Don't look so worried."

"How'd they get in? Sam you were supposed to be locking up, what happened?"

"Don't go blaming me. They were already in before I locked up. I come outta the morgue and they were all over poor Adrian Gates."

Anne looked at Cortez. "Did they..?"

Cortez nodded his head. "He was smeared all around the floor. There was nothing I..."

Elle-May gently caught his arm and spoke softly.

"I'm sorry Sam, thank you for warning us."

197

He looked at her and nodded. "Where'd they come from? How many more are there?"

As the group raced up the hallway the sound of gunfire could be heard from the town.

****

"Brad even if this dummy is right, and I ain't saying he is, I owe him for a lump on my head."

Eastman looked wearily over at Benteen. He could tell it was going to be a long night. "The only one who owes anybody around here is me. He saved my butt tonight."

Benteen was having none of it. Gun battles in the street, even Mary killing Firth was one thing. But conspiracy theories and mad generals was smack bang on planet Emmet. However, facts were facts and this guy had given up his freedom, endangering his own life to warn them. Benteen stood cradling his shotgun and nodded towards Eastman.

"If some guy does have a missile, or whatever the hell aimed at us, then let's just evacuate. Get out."

Taylor slapped his head letting out a frustrated groan.

"I already told you, the military are monitoring your wave bands they can hear everything you say. You both hearing me right? What do you suppose Stone would do if you lot suddenly made for the freaking hills?"

Eastman glanced over at Benteen and nodded. He was right of course, such an exodus would provoke Lord knows what kind of reaction. But there was something he still didn't get.

"Say they do fire that thing off; is it big enough to take out that base as well?"

Taylor moved to the table and picked up a map of the area. After studying the map for several long seconds, he pointed to Armstrong and followed with his finger to the base.

"You got a point there. No, no it's not. It's an airburst warhead; you'd need something to penetrate all that rock." He continued talking almost to himself. "Yeah, but they'd already know that. It has to be two weapons."

Benteen raised his eyebrows and shot Taylor an angry frown.

"What in hell's he gibbering about now?"

"Look Deputy dog, one missile and fizz goes your little town and everything else in three to four clicks. But they'd need a second one to explode below the ground for that base. Got it?"

Eastman clicked his pen top up and down repeatedly. "Yeah, we get most of that but, what are you driving at? We're still gonna get melted."

"Not if we grab one of those warheads."

"And why the hell would we want to do that?" Benteen snarled.

"They need two missiles, one for us and one for the base. They have to detonate them at the same time. If we grab one it could buy us some time and..."

Benteen held up his hand and glowered at Taylor. "Slow down there bonzo. Why exactly do they need to fire them things at the same time again?"

"To complete the mission. They need to destroy both targets at the same time. As soon as those things go off no more secret. They're left with miles of scorched earth and no damn town and one mother of an explanation to make."

"So they high tail it before anybody shows up." Eastman looked down at his desk in silence. Taylor pointed to the location of the military camp on the survey map.

"It's not just the warhead we need to take down. We gotta lift this comms blackout and get outside help."

"Oh Brad, will you listen to this guy. Take out this, take out that. Who the hell do you think you are, General freaking Patton?"

Eastman raised his hand to quiet Benteen; he wanted to hear more. "How'd you reckon to do that?"

"They're using frequency jammers, blanking out everything except for the bands they need. We take that out and no more black out."

"So what we talking about here, some kinda transformer units?"

Taylor waved his hand at Eastman. "Nothing so complicated. They look like oversized ghetto blasters mounted on 6x6 trucks. They're easy to take down."

He stopped and looked at Eastman and Benteen before he continued.

"It's the location we'd need to worry about."

Eastman viewed Taylor with mistrust. This was one of those 'in addition' moments he so hated, when folk added something else on. It was rarely if ever, a good thing.

"What's wrong with the location?"

"When I was captured, they drove past the units, now they're not armoured so they'd be easy to..."

Eastman repeated his question. "What's wrong with the location?"

"Well...It's pretty near to the camp."

Benteen fixed Taylor with a scowl, jabbing his finger at the map. "How damn near?"

Taylor drummed his finger tips on the desk top. "Right next to the main entrance."

"I knew it! I freaking well knew it!" There had to be a catch to all this crap. "You want something outta that base and we're the God damn distraction."

"Taylor if you think we're declaring war on the US Army then..."

"Look at it more like a guerrilla war. All we need to do is whack those jammers then get out ASAP."

Eastman stared at Taylor, mouth slightly open and then sank back in his chair.

"That's not about to happen. We're not in the army. I'm not putting my people in that kinda danger."

Taylor peered intently at Eastman before continuing.

"It's gone too far now. You don't have that choice anymore."

Eastman let out a deep sigh and rubbed his hands over the sides of his face. He looked at Taylor then spoke slowly. "How'd you reckon we do this?"

"Now that's about nine miles past enough," Benteen spluttered. "What in hell are you asking him for?"

"Gerard I want to hear what..."

"How exactly did he get in charge?"

"Simmer down will you. He's not in charge. He's advising us."

Benteen strode over to Eastman and pointed his finger at him like a loaded pistol. "Let's get this right here. You're taking advice from this fruit? You're as screwy as he is!"

Eastman rose from his seat and glared at Benteen and countered in a low icy tone. "You ever heard of the expression 'know your enemy'? Well he does and we need

him on this. That's that."

Bodien's voice broke the tense atmosphere. "This is Bodien to all units. We have a situation at the health center. Send help. Over."

Eastman reached over his desk and spoke urgently into the handset.

"This is Eastman, report. Over."

"Yeah Brad, we got them things all over the place. Over."

"Jedrey, is everyone accounted for? Over."

"Everybody bar Norris Zillman. Over."

Eastman shot the other two an anguished look before continuing. "How many of those things you got. Over?"

"We ain't sure. Over."

"I want you to barricade and use whatever the hell you got, but keep those freaks out. You got that? Over."

"We gonna secure ward one, that's were all the patients are. Over."

"Keep them folks safe, Jedrey. We're on our way. Over."

"Yeah, well don't spare the horses. Over."

"Sit tight. We'll be there in five. Over."

"See you then. Over and out."

Taylor looked from one man to the other and slowly shook his head.

"You both realise they've just picked that up, yeah."

Eastman took a key from his drawer and tossed it over to Benteen.

"Grab yourself some M16's and meet me there."

"Sure thing boss."

Benteen reached up, snatching the key from mid air and nodding to Eastman before racing off for the armoury, leaving the other two men behind. Eastman headed for the door then stopped and looked back at Taylor, puzzled.

"What'd you mean?"

"I reckon I just heard that 'big red button' go click."

CHAPTER – TWENTY-TWO

Pistol in hand, Kate Black cautiously pushed open the glass door leading to the nurses' station. She controlled her breathing, hoping nobody had seen the bead of sweat run down the side of her cheek. She'd had shots fired at her before and sent some back too. She was no stranger to this kind of pressure, but these creatures scared the hell out of her. Your average scumbag with a gun was hardly going to make citizen of the year, but at least they were human.

Sarge tapped her elbow, screwing up his face and pointing to his nose. Yeah, she could smell it too, that rank, sweet stink of rotting meat. They had to be someplace near. She moved into the open space using her weapon to cover all the possible areas as she did so. Although she was an experienced police officer, she was happy to have Sarge and Miguel Bonzzoni covering her back. Sarge fanned out towards the passageway leading to Anne Lenski's office, while Miguel stayed behind her, clutching his baseball bat.

Kate gave a slight whistle and pointed to the open fire doors to the left of her, wafting her hand in front of her face. All three moved warily towards the source of the foul odour. As soon as they stepped through the double doors they could see the creatures at the far end of the corridor, pounding on the locked fire doors. Undetected, Kate ushered the other two back into the relative safety of the main hallway.

"You got enough bullets for all them devils?" Bonzzoni pointed to the ammunition clips on her utility belt.

"She's got more than enough. But shooting rounds down that corridor gonna give us more problems."

"Sarge is right. There's a whole bunch of oxygen tanks right behind them. It'll only take one stray round to blow this place sky high."

"Ay ay ay. But we can't let them bash the doors in. What about all the people in there?"

He was right; they had to draw the things away without any shooting. Once they'd been seen, Kate and the others would need to move fast. The idea made her uneasy, it would be like ringing the dinner bell and she didn't like what was on the menu. She'd seen what was left of Adrian Gates. The question was how to pull it off?

"Ten hut! I've never seen such a God damn collection of maggots in all my life. You, with the eyeball, how in hell did you pass the medical?"

Bonzzoni looked on in horror as Sarge bellowed out drill instructions. Gradually the ghoulish recruits turned about to face the source of the commotion. One by one they started to shuffle forward down the passageway. Miguel tugged at Sarge in an effort to shut him up.

"Sarge! Sarge you gotta to be quiet. Please. This no time for you crazy things here!"

Kate eyed Sarge up and down. "Not exactly what I was thinking... but it works for me."

"Okay well you wanted them out. You on the end, keep up you ugly freak."

Miguel threw his arms up in a gesture of hopeless despair as the things continued their advance. "You are both mad. I am with mad people."

"Miguel Bonzzoni get with the programme here! I'm gonna march these damn things outside to the ambulance bay. All you gotta do is watch for anymore of them. You got that?"

"Yeah, yeah is no problem. I can do."

She had to hand it to Miguel, he was scared stiff but he wasn't going to run out on them. Sarge was just plain crazy, but it was a good crazy. She watched as the unholy procession filed past the nurses' station. They were slow but it wouldn't be good to get caught with them in a tight space. Although they'd seen the things enter the building, she wasn't sure how many had come in the first place. With all the din Sarge was creating, she'd be surprised if they couldn't hear him across the border.

"Left, your left, left right left!"

Sarge's voice rang out across the otherwise deathly still health center, as he led them to the main doors.

"Kate I'm gonna take these maggots out to the bay. You and Miguel double back and shut the doors. Affirmative?"

"Great plan. What about you?"

"Hell, I'll take my chances out there. They move like a stone in Death Valley. I can't see any problems."

As they left the building, Kate caught Sarge by his arm.

"I'm not leaving you out here with them. You're gonna lead them away and then I want you back with us."

Sarge watched as the last of the creatures left through the door then he looked at Kate. "Now listen here, I don't think there's gonna be enough..."

She rounded on him. "Now *you* listen here. I want you with us and that's an order!"

Before he could argue the whole area was bathed in red and blue light as a police siren cut through the air. The three shielded their eyes from the glare of the car's main beam, pointing directly at them. Then they heard Eastman's voice over the PA system.

"You folks all right?"

"Jeez Brad are we glad to see you."

Eastman walked around the side of the car and shone the search light directly at the creatures, which were fast approaching the vehicle.

"Kate, is everybody okay in there?"

"Don't know. Didn't get that far. But they're holed up in there sure enough."

"We can't let them escape into town and we can't capture them. It's too dark and too damn dangerous."

She knew the answer before she asked the question but she still needed to ask it. "What d'you mean Brad?"

"I know it's tough but we're gonna have to put them down. We can't risk them getting away. I'm sorry, that's the way it's gotta be."

He was right of course, it just felt wrong. She'd seen what they'd done to people, but this was just like murder. Cold blooded murder. She watched as the things headed towards Eastman's car. It would only take seconds for them to get close enough to become dangerous, but she couldn't shoot them, not like this. Full of uncertainty she slowly brought her pistol to bear at the lumbering horde.

A second police car arrived and out jumped Benteen. He calmly walked over to Eastman and threw him an M16.

"What we gonna do, Boss?"

"Shoot them. Shoot them all," came the grim reply.

Kate shut her eyes as the sound of assault weapons ripped through the cool night air.

****

Eddy Joe crouched down alongside Austen Colt behind the cinder block wall.

"What you got Austen?"

"Harry's popping rounds into Charley's back yard and we heard some shots over at Clancy's place too."

"Yeah we got us a town full of spooked people here. I just pulled an arrow outta Fred Clark's leg."

"An arrow! Now that's extreme." Ethan Mason peered around the corner. Ray Johnson inched forward. "I heard Mary Firth killed her husband, deader than hell."

"More like murdered. He was a good guy." Tom Price stretched out his cramped legs.

"Hell, where you been for the last thirty years? She ought to get a God damn medal. Nobody gonna miss that sap," Austen Colt snapped back.

"Eddy Joe what you going to do about Harry?"

"Ethan's right, he's most likely gonna get some folks killed like this."

Eddy Joe nodded his head at Johnson, and then cupped his hands over his mouth. "Harry. It's Eddy Joe with some of the guys. There ain't nobody here except us. Stop shooting."

He motioned to the others to stay behind cover and then stood up and started walking towards the end of the yard. As he did so two bullets thudded into the block peppering fragments of concrete over them. As he scrambled back behind cover, the group looked at Eddy Joe for the next move, but it was Colt who responded.

"*That is a – freaking – nough!* Harry, you send one more God damn round my way, and so help me, I'm gonna start shooting back." He pulled the cocking leaver on his AK 47 back. Eddy Joe shot Colt an anxious look then Harry's voice drifted across the night air.

"Sorry boys, I guess I got carried away for a while."

"Yeah, try that again and you will be," Colt muttered under his breath to the others.

"What was you shooting at anyways?" called Price from the safety of the wall.

"Some of them darn vampires in Charley's yard. I didn't know it was you guys."

Mason stifled a chuckle and winked at Johnson. "Vampires? Yeah, sure."

Eddy Joe tentatively moved out from the wall and stood in the sidewalk.

"Yeah well, there ain't anybody except us now. Shut your window and go back inside. This is police business."

They heard Harry's window slam shut and the group got up and walked over to the squad car. Colt eased the AK 47's spring forward and slipped on the safety.

"What you gonna do now Eddy Joe?"

"Gonna head up to Clancy's and try my best not to get shot at again."

He climbed into his car and as he started the engine a second police car drove into the street and pulled up alongside. Mitch Chattman rolled down his window. "Heard some shots, thought I'd best come and check. Everyone okay?"

Eddy Joe nodded at Chattman. "Appreciate that Mitch, but we got it covered."

"Either that or Harry run out of bullets," echoed Johnson with a dry smirk.

The men burst into laughter as the tension was swept away. However, the moment was short lived as the sound of sporadic gunfire sounded in the distance. Mason pointed in the general direction of the racket. "Sounds like Harry's not the only one."

"You want me to chase that down?"

"Yeah. Mitch, I'm gonna check on Clancy."

Eddy Joe inadvertently shone his flashlight in Chattman's face.

"Say buddy, you don't look so well."

"It's nothing."

He covered his face with the back of his hand to block the beam.

"I'm just worn out, that's all."

Chattman wound his window up and drove off in the direction of the shots. Colt watched the car drive away then placed his arm on Eddy Joe's door and peered inside the vehicle. "Hell, that boy looked as rough as sandpaper."

****

"Well that's the last of the trucks, we're on our own."

Harper opened one bleary eye and let out a noisy yawn, tugging his sleeping bag up to his chin.

"Smithy you got a voice like a fog horn. Wake me up when it's chow time."

Harper shut his eyes tightly in a vain attempt at blocking out the grey light of day. He'd enjoyed the best night's sleep since this lousy operation had started. Even the wooden floor of the pre-fab hut was better than hard ground. But now thanks to Smithy stamping about he was wide awake.

"Will you listen already? The chow hut's gone. Everyone's gone, well almost everybody that is."

Harper rubbed the sleep from his eyes with the heels of his hand and glared at the cause of his frustration. It was way too early in the day for all this bull.

"Gone you bum, who's gone?"

"The whole unit that's who. They been pulling out since we got back to camp. Only us and third squad left, sleeping beauty. Don't tell me you never heard any of that?"

Harper ignored the sarcasm and scratched his head. They could've moved the hut with him in it and he'd been none the wiser.

"Where are Dodge and the kid?"

"Wyllie took them to look for a trailer or something."

Smithy took his helmet off and lent up against the wall then popped some gum into his mouth.

"What's he doing, taking them on vacation?"

Smithy shot him an irritated look and threw the wooden shutter open letting in even more light.

"How should I know? Do I look like the information service or something?"

If the unit had withdrawn it was hardly for a good reason. At Mercy Falls, the military had pulled out all the fire crews and replaced them with some of the guys. Then they'd connected the fire trucks to gas tanks. The fires had burned for days. There'd still been people in the place. Not even Bourbon had managed to drown the screams out. But that was all behind him now. However, it looked for all the world he'd drawn the crap detail again. Kicking free of his sleeping bag, Harper sat up and rubbed his palms over his stubble. He stretched and yawned again and struggled to his feet, as the wooden door crashed open.

"What's wrong Harper, you need a personnel request or something? Haul ass!"

Corporal Wyllie's brutish frame blocked the open doorway. He was a powerful man with an unpleasant surly face and bad breath. Harper hated every inch of him. Directly behind Wyllie, were a dozen soldiers clustered, awaiting orders. Most of them looked to be from his squad, but he couldn't see the kid anywhere.

"What's up, Corporal?" Harper asked as he started to put his equipment on.

"You are, at last. Now stow that crap and get your butt outside."

Wyllie stomped off outside, barking out orders as he did so. Harper looked over at Smithy who gave him a wry smile.

"You heard the man. Move your tush."

Harper collected his M16, put on his Kevlar helmet, and went outside to join the others, Smithy close at his heels. Harper scanned the deserted camp area. All the tents had gone, as had all the vehicles; only the pre-fabs remained. The place looked like an outdoor concert, the morning after. The silence made him shiver in the early morning light. His eyes eventually came to rest on Wyllie and the other men. They were gathered around a small flat bed trailer. It looked after all that the possibility of a vacation was still on the cards. Dodge glanced over at Harper.

"Hey! Real nice of you to join us, man."

Harper moved over to stand by Dodge. "Well someone's got to keep you apes in line. What's all this about, anyway?"

"Search me. Wyllie come looking for us, said he needed this piece of crap."

"Where's the kid?"

Dodge shrugged his shoulders and gave Harper a blank look.

"He sent him to get Rai and that King guy. But that was ages ago."

Well at least Wyllie wouldn't be in charge of the group, mused Harper. Rai wouldn't take any more of Wyllie's guff. Although this King was a whole new ball game, he oozed slime from head to toe, kinda like a slug with legs. He was the type of man who you never quite knew whose side he was on. He wasn't sure who was the worst, Wyllie or the spook. It all seemed to be adding to this already festering pile of sewage. Taylor eyed the small group.

"This it then?"

Dodge looked over at Harper. "There's some guys over at the jammers and the General's HQ section, but yeah we're about the last ones."

"Kinda spooky eh guys?"

Harper turned to look at Smithy but said nothing. As he fell in with the rest of third squad he could no longer resist his curiosity.

"Hey Corporal, what's with the box cart, anyways?"

"Ask Sergeant Rai. We don't want to be late; we got us a town to kill."

He gave Harper a smug look then ordered the squad forward.

****

It had been a tough night and Eastman welcomed the sobering light of day. People had spent half the night shooting at shadows but as far as he could tell, the only creatures in town had been at the health center. Ron and his guys had cleaned the parking bay with about a ton of chemicals. They'd killed eleven of the creatures, not one of them local, and not one of them with any kind of ID. Anne had placed them in cold storage. In fact he'd just completed checking the building when she called him into the lab. She was the happiest he'd seen her since the beginning of this thing, but there was also anxiety on her face.

"Has everything settled out there?"

"Apart from the three dead you already had in here and I suppose poor Adrian. No further additions."

He placed his hat on the work surface and gave her a faint smile.

"You say Taylor just turned himself in and... I don't get him."

"He could've kept on running, but he came to warn us." Eastman gave her a serious look and then continued. "Anne, could his story about the weapons be right? I mean would they be dumb enough to use them?"

She lowered her gaze and nodded slightly.

"Oh yes and they would too. They can't risk a breach in the line. Where's he now?"

"I left him in the station. I thought it best to keep him off the street. Folks are still a mite jumpy."

"Do you think he'll be there when you get back?"

"I don't see why not, he walked in on his own. But even after what he said, I'm still not sure if he's telling me the truth."

"Brad, what will you do about Mary?"

"Mary? Now you didn't haul me in to talk about all that last night, so you'd better tell me what you want before you burst."

She reminded him of Helen when she'd something big to say, like the time she got her degree. She'd danced around the living room waving that certificate about like a lottery win. She'd been fit to explode. He smiled at Anne and bid her carry on. She turned away from him and flicked on the wall projector, bringing up two images on the screen. He recognised them from the previous Biology101 lesson.

"Yeah, I know. The first one is the normal cell and the second is the infected one. Right?"

"Very good, I'm impressed. I knew there was more to you than a tin star and a big gun. Now, how about this one?"

She brought up a third image next to the others. At first it seemed identical to the second one, then he looked harder. No, it was different. It had the same ball like appearance but lacked the tendrils of the first image.

"I guess I'd have to say its some kinda...what's any of this to do with Taylor?"

He threw his hands up, giving up on the game. She looked at him hard and waited several seconds before giving her reply.

"Taylor has certain anomalies in his body chemistry that I can't explain." She paused before continuing, "Infected cells constantly change and reproduce until all the healthy cells are destroyed. That's why I haven't been able to treat this thing. It won't stay still long enough." She pointed to the third image. "These are something new."

Eastman walked up to the images for a closer look and hesitantly touched the image. He shrugged his shoulders and turned to face Anne. "They look the same to me."

She joined him at the screen. "Alike but worlds apart and that's the paradox. When I introduced this third example to the infected cells it attacked and destroyed them within seconds." She stared intently at the images, her eyes wide. "Brad they killed them. Wiped them all out!"

"So what's that..?" The implication of what she'd just said hit him like a Greyhound bus. "You mean like... like a cure. Anne, have you found a cure?"

The excitement of this incredible discovery rushed through him. Could this be the break they'd been looking for all this time? She put her hands to her face and breathed out hard. However, as she spoke he detected uncertainty in her voice.

"It's too early to tell. It's not all good news. When I introduced the third example to healthy cells it killed them too." She gave him a slight smile. "At least it's a start."

He caught her arm and gave it a reassuring squeeze. "Hey, don't sell yourself short; this could be it you know."

"I've got lots more to do on this before we start putting flags out. If only I had a city hospital to work with."

"To hell with the city you've come this far on your own. Take some credit here."

"Brad the thing was under my nose all the time, all I had to do was a simple test."

"Where'd you get these cells? Damn!" Eastman looked back at the three images, then back at Anne.

"Brent Taylor!"

"Yes, the vey same."

****

Steedman was immersed in doubt. He sat dejectedly staring at the operations map, with its little red dots. The final phase of *Operation Viking* was drawing to its relentless close. And there was nothing he could do to stop it. Unless there was some type of miracle, in just a few short hours the target area and all the potentials would be vaporised. He scoffed at the terminology they used to describe the town and its people. It was as though by using euphemisms like these, it somehow created a barrier between real people and statistics. In truth they were about to commit mass murder.

Almost everyone had been withdrawn from the camp during the night, leaving a small HQ group and enough personnel to operate the ECM equipment. The jammers would need to be operated until after the devices had been exploded. As far as he knew both weapons were being prepared for use. Can't fault the US Army for efficiency, he pondered. His thoughts were disturbed as General Stone and King walked into the room.

"Colonel, Intelligence says that the potentials have lost control of the situation. I want the operation brought forward."

"What happened General?"

"The drones recorded sporadic gunfire through the night and there was a serious incident at the hospital, involving a number of 'infected'. We have to move now."

"Did they gain control?"

Stone shot an irritated glance at Steedman. "That's no longer our concern. If there's some kinda breach from that base, we don't want those things rambling all over the damn countryside, now do we?"

"Colonel, what's the status with the missiles?"

Steedman rarely agreed with Stone on anything, but like the General, Steedman had a dislike of King. He studied the man carefully before replying.

"Major Naughton has missile one ready to fire; he just needs the launch codes from the General. Missile two has had the warhead removed and is waiting for you, Mr King. Staff Sergeant Rai will collect the device and provide your escort."

"No, I want Rai topside. We still have to provide security until this is all over."

"Yes Sir. Then it'll be Corporal Wyllie leading third squad."

Stone was right; they had to maintain security until the last possible moment. With so few men they couldn't afford to compromise the mission.

"General, tell Naughton not to arm the warhead. I'll do that myself when we get to the site. But I'll need the firing codes from you."

Stone gave King a reproachful stare. "And I suppose you know how to arm the missile?"

"All you got to worry about is giving me enough manpower to haul that damn thing down there."

"My men will get you there, but after that you're on your own. Whatever mission you have, that's up to you. Are we clear on that King?"

"Yeah, I kinda thought that anyway. Colonel, how am I meant to get in there?"

"Wyllie will blow the doors with your say so. Then it's up to you."

Steedman brought a map of the underground base to show King.

"I've calculated the area you need to maximize the weapons blast. If you don't get in far enough, the energy will blow out of the door. You're going to need to get at least to this point." He indicted to an area coloured red. King gave Steedman a worried look. "Hell, that's some distance!"

Stone nodded his head. "Without CCTV we've no idea of what it's like down there or how many infected you're up against."

"Now that's a cheery thought General."

"Look, why don't you just blow the damn place and be done with it?"

King raised his eyebrows. "That would be fine by me Colonel, but we need as much info outta there as we can. There's a possibility Tellermine could've developed a cure. If we can't stop this then... Let's just say I got my work cut out."

"King is there anything we can do to help you?"

"Well General, I'd appreciate some kinda get-away transport being left for me. I've never been one for suicide missions."

"Consider it done. I'll get Corporal O'Rilly to take you to RV with Wyllie."

Stone stretched out his hand and reluctantly shook King's hand.

"Good luck Mr King."

"Thanks. I think I'm gonna need it."

"This might come in handy for you." Steedman gave King a compact GPS device. King took the device, nodded and left the room, closing the door behind him.

"Colonel have you briefed the missile party about King?"

"They'll be ready for any problems. They know exactly how to deal with Mr King, Sir."

"Excellent. I don't want any mishaps at this stage of the operation. I needn't say; King is expendable."

CHAPTER — TWENTY-THREE

Taylor opened his eyes and tried to focus on his surroundings. Everything took on a dreamscape appearance, soft and fuzzy. He was in a type of medical room, judging by the hospital equipment and the reek of antiseptic wash, lying in bed and wearing a hospital gown. As he tried to move, he became aware he was strapped down. His head ached in confusion from the dreadful images of death and blood still in his mind.

"Good to see you awake Mr Taylor."

Taylor's eyes came to rest on a blurred figure in a lab coat. "Where...Where am I?"

"You're safe and over the worst part. You don't know how lucky you are."

Taylor looked at the man, unsure if he was still dreaming, everything was vague and wrong.

"How long have I been here?"

"Over four days. Quite remarkable. The TS's don't last longer than three."

Taylor felt a sharp pain in his arm and looked down to see the man withdrawing a syringe from his forearm. Almost immediately his head began to spin and his eyes clouded over as he sank back on the bed. He could hear the man's voice drifting on air.

"Just something to make you sleep," said the business-like voice.

****

Taylor woke as a distant voice echoed through his head. Slowly and unsteadily he lifted his head towards the direction of the sound. He felt as though he was drunk but without the pleasure of arriving at that state.

"Congratulations, Mr Taylor. I think it's fair to say, you've actually survived the infection. In fact it would seem you've beaten it."

The voice emanated from a thin, smartly dressed man standing a few feet from him. Taylor managed a weak whisper.

"Are you the guy I saw yesterday?"

"You remember Dr Landon? That was three days ago, impressive. No, my name is Dr Tellermine; I'm the director of this project."

The name struck a chord in his addled brain but Taylor couldn't place it. Visions of Lenox and the horrors in the basement flashed before him. That was no dream. The man standing in front of him was the cause of it! Although right at the moment there was not a lot Taylor could do about it.

"How do you feel?"

Tellermine stepped forward and peered in Taylor's eyes with a small bright pen torch. Taylor shut his eyes tightly, turning away. The bright light shining in his eyes made him feel sick, even though his eyes were screwed shut.

"I'd feel a lot better with that out of my face."

"Ah yes, sorry." Tellermine clicked off the light and stepped back a few feet.

"I feel like I've been hit by a semi. What'd you mean 'survived' the infection?"

"Taylor, how much of what has happened to you do you remember?"

"I'm not sure. I'm not even sure if this is a dream…"

Tellermine thumbed through the pages in his file and looked at him.

"You were infected by some of the TS's. You've been recovering for the last ten days. To date all the infected TS's have not lasted more than three days. Consider yourself lucky."

Vivid pictures of blood spattered corridors and creatures snapping at him scratched through Taylor's head like broken glass. But try as he might, he was unable to salvage any further memories. All he knew was that he had to get more from this man.

"Infected, infected with what?"

"We can talk later."

Although Taylor felt like passing out, there was a lot more he needed to learn about what was going on in this madhouse.

"I want to know right now! What happened to me?"

"You really are very persistent. After your little visit things got a bit out of hand. Your own fault really, you were bitten by the creatures you released, passing the virus onto you."

"Where'd this bug come from?"

"Really, such a short memory span. We developed... or tried to develop a cure for Diabetes. NB33, but after some early success all the TS transformed into the creatures you saw with the late, lamented Dr Lennox. You however, are the exception to the rule."

"What's so special about me?"

"As an individual absolutely nothing; you're an exact replica of the rest of the dross out there. But medically..." Tellermine seemed to grow in stature as he went on, "You're a marvel. A medical marvel. Imagine how astounded we were to discover that in order to beat the virus, your whole body chemistry altered itself."

"What do you mean my body chemistry's altered? How the hell is that possible?"

"I can see that you are not yet able to take all this in."

"Why am I still here if I'm cured?"

Tellermine studied Taylor for a few moments, his bland eyes giving nothing away. "When a TS changes they become violent wild animals, in fact worse. They lose all

powers of reason, attacking anybody near them. We'd never seen anybody go past the three day period so we could not take the chance with you."

"I can appreciate that, now what is a TS?"

"Test subject."

"You mean the people from the NB33 tests."

Tellermine's eyes narrowed as he peered at Taylor.

"The original few yes. But we needed so much more. You see, once they've mutated they're of no further use. We cannot communicate with them; all they want to do is kill. To understand this change you have to study normal cells. That means healthy subjects. So it's vital to obtain constant supplies."

Taylor felt a sudden rush of nausea as he processed the information.

"You deliberately infected ordinary people with the virus. Is that what you're saying?"

"You needn't sound so surprised Mr Taylor. With all scientific advances comes sacrifice. Arguably, some sacrifice more. But now thanks to you, that could be a thing of the past."

"Tellermine, you're the freaking original mad scientist."

"Mad? I don't think you fully appreciate the unique position you're in. I have hundreds of those useless failures in cages. I've had to use the homeless, illegal immigrants, and all manner of human dregs. But you Mr Taylor, you are invaluable to me. Working together we could accomplish great things."

The guy was a bigger loony tune than God damn Daffy Duck.

"What if I don't want to accomplish great things?"

"There are many tests and questions I need to ask of you to narrow down the cause of your immunity. When I've established what that is, your blood will be used to develop a vaccine."

He leant over Taylor and stared directly into his face.

"But you would do well to consider this; I only need your heart to supply the blood. If I so wish, I could stop your brain and lock you in hell for eternity."

Taylor felt a sharp sensation on the back of his hand and looked down to see a syringe being emptied slowly into a line in his arm. Instantly he began to experience a warm floating sensation. He tried to hold Tellermine in focus but his eyes felt like cinder blocks as he began his slow spiral into blackness.

****

Dr Landon's face was inches away from his own, as Taylor felt the other man tugging at his bonds.

"Come on wake up we've got to get out of here!"

"What's..? What's going on?"

"I'm getting you out of here." Landon threw some clothes at him. "Get changed into these. We don't have much time."

With difficulty, Taylor sat up on the bed. This Landon guy seemed to be helping him escape but why? Could this be some kind of trick? Getting Taylor to think he needed this guy and allowing Tellermine to gain his trust? Melodramatic maybe, but nothing seemed beyond the realms of possibility.

"Look Taylor, I gave you some shots, they should make you come around faster. But we've got to move."

Painfully slowly, almost in reverse, Taylor struggled to get into the change of clothes and discarded the grubby hospital gown. His legs trembled as he got to his feet holding firmly onto the bed frame. Then he noticed the bite marks on his wrist and shoulder. Painful memories seared his mind at the realisation of what had happened. It had all been real after all. Lennox, the creatures and the last ten days were all of it real.

"Where we going?"

Landon helped Taylor on with his boots. "Tellermine's been busted. There are guys all over the place, arresting everyone in sight. He's escaped with his team but they're sending people for you. Now, no more questions. *We have to go!*"

Taylor reached down and grabbed the other man's collar. "Why should I trust you? You're part of all this."

"Dr Lennox was one of the few people who knew we'd gone wrong. I only wish more of us had supported him."

"Sure? Look at all those people you got caged up."

"Becoming a test subject is one hell of a deterrent, Taylor. You want to stay here and wait to be captured that's up to you. I'm off."

"Hold on here, if these guys are raiding Tellermine's house of horrors that means they're the good guys. Right?"

Landon pushed Taylor's hands away, straightened his shirt and got up, moving briskly towards the door.

"Taylor, you're a valuable commodity now. There are no good guys anymore. You're on the market for the highest bidder. And everybody is a player. Now can we get the hell out of here?"

He'd very few options open to him. If Landon was correct Taylor was now highly sought after. The thought of further tests did not appeal to him. The more distance he put between him and this place, the better.

****

The brilliant morning sunshine glared in Taylor's eyes, making them water as he followed Landon through the maze of buildings. Days of inactivity and sedation had taken their toll on him. Landon stopped and held up his hand and pointed around the side of a small outhouse.

"There's the gate house. Looks as though this lot have replaced all the ZerTon guys."

Taylor made out at least three men in suits standing around a stop barrier, near a black four-by-four Dodge. The distance to the parking lot where Landon's car was parked was not too far from the gate. But even guys armed with pistols could make Swiss cheese out of a car at that range. Taylor hoped Landon had a plan that didn't involve a suicide run.

"Okay, what's the plan?"

"We grab my car and bust out of the gates."

Taylor stared back at him. "Great plan. Got another that doesn't involve getting killed?"

"The barrier is only made of wood; we can crash through that easily."

"Yeah, but guns, they shoot lead." Taylor gave him a disapproving look.

"Got any better ideas?"

"There's gotta be another way out of this place. Think."

Landon looked at Taylor for a moment deep in thought. "Well there's a service entrance, but that's going to be guarded also."

"That's gotta be better than this though, right?"

Landon nodded his agreement.

"My car's the black BMW." Landon pointed to the vehicle parked between a van and another car. "Keep low and we'll use the other cars as cover."

"You've been watching too many movies. That's my line."

Both men set off towards the car and as they drew near, Landon opened the car with a resounding bleeping sound. They halted abruptly as a harsh voice shattered the peaceful morning like a broken pane of glass.

"Stand still!"

They turned to see a man pointing his pistol directly at them, only a few yards away. The last thing Taylor wanted was to enter into a sprint, but there was no way he was going back. The choice was taken from him as Landon raced forward. Two shots hit their mark and the scientist pitched forward, falling between two cars. Taylor threw himself onto the tarmac and crawled to the fallen man as more shots rang out. Landon looked over at Taylor and gasped for air. "Take my keys, get out of here!"

The man was dying. Bright red blood trickled from Landon's mouth, forming a red patch on his jacket. Bright red blood was a sure indication of damage to a major organ. He had moments to live at best. Taylor reached down and took the keys from Landon's already dead fingers. He paused briefly to shut the other man's eyes, and then crawled to the car. He could hear the Dodge start up and drive towards them. As quietly as possible he opened the car door. It would be near impossible for the shooter to know which car was being used; at least that's what he was betting on.

As the man came into view, Taylor shot forward, knocking him high into the air. Then he swung the BMW into a semi turn of clouds of acrid smoke, heading for the gates. The vehicle shot forward as he aimed it directly at the two men in front of the barrier. Taylor braced himself for the bullets, but the two men jumped out of his path without firing a shot. Taylor careered through the open gates and disappeared out of the facility.

****

Taylor knew he was working on borrowed time as he darted about his flat. It wouldn't take long for them to realise who the escapee was and where he lived. Being in the service had taught him to be ready to deploy at a moment's notice, meaning his essentials were always packed. He put his passport into the bag and his wallet with his credit card into his jacket. As he stuffed clean clothing into his holdall, he puzzled at how the men at the gate had allowed him to get away.

He went into his bedroom and took his pistol from under the bed and placed it in the bag. Then he sat on the edge of his bed and thought about his next move. In effect there were two groups on his tail, neither with his best interests at heart. He needed to get out of town and the best person he could think of was Gary Richmond.

Richmond could help him with a safe house, which would give Taylor some room to manoeuvre. But first he needed some cash. There was at least four thousand in his account – his emergency fund. He set about collecting various toiletries from the small black wall unit in his bathroom. Walking back into the living room he heard a loud squeal of brakes, followed by the slam of car doors.

He raced to the window of his second story flat and looked out across the street; four men were pounding up the stairs to his building with weapons drawn.

Taylor leapt back from the window, grabbed his bag and made towards the fire escape. He pulled open the window and studied the deserted back yard below. There was nobody about. Quickly, he hauled down the escape ladder and fled downwards to the ground.

He slung his bag over his shoulder and headed for his 'borrowed' BMW. He'd parked the car out back, near the trash area to keep it from sight. He was delighted that no one had taken an unhealthy interest in the vehicle. He opened the door, started the engine and pulled out onto the main road. Luckily all the men had entered the house. He drove past his own car and turned onto the intersection, completely undetected.

****

As Taylor cut through the rush hour traffic, he pondered about the people who'd raided his flat. There was some kinda power play going on between ZerTon and the unknowns who'd busted them; he was caught in the middle. Yes, the best plan was to get out of town, but with less than thirty dollars in change, he'd need money. There was an ATM at the corner of Jenkins and Dunbar; he'd get his money there. Leaving the car in the parking lot he crossed the crowded sidewalk, heading along Dunbar to the ATM. With his beard and baseball cap pulled down over his eyes, he looked every inch an ordinary guy, and no one paid him the slightest heed.

Taylor fished the card from his jacket, inserted it in the machine and punched in the code. He waited as his request was processed and looked around him. It wouldn't be wise to withdraw all his money; that might attract too much attention. After what seemed an age, he read the 'unrecognised' message in disbelief. Angrily, he jabbed the code in, over and over again. He checked the card, but it was perfectly fine.

He cursed his luck, now he would have to visit the branch. It was somewhere he rarely went; online banking was so much easier. Frustrated, he put his card back in his wallet and walked the short distance to the bank.

Taylor was in luck; for a Monday morning the place was pretty much deserted. After his brief stay behind a large woman with a yappy dog, he found himself at the counter. The bank teller was a pretty blonde, labelled Brooklyn. Where did people get the names for their kids, he pondered? Who the hell would want to name a kid after a damn bridge?

"Good morning Sir. How may I help you?"

The practiced sales prattle skipped from the branch girl, like the flat stones he used to throw in the river as a kid. Her blonde hair had an unnaturally smooth texture, flat ironed into submission.

"I've just tried my card but the ATM says unrecognised."

"Do you have an account with us Sir?"

He read the look of disdain on her face: another bum on welfare.

"Yeah, Brent Taylor. I get my paycheque through on the twenty sixth of every month."

After a few moments the girl looked up from her computer screen with a frown. "Sorry Mr Taylor. I can't find you on our system. Are you sure you've an account with us?"

"I've used this bank for damn near seven years! You'd better check again."

"No need to raise your voice, sir. It's not my fault."

Taylor was conscious of the unwanted attention from the security guard as she moved from the main door. The last thing he wanted was trouble. The woman looked like a Russian shot-putter. Taylor vigorously rubbed his hand across his mouth. "I'm sorry, but do you think you could try once more, please?"

The teller gave the kind of look that went right through him. "This position is now closed. Have a nice day."

Her perfectly ironed hair bounced like a sheet on a washing line as she slammed down the shutter and switched on the 'position closed' sign. Furious, he rattled the shutter and yelled. "Hey. Hey! You still got my card. Hey!"

Before he could protest further, two burly men in suits made their way towards him.

Taylor looked at the space between the men and the door; just enough room, he thought. He did his best to avoid eye contact with them and casually walked to the door. At the last possible moment he turned as if to go in the opposite direction, then ploughed into the men and raced out of the door.

****

Taylor sat waiting for the lights to change to green. Who were these people that could cancel his account? Not just cancel it but erase it completely! Whoever they were, they were only one step behind him. He disliked being predictable, but he had no choice. Richmond was his only chance – he'd have to help. He glanced at the green holdall next to him; hardly enough for a long vacation but it would have to do.

He'd been tempted to call Richmond on the phone but after the ATM it was obvious they were tracking him. A car horn sounded behind him, making his blood boil. His patience was as thin as a New York fashion model. He shot forward and then swung left; he'd soon be outside the office. His jaw dropped at the sight in front of him.

The road was blocked by emergency vehicles and Richmond's once plush office and the buildings either side had been replaced by smouldering ruins. He went to investigate and was soon mingling with the other onlookers. The place looked like a war zone. He pushed his way towards the yellow and black police tape and stood directly behind a policeman.

"Hey officer, what happened here?"

"They reckon it was a bomb – who knows?"

"They pull anybody out yet?"

"Yeah sure, but they all going one way – to the town morgue."

The man looked over his shoulder but Taylor had already gone.

Things were going down hill fast as each door of possibility shut in his face. These people were playing for keeps. He had to come up with a plan 'B' if he wanted to stay ahead and alive. As he squeezed through the throng, his heart sank. A group of smartly dressed men were clustered around his car. Unobserved, he swiftly melted back into the mass of people; time was running out on him.

****

"Hello? Hello? Look if this is one of those calls..?"

"Jane, please don't hang up."

"Who is this?"

"It's me. Brent."

"*You* certainly got the wrong number. There *is* nothing I want to say to you."

Even after six months he could detect the hostility in her voice. But she was his only remaining hope.

"Listen Jane, I know you're still mad at me but..."

"Mad at you. Why you..."

"Look I'm in deep trouble and you're my last chance. Please."

It had been years since he'd needed to use a call box. He twitched his nose; he'd about forgotten how disgusting they could be. He rubbed his scraggy beard; he looked about as bad as he smelt. At long last he heard the voice at the other end.

"Brent, you had nothing to do with Richmond's office, did you?"

"It had nothing to do with me. I swear it."

"What are you mixed up in?"

"I can't say. I don't want you involved in this."

"Oh sure, but you want my help."

She had a point. He had to keep her uninvolved but he also needed her on his side. "There are some people that want a piece of me. I can't say any more."

"So you *did* have something to do with that bomb."

"No! But they may have done it because of me. They know about me working there. Jane, these people are freaking nuts."

"Why do you need my help?"

"You're the only one I can trust. Will you help me?" There was a long silence before she answered.

"Brent, I think you need help. Do you want to come here?"

"No. I'm being followed. We need to meet someplace safe."

He wracked his brains. It would have to be somewhere they both knew and that she'd get right away. Even with the call box, he wasn't sure things were secure.

"Okay, let's play a game. I'm gonna give you a clue but we don't say the name of the place. I know it's complicated, but you never know who's listening."

He knew it sounded like a line from a spy movie, but it was the safest way.

"Don't worry I won't give the game away."

"Yeah, yeah I got it. Remember where we used to sit on that bench, the one with your student's name carved on the arm?" He knew it was a long shot, he hoped she'd remember the spot. He pushed the last of his coins into the phone's hungry monster slot.

"Yes. We used to sit and eat corn chips."

217

He breathed a sigh of relief. "The very same. I'll meet you there in one hour. Can you make it by then?"

"Don't worry, I'll be there."

He replaced the handset as soon as he heard the loud buzzing from the receiver. He smiled confidently. It was highly unlikely these whackos had managed to monitor the call. There was no reason for them to connect an old flame to him.

****

Taylor sat on the faded green metal bench, deep in thought as he watched the near black canal drift aimlessly by. It had been a long time since the spilt. She'd never been able to take the long hours and days away from home. What she needed was a regular guy not a workaholic.

He scanned the length of the canal for signs of people. The place was a popular haunt but not today. It was too early for the lunch-time crowd and way past rush hour. Then he saw Jane walking down the grassy footpath towards him. As she drew near him, her slim body and attractive face reminded him of why he'd fallen for her. The slight breeze tussled her long brown hair as her blue eyes fixed on him.

"Jeez, Brent! You look as if you've been sleeping under a bridge." She sat down alongside him and stared in astonishment.

"Well at least one of us looks good. You haven't changed since I saw you last."

She pulled the collar of her jacket up. "I'm surprised you even noticed. You were never about long enough."

He could hardly argue the point with her and in any case she was completely right. Taylor lowered his eyes and sank back in the old bench.

"Seriously, what's happened, you look awful?" She reached over, affectionately touching his arm.

"I was captured by these people, they drugged me but this guy helped me escape."

"Doctor Landon?"

Taylor was bewildered. "How'd you know his name? I never mentioned it."

"I... It was all over the news. They said you killed him."

"What? *They* killed him and Gary and a hell of a lot of others."

He looked away. "I'm sorry. Look I'm here aren't I? How can I help?"

He looked back at her and stared keenly into her striking blue eyes. "You mean that? You actually mean that?"

"Brent, you need help. What can I do?"

"I gotta get out of town, I need time to think. They've shut my account down and they want me."

"Who do you think is doing this?"

He held his head in his hands in desperation. "I don't know. I don't know if they're from the Government or... I just don't know."

"Why don't you tell the police? Let them sort all this out."

"Can't trust anyone. This has gone way past big. Even the cops could be in on it, hell they could even turn me over to them. I've got to get out for a while."

The shrill tone of her mobile cut through the air. Anxiously she scrabbled in her pocket and switched the device off.

"Who was that?"

"I don't know? It's not important."

"Did you tell anybody about meeting me?"

"Of course not... Anyway, you're not going to leave town without money. How much do you need?"

"It's just a few hundred; I'll pay you right back as soon as I can get set up. Then I'll..."

He stopped suddenly as he made out two cops with another two guys in suits heading towards them. He jumped up and glowered at her.

"Jane what the hell have you done?"

"Brent don't run! You're sick; they're only here to help you."

Taylor gave her a disgusted look and fled into the surrounding woods. He heard the men calling after him, but in moments he'd merged into the greenery.

****

The Montana countryside shot past the passenger window. Taylor turned his head to face the endless road ahead. Only the air conditioning of the huge semi made the journey bearable.

"Hey buddy where'd you say you're headed?"

Taylor glanced across at the driver; he seemed alright, but he was one talkative guy. However, the good thing was that Taylor could make up and say whatever he wanted to.

"Canada."

The driver looked over at him. "I didn't catch your line of work."

"Oh this and that, but I guess it's logging mostly."

"Funny thing that, I was looking at long haul work, like you know, ice trucking. But in the end it's easier driving away from snow, not into it. You see it's my rig, did I mention that? Well I didn't see the point in trashing my only source of income."

"Yeah that's a good idea. Kinda tempting fate I suppose."

The driver nodded and continued about his work and Taylor hoped that would be that.

But to his disappointment the man looked at him and continued with a new line of irritating interrogation.

"Hey, you been following the news about that guy back East?"

"No, I reckon not."

"Oh you're like my old lady she thinks the news is a commercial break. News is educational and education is good for you. I even watch some of the foreign news. I like to think of myself as an educated kinda guy."

"You were saying about this guy, back East."

"Oh shoot yeah. The one that killed all those people. Now that's a real interesting story, don't you think?"

"Why?"

Taylor had the distinct feeling this story was not one he should pursue. However, his curiosity got the better of him.

"Well first up, they reckoned this guy blew all those people away and there's this big manhunt. Then they put the explosion down to a gas leak. Then he kills those cops. Now..."

"So this same guy killed some cops too?"

"Yeah, he killed two cops and a girl near some canal or some place. Human interest, so now you're listening."

The driver aimed a self-satisfied smile at Taylor. Taylor started to experience a deep sense of queasiness as his stomach turned over.

"Who was this girl, what did she have to do with it?"

"Some teacher or something I think. The news said she was just in the wrong place at the wrong time. But the funny thing was that you'd have thought a story like that would have run and run, but it's gone. Almost as if they pulled it."

"What about this nut, did they have any ID?"

"No they never had his name."

Taylor worked hard to conceal his horror. If these people had killed two cops, it was obvious they'd not let anybody get in the way. But if it was a dirty fight they wanted, then they'd picked the right man. He looked over at the driver.

"How far you got to your destination?"

"Less than forty miles to go. There's a truck stop near my last call, look, I'll drop you off. There's gotta be someone headed up that way, we'll ask around. That okay?"

That was the best option he'd get out of this sorry mess. It wouldn't take long for him to reach Burnsville, maybe a few days at most.

****

Eastman looked around his office at Anne and Benteen then broke the stunned silence. They'd all three been transfixed at Taylor's account of the last few weeks.

"Taylor, if you are really immune to all this, you could reverse the process. Stop it!"

"I'm no medic. I'm used to putting holes in people, not patching them up. The late great Dr Landon said Tellermine had a theory that I'd some type of natural immunity, maybe triggered by the infection. But there was a problem. Not only do my antibodies kill NB33 they do a pretty good number on healthy cells too."

"So do we need some of this NB33 as well?"

Anne Lenski looked over at Eastman and shook her head pessimistically.

"It would make little difference. The moment NB33 comes into contact with healthy bodies, it begins the conversion. We have enough examples of that."

She moved forward in her chair and frowned at him. "What blood type were you before this change?"

"O Positive. Why?"

"I ran a full test on your bloods. They don't correspond to any known types, human or animal. The question is can you provide a cure for this virus?"

Taylor rubbed his tired eyes and shrugged. "Tellermine thought that I could be part of a tiny percentage that was immune. But he never got the chance to prove it."

"But what percentage?"

Taylor looked over at her and shook his head. "Landon said there were hundreds of those damned things, all failed test subjects."

"Anne, can you fix all this with his blood?"

"I don't know Brad. I'm going to need lots more tests and ask lots more questions. There has to be an answer to this. But I don't know what?"

"Yeah well, let's not get too carried away with all that Doc."

She looked at Taylor and smiled. "Relax, no sedation or restraints this time around, Mr Taylor."

Eastman massaged the back of his neck, tired after the long night. "Anne, when do you aim to start all these tests?"

She closed her note pad and looked directly at Taylor. "No time like the present."

"Oh, I can hardly wait. But in case you've forgotten there's still the pressing matter of Armageddon to deal with?"

Eastman tipped his head forward. "Yeah well, he does have a point there."

"Okay, I'll give you an arm full for now and you'll have to wait until after for any more."

Eastman glanced over at Benteen who'd sat without a sound through the whole story. "Gerard I hate it when you do this. I know it sounds crazy, but we have to accept this situation..."

Benteen held up his hand to stop Eastman.

"I ain't got any issue with this story; a man gotta be crazy to run into the wind 'cause this medical stuff is good hard evidence, so it supports what he's been going on about. But one thing I don't get, if you're this public enemy number one, how come we ain't heard of you, till now?"

"They want me off the system *not* all over the news."

"Kinda like least said soonest mended."

Taylor nodded his approval at Eastman. "That's pretty good. Yeah, I like that."

"That was something my wife used to say."

"Now you're both cops right? So even all this way out here with the Pony Express or whatever, a guy who kills two cops has to rate, at least a mention on an APB."

He paused and studied the two lawmen. "And you two know exactly what about any of this?"

Eastman and Benteen exchanged a fleeting look at each other. Taylor was right; the case had sunk without so much as a trace. Benteen doubtingly shook his head. "I don't know about that. How could they pull something like that off anyway?"

Taylor leant forward in his chair and held up his hands and extended his blank fingertips.

"Oh easy. Real easy."

CHAPTER —TWENTY-FOUR

"He's dangerous. If we don't get out of here soon, we're going to end up like Osborne." Dr Thornson, a thickset man in a white lab coat paced around the small rock- walled room. The walls, floor and ceiling had been fashioned from bare rock. A single strip light and a small table and chair completed the space. Abruptly he stopped and faced the older man. "We should've left when we had the chance."

Dr Hasslein was not used to being challenged, this was his department, but he had the same opinion as his junior. "I agree with you. It's obvious he's becoming more unstable. But right now he needs us. If the moment ever comes when he does not ..."

"Dr Hasslein, what we're doing here is wrong; evil. I don't want anything more to do with it." Thornson looked at the other man intently.

"Oh please, don't give me any of that 'holier than thou' routine. You knew full well what was going on here. You wanted fame and fortune, like the rest of us."

Thornson looked away, pinching the bridge of his nose between his finger and thumb. "That's before I knew where we got the subjects from. But you, you knew all the time."

"I was wrong, I... I thought we could do some good."

"I think he deliberately infected Osborne with the virus. There were teeth marks on his arm. He exposed him to one of the TS. I also think he started the fire."

"He's paranoid, delusional. He thought Osborne was involved with this 'so called plot'. We have to be very careful."

"If he finds out what we've done..."

"He won't. It's just you, me and Linda. He can't find out."

"I spoke to Dunson just after the lock-down; a lot of his people aren't pleased about things down here. But it's not only the security people."

Hasslein nodded his head. People were unhappy and worried at the direction the project had taken. They couldn't afford further test subjects reaching the surface. Since the fire, the base had been enveloped in a cloud of apprehension. Everybody was on a knife edge.

"Our esteemed leader must know what's going on."

"Of course he does. What worries me is *why* he hasn't done anything do about it."

The high pitch wail of the emergency alarm screeched through the room, startling the two men. Hasslein dashed to the heavy bulk head door and swung it open, beckoning Thorson to follow. The carved rock corridor was a hive of action; lab coated and business suited figures scurried to and fro.

Yellow emergency lights blinked in time to the howling alarm, adding mayhem to the frantic melee. Hasslein and Thornson made their way to a young stern looking woman with short cropped brown hair.

Hasslein clasped the shaken woman's arm. "Linda, what's happened?"

"There's been an explosion on level four."

"Anybody hurt?"

"No, but one of the confinement cages has been breached."

Thornson drew back his head, putting his hand to his mouth. "Lord! How many got into the base?"

"They didn't get *in,* they got *out.*"

"*Out?*" Hasslein looked at her in confusion.

"The blast re-opened one of the old escape tunnels, the ones supposed to have been sealed."

"Don't they lead to the surface?"

Linda nodded her head slowly at Thornson.

"How many got out this time?" His face was pale and drawn, the days of stress finally getting the better of him.

"Twenty six, but five were down for termination in any case." Thornson guided the others into a small rocky alcove set away from the bustle of the main corridor. Uneasily looking all around them, he spoke softly but with urgency.

"We can't afford to wait any longer. We must act now while we still can."

"Calm down! What we can't afford to do is draw attention to ourselves."

"Yes Thornson we don't want to end up in a confinement cage."

"All I'm saying is..."

"Dr Hasslein."

All three spun about to face the man in a suit standing a few feet away from them: a tall man with dark piercing eyes.

"The director would like to see you Doctor."

"I've got work that..."

"The Director means now." The man undid his jacket button briefly exposing the handgun tucked into his belt. "He's very insistent."

****

"Come on Luke, we gotta keep going."

Zach Clayton brushed thick green branches away, clearing a path through the tree line. Luke was moving much slower; his leg was showing signs of infection. He knew he should've taken Luke to town sooner, but the injury hadn't looked that bad. He'd managed to patch the hole in Luke's leg back at the cabin; now he needed a doctor. Luke's face was wracked with pain as he forced himself through the dense trees. It was hard to keep up. He couldn't manage another step.

"I'm all done in."

"I know, but there ain't no telling how many of them things are about here."

Uneasily, Zach scanned the surrounding wooded landscape.

"How far we got to go till town?"

"I reckon we're somewheres past the Airbase, so it can't be far now, but we gotta keep going."

It was obvious it wasn't safe to use the track – too many military patrols. Avoiding the creatures had forced them into the woods; the problem was that neither he nor Luke had walked this area for years. Sure, they'd been up here in vehicles, but that was a darn sight different to walking the ground.

"Zach I gotta stop, my leg's bleeding out real bad now."

Luke stopped and steadied himself using a tree, sliding slowly to the ground. He could go no further. Zach looked at the improvised t-shirt bandage on Luke's leg. The bright yellow garment was now dark red, soaked with his brother's blood. He needed to re-dress the wound and bent down to unwind the cloth. Luke winced in pain and raised his hand to his eyes.

"Luke I'm real sorry about all this, the crash, your leg... I should've taken you to town yesterday."

Luke jabbed his finger at his brother.

"Ain't your fault about them crazy army guys, I mean who'd have reckoned they'd done that? That was extreme, man."

"All the same, I should've gone to fetch help and..."

"No way you was gonna leave me on my own and no way I was gonna let you walk away with all them 'whatevers' about the place. Where'd you reckon them ugly crap heads come from?"

Zach unwound the bandage and grimaced as blood ran freely down the leg, pooling on the hard floor.

"They gotta be some kinda of military experiment or something. Those guys made roadblocks to stop them things getting out, maybe us too."

"So that means..." Luke stopped mid sentence pointing to a thick clump of greenery a few feet behind Zach, "I reckon I heard something over there."

Zach turned his head and followed the direction of his brother's finger. The bush exploded in a frenzy of motion as two of the creatures burst out and advanced towards the stunned Claytons.

Zach found himself transfixed by the thing in front of him as it snarled and drooled. Before he knew what was going on, a sharpened stick erupted from the putrid face and the creature toppled forward onto the rocky ground. Jimmy Red Cloud pierced the second ghoul's temple, instantly destroying the brain. Zach looked at Red Cloud in bewilderment. "Hell, JRC! You just scared the crap outa me!"

Jimmy sent a disapproving stare back at Zach and pointed his makeshift spear at his brother.

"Now I told you before – Jimmy, Jimmy Red Cloud or Red Cloud. JRC makes me sound like a damn cleaning product." He gestured towards Luke. "What you doing up here?"

"We had us a problem with some Army guys," said Zach, looking down at Luke. "We didn't do so well."

"You and me both." Red Cloud walked over to join the two brothers.

"Jimmy you gonna help us get to town, dude?"

Red Cloud looked at him and then at Zach. "You never gonna make it with his leg. Where's your wheels man?"

Zach continued to dress Luke's leg. "The Army trashed one set and the Beast is on the other side of town. Say Jimmy how come you're up here?"

"I was on my way to see Bill Merka when some of them things jumped me. I was lucky to get away. Tried to get back home but the Army shut the whole place down."

"Yeah, we've been dodging them boys and those drones." Zach stood up and looked at Red Cloud. "What about Merka. He have any idea what's up?"

Red Cloud shook his head sadly. "I figured I'd go ask just that. But someone's blown his head all over the wall. I thought the cops would get it wrong and blame me, so I hid out by the tower."

Zach smiled and helped Luke to his feet. "That be about right for that bunch. Jimmy, me and the boy here, we ain't much on tracking and I gotta get him to town. We could use your help here."

Red Cloud took a long look at the desperate pair in front of him. "Okay, but we keep to the woods and stay off the roads until we hit town. We ought to be there in a few hours, but that's gonna depend on his leg."

"That ain't no problem, you guys gonna have to keep up with me."

To reinforce his point, Luke walked painfully forward. "If we follow on from here, we gonna come across the foundations for the old Air Force huts. Then it's a straight run to Armstrong, okay guys?"

Red Cloud took the lead, the other two following behind. They'd only gone a few hundred yards when Red Cloud called a halt. He gestured to an open space set in between them and the next section of woodland. They could make out the crumbling foundations of the old wooden huts, barely visible under the encroaching plant life. Red Cloud's eyes darted about the surrounding area.

"We need to cross that ground fast. We don't want to get caught out in the open."

"Ain't there another way Jimmy?"

Red Cloud nodded his head at Zach. "Yeah, but we'd have to back track on ourselves and find the road so..."

The ground beneath their feet began to tremble violently and then a section of land exploded upwards, sending clumps of debris high up into the sky.

"Freaking butt-wipes done shooting at us again!" Luke shouted out furiously.

"Hold on, that came from *below* ground."

They stared at the smouldering hole a few yards in front of them and then the smell hit them; the stink of rotting meat.

"What the hell is that smell?"

First one creature climbed out from the bowels of the ground, followed by another and still another, as the ground continued to spew its rotting harvest into the light. Now with more creatures than they could count, it was time to leave. As the three men sped away from the gruesome gathering, Zach stopped to look back.

"Where the hell did they all come from Jimmy?"

"The old men talk about the time the dead will battle the living for the earth. I think hell's about right."

****

The station house was crammed full of people – Eastman's rag-tag army of volunteers. Hardly America's finest, though it did him good to see so many people answering the call. He'd gone over the plan outlined by Taylor, and even placed people into groups. That should have been enough but looking at some of the confused expressions around the room, perhaps it was worth going over the plan one more time. He held his hands above his head then brought them together, like a gunshot.

"Just so long as we all got this, I'm gonna run this by you one more time."

As Eastman started to explain, he looked up at the man who was walking towards him. It took him several moments to recognise the clean shaven man was in fact Taylor. It seemed he'd taken Eastman's advice and cleaned his act up after all. Taylor made his way through the horde and sat next to Eastman and Benteen. Eastman eyed him up and down.

"You spend all my money Taylor?"

"Sure. I do want to look my best."

Eastman nodded and walked over to the flipchart by Clara's desk, turning the pages back. He sure as hell was not prepared to wade through another half hour's worth of this. This was going to be the abridged version.

"Group one with Gerard and Taylor, you locate and grab that weapon..."

"Suppose it isn't there. Suppose they got this thing someplace else, what then?"

Taylor looked over at Danny Hardman – "Mr..?"

"Hardman. Danny Hardman."

"Mr Hardman, that base or rather beneath that base is the most effective position they can use that warhead, it'll be there."

Eastman nodded his appreciation, and then Oscar Majors called across the room, "If those Army boys haven't already got through that wall you mentioned, how we gonna get in?"

"Oscar, it's amazing what a little Nitro can do in the right hands – as long as we in the Sheriff department don't bust him."

Benteen smirked at Boulle, who sat expressionless at the rear of the room.

"I'm sure we all fully appreciate your kind donation Mr Boulle. Group two, now that's me and Sarge. We're gonna hit those jammers."

He gestured at Vince Langley and Pat O'Brien – "You guys be ready to go as soon as we take them out."

"We're gonna pump out as many emails and such as we can. Now as well as that, everybody got to ring as many people as they can."

Lenny Kovak had been strangely quiet throughout the proceedings but he called over to O'Brien, "You said a while ago that transmitter you got will reach New York. What if it doesn't work or gets destroyed?"

"Then Lenny, everybody's gonna have one hell of a long distance bill. As soon as the air waves are clear, we got to use every God damn electronic communication we got."

Eastman gave O'Brien the thumbs up sign and then invited Sarge to comment.

"Sarge you want to add anything here?"

Sarge stared at Eastman for a moment. "No, I've already said what I wanted."

Eastman was surprised at Sarge's distinct lack of enthusiasm. Here he was with a mission and yet... something was wrong. He needed to know what, but now was not the time.

George Lee looked at Taylor and raised his hand.

"I got me a question Mr Taylor. Them electronic gizmos. Where we got to hit, to make 'em go bang?"

"Well you may get them to go fizz, but there's nothing in them other than a pile of electric circuits. You just need to hit them as many times as you can."

"He's right," said O'Brien, pointing to the chart with the map of the camp and jammers, "The only time we gonna know for sure those God damn things are cooked, is when we get the waves back."

"Brad, that's all just fine and dandy. My worry is that you and Sarge don't have enough firepower for this. You're gonna need to take those army guys and the stereo box things out and..."

Sarge's voice rang out across the crowed room – "So we need more fire power to kill Americans, that what you saying, Colt?"

"Them boys only gonna get themselves killed if they try to kill us, that's all I'm saying."

Eastman looked over at Sarge and the military group sitting with him. Some were reservists, others home on leave, but all had awkward looks on their faces. Ed Callan was deep in conversation with Sarge. He was a major player on the military team. Eastman had known the boy all his life; Armstrong had always been too small to hold him. It had been no great surprise when Callan left to join the Marines. After the war, some said he'd developed a taste for it. Eastman was glad to have a Recon Marine on his team.

"Sarge you and the guys okay with this?"

Sarge dipped his head forward low and looked left to right before fixing his eyes directly on Eastman.

"Sheriff, we got guys from the army, marines, air force and the navy here. Now each one of us was born and bred in Armstrong." He paused and looked about the room before he went on, "When you asked for help every last one of them stepped up."

Eastman nodded towards the small uniformed group.

"And we appreciate all you've done."

Sarge pointed in the direction of the mountain. "Those boys up there, they took the same oath and salute the same flag as we do."

The volume of chattering dropped to zero as Sarge got to his feet.

"I've got more years of service than you can shake a stick at. But I've never shot at another American, let alone another serving soldier."

A nervous murmur went across the room as Eastman's little army started to voice its concerns. Eastman had to do something; if Taylor lost confidence in them, he'd walk.

"I'm against drawing on our own too, but it isn't like that. These boys mean us harm, and we're gonna get killed for something that's not our doing. We never asked to be involved in all this. No one asked them here and no one wants them."

Sarge met Eastman's eyes and addressed him like a defence lawyer in a courtroom battle.

"Brad, like most other folks in this room, you have never been in real combat." He looked around at the others in the room, "And I'm not saying that's a bad thing. But war is not all about the generals, or the flag or even your country. It's about the Joes around you, kinda like a brotherhood. You fight for the man next to you."

Without the military the others wouldn't stand a chance. Eastman summoned all his conviction and tried one last time.

"You're right; most of us can't even begin to think what combat's like. But we're all in this together and this is life or death." Eastman pointed to the military section. "Looking about this room, you guys owe your family and friends as much loyalty. It's come down to them or us. This is our town and our people. I'll break every rule in the damn book to keep us all safe."

Sarge gestured towards Taylor. "And what about this guy? Why's he so important?"

"Listen, I'd like to tear this guy apart." All eyes turned to Benteen as he raised his voice. "But he knows how to do this and we'd all best listen to him and do something while we still can."

Sarge gave Taylor a long hard stare. "Is he right, can you sort this out?"

"Yeah, but we can't do this on our own." Taylor swept his arms around in an arc at the people gathered about him. "We need you and your guys. It's time to pick sides."

The crowded room fell silent, each person awaiting the verdict, every eye fixed on the group of camouflaged figures. The whole mission was now looking ever more like a suicide run. Then, after what seemed like forever, Sarge broke the silence.

"We've come to a decision," – he paused momentarily – "Brad, we're with you."

Ethan Mason called out over the buzz of noise and addressed Taylor, "Now I get why we can't leave the town in large numbers, Brad's made that real clear. What I don't understand is what's the difference in that and us attacking these people? We still gonna leave the town."

"Yeah, Ethan has a point there. That's gonna make them madder than hell," Ray Johnson called over to Taylor. "This whole operation's been about them containing this threat. They've cut you off from the outside world. The only reason you've stayed safe for this duration, is because you posed no direct threat to them. That's all changed now and judging by what this guy," – he pointed at George Lee – "has told us, the military have pulled out. The only reason they'd do that is to fire off those missiles."

"So what is the damn point?" Tom Price threw his hands up in utter frustration. "If they're gonna use them, why not make a run for it?"

"Our one and only chance, is to move fast and shut down one of those weapons and free the airwaves. You start an evacuation and they're most likely to call an air strike down and still fire the damn missiles."

Eastman called order and waited until everyone had stopped talking.

"Okay now we all know what we gotta do, let's go take our town back."

****

Austen Colt headed towards the group of men with a grin on his face.

"Well no need for any Nitro, Boulle. Someone's had a damn good go at that door."

Benteen moved forward to greet Colt. "What you find?"

"The door's been blown off; there are a few of those things – dead – and a Jeep. There's a bunch of tracks leading down a tunnel."

"So that's gotta be the base then?" Hardman ventured, looking at the others.

"Okay let's move out. Austen you go left and Boulle, you keep right."

Benteen turned to the others, "The rest, you're with me."

"What about me?"

"Taylor, I want you where I can see you. You pull any stunts with us and I'll nail your butt to the nearest tree."

"Thanks for the vote of trust."

"I'd trust you more if I knew why you were so hell-bent on going into that hole."

Without a backwards glance, Benteen led his group out of the trees and set off for the base, a few hundred yards away. He had a mixed bag with him: Ethan Mason, Ray Johnson, James Burke, Tom Price, Roody Goldsmith, and Danny Hardman. Hardly heavy duty, any of them, but they were eager to help.

After a short trek the group arrived at the base. Benteen and his group used the greenery for cover as Boulle and Colt worked around the dilapidated structure. The Army Jeep lay abandoned with a number of dead ghouls strewn on the ground nearby. Both Boulle and Colt disappeared into the building and then reappeared moments later. Benteen held his hand high in the air and the whole band moved silently forward.

"Keep your eyes open and your wits about you. This could get heavy."

Benteen gestured at Taylor to move forward, "You'd best go first."

"Just you hillbillies make sure you don't shoot me in the ass."

Taylor switched on his flashlight and surveyed the opening. The wall section had been blown out, leaving a door-sized opening to gain access. The ad hoc doorway led onto a long dark corridor, with more dead creatures on the floor. Taylor turned as he heard the sound of rubble crunching underfoot. Benteen stood alongside him.

"I kinda guess they come this way then? What's your plan?"

"We're not gonna get much done standing about here. Your bunch ready?"

Even though he couldn't tell in the gloom, he could imagine what their faces looked like.

"Roody, Danny you stay up here. I don't want anybody getting around back of us. We may have to get out in a hurry. The rest, follow Taylor."

Benteen gave him a wily look before they began the journey into darkness. The flashlights flitted about the dank, cavernous tunnel as the party carried on. The bulkhead lamps dotted around the walls hung lifeless in the pitch black. They'd only travelled a few feet when suddenly Taylor hissed at the others to switch their lights off. Bobbing towards them were four high power flashlights.

"We got company! It's the military watch..." Taylor's sentence was cut short by the harsh tones of Corporal Wyllie booming though the cavern.

"Advance and be recognised!"

Taylor nudged Benteen's arm and whispered to him, "Let me do the talking."

"Advance and be recognised!" The repeated command echoed once more.

"Captain Brent Taylor, US Army Rangers. Where's your CO, soldier?"

The beams of light got ever closer until they stopped directly in front of Taylor.

"I'm in charge here Sir. Corporal Wyllie, third squad."

Wyllie was flanked by Harper, Dodge, Smithy and Ford, all aiming their rifles waist high at the other group. Wyllie continued, "This is a restricted area, mind telling me what you're doing with these civilians Sir?"

Even in the dazzling artificial light, Taylor could make out the tension on the soldiers' faces. He had to act fast. The best way out of this type of situation was to take charge: look as if you had the right to be there. At least that was the theory. Taylor hoped he could still sound like an officer.

"I've got orders from General Stone to deactivate the device, Corporal."

Taylor started forward but Wyllie blocked his path.

"Sorry Captain. I need to see the orders first."

"This is verbal, Corporal. You can call the General yourself if you want."

Wyllie stepped back a few feet and levelled his M16 at Taylor.

"I'm gonna have to see some kinda ID here, Sir."

This guy was good, maybe too good. The tension in the cave was almost unbearable with each side unable to predict the next move. Suddenly Harper cried out, "Wyllie, he's that guy who escaped!"

The sounds of weapons being cocked and safety catches releasing reverberated around the cave. In an instant both sides were staring down their gun barrels at each other.

Wyllie kept his weapon aimed at Taylor.

"Listen, there's a doctor working on a cure for this. All we're asking for is time."

"Cure? There's no cure. This is God's punishment for the evil in that town."

Wyllie almost spat the words at Taylor as his voice rose in pitch. "That town needs to burn and you all need to burn with it."

"How about I jam that M16 up your ass, for a damn start?"

Wyllie gave Benteen a dark look and aimed directly at his head.

"Go ahead and try."

It was all going dangerously wrong, it was clear this guy was unhinged. However, Benteen was not exactly contributing to détente. While the reactions of the other four soldiers didn't seem to support this guy, Taylor wouldn't chance them when the lead started to fly. In fact in the next few moments he knew somebody was going to cut loose. As Taylor worked out which of the soldiers to hit first, Ford suddenly lowered his rifle and stepped back from the others.

"I've had enough of this crap! I'm not going down for the death of a town."

Wyllie gave him a hateful stare. "Keep your damn weapon on them, you lousy maggot!"

"Shove it! I'm gonna shut that freaking thing down."

With that, he broke away from the others and stormed off into the dark tunnel.

Wyllie was beside himself with rage as he stared after Ford. The remaining three soldiers kept their weapons trained on the townspeople, uncertain as to what to do next. Abruptly, Wyllie stopped and took aim at the retreating soldier. The red aim point of his M16 darted about on Ford's back until it finally come to rest on his neck.

"Ford! Ford you come back right now. Do you hear me? Ford!"

The flash of Wyllie's M16 lit up the cave like daylight, accompanied by a deafening roar, as he sent two rounds into Ford's back. The impact of the high velocity 5.56mm rounds sent the boy crashing to the ground. Almost instantly, Wyllie's head exploded as Harper squeezed two shells into him.

"Jeez Harper! You gone crazy?" wailed Smithy as he looked from Wyllie to the shooter.

"Yeah maybe, but not as mad as he was."

"Okay, let's be cool about this," cautioned Taylor. "Now we don't want to shoot any of you and we sure don't want you to shoot any of us."

"Smithy, go check on Ford," Harper called over, never taking his eyes off the other group. Smithy flicked his eyes at Harper. "Yeah, but what we gonna do now?"

"Go check on Ford. Now!"

Slowly, Smithy lowered his rifle and began to walk backwards, away from the two groups, keeping his eyes on the crowd from Armstrong. Then he turned around and continued into the cave. When he drew alongside the still body of Wyllie he stopped and called back.

"What about Wyllie?"

"Pop another in him if he's still twitching!" said Harper.

He looked at Taylor then gradually brought his weapon down.

"Now what's all this about a cure?"

Taylor returned Harper's look, hesitated, then brought down his weapon. He reached over and caught hold of Benteen's barrel and slowly pushed it towards the ground. Although the situation had calmed dramatically from a few moments ago, it was obvious it was far from resolved.

"There's a lady back in Armstrong working her butt off to put a stop to all this. She's got a chance of finding a cure."

He paused; it wasn't good to give too much away at this point.

"Now, you people go blasting that town and that's it. Game over. No more cure. It'll take just one of those things to get away. *Just one*."

"Hey guys, the kid's all right!"

Harper un-cocked his weapon and flicked it to safety, then put the M16 onto his shoulder. He made his way down the tunnel, Dodge following after him. Harper called down the tunnel, "Smithy! Get him topside and use the vehicle to get him outta here."

Benteen gestured back up the tunnel. "You'd best take one of us with you. I got two guys at the entrance. With all this shooting going on... well, it's best to be safe."

"I'll go," said Johnson, stepping forward.

"Harper, we need to stop that missile. Show me where it is and I'll make it safe."

He nodded at Taylor and pointed into the depth of the great rock passageway.

"Yeah sure, follow me."

Taylor beckoned to the others then glanced over his shoulder to see that none of the townspeople had moved. Benteen walked over to him.

"About time I reminded you who's running this. I'm the law and I'm in charge."

Taylor rounded on him; there was no time for any of this.

"Well Mr 'I'm in charge', after you disarm this state of the art weaponry system, without setting the damn thing off, mind telling us what your next move is?"

"Yeah, well...I –"

"Oh hell, lighten up Gerard, you ain't no Tom Cruise." Colt pointed to Taylor.

"This dude ain't done so bad."

"Yeah, at least we're all still alive," Burke agreed, standing beside Taylor.

Out-voted and outnumbered, Benteen had no option other than to stand down.

"Don't get no big ideas down here, Taylor. These folks are my responsibility."

Harper called out to Smithy and Ford as they drew near to the group, "That was a real wise ass thing you pulled back there, kid." Then he gave him a broad grin, "but I suppose you did all right."

"He was lucky the armour took the worst of it, but his arm's messed up."

Smithy had applied two field dressings to Ford's shoulder. Shaken, Ford looked at Harper and smiled nervously at him. "You think my arm's gonna be okay man?"

"Nah, they'll take one of your legs off," Harper said, shaking his head.

"Legs?"

Dodge winked at Smithy. "I had this cousin who went in to get his tonsils done. Some clown turned the gurney around and now the guy sounds like Alvin and the Chipmunks."

Smithy leant forward and pointed directly at Ford. "Yeah and he ain't lying neither."

Both groups erupted into chuckles and laughter; even Benteen had to smile. Smithy held onto Ford, and together with Ray Johnson, they left the others and made their way up to the surface. Harper and Taylor led the way, while Benteen and the rest walked behind them. After a short time they came to a set of stairs and a lift. Harper waved his hand towards them. "Lift's out. We'd better take the hard way."

****

The men stood at the bottom of the stairwell; the space was similar to that of the entrance level. It had the same look of having been carved out of the ground.

They continued past some small rooms and a storage area, then Harper called a halt and pointed to the device on the box cart.

"That it?" asked Benteen dismissively, training his beam over the objects.

"Yes that's it," answered Taylor, moving in for a closer inspection.

"You know what this thing is Harper?"

"It's a heat weapon, sure."

Taylor moved in still closer. "I take it you didn't set this up then?"

Harper joined Taylor near the device and gave a puzzled stare. "Why, what's wrong with it?"

Taylor pointed to a small square cavity where two disconnected leads dangled down. "If you had, you'd have noticed that the timer's missing."

Dodge shook his head and looked at Taylor. "What's this about a timer?"

"It's about the same size as an iPad. It should have an LED, counting backwards. You know, kinda 5, 4, 3, 2, 1, bang!"

Benteen pushed his way to the front and eyed the two soldiers with suspicion. "Timer? What they done here?"

"There should be a programmable timer unit on the damn thing, but it's not there."

Harper looked at Taylor and gave an indignant shrug. "We never had anything to do with this; we let King do all that crap and..."

"King! King was in charge of this?"

"Yeah we just provided the muscles and hardware. He set it up and went looking for some guy's lab. We didn't hang about."

"Hell, if this bozo's taken that timer thing, then that's our job done. It's harmless."

Taylor gave Benteen a pained laugh. "King may have taken the timer but the thing is still armed. He's only gotta plug it in and we're back to square one."

Price pointed at the warhead. "You know about these things. Can't you disarm it?"

Taylor gave him an irritated look. "I don't have any tools and in any case, he's probably booby trapped the booby traps. We'd be doing the job for him. Harper, this guy with the lab, it wouldn't be Dr Tellermine would it?"

Harper nodded at Taylor. "Who is this guy anyways?"

"He's the creep who started all this. Benteen, we got to get that timer back, then blow this place the hell up."

Benteen looked at Taylor in bewilderment.

"You gone loco or something? I thought the idea was *not* to pop these things off. All of a damn sudden you want to blow one up."

Taylor looked from Benteen straight at Harper; he had no time for banter.

"Where's the second missile located?"

"Well yeah, but..."

"No time for buts, we're all on the same side now."

"Sure. About half a click from the camp near the ECM jammers."

"Benteen, we gotta get word to Eastman. He's got to take that missile down, right now."

Ethan Mason rubbed his finger anxiously over his top lip as he looked at Taylor and Benteen. "What about us? What are we gonna do?"

Taylor pointed his light at the darkened stairwell leading to the unknown. "We're going down there."

CHAPTER – TWENTY-FIVE

The group picked their way through the debris strewn corridor of the third level. Fire damage was apparent throughout the whole area; the heavy reek of smoke and charred flesh hung in the air. Something bad had happened here and everyone could feel it. Taylor scanned the hewn out corridor before them, desperate to locate Tellermine's lab.

Hopefully there'd be something he could pass on to Lenski, but he felt sure King would have found anything useful by now. In all probability he'd now be on his way to the warhead. However, that particular information would not be finding its way to the others.

"This King guy, how'd you know him?"

Taylor turned to Harper. "I had the pleasure of working with him in the war."

"You were both spooks then?"

Taylor gave him a hard look. "I told you, US Army Rangers. King had his own agenda."

Taylor stopped as he arrived at a fork in the passage; he looked back at Benteen who called a halt. One path ended in a large metal door, barred by a hefty metal rod that slid through the handrails. The second path snaked around a bend into total darkness. Damaged bulkhead lamps blinked like deranged signal lamps. Dodge lit up a plastic wall map with his helmet light. "Hey, what's that guy called?"

Taylor and the others gathered around the map. It gave directions to all locations on the level, including the 'Restricted Area and Medical Research Lab'.

"That what you're looking for?"

Taylor smiled at Dodge but before he could answer, a guttural snarl drifted around the darkened corner. All eyes turned to the bend and the group aimed their weapons in the same direction. After what seemed an age, one of the creatures scrabbled over the rubble and lumbered towards them. Taylor held his hand up and whispered to the group, "Nobody shoot, we don't want them to..."

Ethan Mason fired at the creature, killing it instantly. The gunshot rebounded like a base drum. Benteen was furious. "What in hell did you do that for?"

He marched up to Mason and snapped in his face, "I sure hope he was on his own!"

Boulle held up his hand to quieten the others and turned his head towards the bend in the corridor. "I reckon that's some of its buddies coming, right now."

The sound of the advancing ghouls resonated about the confined space.

"Let's spilt!" Tom Price yelled, racing past the others towards the other end of the passageway. Taylor watched as the horde of flesh eaters advanced on them. So many in such a tight space could well prove difficult. Sure, they had enough firepower to deal with them, but the noise would bring every festering ghoul in the base down on them.

"Hey guys, in here."

Taylor spun around at Price's voice. The man was frantically pulling at the set of barricaded metal doors, trying to dislodge the shaft. There was something not quite right about the set up. Taylor looked again; the metal rod had been jammed through the door rails from the outside. It wasn't to keep things out; it was to keep things locked in. Taylor caught sight of a discarded metal plate near the door and recoiled in horror as he read the roughly painted note: *Keep out! Infected inside!*

Price wrenched the bar out from the rails but even before it hit the ground, dozens of creatures burst out from the doors. The others could only watch as the things fell on the helpless Price, tearing him apart as they ate him alive.

****

Eddy Joe stood with his arms spread across the roof of his squad car; the warm metal felt good against his bare arms. He was making the most of this short interval; Main Street was all but deserted, which in his view was just as well. It wouldn't do to have too many folk about. Most had gone home to wait it out. Preacher Goodman and Father O'Donnell had held a combined service some time back, but now the church was empty.

He glanced at his watch; Brad and the others had been gone near two hours. So far, no great fire ball in the sky. Emma and the kids had taken to the old bomb shelter under the house. Eddy Joe knew he should have sent her off to Ma's, but now it was too late. After all the time they'd lived there, who'd have thought that anybody would ever need the shelter. Sure he'd made it into an extra room — Gerard had helped paint the walls – but that was a long time back.

Yeah sure enough, he'd been a cop an awful long time. It had just been him, Gerard and Eastman for a while. Just straight forward police work but he couldn't imagine doing anything else. Now the notion that Armstrong was the centre of some kinda Top Secret stuff was beyond him. Still, here he was, standing waiting for whatever came their way.

He looked up as Kate Black pulled up in front of him in her squad car. She was a fine looking girl but she was as tough as anybody he knew.

"Hi Eddy Joe, I got to talk to you." She closed her door and walked over to him. "I think we have us a problem."

She looked worried, as if there wasn't enough already going on.

"I hope it ain't a big one."

"I just got through with the Clayton boys. Said they'd seen an army of those things headed our way."

His face lit up and then he burst into laughter. "Shoot! Them boys are born liars; they've never known nothing else. I reckon they..."

"What about Red Cloud? Is he a liar too? Because he said exactly the same thing."

Eddy Joe stopped dead. The Clayton brothers were one thing, Red Cloud was different. "Okay, get hold of Mitch, tell him go take a look, will you?"

She shook her head and sent him a blank stare. "I don't know where he's at. I can't reach him."

He gave her a mystified look in return. That had to be one of the dumbest things he'd heard today. "What you think we got these for?" He patted his radio set and smiled.

"Yeah, well that looks like something else I got to tell you about. When's the last time you used that?"

He keyed the handset. "Eddy Joe calling Kate. Do you read me? Over?"

"Kate not reading you, 'cause all the radios are down. Over."

She jerked her thumb at her squad car. "And they're down too. Clara said the whole system's dead."

"Even the CB's?"

Slowly she nodded her head. "We got no communication with anybody."

"Yeah, we do. Us. You go get Jimmy, have a look what he's about." He got back into his car. "I'm gonna chase down Mitch."

****

Eastman watched from the grassy ridge as Sarge skirted across the broken ground towards him. The guy was in his element. He grinned as Sarge crawled up alongside him and the others to make his report.

Sarge lay against the crest and lifted the visor on his fatigue cap, wiping the sweat from his eyes. "There's six or seven guys, mostly M16's and some heavy duty stuff too."

Eastman frowned; anything heavy duty he could do without.

"How heavy duty?"

Sarge brushed the dust and grime from his M16. "A grenade launcher, two M60's and a 50 Cal. That heavy enough for you?"

Eastman shut his eyes. "That's more than enough artillery, thank you." He edged back up to the top of the ridge, taking care to keep his head low. The position lay about 800 dusty yards off no man's land, tucked neatly behind a long ridge. To the rear was a second ridge and beyond that, the mountains. The only things visible were the two ECM towers, standing out like some type of modern art against the natural landscape. To the left and right of the target stood rows and rows of razor wire, glinting in the warm afternoon sun. Bodien sidled up to Eastman and looked out across the barren moonscape. "How we gonna do this, Brad?"

"First we get in closer, then..."

"Why don't we just blast holes in those darn boxes like that Taylor guy said?"

Sarge gave Glyn McDowall a sharp look before making him wish he'd never asked.

"The targets are beyond the effective range of the M16's. But the good news is that they can't hit us either. Bad news – we gotta get closer. The hunting rifle's got the range, but not the volume of firepower we need for the ECM's."

"Why can't we hunker down, get in real close then rush them? That would do it."

"McDowall, even at this range, that darn fifty can blow a hole in a block wall. We rush those positions across open ground, and it'd be like re-creating God damn Gettysburg!" said Sarge, scowling.

Not to be outdone, McDowall pointed smugly at Ramon Tuco and gave a devious smile. "How about we use him to draw their fire then rush 'em?"

Sarge went right up to McDowall's unpleasant face. "How about I kick your sorry ass over that ridge and use *you* for target practice?"

Eastman held up his hand and moved in to separate them. "Sarge, can we use the game rifles to pin those guys down and move in with M16's?"

"Yeah, that would work. We got to hit them all over at the same time, divide their firepower. But we got us another problem."

Eastman frowned as he looked at the military man. "Now he hits us with the 'additional' problems. Mind sharing with us simple folk?"

Sarge dismissed Eastman impatiently with a wave of his hand. "I was getting to it... George Lee may have found one of the missiles."

The others listened in stunned silence as they waited for him to continue.

"There's a clearing just beyond that ridge," he pointed a few degrees right of the position in front of them, "with a launch pad complete with missile."

"Jeez Brad, we got us two targets!" called out Bodien.

"Oh just great. We start on them," said Paul Washington, jabbing his finger towards the ridge, "and them others are likely to fire that darn rocket!"

Washington was right. Any kind of direct action against the ECM could well bring a whole bunch of trouble down on them. This was another of those 'additional' problems. It was obvious that they had to take out both of the targets but which one first? Eastman shot a desperate glance at Sarge. "You got any ideas here Sarge?"

Sarge looked around the faces of the men sitting nearby, then pulled his peak down. "The mission is to put the ECM's out of action but we got us a slight issue. In doing that, we risk triggering the very thing we're up here trying to stop."

"Yeah, we kinda got that figured Sarge. What we gonna do to sort it out?"

Sarge gave Bodien a dry smile then continued his briefing speech, "You want to take a bridge; you take it from both ends at the same time and..."

"Maybe, but this ain't no damn bridge Sarge!"

Unused to being interrupted in military matters, Sarge rounded angrily on Washington.

"That's real observant of you there Washington, but the principle *is the same*. We need to hit both targets at the same time."

McDowall covered his face and let out a stifled cry. "So what, now we gotta blow up a God damn freaking nuke as well?"

"Then maybe not."

The group whipped around to see Ed Callan squatting just to the left of them, dressed in his marine combat uniform and cradling an M16. His eyes seemed old in sharp contrast to his youthful face.

"Well Ed, speak up."

"They got a medium strike bird all gassed up and ready to fly. But what we need is the command vehicle alongside it."

Eastman nodded thoughtfully at him. "So we take that out, then what?"

"The weapon is more than likely being controlled from here. We shut that baby down and they can't fire. They could launch from someplace else I guess,

239

but it ought to give us the time to frag the jammers."

"What, we just pop some rounds into the gas tank?"

Callan looked at Washington and gave him a faint grin.

"Nope. The thing is armoured, rounds zipping off the hull is gonna give the game away. We need to destroy the truck pronto, before anybody can react."

Bodien gave Eastman a worried glance. "We got nothing to take down armour, Brad."

Sarge cleared his throat. "Reckon I could help out with that."

He slid across the ground to a large green holdall and sat with his legs astride the bag, watching the others as they drew near. He began to unzip the canvas bag. Eastman's eyes widened as Sarge produced what looked like a small rocket launcher, followed by other assorted military hardware.

"Now Sarge, I know you don't have a licence for that stuff." Eastman was amazed at the bag of goodies.

"Some stuff I was saving for a rainy day."

Bodien scratched his chin as he looked at Sarge. "Most folk would likely have a rain coat for that Sarge."

McDowall pointed to the rocket launcher. "That some kinda bazooka you got there!"

Sarge gave him an annoyed glare as he extended the small tube to double its length. "Bazooka? Dumb ass! This is a 66mm LAW anti tank launcher. It'll sort out any armour they got over there."

"Hey, we can kill that truck," Tuco continued excitedly, "and then those electronic things, all with that Baz... I mean anti tank thing."

"Hold the parade. The 66 is a one shot disposable weapon. You get to use it the once."

Washington jammed his baseball cap tight on his head. "Back to 'plan A,' I suppose."

Sarge continued to rummage around in his bag then gave a satisfied grin as he found the object of his search.

"That's an amended 'plan A'."

"Grenades!" Bodien cried out in astonishment.

Eastman reached into the box and picked one out as if it were an apple. Now at least they had a fighting chance. But the best way of using these weapons was to get in close, very close. He turned the small but deadly metal sphere around in his hand.

"I'm not gonna ask where you got all this from Sarge, but do they work?"

"You just pull the pin and count to three. Like in the movies." Sarge clasped his hand around Eastman's hand and the grenade. "Then throw the darn thing as hard as you can. Just remember Uncle Sam gives the contract to the cheapest bidder."

Eastman gave Sarge an awkward look then handed him the device. "Okay it's about time we showed those bums we mean business." He leant forward and beckoned the rest closer. "Now this is what we're gonna do."

****

Eddy Joe had problems with the sheer number of creatures headed towards the town. The video Kate had taken with her phone had sealed the deal; there had to be damn near a hundred, maybe more. The only saving grace was that the blasted things only seemed to use two speeds, very slow and stop. It was almost forty minutes since they'd first appeared; enough time for him to get some of the guys to throw up basic defence lines.

"That's about as good as it gets."

He nodded slowly at Kate then looked at his band of warriors. It was obvious that Brad and Gerard had taken their pick of the best. There were no more than twenty armed men and just two automatics between them. He was expected to hold the line with this motley crew. Hold the line he thought, this bunch could hardly hold their water. The crude barricade slung across the street was no better. A couple of cars and some odds and ends of timber wouldn't stop the creatures long. Where the hell was Mitch?

"Hey Eddy Joe. Where'd the Judge go, planning the war?" Oscar Majors mocked.

"I don't much care where he's at, so long as he's outta my hair."

Eddy Joe laughed with the rest of the group. "How can he go and elect himself Mayor anyways?"

Puzzled, Jim-Boy looked over at Majors. "Sure he can – he's the Judge."

The conversation was cut short as all eyes turned towards the arrival of Virdon's fire car. He pulled up alongside the defensive line and called Eddy Joe over to him.

"Is this it?"

"It's the best we could come up with." Eddy Joe shook his head glumly at Virdon.

"I got folk strung out all over town but this here is the most likely place they gonna reach first."

Virdon sighed, surveying the sorry excuse for a line. "This ain't gonna hold long."

"I figured that, so I got us a fall back position over at Mendemus Road."

Eddy Joe indicated to a series of ramshackle barricades less than a block behind them.

"What then?"

Eddy Joe whistled through his teeth as he turned to Virdon. "By the time that comes around, there won't be much point in hanging about here. Folks are gonna want to get off home."

The two men exchanged dejected glances; there were no options left. With all the comms down, they were on their own. They could only wait for the coming onslaught.

****

Britney and Marv hurried through partly deserted streets; here and there frightened people scurried about, barricading their homes. Marv watched Mrs Cornelius ushering her two small children in from the front yard. Mr Cornelius was nailing heavy boards onto his new window frames.

Passing onto Zanuck Drive, Marv became aware of Britney clasping his hand tightly. Altogether, not an unpleasant feeling – in fact he was enjoying it – but he had to get her home. It had been some time since the police ordered the street to be cleared; he didn't want to hang about to find out why. Britney stopped abruptly, pulling him off balance as she did so.

"Marv, you really think the army will bomb us?"

He tried his best to reassure her. "Of course not."

"You are *so* not a good liar. Now, how about the truth?"

He considered his reply before he spoke. "They're running scared and people do dumb things when they get that way. My dad reckons they see us as a threat."

She stared deeply into his face. "But we're not the threat; those creeps are to blame."

"Yeah, but the army don't see it that way."

He looked down at the sidewalk, unable to meet her gaze. She tugged at his hands. "But they wouldn't do that to us Marv, how could they?"

"We bombed all those villages in the war 'cause we thought they were strongholds. People do dumb things."

"*But that's our own army out there.*"

"Nothing worse than someone who thinks they're in the right."

"Oh Marv, I'm scared."

"It'll be all right, you'll see."

He held her shoulders and looked into her face; she was scared but then so was he. "Anyway, Eastman and the others are gonna get us back on line."

"Marv you don't believe that some old radio dude will stop this do you?"

He took his phone from his pocket and flashed her a smile. "Yes, and so should you."

"Who's the first person you gonna call?"

"Pat O'Brian said you just gotta call everyone and anyone. How about you?"

"You."

Suddenly she leant forward and kissed him firmly on his lips. Every inch of his body tingled until the only sensation he could feel was her lips on his. Gradually, they stepped back from one other and stood in silence, staring into each other's eyes.

"Come on, we'd best get you home." He took her hand and started forward.

"Marv look, there's a cop over there, let's ask him what's going on."

She pulled him towards the figure of a deputy in the doorway of Lewis Dixon, the shoe shop.

"They got more things to worry about than us."

He made an effort to draw her back but she pulled away from him and sped across to the sidewalk. The green-jacketed deputy seemed oblivious as Britney called out to him but then, without warning, the deputy lashed out and grasped her by her long brown hair and bit deeply into her bare arm. She screamed as Mitch Chattman continued to gnaw into her flesh.

Marv could see Britney's lips moving, but there was no sound. He shut his eyes tightly and clasped his hands over his ears, shaking his head as if to clear the image. Marv's tear-filled eyes sprang open at the sound of a boy, screaming. It took him a few moments before he realised that the boy was him. He flung himself at the thing that had once been Mitch Chattman. With little effect, Marv rained blows down on the abomination that had torn his dreams apart.

A tyre iron flashed past him, splintering Chattman's skull and sending blood and bone splashing over the large shop window. As the now lifeless body crumpled before his eyes, Marv raced to Britney. He looked in despair at the ugly teeth marks on her arm. They embraced each other tightly, each fully aware of the inevitable outcome.

"I think is time to get her to the hospital."

Miguel Bonzzoni stepped forward, clutching the bloodied tyre iron as he moved towards the youngsters. Marv had been completely unaware of his presence. He allowed Miguel to lead them forward, though in his heart he knew there was no longer any point.

****

"Damn, damn, damn!"

Anne Lenski slammed her palm down onto the lab table, rattling the test tubes as she did so. Taylor's blood cells were attacking the human cells with the same ferocity with which they attacked infected cells. She'd exhausted all the test combinations with this last infuriating batch.

"No point in asking if you got a cure then Doc?"

"I just don't understand it, Sam. I've tried every test combination I know. It just has to be one of them."

"Yeah, um... hey, I wonder how the guys are doing up there?"

She'd been so immersed in her work, she'd totally forgotten about Brad and the others. She felt a wave of shame wash over her; while she'd been in her own bubble, Lord knows what could have happened.

"Any news Sam?"

"Nope, not since all the radios went down. 'Less of course you count the Judge, but that ain't exactly news anymore."

Her face full of curiosity, she leant towards Cortez. "What's that about the Judge?"

"Jeez, Doc you really had your nose in them books. Carmille took over right after the guys left."

She stared at him bewildered. "He can't do that. Who'd let him get away with it?"

"Well you tell him that." Cortez gave her a brief smile. "Called a meeting at the Court House then elected himself the new mayor. Way to go."

"Nobody said anything?"

He looked at her and slowly shook his head. "Would you?"

She sat back in her chair. Carmille held the town with a grip of iron, but she'd always thought him a stickler for the law. He'd have a fight on his hands when Brad got back. *If* Brad got back. She brushed the thought aside; it did no good to tempt fate.

"Has Elle-May come back from the fire house yet?"

"She went back out with two of those army nurses after she sent everybody home."

Anne nodded; there seemed no point in keeping staff at the health center when all the patients were gone, apart from those in isolation. And they were now well beyond any medical help she could provide.

"Sam, could you bring me some of the samples we took at the morgue please? Can you bring them in the red plastic box?"

She needed the samples, but she needed her space even more. Cortez was hardly her first choice after Conrad Brown. However, in fairness to him, Cortez had offered to stay, along with Elle-May and the two army girls. Conrad had failed to turn up for work and there was still no sign of Zillman. She had a dark suspicion as to what had happened to them.

"Yeah sure, I know the ones." He turned back from the door as though he'd forgotten something. "That kinda reminds me, Doc. Went by Zillman's place this morning. He was packing his truck, said he was gonna split."

"Well at least we know where he is I suppose. Thanks Sam."

As he left the room, Anne took a sip from her coffee and grimaced at the taste of the ice cold liquid. She thumbed through her notes; there had to be something she'd missed. Fully engrossed in her task she failed to notice the door slowly open behind her.

"Don't want to disturb you, but you got something I need."

Surprised, she turned to see Barney Branigan leering at her from the doorway. She'd never felt comfortable around the man.

"We don't often see you in here Mr Branigan."

"Not surprising since you barred me." He gave her an odd grin, the type of grin that rarely meant well.

"Yes, well my staff aren't here for your personal amusement. What can I do for you?"

He moved closer; she could smell his bad breath. "You got something I need, honey."

"And what would that be?"

"I just want that cure you got for this virus thing. Then I'll be outta here."

Cure! Was he mad? She was a million miles away from any cure and he would certainly be the last person in the line. However, the last thing she wanted was to antagonise him. Cortez would be back soon anyway; all she had to do was stall.

"What makes you think there is one?"

"We know what you've been up to. You been experimenting on people. I just want my share that's all."

"I don't know where you got that from but..."

He strode over to her and growled in her face, "Don't play dumb with me, lady!"

She backed away from him until she bumped into a chair.

"Suppose I did have a vaccine – it would be for everybody, not just for one person. Why would I give it to you?"

"Cause it would save you a lot of pain." His mouth opened in a grin, revealing his yellow teeth.

"Be sensible, there are armed men out there..."

Branigan advanced on her, his face full of menace. "I reckon they're gonna have their hands too full to worry about little old me."

There was an ominous air to that last remark; it made the hair on the back of her neck stand up. "Why? What makes you say that?"

"I turned out all those freaks you made. They ought to be heading onto Main Street."

"You moron! Do you know what the hell you've done?"

"Just give me that damn stuff you lousy broad, or I'm gonna start slicing bits off!"

She looked down to see Branigan holding a large brass-handled hunting knife at her stomach.

CHAPTER – TWENTY-SIX

King loaded his second ammo clip into his pistol, cocked the 9mm and stepped over the dead creatures at his feet. That had been close – too close. He looked down at the grotesque, misshapen bodies. The whole base was filled with the pungent smell of burning. Far stronger was the reek of rotting, burnt human flesh. It smelled like a garbage dump, a human garbage dump.

As he continued, he scanned the surrounding area with night vision gear. Crumpled bodies and various pieces of rubbish littered the floor. King walked a few yards, then stopped to check his GPS from the corridor number attached to the wall. He smiled, then resumed his progress until he came across a large metal door marked 'Medical Research'. Light flooded into the corridor and he darted forward, pulling the door closed behind him. The last thing he wanted was another run in with the creatures; he'd been lucky last time.

He removed his night vision gear, feeling helpless as his eyes adjusted to the harsh light. He was in a tight enclosure with several small rooms built into the rock face. He made his way towards a room marked 'Restricted Area'. Cautiously, King pulled open the door and went inside.

Two rows of six blank computers occupied the gloomy room. His eyes systematically searched the confined space. King caught sight of a green power light blinking at the far end of the room. His footsteps echoed over the wooden floor as he walked to the source of his curiosity. Two blank VDU's sat on a separate table just to the left of a metal door. King clicked on the standby switch and was surprised to see information being downloaded onto a USB pen. He stared intently at the screen. Why would some random computer be powered up and downloading onto a pen drive? Intrigued, he reached over to the gadget.

"Please don't. It hasn't finished yet."

King whirled around, ready to confront the cause of the sudden interruption.

"Out! Where I can see you," he ordered, aiming his pistol at the desk to his right.

A small, timid man in a dirty lab coat emerged from underneath the table; he stood a few feet from King, bathed in the light from the VDU's.

"And who might you be?"

"Hasslein. Dr Hasslein, head of Research Amendment," the little man uttered, fearfully.

"Where's Tellermine?" King snapped back.

"He... he ran out on us; left us all to die."

"Taking all the research with him..." King sent a savage kick to the table, sending it crashing onto its side. Hasslein winced and moved back at the outburst. "But it won't do him any good, not without my amended notes."

King lowered his pistol and advanced on the terrified man. "Why not?"

"He only took part one of the material. The part that creates the mutations."

Hasslein clasped his hands together, almost gleefully. "He needs part two – the amended research – and without that, he has nothing."

King pointed to the pen drive. "And all that is on this USB?"

It took the man a few moments before he replied. "Yes. I managed to save almost all the data."

He checked the download progress, smiled, then ejected the stick. "This will give us a way to redress the virus."

King holstered his pistol. His eyes bored into the other man. "You're telling me you have a cure for this chaos?"

Hasslein took his glasses off, rubbing them on his coat. "As soon as I can re-assemble the data, yes, this will cure the infection."

"What do you mean *re-assemble?* You either got a cure or you don't."

King strode across to Hasslein, forcing him back against the wall.

"Well maybe not quite ready – it's very complicated, you know."

King reached over and slowly, deliberately, straightened the man's tie, while staring directly into his eyes.

"It's been my experience that things are never as complicated as you think they are. Things *are* or things *are not.* Now, I'm gonna ask you the same question, but you'd better have a different answer this time." He stepped back and gave Hasslein a menacing smile.

"The data is fragmented, disjointed, like a jigsaw." He held the pen drive up to the light, reflecting its shiny metal casing. "It's all here, but it needs to be assembled."

"And you would be the only one to do this, right?"

"There are two others who could do it but…"

"Where are they?" King's voice took an animated edge as he pressed for information.

"Through there." Hasslein indicated to the door behind King. King waved his arm at the door. "More for the party."

Hasslein opened the door, allowing Peel and Thornson into the room.

"Thank God! Are you the rescue party?" Thornson turned from King to look at Hasslein uncertainly.

"Rescue party? Oh yeah, that would be me," said King, smiling at the others.

"Are you the only one?" Peel asked, stepping up to King.

"This is Doctor Lynda Peel and Doctor Thornson, two of my research associates."

"Are you the only one here Mr...?"

King looked right through the woman as if she wasn't even there. There was an uncomfortable silence.

"How'd this place get in such a mess?"

"After the first fire, Tellermine became paranoid; thought there was a spy down here."

Peel took up the story. "One of the holding pens was breached. When the first test subject made it to the surface, Tellermine thought they'd shut him down. We think he deliberately started the second fire, but then he took it too far."

Thorson looked at Hasslein then continued grimly, "Yes, way too far."

"Go on."

Slowly and somewhat uneasily, Hasslein began. "Tellermine introduced a 'hyped up' derivative of NB33 into the base sprinkler system."

He paused briefly and rubbed his hand over his eyes. "Anyone caught in the downpour was instantly infected. Rather than days, the transformation took place in hours."

He halted, unable to carry on. Doctor Peel took his hand. "The creatures went on a rampage, hunting everyone else down. Then Tellermine released all the secured TS into the base. It was a bloodbath."

King sat down in one of the many chairs, shifting his gaze between the other three. "See, what bothers me is why he took off... leaving you three with the 'wonder' drug."

"Because he thinks he has the wonder drug."

King shot a glace back at Thorson. "And why would he think that?"

"We copied the master files, then we corrupted the originals. And for added insurance we encrypted the whole lot."

Hasslein nodded agreeably at Thorson. "He's quite correct; by the time Tellermine gains access he'll find the data of no use."

"Until he works it out for himself..."

Doctor Peel shook her head at King. "It will take him months if not longer and by that time our cure will be available to anyone who wants it."

King stood up and began to study his GPS.

"According to this, that door leads to the main exit. After you Doctor Hasslein."

"That way is blocked under a ton of rock."

Hasslein walked to a computer and showed King CCTV images of the tunnel.

"And if you go this way you run into them."

The small black and white screen was crowded with the creatures. King turned away from the screen and looked at his GPS. He tracked his finger over the tiny screen for another way out.

"Didn't you say you were the only one of your group? Then who the hell are they?"

King hid his irritation from the others as Taylor's face stared back at him from the CCTV screen.

"I've no idea, but I'd say they're no rescue party."

"But there are soldiers with them. They must have come to rescue us."

Hasslein pointed at the grainy TV pictures, almost in desperation.

"What would *real* soldiers be doing with the very people they're meant to be containing?"

Thornson was confused – "Are you saying they're fakes?"

"That cure is worth a lot of bucks to a lot of desperate people, starting with them." King glanced at the GPS, his face glum. "They're about two corridors away from us. I want to put some distance between us and them."

He pushed the inner door open to reveal a large bulkhead door leading to the blocked passage.

"Sorry, that's the only way out."

Hasslein shrank away from the door in dismay. "We can't get out that way. I've already shown you!"

"We wouldn't last five minutes out there with those things. I won't go!"

Peel's frightened face looked for support from the others. King brought up the TV section containing the creatures and stabbed his finger at the screen.

"Eight, nine, ten. Ten! That's no big deal."

"You propose to fight through that lot with *us*?"

King gave Thorson a bland smile. "I can't risk a fire fight with that other crowd. There aren't too many of those things, besides they don't shoot back. Trust me, that's always a good thing."

Hasslein waved his finger at King, shaking his head in disagreement. "I still don't like it; there are too many TS's."

"The door they're all clustered about, leads into the mess hall…" He drew his finger along the GPS display, "…and that leads directly to stairwell 3. That people, takes us the hell outta this bone yard."

"Look, you may be used to all this gung ho stuff but…" Thorson trailed off as he watched the reactions of the other two. "Don't tell me you're going along with this?"

"My mission is to convey all research material and survivors to safety. Period. That's exactly what I intend to do…" King paused as he observed the small group's reaction before continuing, "…but you have to trust me."

Peel looked at the two men, almost pleading with them: "I don't want to die down here."

King looked earnestly at them. "Then trust me to lead you all out of here."

"Okay, okay. Now please get us out."

"Consider it done, Dr Hasslein. These things are like any other predator; they hunt with sound and sight. As long as we can get to that mess hall, we're in with a chance. So we have to keep silent."

He steered them to the outer door then paused and held his hand out to Hasslein.

"I'd better take the stick, just in case."

Reluctantly, Hasslein handed King the device. "This could save a lot of lives."

"Don't worry. I'll make sure the right people get it."

He took the stick and slipped it into his jacket pocket. Warily, he pulled open the metal bulkhead door and moved into the dimly lit corridor. The only source of light came from a neon lamp near the door. A quick visual inspection offered no possible route of escape; it would have to be through the mess hall. King signalled the group to follow him. They'd travelled a few yards when King stopped dead, smacking his jacket pocket in frustration.

"Damn! I left the GPS on the table." Peel peered fearfully into the shadowy tunnel ahead of them.

"Leave it, we don't need it. You have to stay with us."

"No can do. That's our only chance out of here. Look, I won't be long." King started back towards the open door. Urgently, Hasslein called after him – "I'm sure I could…"

"I want the three of you watching that corner. Don't take your eyes off it."

They watched as the uniformed man sped back to the door. Hasslein turned to the others.

"We'd best do as he says; I don't want them creeping up on us again."

The three stood like watchful sentinels, mindful that the slightest noise could attract danger. Suddenly, Hasslein screamed out in pain as a bullet ripped through the rear of his thigh, toppling him to the floor. As he rolled around in agony, he was astonished to see Thornson and Peel fall with similar injuries. He tilted his head in time to see King disappear through the door. He cursed the man and then fell silent at the sight of the ever hungry ghouls advancing on them.

"Ding dong. Dinner is served," said King. Safe inside the lab, he locked the metal door and reached into his jacket, producing the GPS. Then he located Taylor on the CCTV.

"Need to do better than that Sport."

King left the lab as the high-pitched scream of a woman penetrated the wall.

****

Eddy Joe stopped his patrol car on the corner of Biderbeck Road and Honorious Avenue. He left the vehicle and walked over to Kate who was standing by her car. Eddy Joe's jacket was torn and his face bloodied.

"We couldn't hold them, they broke our lines. I told the guys 'shoot at the head' but folks panicked…" His voice rose with anxiety as he continued, "Those damn things kept getting back up; even full of holes they kept coming."

He lent his hands against her car, leaving grimy fingerprints on the metal surface.

Kate stroked his arm and spoke softly to him.

"Where'd they go?"

Frantically he rubbed his hands over his face, as though brushing away cobwebs.

"They swarmed all around like locusts, looking for people to eat. After that, the guys wanted out. I sent what was left of them home."

"You did what?"

He pulled away. "Don't you get it? They'd had enough, damn I'd had enough!"

"Look, we gotta get organised, go at them again. You and me. It's our duty."

"I know all about duty, but times like this you gotta look to your own kin."

"This town is our responsibility – we owe them that," she said, squaring up to him.

"I got responsibilities as a father and a husband. If there's some nut about to roast this town then by damn, I'm not spending my last chasing about here."

He thrust his finger at her, his face flushed with anger.

"I'm gonna spend it with my folks!"

She dropped her gaze and looked at the sidewalk. He placed his hand on her shoulder then walked back to his car. As he drove past, she called out to him, lifting her hand to wave him off.

"Good luck."

"I'll leave that with you," he said, before driving off towards Honorious Avenue.

Disappointed, she watched as his tail lights vanished from sight. Maybe he was right; maybe it was best to go home. After all, what could she do on her own, against dead things that wouldn't stay dead? Maybe she should go home. She started the engine, then turned her head at the sound of nearby gunfire. She looked back up Honorious Avenue, shook her head and drove in the opposite direction, towards the shooting.

****

"I think you have gone far enough."

Branigan let go of Anne Lenski's hair and turned to face Miguel Bonzzoni, standing in the doorway with Marv Glitzman and Britney Patrick.

"Yeah, and I think you'd best mind your freaking business, unless you want some of this?"

He held up the knife, its razor sharp blade glinting in the artificial light. Anne took the opportunity to move away from him and stand with the others. She smiled at the two youngsters but her face fell as she saw the bite on the girl's arm.

"You can leave. I will not try to stop you," said Miguel Bonzzoni, lowering his weapon. He stood away from the door, ushering the others aside as he did so.

"Don't give me orders little man. I ain't leaving till I get what I came for."

"What's he on about Dr Lenski?" Marv looked at her as he held Britney tightly.

Anne shook her head dismissively at Branigan. "Nothing, he's drunk."

"Damn! 'Nothing,' she says. Well ain't that rich. While we been dying, she had a cure all the time. Tell them!"

"Please help me, I've been bitten," said Britney. With an effort, she held up her arm to display the teeth marks.

"He's talking garbage. There is no cure!"

"That's right. You gonna let her turn like you did all the rest, but not me. I'm gonna use that stuff you got."

Branigan looked at the array of slides and phials on the desk behind him. He started to examine some labels, while roughly pushing everything else aside, unsure of what he was looking for.

"Just give him what he wants. She's getting worse." Marv pleaded with Anne – anything to get rid of Branigan. Oblivious to the others, Branigan continued in his wild search, smashing glass containers on the floor.

"It has to be one of these blasted things."

"None of them work. Why can't you see that?" Anne roared back at him.

"Then I'll grab the stinking lot!"

He started to thrust sealed ampoules into his coat pockets then moved for the open door. The others moved aside, giving him free access, all except Anne Lenski. She had to at least try to warn him. "Branigan, just listen to me for a second. You've no idea how dangerous that stuff is. It's likely to kill you. Do you understand that?"

As he stared into her face, it seemed for one awful second as though she'd pushed him too far.

"You're lucky I don't kill you." And with that, Branigan barged past her, marching up the corridor, away from them.

"Why you leave that pig take the medicine?" said Miguel Bonzzoni, throwing his arms into the air and shaking his head, "...I don't get you."

She looked on miserably at the mass of broken glass and blood samples on the floor. "If he takes any of those, he'll end up dead."

****

"Taylor, we're about lucked out on this dumb mission. You'd darn well better have a good plan!"

Benteen rested against the rock wall. This guy seemed to have had some kind of plan a while back, but after the three bodies by the lab, Benteen wasn't too sure anymore. They'd doubled back and gone through a whole mess of corridors and seemed no closer to finding the guy with the bomb. Taylor looked at Benteen with weary eyes. "That sign back there said Tellermine's lab is just up ahead." He pointed in front of them towards the partly blocked tunnel. Benteen flashed his torch down the tunnel; it branched off into three directions. Some boulders had fallen onto the path, the whole area looked unsafe. He shot a doubtful stare at Taylor. Everybody, even the soldiers had been shaken by Tom's horrific death. It was one thing Taylor pulling heroics with his life, but risking other folk, that was quite different.

"What makes you think you gonna find this Tellermine here? If he's that smart he's gonna be long gone."

"I'm not looking for *Tellermine*; I want anything of use our good doctor left behind. If it's anywhere, it'll be in there."

Austin Colt cut into the conversation. "What about this King character? Don't we need that timer?"

"We certainly do."

"Yeah, sure we will. He's long gone." Benteen scoffed, laughing loudly.

It must be clear to even Taylor that King would have long gone, Benteen concluded. What worried him was the possibility that bum could be about to set the darn warhead off, with them still down there.

Taylor shone his light onto a metal object on the floor. It was an empty pistol clip. "Found this near that lab, too," he said, handing Benteen an empty pistol magazine. "It's from the same type of weapon as this one. I'd say there's a fair chance he's about somewhere."

"You want us to go with you Sir?"

Taylor nodded his thanks to Harper. "That could be a good idea. But King is one seriously messed up individual."

"So what, we just hang about waiting on you then, do we?"

Benteen was sick of all this bull; he'd followed Taylor about like a lap dog for hours. They'd fought through an army of those foul things and now Taylor didn't need them anymore.

"Benteen, this guy is nuts, he kills for fun. Anyway, you'd better get your people topside. It's all over now anyway, one way or another."

Benteen cast a distrustful eye over at Taylor and the soldiers. Could it be that this guy wanted him out of the way? Had that been the plan all the time? What if...?

"Stay sharp. We got some of them things coming up behind us!"

Benteen looked to see Boulle running towards him and pointing behind him. The group peered into the tunnel's half light. Within seconds they could hear the clamour of a large group of ghouls, staggering towards them.

"Benteen, can you hold them off? I need time in that lab."

"Sure, but the more clatter we make the more of them gonna show."

"Hold them as long as you can, then pull out. We'll make our own way."

Benteen tapped Taylor on his shoulder. "Just so long as you remember where you gotta bring anything you find."

Taylor gave Benteen a deep frustrated sigh as he eyed up the big cop. "You still don't trust me after all this?"

"Nope. There's something that ain't right about you." Benteen turned and called out to the others, "Okay boys, let's send these freaks straight back to hell!"

The cave lit up like the fourth of July and with about as much noise. Rifle and pistol rounds ripped into the advancing horde, sending congealed blood and putrefying flesh fragments through the air. Still the relentless snapping, snarling ghouls kept coming, driven by their terrible hunger. With a noise like a thunderclap, tons of rock came smashing to the ground.

Benteen spun around only to be confronted by a new wall of rock and a thick cloud of dust. Dodge lay on the floor with his leg bent backwards. Taylor was nowhere to be seen. Benteen ran torwards the two soldiers.

"Where'd the hell Taylor go? Anyone see Taylor?"

Harper looked up at Benteen and pointed to the rocks. "Yeah, he's under that!"

Benteen looked at the mountain of solid rock in front of him and then at the approaching creatures behind them. They were trapped.

****

Chris Emery sat on his beloved bench overlooking Grant Park. The bench had been donated by his father after Emery's mother died. It now bore the names of both parents. Everything in the park was as it should be: the wide selection of flowers neat in their beds radiated a resplendent array of colour. The closely mown lawns and pruned trees completed the picture perfect image of the park. Even during the hot spell, not one scorch mark or dry patch could be seen. Lance Kronberg was every inch the expert gardener.

Emery could feel the warm sun on his face and hands as he looked over at the clock tower at the other end of the park. He squinted, but it was no use: he'd forgotten to wear his glasses. He wasn't even sure where he'd left them but perhaps Beth would know. He stared thoughtfully at the two Civil War twelve pounder 'Napoleon' cannons either side of the iron gates. They'd been there since ever he could recall, one Confederate, the other Union; a continuing reminder of the futility of war.

Emery enjoyed this weekly ritual and now that he'd retired, he intended to do it more often. Even so, the park, indeed the whole town seemed inordinately quiet. Perhaps it was one of the many public holidays the town observed. He was relatively sure it was not Christmas, because of the absence of the great tree. He forced himself to concentrate harder.

Why was it that he could remember certain things with qualified accuracy and yet not others? In point of fact, carpet slippers. He looked down at his feet, the rest of his attire was passable, but carpet slippers would simply not do.

Deep furrows creased his face as he tried to recall what that charming army nurse had said earlier that morning. He was sure it had been something important, if only he could remember what? This memory thing was distracting indeed. He turned his head towards a sudden commotion off to his left.

Several people were milling about by the new bird feeder; it made him cross to see the damage they'd caused to the small wooden fence. Most likely drunk; not that this gave them carte blanche for wanton destruction. He could not allow this type of disgraceful behaviour; shaking his head crossly he started towards the odd little group.

"Someone is going to have to pay for this damage you know," Emery said, pointing to the broken fence. "This park is for everyone's enjoyment, not just yours."

Halloween! Yes, that was it – Halloween. He looked with admiration at their costumes, so convincing and such incredible detail. The wounds and makeup almost looked real. In fact, these boys could give one of those horror movies a run for its money. However, at least they seemed to be taking notice of what he was telling them. They'd stopped their activity and were now staring intently at him.

They appeared still to be 'in character' and he began to find them unsettling. The group moved forward and he instinctively backed away from them. As they closed around him, suddenly Emery recalled what the nurse had said to him – yes that was it!

"Get away old man!" Red Cloud screamed out his warning. But he was too late and too far away. Red Cloud turned his head as the creatures began their frenzied feeding. There was nothing left to do but leave the park and head for home. First he needed to find something with which to defend himself; then, he needed a plan.

From what he'd seen of the creatures, they had pretty much free run of the town. Apart from the dead, the only people he'd encountered had been running away. Those people who had stayed indoors were now shooting at anything moving. It was like the Wild West – Red Cloud considered this a very unhealthy place for a Red Indian.

As he left the park he walked down Thomas Street and stopped outside APP Sports. Looking through the broken window, he'd hoped to find something of use, but now that looked unlikely. He pushed on the door and went inside, crunching broken glass under foot as he did so. His heart sank at the empty gun racks in front of him. Then he caught sight of a solitary bow at the end of the counter. He picked the bow up inspecting it carefully for any damage, drawing the string back and letting it go with a loud twanging sound. It was hardly an Indian hunting bow, but it would have to do. He gathered as many arrows as possible, then selected a rucksack and began stuffing it with various items for his escape. His dark brown eyes glinted with pleasure as he spotted a Tomahawk in the knife section. Typical white man, take all the guns and Bowie knives but leave the Indian stuff behind. He smiled as he left the shop; at least now he was in with a chance.

****

"You reckon that's the last of the gunfire O'Brian?" Vince Langley paused for a moment. "Then again, maybe that ain't such a good thing."

O'Brian lifted his US Navy cap onto his head. "Either we run outta bullets or those things run outta people."

Both men were in O'Brian's radio room; it had all the refinement of a cave. The white washed walls had long since surrendered to a dirty grey. The old metal door had more rust on it than a sea wreck. But it was here O'Brian spent most of his time, engaged on a series of endless radio projects, which he somehow never quite seemed to complete. In contrast, the rest of the tiny room was crammed with the latest state of the art telecommunications gear. O'Brian checked the signal strength once more and cursed. The line was still on zero and that meant the ECM was still operational. Langley tapped the monitor window with his finger and let out a sigh. "I was sure we'd have heard something by now. I don't like all this waiting."

"That's all we can do – *wait*."

"I guess you gotta be used to all this excitement, I mean being in the navy and all."

O'Brian took a small swig out of his hip flask and reclined in his easy chair.

"I spent twenty years in the US Navy, I been in three wars and a hell of a lot of other stuff, but the closest I ever come to a real fight," he raised his flask, "was after too much of this crap. Fella, we both in the same boat here."

A sudden pounding at the door sent both men rocketing up from their seats.

"Who in the God damn hell is that?"

O'Brian shot an angry look at Langley, and then selected a large wrench from his tool rack. Both men padded towards the door, fixing their eyes on it, as though they could see right through.

"Come on guys, it's me, Oscar Majors. Open up!"

O'Brian sent his reply back like a broadside. "Go someplace else, we're busy in here!"

"Guys!" Majors sounded terrified as he pounded on the door.

"Best let him in Pat, before he brings half the county down on us."

O'Brian looked at Langley, then hesitantly reached over and lifted the heavy bolt. Majors flew into the room as though the devil were on his heels. Desperately he clutched at the two men. O'Brian slammed the door shut and glared at the panic stricken man, pushing his hands away.

"Where's the God damn fire!"

Langley was altogether more sympathetic in his approach as he led Majors to a chair. "Take it easy Oscar, you gonna do yourself an injury. What's up?"

The man was a mess; he looked as though he'd come last in a cross-country race. His clothes were covered in dust and his trainers had dried blood over them. But it was his face that told them the story. Even safely in the radio room, his wide eyes darted about like a buck caught in headlights. Something bad had happened: they were about to find out how bad.

"Those things are all over the town, they're killing everybody!"

He buried his face in his hands, rocking himself gently in the chair. He looked every inch a broken man. O'Brian shook him roughly.

"What about the cops? What about the patrols? You guys had a line out there."

He shook him harder and Majors exploded – "*Gone!* They're all gone. Eddy Joe went down under a ton of those freaks. He never got up. I saw Mitch Chattman dead in the gutter. Everybody else ran or ended up the same way. Virdon and his guys were putting out a fire then the things swamped them. It was all over. I just ran."

O'Brian and Langley were in shock; they knew these people. It couldn't be possible they'd all gone. How many people had died and how many more would die?

"Everybody and their damn uncle's neighbour got some kinda gun in this town. You telling me those things went right through everyone?"

Majors stared directly into O'Brian's eyes, tears cutting lines down his grubby face.

"I shot one, five, six times. It just got right on up. We didn't have the firepower."

"Abe McReedy got a shop full of firepower, right Vince?"

Langley slowly nodded his stunned agreement, lost for words.

"We tried that already. It's sealed up tighter than a drum..." Majors rubbed his hand over his eyes.

"Well then Majors go get Abe and open the damn place up then!"

"It ain't as easy as that O'Brian. Abe's got himself some new friends. Last time I saw him he was chewing on Ed Corbyn's innards up on Armando Drive."

"Shoot! That's less than a block from here!" Langley's eyes sprang open in alarm.

"Guess he ain't gonna want his radio back now?" O'Brian walked back to his workstation, apparently unfazed by the grim news.

An uncomfortable silence filled the room until it was broken by Majors.

"Say, O'Brian, you sure all this junk works?"

"Junk? This is highly sophisticated electronic communications equipment. Junk!" O'Brian threw the words back at him and busied himself in his work.

"Sorry. All I meant was, the guys ought to have got back to us by now."

Majors stood up and walked to the large town map mounted on the wall and began staring at it. All three men turned about at an unexpected banging on the door.

"This is getting God damn ridiculous! And who the crap is this now?" yelled O'Brian, flinging his baseball cap onto the workface, his weathered face an unhealthy shade of crimson. Majors gave Langley an uncertain look. In return, Langley grimaced back at him.

"Well, ain't one of you gonna see who the hell this is?" said O'Brian, jerking his thumb in the direction of the sound.

Langley shrugged his shoulders before looking at Majors and nodding towards the door. Reluctantly, the shopkeeper edged forward and called out. There was no reply other than the steady thumping sound. Langley selected a hammer and went to stand next to the other man. Majors looked at the hammer and then gave him a surprised gaze.

"You never can tell." Langley eyed the hammer then smiled. "Best open up Oscar, see who it is."

Majors slipped the latch and slowly opened the door a fraction, peering gingerly through the open space. He drew back in horror and then violently slammed the door shut, frantically bolting the door.

"Freaking hell! It's like the God damn Muppet Show in here." O'Brian turned away from his work and glared at the latest interruption. Majors stood with his back to the door, his face pale and his eyes wide in terror.

"O'Brian, you wanted to ask Abe about the keys? Well now's your chance, he's out front. Only he ain't on his own."

The three men looked around them as dozens of the creatures strated pounding on the fragile wooden structure.

CHAPTER – TWENTY-SEVEN

Colonel Steedman bustled into the CP clutching an attaché case, his face grim. Stone sat with two soldiers: all that remained of his HQ staff. The General spoke tersely without looking up from his paperwork.

"Colonel, I hope you've got news about King. We haven't heard from him in..."

"Yes Sir. We have a problem with Mr King." Steedman walked forward to stand in front of Stone.

"There are always problems with people like Mr King." He gave the Colonel an irritated look. "What?"

"I don't think King is who he claims to be." Braving the General's cold stare he continued, "Yesterday, one of our patrols found a body."

"Colonel Steedman, the place is littered with dead bodies. Get to the point!"

"The man had been executed. Spook style, hands tied behind his back and a single pistol round to the nape of the neck. Pretty much text book."

Impatiently Stone waved him to continue, hoping the conversation was going somewhere.

"I ran an e-check on him, prints and mug shots. It gave me a restricted access message, but I managed to override it. Turns out the man was a GS2 agent."

"Are you going anywhere with this?"

"I have a buddy who works GS2, King's plates were registered to the GS2 motor pool and the car belonged to the dead man. There is no mention of anyone known as King. He has to be an imposter."

"I knew there was something about that guy. Why am I hearing about this now?"

"It took some time to get the information and I knew you'd want hard facts General."

Stone nodded his appreciation, but then his face took on a vexed look.

"Thing is, who the hell is this King?"

"No one. He doesn't exist. I ran a full e-check on him: all blank. None of the agencies has him on their books, or at least none will lay claim to him."

"How the hell could he walk into this operation without us knowing who he is?"

"General, he had clearance from the top and he just... just looked as if he belonged."

Stone pointed to the attaché case still held by Steedman. "Is that King's case?"

Steedman nodded and plucked out a solitary brown A4 envelope. "I went through his room and this is all I could find."

Stone read the envelope label out loud. "GS2 Restricted Access. These are the 'need to know' orders he was keen for us not to see. Let's see what all the damn fuss was about."

He took a metal rule from the desk and sliced the bulging envelope open. Holding the envelope by its opposite corners, Stone slid the contents onto the desk.

"New York subway timetables. What the hell is this?"

Stone roared and sprang to his feet. "Colonel, I want that damn spook back here ten minutes ago! And I want direct fire control over those warheads."

****

Taylor wished the marching band in his head would go play someplace else. Painfully, he opened his eyes and almost instantly he was sorry he had. King was standing a few feet away looking down at him. Of all the people he could think of, it had to be King.

"Glad you could join us Sport, saves me having to kick you awake."

Taylor took his time getting to his feet, taking every second to assess his new surroundings. He was in some type of small office, not as basic as the rest of the base. The room had plastered walls and tiled flooring. Metal filing cabinets lay at either side of the room. Behind King was a large desk with a computer. This had to be Tellermine's office.

Taylor looked over at the other man. "Sorry to disappoint." Taylor could not work which hurt the most, his head or raw elbows. "How'd I get in here?"

"I dragged your sorry ass in. Couldn't risk any rocks landing on you."

Taylor winced as he tensed up his body. "What about the others?"

King drew his finger across his throat and gave Taylor a dry smirk. "You rolled clear. Gave your head a crack, the others, not so lucky."

It saddened Taylor to think of all the people who'd died to get him where he was. He'd make sure it had not been in vain. To King's left was a desk with the timer on it. Above all else, that had to be his priority. Taylor motioned to the desk and moved forward.

"Why'd you disconnect that device?"

"Stop that fool Stone from toasting my butt." King moved back a few paces and placed his hand on the device.

"How come? I thought you were his errand boy?" Taylor circled around the other side of the table until he was within reach of the small box. He didn't know what King was up to, but he needed the timer.

"I'm no one's errand boy! I couldn't trust him any longer."

It was obvious that he'd struck a raw nerve. Something was rotten and it wasn't just the piles of dead. "I take it Tellermine's split?"

King nodded. "Real nice guy. He burned the place, made everybody zombies then let them loose."

"You get that from those three geeks you killed? In any case when did you switch sides?"

Taylor was playing chess again but this guy was no Eastman. He had to push his buttons carefully.

"You were always that little bit too smart, Sport. But I never changed sides. I just increased my opportunity. I've made more money from this job than any other in my whole life."

"*That's it?* The money?" Taylor crept ever nearer to the desk.

"You've no idea how far this has gone man." King took his hand off the device and pointed at Taylor. "This goes way beyond Tellermine or this containment crap. It's always been about you. Do you know how much you're worth? Do you?"

Taylor felt a nasty sensation creeping into him. This had sunk below corporate greed and it went beyond this messed up containment operation.

"Who you working for?"

"Working for? I decided to go independent. I'm gonna sell you to the highest bidder. Imagine NB33 as a weapon…" Kings eyes glazed over as he continued, "…Now imagine how much you'd pay for a cure."

All the time Taylor had thought it was about big business and cover ups, this maniac wanted to make the thing into a weapon. No wonder King had let him escape; he was in it for himself all the time.

"King, you need to think about this a second. *King Business Enterprises* is one thing but turning these freaking things into weapons is total insanity!"

"So is the nuclear arms race. If someone gets the edge then the rest will pay to get it back. So you're wrong, it is just business."

"What if some tin pot terror jerks get hold of NB33? What if…?"

King smashed his hand down on the desk and glared at Taylor. "Enough! I'm controlling this and I'll sell it to whoever the hell I want to!"

"What if I don't want to play ball? You gonna need me alive."

King pulled out his pistol and with his free hand pointed to a small medical cool bag on a nearby desk. "Open the bag."

Taylor did as he was ordered. It contained several small glass sealed bottles and syringes. Puzzled, he looked over at King.

"I took a crash course in phlebotomy. All I need is your blood."

King cocked the pistol and aimed it at him. "Dead or alive, you decide."

Taylor knew he had to get the advantage over King and he had to do it fast. He picked the bag up without closing it and walked over to King.

"Okay, how exactly do you think we're getting out of here in one piece?"

The other man's face relaxed and a slight smile swept over his features as he lowered his automatic. Here was a man who could taste power. The last thing he wanted was to mop up a dead man's blood. This could well be enough to give Taylor the edge he needed.

"Glad you got with the programme, Sport. It's down the corridor then up some stairs. I'm pretty sure that's how Tellermine left."

Taylor pointed to the forlorn timer still on the desk. "You gonna use that?"

"Gonna have to. I'm not leaving anything down here for anyone else to use."

"Yeah well, what about General 'inconvenience'? As soon as you wire this up we're both yesterday's news." Taylor grinned smugly as he patted the device. King smiled back at him. "Ain't gonna happen buddy. I modified it, changed the firing codes."

"How'd you… don't tell me, another crash course slotted between manual handling and time management, right?"

"A lot of effort and money has been sunk into this…"

"And all for you to clear them out and cut yourself a new deal."

"Why the hell not? Tell me that? I took the risks, I'm the one stuck in all this filth." King's temper yet again got the better of him as he sent a chair hurtling into the wall.

"What about me? I mean, without me you don't have Jack…"

King gave Taylor a devious look. It was the look that allowed Taylor to make up his mind; in a way it sealed King's fate. In one fluid motion Taylor's fist smashed into King's jaw. Caught off guard, he flew backwards over the table, swiftly followed by Taylor. Both men engaged in a savage fight for survival. Gaining the upper hand, King broke away from Taylor and drew his pistol. In a desperate last gamble, Taylor rammed a table into King, forcing him into the wall. However, King succeeded in loosing off two rounds. The first bullet went wide of its target but the second sliced through Taylor's arm. But it was not enough to stop him beating King to the floor with a desk lamp. This was one fight Taylor could not afford to lose.

Satisfied that King was no longer a game player, Taylor tore a strip from his own shirt and bound his wound. Although only a graze, it was best to control the bleeding. Then he noticed the timer lying on the floor. Reaching down, he picked up the device for a closer look. It seemed intact but as he tried to access the control system his plan fell apart.

Each time he pressed the timer the word ERROR glared back at him from the LED. He covered his face with his hands, swearing repeatedly. The all important timer function was inoperative. There was no way to safely explode the warhead. He had failed. His eyes narrowed in concentration as he scrolled through the menu bar. He smiled briefly as he read the new LED message: MANUAL OPERATION ENABLED. Then his face sunk in desperation. He rubbed his forehead, sweat trickled into his eyes, making them sting. Well at least there was one way to explode the damn thing, although maybe not the best.

As he collected the device, the hairs on the back of his neck stood on end. Even before he turned about, he knew what he'd see. Several creatures had gathered in the doorway; the pistol was nowhere to be seen. He backed away as the creatures pushed forward.

****

Sarge was satisfied he was well within the LAW's effective range. This was no time for any mistakes. He settled himself into a secure firing position overlooking the target. Both control vehicle and missile were less than a hundred yards from him, and about half that distance from each other.

He scrutinized the surrounding area. The missile site had been well placed, with trees covering all four sides. It was perfectly hidden away from any unwanted attention, but not well defended. A heavy frown creased his forehead; they'd made no attempt at a permanent defence. In all probability these guys had only recently placed the firing unit here. Still, there was no excuse for sloppy work. A further two vehicles had accompanied the unit but these were situated at the far end of the clearing. He was good to go.

George Lee and Callan had the two guards standing near the Humvees covered. The rest of the detail had to be in the control vehicle; it'd be like shooting rats in a barrel. He sighed as he contemplated the next move. He had to deny them the tactical advantage of firing the missile – that meant taking the truck down first. That also meant certain death for the guys inside. The war felt like a million years ago. They'd given him a medal for saving American lives back then; he sure as hell would not get one for killing Americans. Nevertheless, that's what he needed to do.

Sarge looked about the peaceful meadow one last time; clusters of little blue flowers broke up the sea of green grass. Everybody was in place and waiting for him to take the shot. He brought the LAW out from his pack and extended the weapon, ready to fire. Clicking the safety off, he aimed at the objective. No time for hesitation now, he squeezed the trigger and watched as the flaming projectile screeched towards the helpless target.

The explosive power of the 66mm armoured piercing round lifted the truck into the air. Then the twisted wreck slammed back to earth, belching fire and thick black smoke. Two simultaneous shots rang out. Sarge shut his eyes as the sound of cheering broke out across the meadow.

"Sarge, you did it!"

Max Koneg and Bill Gardener had scrambled up behind him, broad grins spread across their excited dirty faces. Sarge was in no mood for celebrations.

"All I did was kill a bunch of Americans." He pitched the now useless LAW over the tump and watched it roll down the steep incline. Koneg craned his head around to look at Sarge. "Yeah, but think of all the folk in town. They're safe now. Sarge, you gotta leave the war be."

"Max is right Sarge, that's all behind you. Hell! Everybody gonna know what you did today. Things gonna be different from now on."

What the hell did they know? It wasn't the IED or a sniper's bullet or even his PTSD that had brought his long and eventful army service crashing down. No, none of those things. It had been that damn pinprick in his thumb. Everything else, the army had fixed. They'd even set him up training grunts, but what they couldn't allow, was a soldier with Type 2 Diabetes. There was nothing they could do about that. Sarge looked straight ahead and silently led the two men down towards the missile.

"What we gonna do with that missile Sarge?"

Sarge looked at the Deputy; he didn't have the heart to tell them the missile still posed a danger. At any moment it could be launched remotely.

"Nothing. We don't want to risk setting the thing off. Keep the guys at their posts, in case anybody shows up to collect."

Jeb Doyle came running over to the small group waving his arm towards the far end of the meadow. "Hey guys, you see that? Robert Pool took off in one of them army trucks."

"What in the hell for?" Koneg exclaimed, holding his hand up in bewilderment.

"To save his own lousy drunk ass! I knew that jerk was no good." Gardener scowled as he spat after him. Sarge followed the vehicle's dust trail as it sped away. Maybe Pool had the right idea. After all, who were the dumb asses now?

****

Eastman was in a desperate fix, pinned down yards in front of razor wire, his only defence a low dirt ridge. All hell had let loose after the explosion from the missile site. It had been the longest few minutes Eastman could ever remember waiting for the second explosion, but thank the Lord it never came. He watched as the 50 cal tore great lumps out of the ridge he'd just crawled from. The clamour of war was all around him, a dozen or more different calibers zipping through the air.

Most of his guys were Sunday shooters, couldn't hit anything two foot away and those that could shoot, were pinned down like him. Another 40mm grenade exploded nearby, showering him with brown earth. He dusted himself down and looked at Bodien next to him.

"Jeez that was close Brad."

Bodien was right; the guys on the 50 cal could not depress the weapons barrel enough to hit them. But the guy with the grenade launcher was getting too damn near. Soon he'd land one on top of them. They had to move in closer.

"Jed, we gonna have to move soon, or we're gonna be spread over this chunk of dirt."

"Reckon we ought to try another grenade?"

Eastman shook his head in dismay. He looked at the mess of tangled wire. They'd just about succeeded in reaching that distance, let alone the ECM. What they wanted was a diversion.

For the second time that afternoon, Eastman was drawn to a long shallow ditch a short distance away. There was absolutely no cover between him and the ditch, only deadly open space. Hardly ideal, but as O'Brian would say, 'any port in a storm.' He had to know what was going on; he couldn't coordinate the attack hidden behind a ridge.

"Jed, I'm gonna make a dash over there." Eastman nudged the other man's arm and pointed towards the ditch.

"Hold up there boy, that ain't exactly the best plan you ever did make."

"I got no option. You cover me, because when I move, that grenade launcher is gonna be right on my tail. You gotta get him and then I'll cover you."

They readied themselves and after a brief countdown, Eastman made his move. He cleared the distance and rolled into the trench, as M16 rounds kicked up a dust storm around him. A blast of automatic fire, followed by a triumphant rebel yell, was exactly what he wanted to hear.

From relative safety, he signalled Bodien to stay where he was. Even though the 50 cal was unable to hit them, it still had to be dealt with. Eastman tried to sight his M16 on the target; the weapon's elevated position made it impossible to hit both of the gun crew. Even with one person, the weapon could still be operated.

Despite the constant barrage of gunfire resounding through the valley, barely anybody had actually been hit. Heading towards the far end of the compound on the track, Eastman could make out a dust cloud. Army reinforcements were on their way. Damn! Now was not the time for caution, he had to act before it was too late.

Selecting one of the remaining grenades, Eastman leapt to his feet and sprinted to within feet of the 50 cal. The lever fell with a metallic ping as he pulled the pin and hurtled the grenade. In the blinking of an eye, both soldiers were dead and their weapon out of action.

"Jed, about time you used that pitching arm you're always on about. We got some gate crashers." Eastman pointed to the now visible Humvee as it shot past the checkpoint. Bodien broke from his cover to join the Sheriff and both men ran to the edge of the razor wire. Each threw a grenade though both fell short of their marks, the explosions only served to throw up dirt and make a hell of a noise. Suddenly, 7.62 mm M60 rounds started churning up the ground about them. Dangerously exposed in the open, both men dived onto the floor. The distinctive bark of an AK47 cut through the din and moments later, the M60 fell silent. Both men were surprised but elated to see Austin Colt stride towards them. But this was no time for a joyous reunion. The Humvee drew near – they'd run out of time.

****

Robert Pool held the steering wheel ever tighter, willing himself onwards. The soldier at the crude checkpoint quickly lifted the barrier and Pool drove into the clearing. Too late, the soldier realised his mistake and began firing at the Humvee at point blank range. M16 rounds bounced off the armoured shell as Pool picked up speed, throwing up large clumps of dirt.

Pool fixed his eyes on the impressive black ECM towers at the opposite end of the glade. He watched in the distance, as two cops destroyed some kind of big machine gun. Then they set about attacking the towers. But the men were too far away to make any effect on them. Unseen by the cops, soldiers ran out from a truck and raced to counter the hopeless assault. Pool hit the horn in an attempt to draw the soldiers away, anything to gain time.

It took moments for the three men to identify the new threat and they instantly started firing at the approaching Jeep. Pool found it hard to see as the high velocity rounds chipped away at the armoured glass. He kept his foot hard down on the gas pedal, as though he wanted to put his foot through the floor. He hoped the vehicle would hold together long enough for him to complete his mission.

Soon his long journey would be concluded; the ECM towers loomed closer. But they were just a means to an end. He wanted to end the suffering – his own personal hell. Losing his wife to cancer had been almost too much to bear, but then his son also… it was too much. He'd made a few half-hearted attempts at suicide, but deep down he knew he was a coward. He fooled himself into thinking it would all get better; it never did. It surprised him how few bottles it took to forget things, although never quite everything.

Sure, Lenski and Tony had helped, but Tony was gone now. Pool couldn't go through another rehab programme again. He picked up the flask from the seat next to him and stared at it. He could smell the whisky. It would be so easy to turn around and –

Disgusted with himself, Pool lobbed the flask into the back of the vehicle.

He aimed the hood of the heavy vehicle at a cluster of gas cans near the generator. He shut his eyes and smiled.

"It's all right now, I'm coming home."

****

Eastman threw himself to the ground as the Humvee crashed into the generator. A massive spiral of orange fire engulfed the ECM towers and the shockwave hit the ground like an express train. Stunned, Eastman clambered to his feet; the towers were no more than red-hot twisted metal. As he regained his hearing he became aware that the gun battle had ended.

Then his radio sparked into life, swiftly followed by dozens of ring tones from all around him. Bodien punched the air, full of delight.

"Damn it Brad, we're back on line!"

Eastman started to flick through his radio channels; the airwaves were full of voices. The whole town was talking at once. There were things he had to do, but first he had to ensure the fighting did not resume. It would only take some hot head to start it all over again.

Eastman gestured to his radio.

"Now let's see if I can get these guys to give in."

"Yeah, but what frequency they gonna be on Brad?"

"They were the ones spying on us remember." Eastman smiled as he saw the penny drop and Bodien's eyes lit up like a slot machine.

"This is Sheriff Bradley Eastman, Armstrong Police Department. All military personnel in this vicinity are ordered to cease and desist hostilities immediately. Or you will be arrested!"

"Did that feel as good as it sounded Boss?"

Eastman looked over at Bodien, waited a few minutes then repeated the warning. He hoped that they'd see the game was over. It was pointless continuing fighting. However, what if they wanted to carry on? He didn't want to go there. Suddenly his radio crackled.

"Sheriff, this is Leo Spelvin. Those army guys are putting their guns down. I think they've given in."

"Okay Leo, keep me posted." Eastman gave Bodien a smile. "Jedrey, bring the guys down and start rounding up these bozos." He tapped Bodien's arm and gave him a more serious look. "Do it real easy, I don't want any trouble. You hear?"

"Max Koneg to Brad Eastman. You there, Brad? Over."

Eastman held the radio away and rapidly cranked down the volume. "Yeah. No need to shout Max. What's your situation there? Over."

"Sarge took the truck out and we got that missile in the bag. Well done Brad – you did it. You did it man!"

"Not exactly me. Some Humvee crashed into the jammers and set a bunch of gas cans off. The whole lot went up." He waited for Koneg to reply but the airwaves remained oddly soundless. "Max, you still there? Over."

"That Humvee it… Robert Pool took off in a Humvee a while back. Foster said it was headed towards you. Over."

Eastman stood watching the fire streaking into the afternoon sky and said nothing. There was nothing to say. His thoughts turned to Robert Pool. Armstrong saved by the town drunk? Now wouldn't that be something else.

****

"Sir, we just lost contact with Control One." The soldier adjusted his headset and turned to General Stone. Stone got up from his seat and walked the short distance to the operations desk, deep lines of concern spread over his face. "What d'you mean Green?"

"Sir there's no communication with the vehicle or the operator's comms. I should be able to raise at least one. I think the vehicle's been destroyed."

"That's it then. I want Warbird Two detonated right now!"

"General, shouldn't we get more info? We need to..."

"*Wait*? Colonel, I think we've waited long enough don't you?" Stone cut Steedman dead and pointed down at Green. "Green, start systems operation on Warbird Two."

Green brought up the firing codes for the warhead at the underground base. Within seconds he'd punched in the details. Stone inserted the code key into the fire control device on the desk in front of him. He reached over and flicked off the small plastic cap on the unit, revealing the firing button. He jabbed his finger, depressing the device with a dull tap.

Frantically, Green started pressing his keypad as dozens of messages flashed up on the VDU. Something had gone wrong. "Sir, the programme's not responding. Warbird Two is offline."

"What? Soldier, get that damn thing back online now!"

Green's fingers moved like a blur as he desperately attempted to remedy the situation. Then, after moments of intense activity, he shook his head fearfully and looked up at Stone.

"Sir, the firing system's been disconnected. I've tried to override it, but it's impossible."

"Keep trying man!" Stone turned to the other operator sitting next to him. "Callahan, I want Major Naughton and Staff Sergeant Rai down that base. Find out what the hell's going on."

Steedman moved to stand next to Stone. "General, we have to deactivate Warbird One. If the potentials get hold of that missile we..."

"Deactivate? Like hell! I want that missile airborne. This has gone far enough."

As Steedman was about to argue his point, he noticed that the ECM monitors were showing no power output. He crossed to the console for a closer inspection, but the LED registered nil output. Steedman signalled to Callahan to join him. "Callahan, check this out."

Callahan checked and re-checked the readings and after a few moments, turned to look at the Colonel. "Sir, the ECM's are down. The target zone has got full comms back. And..." His voice trailed off.

"And what?"

"Colonel, I'm picking up two way communications. Sir, they're talking to the outside."

"Good Lord." Steedman raised his fingertips to his temples. "Put it on speaker."

The operations room was flooded with the din of a whole town, speaking as one. But it was one solitary voice that leapt out at them; one voice that stood out from every other.

"This is Sheriff Bradley Eastman, Armstrong Police Department. All military personnel in this vicinity are ordered to cease and desist hostilities immediately. Or you will be arrested!"

"Damn! Steedman you still want me to wait?" Stone turned to Green. "I want that bird launched in the next ten seconds!"

Green tapped the firing codes into his console and after a few seconds nodded his readiness to the General. Everything was now in place for the destruction of the town. Stone inserted his second key and flipped open the firing lid, placing his finger directly over the activation button.

"General! Think of what you're doing. That town is talking to the outside world. This mission is compromised. You push that button and you're the biggest mass murderer in American history." Steedman took his pistol and aimed squarely at the back of Stone's head and waited. "I'm begging you, don't do this."

Stone's finger hovered over the button; beads of sweat ran down his face, into his collar. The veins in his temples stood out, fit to explode. Steedman's finger tensed on his trigger. Stone's head slumped low between his shoulders and he closed the plastic lid down.

"Green, shut the programme."

Steedman replaced his pistol in its holster and walked over to the desk. "General, I think you made the right call Sir. But I need those fire control codes from you."

Without uttering a single word, Stone gave him both keys. He slumped into his chair and looked up at Steedman.

"I had my orders Colonel. You can't go far wrong, following orders."

"Isn't that what they said at Nuremberg, General? I'm going to disarm that missile and go help those people down there. Operation Viking is hereby cancelled."

He gave Stone one last look before leaving the room.

****

Taylor stood in the gloom of the entry tunnel, completing the last of the connections on the timer. The device was now reunited with the warhead but he was loath to switch the gadget on. There was a possibility that the second the timer took power from the warhead, any commands sent from Stone could detonate the device – as if it were a demented print machine, suddenly clearing, and all the print jobs arriving at the same time.

He looked at the plastic connectors and shook his head. Taylor did not entirely trust King's sudden DIY skills to hot wire state of the art missiles. He'd only connect at the last possible moment, by which time it would hardly matter anymore. Deep in thought, he skipped his flashlight around the rocky warren. At least they wouldn't be able to use his blood now; at least Lenski would be smart enough to make use of the samples he'd already provided.

He stared at the power switch; most people had no idea of the exact time and means of their death. Taylor knew that pressing the switch would be his last ever act. It was like pulling a grenade pin and then waiting for the darn thing to cook off. Yet he was strangely calm, he felt no panic or fear holding the plastic connectors. He shut his eyes and –

"Taylor! You God damn butt wipe! What in hell you still doing alive?"

"Benteen!"

"Who'd you think I was, your mother?"

Taylor watched as Benteen trudged towards him, limping badly. As he got closer, Taylor could see that Benteen had been wounded many times, even in the poor light it was obvious he was in a bad way. Then he spied the wound on Benteen's bare arm.

"Have you been...?"

"Yep. My arm, my neck, they even got me on my leg. Real hungry critters."

The big man leant against the cave wall, resting his chin on his chest.

"Anybody else get away?"

"Everybody. We thought you was dead, then a whole swarm of them SOB's showed up. We followed the stairs up, just like you said, but someone had to hold them back."

Benteen swayed sideways but Taylor propped him against the warhead trailer.

"You got this blasted box of tricks working yet, boy?"

"Yeah but Houston, we have a problem. King damaged the timer… means it can only be fired manually."

Taylor dabbed at his chin and stared at the floor.

"Oh that's just great. Kinda like a damn suicide bomb!"

Taylor shook his head. "No, a lot like a damn suicide bomb."

Benteen pointed to the bullet graze on Taylor's arm. "You been bit too?"

Taylor gently patted the wound. "No, that punk King shot me."

"Nice company you keep there, son. Okay, so I kinda think I out injure you! So how's this pile of crap work?" Benteen stepped forward to get a better look at the contraption.

"You sure about this? I mean..."

"Ain't fixing to end up like Al and them others. How's it work?"

Taylor stared at the big cop a few moments before carrying on. "These plug into the connector here," he said, pointing to the device, "that gives you power. Then the menu comes up, you scroll down until you come to manual operation."

He paused and looked up at Benteen.

"Yeah, yeah. Even I can operate the DVD. Just show me how to shoot the damn thing boy!"

"Manual operation gives the fire or safe option. No prize for guessing which one you want. It'll highlight fire, you push okay and that's..."

"Will it work? You said it was damaged."

That was the big question: would it work? And could Benteen work it? Still, the guy was prepared to give his life for what he believed in. Taylor wasn't even sure what he believed in anymore.

"It's got to."

"How long you gonna need to get clear?"

Benteen was getting worse, his breathing was slow and laboured and he had difficulty keeping his eyes open. But people like him were made of stern stuff, or at least that's what Taylor was counting on.

"This thing's been positioned to maximize the energy release. Nearly all of it will hit the base interior. But we're gonna have a lot of back blast, maybe as much as half a click. I'd say about five minutes."

He knew it was a lot to ask, considering the guy looked fit to keel over at any time. But not only would Taylor have to get out of the base, he'd need to get clear of the blast zone. Something that burned the very air was best kept well away from.

"I'll do the best I can. But don't drag your feet."

Taylor looked directly into the other man's eyes. The guy had to be the most unpleasant, unlikable individual he'd ever encountered. Yet here he was, about to lay his life down so Taylor could escape. Exactly what did you say to someone like that?

"Taylor, I always fixed on you being no damn good, I never realised you'd be the death of me."

Both men laughed, Taylor nodded his head and turned on his heel, disappearing into the gloom. Drenched in sweat, Benteen braced his back on the trailer and eased himself onto the ground. Every inch of his body ached; even breathing hurt, all he wanted to do was to shut his eyes and sleep.

****

Benteen's eyes shot open. Damn! How long had he been asleep? He cursed his broken wristwatch; there was no way of knowing if Taylor had got clear. He doubled up as waves of pain swept over him. His gut felt like it was on fire and his head felt ready to explode. He knew he had to stay focused on keeping alert. Next time he might not be so lucky. Next time... The thought of turning into one of those crap heads turned his blood to ice. He'd be better off ending it now, and that's what it was all about. This was Gerard 'T' Benteen's last stand.

He shot bolt upright at the sound of gravel crunching nearby and shone his flashlight in the direction of the sound. Some distance away, a ragged line of creatures was heading towards him. Instinctively, he touched the bite on his neck as he looked at the gallery of misshapen faces snarling at him. The wound was now oozing a foul, thick liquid. He struggled to his feet, took his pistol and gunned down the advancing abominations. He fumbled in his ammo belt for another magazine but found nothing. All the pouches were empty. Frustrated, he dropped his pistol into the darkness. From further down the passageway the high pitched wails were coming closer. Soon another wave would be approaching but this time he had no ammunition. With the fading light form his flashlight, Benteen took the small plastic connector between his clammy fingers. With other hand he located the porthole.

"Come look what I got for you, you God damn freaks!" Benteen's laughter echoed around the cave as he switched on the device and power surged into the timer.

CHAPTER — TWENTY-EIGHT

"O'Brian! Ever thought of using blocks when you threw this place up?"

O'Brian scowled back at Langley. "You know how much alimony is these days? And I got three of them bleeding me dry!"

The small wooden shack rocked under the relentless onslaught of the creatures outside. Several wooden panels had been forced open, revealing chinks of light from the outside world.

"How many of them are there, do you reckon?" said Majors, hammering the last of the nails into the damaged panels.

"Do you think I got some kinda X-ray vision going on here? How the damn hell should I know? Help me get this against the door."

Majors shrugged and joined O'Brian in dragging the metal cabinet to the door. O'Brian watched him closely. Now was not the time to come un-glued. The wails and groans from the creatures were starting to prove too much for the shopkeeper. Majors held his hands over his ears and shook his head from side to side.

"Why can't they just shut up? Shut up!"

"Stow that crap, sailor! Don't go lame on me now."

Langley moved in between the two men. "Take it easy will you. Them things are about enough for anybody."

"I've had about all I can take of this sorry son of..."

O'Brian was cut short as the little room was filled with voices. The radios had erupted into life. The men stared at the sets, unable to comprehend what was happening. They'd waited for what seemed like forever to hear something other than harsh static. Now the powerful radios were picking up calls from all over America.

"This is Burnsville News Channel calling Armstrong. Is anybody online?"

O'Brian almost pulled the mic off the table in his excitement as he responded to the call.

"I read you. This is Pat O'Brian. We read you loud and clear Burnsville. Over."

"This is Karolina Frost BNC; we've been getting some pretty wild stories from you folks out there. What can you tell me, Mr O'Brian?"

He looked over at the other two, his face divided by a wide grin.

"You gonna have yourself one hell of a story here, lady. The town is under attack by some kinda terrorist group. I don't know how many dead we got, but these guys are all over the place. Over."

Majors pointed in horror at one of the damaged sections of the shack, as several creatures forced the gap wider open. Grey, decayed hands grasped at the air in a vain attempt to feed. Langley swatted at the hands with his claw hammer, allowing Majors to close the breach with the table. The three men knew it would only be a matter of time before the ravenous things got inside.

"Mr O'Brian, do you know why they're attacking you? What do they want?"

"They got some type of missile set up, I reckon they're gonna shoot it off at some place. You gotta send help. Over!"

As O'Brian continued his talk with the news station, Majors moved to stand with Langley, a confused look on his face.

"Terrorist missile? Why not tell her the truth?"

"Cause folks still recall the Super Bowl and Times Square bombings, Oscar. Terrorists are real: you go on about zombies and she gonna switch off."

Both men looked skywards at the sound of footsteps clattering around on the tin roof.

"How the hell they get on the roof?" Majors jerked his finger upwards in disbelief; the things could hardly move in a straight line, let alone clamber onto the roof. Things were now well beyond normal.

O'Brian called across from his radio bench. "Fellas, we gotta keep transmitting. The net's crashed and the landlines are overloaded!"

"Ain't surprising, it was never made for this kinda use." Langley shrugged, rubbing his cheek. "But we did get out to people, right?"

O'Brian gave them a huge smile. "Hell yeah, I got CBS, CNN and a whole bunch of others waiting on the line. We're big news guys."

The sound of gunfire drowned him out as volley after deafening volley rang through the air. But almost as soon as it had started, the gunfore stopped and the small shack returned to total silence, except for the incessant radio babble.

"Reckon we ought to take a look boys. Majors, you..."

"Ain't gonna be me. Your damn shack, you look!"

Majors defiantly shook his head and levelled his finger at O'Brian. Moving to the back of the room he stood with his arms folded, distancing himself from the events.

"God damn interruption after interruption. Like being married all over again!" O'Brian thundered over to the door and flung it open, then stopped dead in his tracks.

"We heard you broadcasting and figured you'd need some help up here."

O'Brian stared speechless at Kate Black and the small group of townspeople congregated around the door. All around them were dead creatures; Abe Mcreedy lay with an arrow embedded in the side of his head. It had been a massacre, but a type of massacre O'Brian agreed with. He pointed at McReedy and gave a dry smile.

"Who'd you get to help out, Geronimo?"

"I heard that, Paleface!"

O'Brian looked up to see Red Cloud's grinning face peering back at him over the edge of the corrugated roof. "Get off my freaking roof, you crazy God damn Indian!"

Benny Arnold ran up to the group, pausing to catch his breath. "Guys, my wife just rang me. Said we're all over the news stations."

He caught Kate and Red Cloud by their arms. "There's a whole bunch of people headed out here."

Jim Boy stepped forward. "Now we all done with this crap, we all safe right?"

Sam Glitzman waved his fist in the air with delight. "He's right. Now we're all over the news they can't do diddly-squat to us."

A high-pitched boom sliced through the air like a hot knife through butter. The immediate skyline turned fire red and even at this distance, they could feel the hot blast of air wash over them. They watched, eyes wide in fear, as the red sky continued to grow and grow until it threatened to engulf the sun.

****

The squad of heavily armed soldiers advanced on Eastman. Heston Street was deserted except for Eastman and the soldiers, the two factions closing in on each other. His pistol held low, Eastman kept up his pace, rapidly closing the distance between the soldiers. Eventually they came to a halt, each side now unable to pass the other.

The lead soldier swept his gloved hand across the thick red pen lines on his plastic covered map. "Sir, we've cleared through these sectors. We're gonna link up with some of your people, two blocks from this point."

Eastman took his shades off and looked at the thickset New Yorker in front of him. "Sure, best take it easy. There's a whole bunch of scared folks out there with lots of guns."

The man gave Eastman an uneasy smirk. "Yeah, no need to say that twice. We're headed past the precinct; you can tag along if you want?"

Eastman held up his hand, declining the offer. "Nope, I'm going the other way. Some people to check on."

He walked off, leaving the soldiers behind him as he continued up the road. The town was a mess. Trash cluttered up the sidewalks, the occasional abandoned vehicle blocked the street. His nose twitched at the same chemical odour he'd first encountered with Pool. There was something else in the air – the stench of decay.

A group of soldiers were loading some dead creatures onto the back of a truck. Eastman paused briefly to look at bloody handprints smeared across shop fronts. It would be some time before he'd get an accurate death toll. Warily, he moved through the strange and surreal, deserted streets. Finally the health center came into view. Two military trucks were parked directly in front of the main entrance with a number of busy soldiers. One of the men nodded to Eastman, who in return touched the brim of his Stetson and walked into the building.

"Sure glad to see you, Sugar."

Eastman winced at Elle-May's unexpected bear hug but managed to smile it off and gain his freedom.

"You ever quit nursing, try wrestling. Well how'd it go back here?"

"It could've gone a whole lot worse. When that darn thing went off... Well you can just imagine. But everybody's where they ought to be, all except for Norris. Lord knows where he's at." Lowering her voice, she moved her eyes in the direction of a group of army medics walking past them. "We picked up some extra staff, but after what they tried doing, I'd rather trust a snake."

"Makes two of us. Where can I find...?"

"In the lab, I reckon she must be about done in by now. She's worked through the whole thing."

"Yeah, reckon so. Thought you'd like to know, Jedrey said he'd catch up with you directly."

He smiled as Elle-May patted her hair. Even after everything that had gone on, there was still time for romance, for some. He turned away and set off up the corridor, the short distance to the lab. He pushed the door open.

"I heard someone was in need of a rest in here?"

Anne rushed at him, wrapping her arms around him, burying her head into his chest.

"I think you just popped another one of my ribs…"

Instantly she released him, her face full of concern as she stared back at him.

"Are you hurt Brad? Let me check you out."

"Any more of this and I'm gonna need some serious medical treatment. But it sure is good to see you."

He stepped forward, clasped his hands around her slender shoulders and smiled.

"Brad, did we manage to get any news coverage?"

Eastman laughed, nodding his head as if at some unspoken joke.

"Don't tell me you haven't heard O'Brian all over the radio? He's a regular celebrity. He's got all the big stations lined up for interviews."

"It'll be the book followed by the movie and then who knows what else?"

They looked at each other and burst into laughter at the prospect.

"Is it true about Robert Pool?"

"Yeah, if it hadn't been for him we'd…"

Anne nodded sorrowfully at Eastman. "How come the military changed sides?"

"After the first missile went off, this Colonel Steedman guy turned up. Said he'd taken over from the General and offered to help sort this mess out."

She read something in his face that betrayed his unhappiness with this sudden turn of events. She studied his face and waited for him to continue.

"King was some type of double agent, working for another bunch. Steedman wasn't even sure if any of this was legal. All those people killed – for what? So some suits could make an extra buck."

"Brad, if this man's here to help, then let him get on with it. They owe us that."

"That's just it. This morning they were all set to nuke us and now we're all supposed to be God damn pals!"

Reaching over, she caught his hand.

"Don't knock it. Use the situation and use them."

Eastman clasped his hand over the top of hers and gave her a begrudging smile.

"I know. But the whole thing sticks in my craw, that I gotta have these punks in our town. Now that Steedman's operating outta my station house – made it his CP – I needed to get away, bedsides it gave me a good excuse to come check on you."

"You don't need an excuse for that Brad. I mean...Want to hear some good news?"

"Is there good news anymore?"

"I've solved the car crime for you and I know who's behind it. Want to hear more?"

"This, I just gotta hear."

"I've been treating Luke Clayton. He told me he and his brother have been stealing cars to order for... Norris Zillman. What about that?"

Eastman narrowed his eyes and then erupted into a fit of laughter but quickly stopped at Anne's cross expression.

"I'm sorry but... Anne, look, those two are small time, they don't have the brains to run something like that. And Norris Zillman. Oh come on. You've been had."

Anne stared back at him, her arms folded indignantly.

"Sam Cortez went by Norris' place to see where he was. He couldn't find him, but Sam said he found a garage full of all types of vehicle parts. You and Gerard can go and take a look."

Eastman looked away and let out a deep sigh, the smile now replaced by a dark, gloomy expression.

"Did Gerard and his group get back okay?"

"He stayed behind for the others to get away."

"He's probably on his way back right now and..."

"Even if he made it out, that bomb scorched half the mountain side. I checked; no one's seen him since."

Sadly, he fixed his gaze at the green tiled floor.

"I'm sure he's alright."

His lips turned up in a half-hearted smile.

"What do you think's gonna happen to Stone, now that everything's out in the open?"

She raised her arms, turning her palms upwards and then sat at the desk.

"It's the army – who can tell? It could go one of two ways. They could sacrifice him in a congressional investigation or try for a colossal cover up."

"I'd damn well like to see them try!"

Eastman slammed his fist down hard on the desk, clattering what remained of the test tubes and making Anne jump.

"At least we have Taylor, if he'll talk that is. Where is he anyway?" she asked.

"Colt said they had a cave in down there. Taylor was under it."

"Oh no. No!"

He moved forwards to comfort her. "I know, but he knew the risks."

"It's not just that. Branigan bust in here and took all Taylor's blood samples. Without new ones we're back where we started."

"How'd he know which ones were which?"

"He didn't. He took the lot. None of them are any good, Taylor's blood is lethal."

"What you gonna do now?"

She rose from the seat and headed for the door.

"I have a ward of new patients with the kinda injuries I can treat this time. How about you?"

Eastman opened the door for her and walked out behind.

"Time I took this town back and then I got me a long overdue appointment with the Judge."

****

Branigan slumped forward on the bench and looked at the foul smelling black vomit covering his feet. He couldn't remember the last time he'd felt as ill as he did right now; his whole body ached. It was all that fancy Lenski's fault. She'd deliberately given a bad batch of that crap to get back at him. She could've told him which one to take. She thought she was so damn smart – better than everybody. She was just another college smart-ass and he knew what women like her really needed.

Without warning, Branigan vomited again. He fought the urge to pass out as the thick black sludge splashed onto his lap. If only that lousy thing hadn't scratched his face – there was no telling what crap he'd caught from her. But he knew one thing; he'd sure as hell make Lenski pay. He'd been quick off the mark but the only thing was, he'd not known which of the drugs to take, so he'd tried them all.

He raised his head at the sound of nearby voices. One, he recognised immediately. Part time retard and full time white trash – Jim Boy. He'd have to do. Branigan had to get back to hospital – that witch would have to help him. Then she was gonna pay, like that freak in the car.

Branigan staggered to his feet, the stomach cramps were getting worse, and it was now difficult to even stand. But he had to get help. He clutched the metal framework of the bench and lurched forward. He could hear the voices getting closer, he tried to call out, but his voice sounded more like a growl. Desperate to clear the gunge from his throat, Branigan stumbled out on to Ryker Street. The two figures in front of him were blurs as he reached out for help.

"Watch out!" screamed Zach, pointing frantically to the monstrosity directly behind Jim Boy.

Jim Boy spun around and fired his pistol into the creature's head, sending blood and brains onto the sidewalk. He stood shaking while Zach walked over to the dead thing sprawled in front of them.

"Hey, you just blew Barny Branigan away man!" Zach exclaimed, stepping away, astonished.

"What?"

"Yeah, no sweat though, he was a zombie. Come on let's move it."

"That *is* enough! I'm done with this town."

Jim Boy held his hands to his head, shutting his eyes tightly.

"No argument from me. First we get 'The Beast' then we go get Luke."

"And then we go, right?"

"Nope. Then we get my money from Zillman. Then we go."

Zach reached over and took the pistol off Jim Boy. He tucked it into his belt; best to play it safe.

"I still don't get it. How come nursey boy is Mr. Big?"

"I told you, it's a cover… and I'd be real careful there buddy with that talk, unless you wanna end up as a freeway support."

He caught Jim Boy's arm and dragged him forward. This was no time to hang around.

"You sure we all talking about the same guy here?"

"He runs four chop shops outta Burnsville. He's a real *badass*."

Both men rushed across the street and turned up a deserted side lane full of upturned trash cans. Zach broke into a broad smile as he glimpsed the big orange four-by-four at the far end of the lane. He raced up to the monster car and patted it affectionately, completely ignoring the other man.

Irritated, Jim-Boy blocked the access to the driver's door. "You ain't playing me for no fool, Clayton? You even hearing me?"

Zach jabbed his finger into Jim Boy's chest. "You want to come with me or not?"

Jim Boy winced and then nodded as both men climbed into the vehicle and sped out of the lane, throwing up clouds of dust as they raced off.

****

"You people should be more selective about who you let in this place."

"I heard you were dead."

Eastman looked over at Taylor; the guy was a bedraggled mess, but at least he was still alive. Nothing surprised Eastman anymore. He shot Anne a glance as they walked down the empty street.

"Never the less, Mr Taylor, we're very happy you're not."

Eastman led the others away from the street into an empty shop, out of sight. The only sound that could be heard was the crunching of glass as they stepped into the storeroom.

"I'd have to go along with you there. Like that guy said 'the tales of my death were greatly exaggerated'…" Taylor crossed over to the other two and studied Eastman's face before continuing. "Benteen wasn't so lucky. Sorry, he didn't make it."

"How'd…? What happened?"

Taylor spoke softly, his usual brashness gone, as he answered Eastman.

"He was in bad shape. He didn't want to end up like one of them."

"So he stayed behind to keep the missile safe?"

"He did more than that. Someone had to press that big red button and that someone would have been me, but for Benteen. He saved my ass."

The three stood without a sound, as though mourning Benteen. It was Eastman who spoke first.

"How'd you come back?"

"I ran into Major Naughton and a Staff Sergeant and persuaded them that hanging around would be less than healthy. Then…"

"I think what Brad means is *why* did you come back?"

"Well… I… as soon as I work that one out I'll be sure to let you know."

"Anybody, apart from those army guys, anyone else know you're back in town?"

Taylor shook his head.

"After they dropped me off, I kept low. Those two would just take me for one of you lot in any case."

"Thing is, we got us a situation here."

Eastman drew his finger lightly over his troubled brow.

"You're still under arrest for multiple homicides, not to mention escaping while in custody. What to do next?"

"You sound like that idiot judge. You can't..."

Eastman held his hand up like a traffic cop and waited until Anne had stopped raging.

"Taylor you have to appreciate these are all serious charges. However, since all documentation has yet to be added to the police computer systems, and I don't have any prints and the said suspect was buried under an A-bomb, I don't have a lot to go on. Now that's the situation."

Taylor dipped his head and shrugged.

"Yeah, I can see that could be a slight predicament."

"Plus a number of witnesses last saw the late Mr Taylor buried under a rock slide. That would seem to point to his demise." Anne wagged her finger at them to highlight the point.

"I would have to agree with you Anne. Hard copy records could easily get lost with all that's gone on around here."

"Not to mention Brad, you don't have time to chase any of this down."

"True. The law can't chase what isn't there."

Almost sidelined by the exchange, Taylor spoke up. "Do I take it that you're letting me go?"

"We all got choices to make; Benteen made his and this is me making mine."

"Yeah, but not always good ones."

Eastman placed his hand on Taylor's arm. "You came back here, now that was your choice. That's good enough for me."

"This is Bodien calling Brad. Do you read? Over."

Eastman keyed his mic.

"Eastman here. Go ahead Jed. Over."

"I'm up top of Regan's roof. There's a whole bunch of army and news guys neck and neck for the town. It's looking like Wacky Races out there. Over."

"That's all good," said Taylor. "The more of a media circus you create Eastman, the better."

Eastman nodded in agreement. Taylor was right; the more TV cameras that came, the safer they'd be.

"Let those news people in Jed, the more we got, the better. Anything else I should know about? Over."

"O'Brian and Lenny just about killed each other over who's getting the best media coverage. But I reckon they kinda worked it through. Over."

Eastman looked over at Anne and Taylor, a large smile on his face. Maybe it was heading for the book and movie after all.

"Roger that. Maybe we ought to start selling tickets, all these extra folks arriving? I'll catch you later. Take care. Out."

"Things are gonna start getting crowded around here Eastman."

Eastman turned to face Taylor.

"There's a SWAT team from Burnsville and a whole bunch of State Troopers headed in here. Now the military may not ask questions about you but the others sure will."

"Time I wasn't here. I'd best be making tracks."

"Hold on there, Mister," said Anne. "You're not going anywhere until I take a look at that arm. Can't have you sloshing blood all over the place."

She stepped forward and took him by his good arm.

"Anne's right Taylor, besides you're gonna need some new kit and I'm gonna need time to organise stuff."

"What will you do after all this, Mr Taylor?"

"I told myself a while back I'd bring Tellermine down and kill him. I guess one out of two ain't bad. But I'm not wasting my life chasing him down, if that's what you mean."

"Glad to hear that. Anne, best get your bag of tricks. I'll get sorted then we'll all mosey up to my ranch. Taylor, you stay here, out of sight."

Taylor jerked his head up. "I already kinda planned that."

"Oh, Mr Taylor I'm going to need some more blood from you when we get to Brad's."

"Blood, blood, blood. What is it with you, Doc? I'm gonna need to wear a crucifix around you from now on."

Eastman coughed loudly.

"When you two are done." He pointed to his watch. "I want us all back here no later than a quarter after. We all clear on that?"

The other two nodded and Eastman left for the station house. He had a lot to do but less time to do it. Soon the town would be stitched up tighter than new boots. Then he'd have one hell of a job getting Taylor out.

****

Eastman and Taylor stood looking out across the wooden fence, taking in the view of Eastman's ranch. The cloudless blue sky stretched on forever; the only evidence of earlier events were the black scorch marks that speckled the landscape. Everything was still, just as it should be.

"Eastman, this place is like a dream, the type of place I've always wanted."

"I gotta agree with you. Helen and me built this place up over the years. Kinda let it go these last few months."

"Sorry about your wife, still you got yourself a fine woman with the good Doctor."

Eastman quickly held up his hand in protest. "Oh, that's not the way it is with us. Her husband died some time back in the war and..."

"I seem to recall this guy talking about choices. Maybe it's time you made yours. Life is a hard game, let alone playing it on your own."

"Well you two seem to be having a cosy 'man chat' – anything I'd be interested in?"

Eastman whirled around like a boy caught with his fingers in the candy jar.

"No. No, nothing at all. Just shooting the breeze. You know."

"How's that arm Mr Taylor?"

"Which one? The arm with the stitches or the one you drained?"

She grinned at him, shaking her head.

"Really, Mr Taylor. Anyway, I've been watching the TV and it seems as though we've made just about every news channel. The town looks more like a film set, media people everywhere."

"We'd best get this done while we still got time," said Eastman, walking to his barn and gesturing them to follow him. He pulled open the heavy green wooden door and looked at the other two.

"What do you think?"

The white two-door Chevy convertible would not have looked out of place in a car showroom. The pristine paint job sparkled as the bright sunshine reflected off its highly polished surface.

"This was Helen's. I got it for her birthday just before she... I could never bring myself to part with it. But now I reckon it's time I let it go."

Eastman produced a set of car keys from his shirt pocket, turning them over and over in his hand. Finally, he extended his arm, letting the keys tip into Taylor's outstretched palm.

"Eastman you sure about all this? I mean..."

Eastman held up his hand and looked at Taylor.

"It's gassed up and I've already loaded your kit and caboodle, with a bunch of extras." He pointed to the trunk and then handed Taylor a brown envelope. Taylor opened the envelope and let out a shrill whistle as he looked inside.

"Jeez, did you raid the Christmas fund or something?"

"There's near two grand. All I could lay my hands on. It'll have to see you through."

"Brad, what happens if he gets pulled over? I mean, he's hardly able to show any ID is he?"

"Sorry Anne, but that's part of the risk. It's that or walk. As long as you don't run any red lights, you ought to be okay."

"Listen you two, I... Look, I really appreciate all this."

"No, it's us who appreciate what you've done."

Eastman paused a few seconds, waiting for her to finish, lost for words. "I don't know what to say to you."

Lenski shook her head crossly and gave Eastman a disapproving stare.

"Well we could always start with 'thank you' swiftly followed by good luck Mr Taylor."

"Who's this 'Mr Taylor' guy? I keep looking around for my father. After all this, please call me Brent."

She leant forward and kissed him on the cheek. "Thank you and good luck Brent."

"Say, any more of that and I could be persuaded to stay."

He climbed into the car and started the vehicle, winding down the window. The engine purred like a cat. "About time you made that choice, Lawman."

Anne cast her eyes at Eastman, who stood silently. "What was that?"

Both watched as the car taxied down the long track before vanishing from sight. They both waved as Taylor sounded the horn. Then he was gone.

"What will he find out there Brad?"

Eastman reached over and took hold of Anne's hand and smiled contentedly as she grasped it firmly. He held her closely to him and breathed in the scent of her perfume. He looked across the paddock and for a moment, he thought he could make out someone on a horse. But in an instant the image disappeared – if it had ever been there at all.

"Did you see something?"

Eastman rubbed his eyes and smiled. "No. Not anymore."

"What about us, Brad? Where do we go from here?"

"We got a lot of folks down there who need us."

He led her to the squad car and opened the doors. "And after that, I reckon you and me got some living to catch up on."

****

Today is the twenty-second, two whole weeks from those events at Hinckle Point. But it feels more like a century since all that madness engulfed my town. Even now it all seems like some kinda crazy dream, all except for our dead, of which there are many. Counting those at the base and the creatures, our new best friends, the military, put the number at around three hundred. The truth is, that's something we will never know.

Today's memorial service was the first time we'd all been together as a 'normal' town since the start of this. I heard a lot of talk about sacrifices and a fine speech from our new Mayor, Veronica Redman, but none of that can replace the people we lost. Fine words, but just words all the same. Gerard and Mitch were buried with full honours. They awarded Gerard and me the Medal of Valour. Since he's no family left, I thought it best to display Gerard's medal at the station house. That way it's gonna feel like he's still about.

We saw the last of the military leave today. They spent the last few days going over the old base but when the media hounds got too interested, they concreted the whole place over. They tried to make it as though it never was, but you can't take back all the hurt that place has caused.

But some good has come out of the mess. Uncle Sam's been throwing dollars our way as if they were going out of fashion. A major logging outfit has bought the old sawmill and that means big investment. So along with a hefty regeneration programme, that's all good news.

But I'd say the best news is that Britney Patrick survived the infection. Anne says the kid has the same immunity as Taylor. It may have been triggered by the bite; some kinda reaction that only occurs in a small handful of people. But that stays with us. So the kid was right after all – she really is one in a million. Things could get complicated if she ever has to have a blood test though.

The Judge retired from office after Veronica got elected Mayor, which most folks agree was about time. Norris Zillman and the Clayton clan just upped sticks and moved out of the area. They can go be someone else's problem. All the charges on Mary Firth got dropped. No evidence, no witnesses and most of all, she'd been through enough.

On a personal note, I've been seeing a lot more of Anne these past weeks. A few movies and some eating out, hardly makes for serious dating. But for the time being that suits us fine. I'm gonna sign out now, I'm taking Anne to that new Italian. A complimentary dinner for two, that sort of thing can never be bad.

Well that's just about all I can think of for now. There's most likely a bunch of other stuff I could say, but maybe that's for another time.

Eastman closed the little leather bound book and glanced up at the wall clock. There was just enough time for him get out of his uniform, shower and go collect Anne. He took off his black necktie, rolled it into a coil and placed it in his hat. He'd only ever worn this formal uniform once before, and that had been a wedding. All he could recall was that it had been a hot day like today.

As he passed the hall mirror he caught sight of his new shiny medal. Appreciation from a grateful State Governor – another darn politician hot on election votes. He took a long look at the face staring back at him and dabbed at the additional grey hairs sprouting on his sideburns. Could he have done more? What if he'd taken more notice of Taylor's impossible tale? The time for recriminations and the 'who should have done what' had long passed. It was no good griping about shutting the barn door. He'd done his best to bring the latch down.

There'd been no news from Taylor, but Eastman had scarcely expected a post card. General Stone on the other hand, was wall-to-wall news. Every magazine, newspaper, radio and TV station across the planet was hanging on the next revelation. The congressional hearing was tearing him apart. Just about everybody who'd ever known the guy was taking the stand. The brass wanted to nail Stone's liver to the senate door. It'd serve the lousy bum right.

Eastman walked into his bedroom and placed the book in its safe hidey-hole. Some things were best kept a secret. Maybe things hadn't turned out so bad after all. Jimmy Emmett was still jawing about 'conspiracy theories' and such, only now people didn't think him so crazy anymore. After the incredible events, no one would ever take anything for granted again. It had been the longest few days Eastman had ever seen; still it was all behind them now. Things had to get better from now on in.

****

The man sat in the small windowless waiting room, lightly tapping his fingertips on his briefcase. His smart dark grey suit complimented the functionality of the room. It wasn't that he was nervous, far from it, he was eager to meet his new employers. He glanced over at the receptionist, engulfed in her typing. Her long, jet-black hair was secured tightly in a ponytail. Her striking Asian features were a welcome change from the made up faces of Western women. He was conscious of this being the third time in the fifteen minutes he'd been waiting that he'd looked at her. But in such a confined space it was difficult to look anywhere else, rather like being in a crowed elevator.

It was not as if he could fill the time reading the many leaflets and information posters dotted around, he'd never mastered any foreign languages. And there were only so many times someone could check their wristwatch.

To his shock, he suddenly became aware of the girl looking directly at him. In panic, he quickly averted his eyes. What if she'd caught him looking at her earlier? Now she probably thought he was odd. He'd never been at ease in the company of females. Personal relationships he'd discovered were greatly overrated.

"I'm sure Party Member Choi will not be much longer."

The girl smiled, staring at him, as if awaiting a response and then returned to her work.

"Your English is excellent. I'm sorry I can't say the same for my Korean."

The diminutive young woman looked up from her work.

"I took American cultural studies at UCLA." She paused uneasily then swiftly added. "A frivolous waste of time, but now I devote myself to serving my country."

"Such devotion to duty, I'm impressed. We in the West can learn a lot from you."

He smiled at her then sat back in the fabric-covered chair. Such discipline and dedication were rare commodities in America. However, the Korean sense of punctuality seemed to need some work. Glancing at his watch, he sighed and resigned himself to an undetermined stay. His wait was short lived as the large wooden brown door swung inwards.

Two Korean men dressed in suits entered the room and walked over to him. The younger man spoke first.

"I am so very sorry for this delay. Please accept my apologies. My name is Mr Choi, Minister for special affairs. This is Mr Haan, the Director of this facility."

The second man smiled and bowed his head slightly. "You are assured of my complete cooperation in this matter."

"The Leader has expressed his personal wishes for the success of this project. I trust I can give him a favourable report by the end of this week?"

"I'm delighted that the Leader attributes such interest to this venture Mr Choi. I can't wait to demonstrate the success of my process."

"You will find us most accommodating."

Choi gestured to the open door, extending his arm towards the brightly lit corridor.

"Please allow me to show you to your work station. You will see we have made every effort to comply with your requests."

Haan followed after the other two into the corridor. "Is there anything you need, Doctor?"

"A constant supply of raw material Mr Haan. That will keep me engaged."

"Raw material?" repeated Haan, his face furrowed in puzzlement.

Choi held up his hand. "This is a political correction facility; you will have all the raw material you require. And you may work without restriction here Doctor Tellermine."

"I'm delighted. That will be so refreshing after that last episode Mr Choi."

Tellermine adjusted his round metal spectacles and looked through the tinted glass onto the compound below. Several hundred political prisoners were exercising to music under the watchful eyes of armed guards. He smiled; at least North Korea would appreciate his work, without the sentimentality of the West. If NB33 could not be used to improve medical science then at least the Leader would find a new use for it. Yes, the new enhanced formula would speed up the mutation process. There was no time like the present to start work. Tellermine smiled, he did so enjoy his work.

THE END

CHECK OUT OTHER GREAT ZOMBIE NOVELS

RUN
by Rich Restucci

The dead have risen, and they are hungry.

Slow and plodding, they are Legion. The undead hunt the living. Stop and they will catch you. Hide and they will find you. If you have a heartbeat you do the only thing you can: You run.

Survivors escape to an island stronghold: A cop and his daughter, a computer nerd, a garbage man with a piece of rebar, and an escapee from a mental hospital with a life-saving secret. After reaching Alcatraz, the ever expanding group of survivors realize that the infected are not the only threat.

Caught between the viciousness of the undead, and the heartlessness of the living, what choice is there? Run.

THE DEAD WALK THE EARTH
by Luke Duffy

As the flames of war threaten to engulf the globe, a new threat emerges.

A 'deadly flu', the like of which no one has ever seen or imagined, relentlessly spreads, gripping the world by the throat and slowly squeezing the life from humanity.

Eight soldiers, accustomed to operating below the radar, carrying out the dirty work of a modern democracy, become trapped within the carnage of a new and terrifying world.

Deniable and completely expendable. That is how their government considers them, and as the dead begin to walk, Stan and his men must fight to survive.

SEVERED**PRESS**

CHECK OUT OTHER GREAT ZOMBIE NOVELS

DEAD ASCENT
by Jason McPhearson

The dead have risen and they are hungry...

Grizzled war veteran turned game warden, Brayden James and a small group of survivors, fight their way through the rugged wilderness of southern Appalachia to an isolated cabin in the hope of finding sanctuary. Every terrifying step they make they are stalked by a growing mass of staggering corpses, and a raging forest fire, set by the government in hopes of containing the virus.

As all logical routes off the mountain are cut off from them, they seek the higher ground, but they soon realize there is little hope of escape when the dead walk and the world burns.

CHAOS THEORY
by Rich Restucci

The world has fallen to a relentless enemy beyond reason or mercy. With no remorse they rend the planet with tooth and nail.

One man stands against the scourge of death that consumes all.

Teamed with a genius survivalist and a teenage girl, he must flee the teeming dead, the evils of humans left unchecked, and those that would seek to use him. His best weapon to stave off the horrors of this new world? His wit.

CHECK OUT OTHER GREAT ZOMBIE NOVELS

DEAD PULSE RISING
by K. Michael Gibson

Slavering hordes of the walking dead rule the streets of Baltimore, their decaying forms shambling across the ruined city, voracious and unstoppable. The remaining survivors hide desperately, for all hope seems lost... until an armored fortress on wheels plows through the ghouls, crushing bones and decayed flesh. The vehicle stops and two men emerge from its doors, armed to the teeth and ready to cancel the apocalypse.

TOWER OF THE DEAD
by J.V. Roberts

Markus is a hardworking man that just wants a better life for his family. But when a virus sweeps through the halls of his high-rise apartment complex, those plans are put on hold. Trapped on the sixteenth floor with no hope of rescue, Markus must fight his way down to safety with his wife and young daughter in tow.

Floor by bloody floor they must battle through hordes of the hungry dead on a terrifying mission to survive the TOWER OF THE DEAD.